THE EIGHTEENTH GREEN

THE EIGHTEENTH GREEN

WEBB HUBBELL

BEAUFORT
BOOKS

THE EIGHTEENTH GREEN

Copyright © 2018 by Webb Hubbell

Hardcover: 9780825308857
Ebook: 9780825307737
Paperback: 9780825309960

For inquiries about volume orders, please contact:
Beaufort Books
info@beaufortbooks.com

Published in the United States by Beaufort Books
www.beaufortbooks.com

Distributed by Midpoint Trade Books,
a division of Independent Publishers Group
www.ipgbook.com

Cover Design by Michael Short
Interior design by Mark Karis

Printed in the United States of America

To:
Suzy, John, Laura, Pete, and George

PROLOGUE

STEVE KOEPPLE WAS A METHODICAL MAN, a man of habit. As head greenskeeper at Columbia Country Club in Chevy Chase, Maryland, he
began his morning as he always did, traversing the course just before
dawn, assessing the condition of the greens and the work needed
to make sure they'd be in tip-top condition before play began for
the day.

A golf course is at its best right before the sun rises—when the
air is crisp and clean and dew covers every blade of grass. To Steve,
Columbia seemed to shimmer as if it were alive and breathing. The
acres of green space and stately trees—a sanctuary of green encircled
by the suburb's affluent neighborhoods and bumper-to-bumper
traffic—took on a life of their own.

This morning the course spoke to him—something was wrong,
off-kilter; it didn't feel right. So far, both the fairways and the greens
were in good shape, and he shook off his unease as he drove down
the long path to the eighteenth green. Climbing out of his cart to
get a better view of the elevated green, he saw a motionless lump
at the far edge.

"What now?" he groused, the tinge of unease returning.

A decent perimeter fence surrounded the course, but critters
found a way in; deer were a constant nuisance, and there'd been a
few coyote sightings. But deer, and usually coyotes, run at the sight
of a golf cart, and this lump wasn't moving. Steve was sure he was
looking at a drunken duffer sleeping it off. It wouldn't be the first
time.

Whoever he was, he wouldn't appreciate being discovered, so Steve approached gingerly. He knew that an embarrassed club member could make an employee's life miserable. A club manager in Virginia lost his job after he'd interrupted a member and another member's wife playing tennis sans clothing on a clay court late at night. The club's board decided that the manager used poor judgment in disturbing the embarrassed couple; at the least, he should have let them complete their match. No job had a shorter life span than that of a country club manager.

He feigned a loud cough, hoping the noise would rouse the sleeping man. No such luck. A broken rake lying just off the green caught his eye, and he wondered absently why it was there. He called out, "Hey, fella!" Still there was no movement. Steve sighed, leaned down, and shook the man. The inert figure didn't move.

Gathering himself, he hurried back to the cart, where he reached for the walkie-talkie under the dash.

"Josh, we've got a problem. There's a dead man on the eighteenth green. Call nine-one-one, now!"

SATURDAY MORNING

1

I WAS OUT OF SORTS, had been all week. I figured it was because I hadn't been able to get in a round of golf for more than three weeks. I was more than ready to get back to my regular Saturday game at Columbia. But as I pulled up to the gate, the security guard stopped me to say the course was closed—no explanation.

I parked and hurried into the clubhouse, looking for my playing partner, Walter Matthews. I spotted him near the bar, coffee in hand, surrounded by a group of grumbling, would-be golfers. He waved me over, and I asked the obvious question.

"What's up? Why's the course closed? It hasn't rained in a week. Don't tell me the President is playing this morning."

Sure, it was a big deal for the President to play the course, a huge honor for the club, but most members would happily forego the prestige. The Secret Service demanded a three-hole gap between the President's foursome and any other group on the course, backing up play everywhere.

Walter gave me a wry smile. "Nope, that guy only plays at his own courses. The greenskeeper found a body on the eighteenth green early this morning. The police have shut down the whole course, even the driving range."

Columbia's clubhouse overlooks the eighteenth green, so we joined others to stare out the large window. Stakes joined by yellow police tape circled the green, and I could see what looked to be a discolored area on the edge of the manicured grass. The green itself was empty, save for a few guards standing off to one side. The lab guys and detectives must have finished their grisly work.

I turned to Walter. "A body? Anyone we know?"

"I hear it's a man named Spencer, Harold Spencer. I didn't know him, did you? The gossip is he only played golf on occasion, but was a regular on the tennis courts and at Friday's poker game."

"Sounds familiar, but I can't place him. Anyone know what happened?"

"Beaten to death with a sand rake, they say. No one knows why he was out on the course last night; so far, it's a mystery."

With no golf in our future, we found a table and made small talk over fried eggs, country sausage, hash browns, and buttermilk biscuits. Walter has been my best friend, golf partner, and client for years. His wife Margaret—Maggie—and I work together at a small antitrust law firm we started after we left my former law firm.

Walter and I tried hard, but our conversation was stilted. I mean, a man had been killed with a sand rake, for God's sake, only a few yards from where we sat. Yet a bunch of golfers, myself included, were eating breakfast and drinking Bloody Marys, trying to pretend nothing had happened. The sorry fact was most of us weren't too upset about what had happened; it didn't seem real. We just wanted to play golf.

The golf pro made the mistake of strolling into the clubhouse. He had no answers to the barrage of questions: "What happened out there? Why can't you open the driving range? Can't we at least play the front nine?"

He left quickly. I scolded myself for being so callous and indifferent about the fate of Harold Spencer.

I was all at sixes and sevens. Truth is, I'm a man who likes routine, and now I didn't know quite what to do with myself. I thought about driving out to the Eastern Shore to meet Carol Madison at her weekend home. Carol and I had been seeing each other non-stop for months, and we'd just had our first serious disagreement over my decision to play golf instead of spending the weekend with her.

Carol was a political consultant—not a lobbyist, but a very discreet, very successful Washington political consultant, whose business was gathering information from the powers that be and feeding that information to her clients and their lobbyists. For example, after several cocktails a senator might confide to Carol that his finances were shaky. She'd pass that information on to her client, who would help straighten out his finances by asking a particular organization to invite the senator to give a speech—in exchange for a generous honorarium. No *quid pro quo* was mentioned, but the senator would remember the favor when the client's lobbyist came knocking.

Carol never acted as a lobbyist, and seldom knew how the information she gathered was used. She preferred it that way. She was a gatherer and conduit of information in a city where information was power, and for that information she was paid well.

Most every weekend when Congress was in session, Carol invited a few select clients to join carefully selected members of Congress and high-ranking officials in the administration at her second home on the Eastern Shore. These house parties provided the perfect opportunity to enjoy a weekend of tennis, boating, and good food while making the right connections in a very private setting.

As of late, I'd been a regular at these weekends, but the weekends were business for her. I'd tried to engage with her other guests, but I didn't have much in common with DC politicos at that level. I also hadn't played tennis since Angie died. I spent all day by Carol's pool, eating and drinking too much. I was tired of missing my usual Saturday round of golf, so at lunch with Carol on Monday I'd suggested an alternative—this week I would play golf on Saturday and drive up on Sunday.

"If golf is that damned important, why not play the entire weekend?" she snapped.

Our lunch ended in stony silence, neither of us willing to back down. By Thursday I'd gotten over my bullheadedness and called to apologize. She continued to huff at my "misplaced priorities and need to have things my way," so I ate more crow, and we made a date for Monday's baseball game.

The more I weighed calling her now that golf was cancelled, the more I thought better of it. I'd stay home, relax, or maybe catch a movie.

We had reached a point when it was time to talk about "priorities."

Carol was my first real relationship since the death of my wife Angie five years ago. But how serious was I, or was she, for that matter? We'd both been going with the flow, avoiding the tipping point.

I loved being with her. She was classy, intelligent, and knew more about baseball than any woman I'd ever known. The sex wasn't bad either—oh, who was I kidding—the sex was terrific. I didn't enjoy the DC cocktail circuit or the power weekends that were an essential part of her business, but I sure didn't want some other guy to fill in as her "special guest" at such events. I was willing to meet her more than halfway.

I felt a jolt at my arm and realized that Walter was handing me his cell phone. "Maggie," he said, grinning.

"Left your phone at home again, didn't you?" she asked with a touch of annoyance.

"Guilty as charged," I laughed. "What's up?"

"Clovis has been trying to reach you all morning. I told him you were playing golf, but I'd see what I could do. If Walter hadn't answered, I would have called the pro shop and had you pulled off the course. He sounds that desperate."

"Any idea what's bothering him?"

"I haven't a clue. You know Clovis, nothing fazes him. But this time—well, I've never heard him so frazzled. It's a bit worrisome."

Walter waited in silence as I punched in Clovis's number.

I'd met Clovis Jones several years ago when I returned to Little Rock to help my long-time friend, Woody Cole. Woody had been arrested for shooting Arkansas's Senator Russell Robinson in the State Capitol Rotunda. Clovis was my lead investigator and provided security for my team during that case. Since then he'd played a major role in every high-profile case I had. He'd saved my bacon more times than I cared to think about, and we'd become close friends. I'd spent a week every spring with him in Arkansas fishing for trout on the White River, and it was easy to talk him into coming to DC to watch the Nats.

Clovis answered on the first ring.

"Thank God Maggie found you. How soon can you get here?"

"Slow down, Clovis. What's up?" I asked.

"Ben is about to mortgage his place and hire that damn fool Les Butterman to represent his daughter. Butterman will take every penny Ben's got and plead her out like he does every poor fool who hires him. Ben's too damn proud to ask you for help, so I'm asking for him—you need to get your ass down here."

Ben Jennings had been—well, not exactly a second father, but a safe haven for me when I was growing up in Little Rock. For as long as I'd known him, he'd owned and run a barbeque restaurant on the south side of town that made the best chopped pork sandwiches, ribs, and hush puppies anywhere, and I mean anywhere. He was a family man to the core. His wife Linda and his kids, Ben Jr., Lee, and Rochelle meant the world to him.

I tried again. "Slow down, Clovis. What are you talking about? Is Rochelle in legal trouble? Why can't Micki handle it?" I held the phone so Walter could hear, too.

"Don't they have television in DC? Ben's daughter is Rachel Goodman, for God's sake, the woman accused of spying for Israel and stealing military secrets. Hell, Jack, she's been on the front page of every newspaper in the country. Where have you been—holed up in a cave?"

First, my golf game had been cancelled, and now Clovis was trying to pull off some weird joke. It wasn't funny. If Ben's daughter was a spy, then I was the King of England.

2

I SPOKE WITH IRRITATION. "Ben has one daughter, and her name is Rochelle. I haven't seen her in years, but there's no way in hell that Rochelle is a spy. Are you and Stella in town?"

Clovis's significant other, Stella Rice, did computer consulting for Walter's companies, so it wouldn't be unusual for the two of them to come to DC unannounced. I expected Clovis to laugh, but his voice remained tight.

"Since you haven't seen her in years, you wouldn't know that Rochelle got married a few years back and changed her name. It's too long a story to get into, but the Rochelle Jennings you knew is now the Rachel Goodman you've been reading about in the papers. You need to come to Little Rock."

I could hardly believe my ears. Surely he was mistaken. Surely Rochelle wasn't the Rachel I'd seen in the headlines. "Hold on a minute," I replied, putting the phone down on the table.

"Walter, any chance I can charter your plane for the weekend?"

"Sorry, but no, you can't."

The awkward silence only lasted for a few seconds, before Walter flashed that sneaky grin I'd come to know and enjoy.

"But you can use it gratis for as long as you need it. I'll ask my pilot to be ready to leave by one o'clock. Does that work for you? Do you need Maggie? We're supposed to go to the symphony tonight but we can cancel."

I was no longer surprised by Walter's spontaneous generosity. Thankful, but not surprised.

"The timing is perfect, thanks. I have no idea what to expect, but there's no need for Maggie to make the trip. But I do need to talk to Ben in person before he hires that shyster Butterman. Sorry, Walter, but I can't get you out of this evening's concert."

I picked up the phone and said, "I should be there around three o'clock your time this afternoon. I'll text you before we take off. See if you can get me a room at the Armitage. If it's booked, try the Marriott. Just don't let Butterman anywhere near Ben until I get there."

"Got it. Ben will be thrilled. This thing's really gotten to him; it's way outside his wheelhouse. I'll give Micki and Sam a heads-up, too. We wondered if you'd fallen off the map, or maybe Carol wouldn't give you a hall pass. I guess I should've called earlier. I'll see you at the airport."

His comment about Carol stung—I hoped he meant it in jest. As I handed the phone to Walter, my mind wandered to what little I had read about the Rachel Goodman who had been accused of espionage.

She had graduated with honors from the University of Virginia, majoring in Arabic Studies, and taken a job with the Justice Department in New York. In the course of her work she had met and fallen in love with a young Jewish Rabbi, Ira Goodman. They had married and soon moved to DC. Two years ago he was the lone American victim of a rocket attack that killed more than twenty people at an outdoor restaurant in Jerusalem. The Israeli government blamed Hamas, but no one was ever arrested.

I heard Walter push his chair back, and I returned to the present.

"Thank you again, Walter. You know how grateful I am."

"I'd ask you to bring back a couple of bottles of Ben's barbeque sauce, but not this time. How on earth could Rachel Goodman turn out to be Ben's daughter?" He shook his head in disbelief, but continued before I could get in a word.

"Here's the thing, Jack. I think the world of Ben, but if the allegations about his daughter prove to be true, I'll have a hard time with this one. I'll keep an open mind for Ben's sake, but . . . stealing military secrets is hard to condone."

I wasn't surprised by his reaction. When the story hit the papers, I'd felt much the same way. Only my lawyer's caution and the presumption of innocence had tempered my outrage. I couldn't imagine any excuse for stealing military secrets and turning them over to another government, even an ally like Israel.

I hurried home to pack and call Maggie. When I told her Ben was about to hire Les Butterman, I wasn't surprised by her reaction. We'd met Les during the Cole matter, and she'd had a visceral reaction to the man. Who wouldn't? Oily, slicked-back hair, bad manners, cock-sure of himself, with a sexist attitude to boot. He was the kind of lawyer who gives all lawyers a bad name.

"Don't you dare let that sleaze bucket anywhere near Ben," Maggie fumed.

"Thanks to your husband's generosity, I'm on my way to Little Rock right now. Sure you don't want to hitch a ride so you can give your regards to ole Les? I know he'd love to see you," I teased.

"Please! I'll get to work setting up a new client file and doing the media research."

Maggie normally opposed our representing anyone unless it was antitrust related. Her enthusiasm surprised me.

"Don't spend a lot of time on this, Maggie. I don't know what kind of relationship Ben has with his daughter, but things can't be all peaches and cream if she changed her name. She may not want his help. I expect all he needs is for me to recommend a decent criminal attorney in DC who specializes in espionage cases. But if it comes to it, are you okay with our getting involved?" I heard her take a deep breath.

"Yes, Jack, I'm okay—mainly because I've learned that nothing will stop you from representing someone once you've made up your mind, no matter what I say. I've lost the argument too many times. I haven't given up, but this time even the press is calling for the death penalty, and you know how I feel about that. There are enough murders every day without the government setting the example."

I smiled as I listened to my English-born friend question the wisdom of our criminal justice system. I knew the real reason she wouldn't argue this time—she knew how much Ben meant to me. I was a sucker for old friends and lost causes. Rachel or Rochelle, fell into both categories.

3

I CALLED BEN'S CELL, but his wife Linda answered. She told me that when Ben heard I was coming, he had snatched his fishing rod from the umbrella stand and headed to Miller's Pond, reasoning, "Well, if Jack's coming, I've got crappie to catch."

"Don't worry—we've already got plenty of food in the fridge. Gifts from friends." Linda taught middle school math for many years, but had retired six months ago. Ben tried to get her to help at the restaurant, but she wasn't having any of it.

I hadn't thought of pan-fried crappie in a very long time. Most Arkansas fishermen will tell you that well-cooked crappie is the best tasting freshwater fish around. Crappies were puny, not more than half a pound. But they put up a heck of a fight and tasted as sweet as sunrise.

I started to call Carol, but thought better of it. She'd be busy entertaining guests and organizing dinner. So I texted her that I was off to Little Rock, figuring I'd hear from her sooner or later. But it had now been a couple of hours. Maybe things weren't back to normal after all.

Clovis picked up on the first ring. Yes, we were expected at Ben's for dinner. We'd eaten at Ben's restaurant many times, but neither of us had ever been to his home. Sam and Micki would meet us for brunch tomorrow at Crittenden's, the restaurant in the Armitage Hotel.

Sam had been one of my best friends in high school, my college roommate, and was now the county's prosecutor. Micki was a defense attorney who'd take on almost anyone with a convincing story—she'd never get rich practicing law, but she'd always be able to sleep at night. She'd acted as my co-counsel on the cases I handled in Little Rock, and this spring saved my butt by helping me defend Billy Hopper, the NFL all-pro wide receiver accused of a brutal murder in DC I looked forward to seeing them both. Sam was the friend you might not see for years, but when you did, you picked right up as if your last conversation had been just a moment ago. Micki . . . well let's say Micki occupies a special place in my heart.

The cab dropped me off at Montgomery County Airpark, just a few miles north of DC. Walter's pilot, a fellow of few words by the name of Abe, pulled up the stairs and settled into the cockpit with his co-pilot. I leaned my seat way back, aware of the privilege. Air travel today is tough and usually unpleasant. Many of my friends prefer to drive rather than fight the hassle of flying. If you can afford it, a private jet is the way to go. No long security lines or luggage hassles, not to mention generous legroom and a well-stocked bar.

As we climbed to cruising height, I immersed myself in articles about Rachel. She'd met her rabbi husband in New York, and they had moved to DC soon after the wedding. He became an assistant rabbi at a prominent synagogue in the District, traveling often to Israel as part of a cultural exchange sponsored by the Israeli government. She earned a Master's in International Affairs at George Washington University and, after graduation, took a position with the Defense Intelligence Agency at the Pentagon, climbing the ladder to become a senior analyst for the Middle East. They had no children.

After Ira's death she took a small apartment in Arlington, keeping to herself most of the time. An anonymous tip led authorities to discover she'd been downloading mountains of information about top-secret weapon systems under development by the Department of Defense and private contractors to a zip drive. The theft was breathtakingly simple.

The Feds were holding Rachel at a secret location while they tried to assess the damage. The Department of Justice and the various intelligence agencies had been oddly silent about what they'd discovered, including whether Israel had recruited her or she had volunteered after her husband's death.

High-level government sources, speaking off the record of course, insisted that Rachel was acting on behalf of the Israeli intelligence service. Our relationship with Israel had come under increased scrutiny. She faced a lifetime in prison or possibly a death sentence for espionage. I could find only a passing reference to her Little Rock connection.

The press interviewed her husband's brother, Mort Goodman, who said, "I don't agree with what Rachel did, but out of respect for my late brother, I'll pray for her soul and hope that life in prison will make her see the errors of her ways." The parents of her husband refused to talk to the press, but a family friend who insisted on anonymity said, "Abner Goodman and his wife Shirley are devastated. What on earth was she thinking? She has disgraced and betrayed the family and Ira's memory." The letters to the editor in the papers were of a similar tenor.

The *Post* reported that prior to her husband's death Rachel had been very active at their synagogue and had coached girls' basketball at the Jewish Community Center in Fairfax. The synagogue's rabbi declined comment, but a senior member of the JCC's staff told the reporter, "You could have knocked me over with a feather when I heard Rachel had been arrested. I've never known a kinder or more generous person. She spent much of her free time coaching and mentoring young girls. She quit coaching after her husband's death, but we all thought she'd return at some point." Other articles reported that she had been outgoing and very supportive of her husband's work both at the synagogue and in the community, but that after his death she had become reclusive and withdrawn.

I expected to read that the FBI had discovered large overseas deposits in her bank account, or that a dark, good-looking Israeli agent had turned her after Ira's death, or that she was embittered after Ira's killing and had become radicalized, but not a word. I couldn't remember a high-profile case in which the press hadn't been fed information by law enforcement off the record. How else could they prejudice the public beforehand?

If you believed what you read, the authorities had her dead to rights. But I had learned that things aren't always as they appear. I had lots of questions, beginning with how an African-American woman from Little Rock met, fell in love, and married a rabbi from Brooklyn.

I closed my laptop and allowed my thoughts to turn to the young college student I'd known as Rochelle Jennings. One weekend, she'd driven with friends from Charlottesville, Virginia to DC for a basketball game between Georgetown and UVA. She didn't want to party all night in Georgetown with her friends, so she was left to fend for herself. Her dad had told her if she ever found herself in DC needing help, she should call me. I was out of town, but she asked Angie if she could sleep on our couch for the night. She ended up staying the whole weekend, and Angie drove her back to school on Monday.

Rochelle would stay with us for a weekend now and then from that day on, bonding with Angie and becoming almost a big sister to our daughter, Beth. I was busy at work so I didn't get to know her well, but her maturity, good manners, and friendly demeanor impressed me. After college, she rented her own apartment. I saw little of her after that, but Angie and Beth would go to lunch with her occasionally. I thought I remembered seeing her at Angie's funeral, but I have to admit that time in my life is still a blur.

Thinking about Rochelle reminded me of her father's history. He was raised on a small farm outside the prairie town of Dumas in southeast Arkansas and drafted into the Army during Vietnam. When he returned from the service, he attended college on the G.I. Bill, but dropped out after a year. He sold barbecue at construction sites out of the back of his truck and eventually opened "Ben's" in Little Rock, just on the outskirts of the now shabby industrial district. It wasn't much to look at, and if the wind blew just right, your eyes burned from the smoke pouring from the big smoker out back. But any weekday you might run into the city's mayor, or the president of a local bank, or ladies from the Junior League, all lined up to get the best barbeque in Arkansas.

Ben had tacked up decades of family photos on the paneled walls: his kids and their friends, pictures from family trips, pictures of the fish they'd caught, and the sights they'd seen. You'd see autographed photographs of state politicians he admired: Fulbright, Clinton, Pryor, Tucker, Beebe, and Bumpers. Republicans were always welcome to pay for his barbeque, but only one Republican graced Ben's wall: long-deceased Governor Winthrop Rockefeller. Six days a week, from eleven in the morning until nine at night, the tables filled with folks eating good barbecue and drinking beer. Benches and picnic tables shaded by huge oaks sat on an empty lot next door and, depending on the drift of the wind, they were full, too.

Ben wasn't a big man—about five-foot-eight with a barrel chest and arms as big as tree trunks. When I was a young man, I'd sit at the counter eating a chopped pork sandwich so wet with slaw and barbeque sauce you needed a drop cloth underneath to catch the drippings. Unless the police were present, and even if they were, I'd wash down the barbeque with a beer. Ben was always ready to listen to my problems, usually stories that involved a girl, my stepfather, or my curve ball. His down-to-earth advice wasn't always what I wanted to hear, but was almost always what I needed. The day I left Arkansas, I spent my last night with Ben talking out my options.

Twenty-five years later, I returned to Little Rock to help Woody Cole. In a matter of days, I was back eating a late lunch at Ben's, picking up where we'd left off. I've been back to Little Rock several times since, and each time lunch at Ben's has been a must. His barbeque alone was worth the trip to Arkansas. My wife Angie used to beg friends to bring a few bottles of his sauce when they came to DC. She occasionally cooked her own, but she could never duplicate Ben's. I want them to serve Ben's barbeque at my funeral. Add Helen Cole's chess pie, and the church will be overflowing.

Abe's voice announcing our approach into Little Rock gave me a start—I must have dozed off. As I watched the square fields of rice and soy beans come into shape below, my thoughts turned to the man who had died last night on the eighteenth green, Harold Spencer. His name sounded familiar, but I still couldn't place it. Could the high-stakes poker game that Friday have had anything to do with his death? At least it had nothing to do with the business at hand.

4

⬦————⬦

CLOVIS WAS LEANING against his black Chevy Tahoe when I walked off the plane at Little Rock's Hodges Air Center. We exchanged an easy hug, and he tossed my bag into the back seat, asking, "No golf clubs?"

"Won't be here that long. What do you know?"

"Not much. *The Demozette* made a big deal about Rachel growing up in Little Rock, ran pictures of her playing basketball for Central High, and interviewed old classmates who speculated on what made her turn into a traitor."

The local paper, *The Arkansas Democrat-Gazette,* is the product of a bitter battle between two papers—*The Arkansas Gazette* and *The Arkansas Democrat.* When the dust cleared and the owner of the *Democrat* ended up buying the *Gazette,* he merged the two papers, and everyone but him called the product the *Demozette. The Gazette* had been an old-line, well-respected publication. The *Demozette* had a conservative bent, but it had gotten better over the years, and at least Little Rock still has a real newspaper, complete with good comics and the cryptoquote.

"Can you get someone to pull those articles for me?" I asked.

"Maggie's got your number. Copies of the relevant papers are in your room at the Armitage."

I smiled. Maggie was always a step ahead of me. She knew I liked to hold the actual paper. Sure, you could dive right to a specific article on the Internet. But you couldn't see the positioning, the ads, the obits, the style pieces, the local sports news—all the components that showed the character and quirks of a community. *The Demozette* still did a good job of that.

"The bad news is Ben has shut down his restaurant," Clovis continued.

"No way. Why would he do that? That restaurant is his life."

"Some jerk painted Stars of David, swastikas, and ugly graffiti on the walls. If you wanted takeout, you couldn't get through on the phone for all the nasty callers tying up the line. His employees and customers were scared to come in, and several of his suppliers refused to make deliveries. I don't know what's come over folks to be so hateful. Maybe it's those guys in the new administration."

"Ben's not scared off easily. Did he have the good sense to call you?" I asked.

"At first he refused my help, but when he closed the restaurant, the assholes targeted his home—bricks through the windows and honking cars driving by all hours of the night. Now I've got guys watching the place, very visible guys. We take care of Ben and Linda and watch the restaurant day and night to make sure no one torches the place. Sam's been a big help with the police."

"I can't believe it. There hasn't been a word about any of this in the *Post*."

"Nope, and not a word in the *Demozette* either. They're spending all their ink reminding people that Rachel is a dirty rotten traitor and that her parents live and work right here in River City. Sam had to go to the publisher to get them to quit running pictures of the house on the front page. Remember how worked up folks got when Woody shot Russell? Well, that was nothing compared to this. I'm surprised we haven't seen white sheets and burning crosses."

"Come on, you're exaggerating."

"You can see for yourself. Little Rock has changed a lot since you left, mostly for the better. But pockets of racism and anti-Semitism still linger, and some people are quick to get riled up. Maybe they're just bored and enjoy the diversion. But Sam's worried, and so am I."

"All this has got to be expensive. I can…" I blurted.

"Put your wallet back in your pocket, Jack. I've got this. You have your hands full figuring out what you can do for Rochelle."

He was right, but I felt guilty. For weeks, Clovis, Sam, and others had been doing what they could to help, while I was completely unaware. I hadn't lived in Little Rock for over twenty-five years, but it was still home.

"I'm sorry, Clovis. I'm the latecomer to the party. Remind me to listen and keep my mouth shut. I didn't even know Rochelle had married, much less changed her name."

"I want Ben and Linda to tell you the story, so I won't jump the gun. Instead, let's go over how to keep you safe while you're here."

I interrupted, quickly breaking my promise to shut up and listen.

"What? Not again! Has Maggie put you up to this?"

"Yes, Maggie and I talked, and yes, she pulled rank, so be quiet and listen. In case you've forgotten, folks remember you as that hotshot lawyer who helped Woody Cole, the man who shot their beloved Senator. Those folks have long memories and short tempers, especially if a little Jack Daniels is involved.

"You've got a reputation for upsetting the apple cart, so to speak. Speculation will run rampant that you're here to get Rachel off. The press will hound you, and those same people throwing bricks through Ben's window will turn their anger toward you. No one knows you're in town yet, but that won't last long. So listen up: you're not to leave the hotel without one of my people or me, Maggie's orders. We'll drop your bag off at the Armitage. Then we'll head to Ben's. Got it?"

I gave him a curt nod and changed the subject. He might be right, but I didn't have to like it.

"Is Stella joining us for dinner?"

Stella and Clovis lived together, and most everyone figured they'd get married; it was only a matter of when. Clovis bought the ring over a year ago, but he still hadn't popped the question. I'd asked why the delay, but he always changed the subject.

Stella looked nothing like my image of a computer genius and an expert in cyber security. She loved skyscraper heels, tight jeans, piercings, and multi-colored nail polish and hair. When she wasn't buried in the depths of a computer system, you'd find her working out at the high intensity CrossFit gym she owned. She'd met Clovis when we worked on the Stewart case together. They were an unlikely pair, but it worked. Love is funny that way.

"Not this time. She's in Charlotte at Walter's data center. Walter's computers are under attack by a sophisticated team of foreign hackers. She'll be there for at least another week."

Walter had tried several times to hire Stella to become head of I.T. for his companies. She'd avoided giving him a definitive answer, but was willing to consult whenever one of his companies had a serious problem. Stella valued her independence.

"She's not much on fried foods anyway," he said with a poorly concealed glance in my direction. "Looks like you've put on a few."

"Okay, okay, don't rub it in. I'm trying to eat better, but I haven't had fresh crappie in ages. I can't wait."

"Me, either," he grinned. "Let's go!"

5

⊱━━━⊰

FINDING NO PRESS outside the hotel was an immediate relief. We walked through the lobby and took the large wood-paneled elevator up to the fourth floor. I changed into a fresh shirt, khakis, and a navy blazer. Within thirty minutes we were parked in front of a one story red brick house with a manicured lawn on Shirley Drive. Nothing distinguished Ben's home from the red brick homes on either side except his had a porch and a porch swing. Well, one other thing: plywood covered two of his front windows.

We pulled into the driveway, and Ben opened the front door almost before we got out of the car. He was wearing a dark grey suit, striped tie, and his shoes had been polished. I was glad Clovis had suggested a sports coat; clearly Ben considered us special company. He showed us into his living room, and I offered him a bottle of cabernet that Clovis had picked up at my request.

"Thank you," he responded, "but you shouldn't have." He verified the usual bromide by opening a closet door in the entry hall that revealed shelves full of wine and bottle after bottle of every kind of liquor you could imagine. My jaw dropped when I saw the quantity and quality of his liquor stash.

Ben laughed. "Business friends and suppliers show up every Christmas with a bottle or two to honor the season. Linda makes me keep it all out of sight. She used to worry Preacher Barnes might drop by unannounced, but not so much anymore. Someday she's gonna make me clean it all out. Maybe we'll have a big party, invite everyone we know, and drink it all."

He waved us into the living room and filled glasses with ice, followed by a healthy shot of bourbon in each. I sank into a well-used armchair, looking around the room with interest. Family photos, mementos, and knick-knacks filled the walls and shelves; needlepoint pillows nestled in the corners of the sofas and chairs. It was a very comfortable room, full of family memories.

Ben handed us each a glass and raised his in a toast.

"Welcome to my home, gentlemen. Drink up."

We raised our glasses, and I took a sip—oh my God, I'd never tasted better. I let out an appreciative sigh. I could tell Ben was pleased with my spontaneous reaction.

I had to ask, "What are we drinking?"

Ben's eyes twinkled. "Well, I did a man a favor a while back. He showed up last Christmas with a bottle of Pappy Van Winkle 20 Year. Linda knows it's expensive and knows better than to pour it on her fruitcakes, but doesn't have a clue what it costs. I've been saving it for a special occasion."

I couldn't believe we were the special occasion, but enjoyed the honor. He shook off our thanks.

"Jack, I know we have business, but let's save it for after dinner. Linda wants to be part of that discussion, and right now she and her friends are fixing dinner. Tell me about that daughter of yours."

Ben had met my daughter, Beth, when we were in Little Rock for the Cole case. I told him she and her significant other, Jeff Fields, were living in St. Louis. Jeff was completing his internship at Barnes Hospital and Beth was working on her Master's in Social Work at Washington University. I expressed my frustration that they still weren't engaged, but acknowledged that conventions change with the times, and that they didn't need my permission.

I knew I'd stepped in it almost the minute I said it. Clovis cleared his throat, and Ben took a healthier sip of his drink, but nothing more was said. We spent the next half hour talking sports: the Razorbacks' upset of Auburn the first game of the season, my Stafford State Cardinals' chances in basketball, and Ben's excitement over the upcoming deer season.

A woman I didn't recognize marched in from the kitchen and

announced that dinner was ready. I'd met Linda several times at the restaurant. She was short, slight of build, and wore her graying hair short. This woman was at least five foot ten, her long black hair held back with several rhinestone barrettes. She looked to be around forty years old or so and was dressed in a long, flowery dress and heels. Large gold hoop earrings shaped her face.

The mystery was solved when Ben pulled out her chair at the dinner table and introduced us to Jasmine White, a neighbor and close friend of Linda's. There were only four chairs at the table. Ben forestalled the obvious question, saying that Linda was in the kitchen supervising dinner.

"She'll join us later," he said, as if the seating arrangement were an everyday occurrence. Before I knew it, Ben had said grace and the door to the kitchen swung open.

Three women came into the room with platters and bowls piled high with crappie, hushpuppies, potato salad, collard greens, fried okra, and lima beans. A fourth woman came in with a chilled bottle of white wine for Clovis, Jasmine, and me. Ben continued to sip on his bourbon. The crappie was cooked to perfection, and the vegetables must have been fresh from someone's garden.

I have to say Jasmine acted the perfect hostess, engaging Clovis and me in conversation about current events, our childhoods, and our favorite vacation spots. Ben ate little, but encouraged Clovis and me to have our fill. It was hard to stop because as soon as we finished one helping, one of Linda's watchful friends would appear to pass around a new platter.

On her third round I begged, "Please, I can't eat another bite. I really can't—I might explode."

The friend holding the serving spoon looked disappointed, but backed away. Clovis tried to suppress a relieved sigh.

Jasmine asked, "Would anyone like coffee with dessert?"

We all declined. On cue, a woman brought in a piping hot apple pie accompanied by a bowl of vanilla ice cream, impossible to resist.

We didn't see any sign of Linda until the table had been cleared. We all jumped up as she peered around the kitchen door, but she still didn't join us. She looked to her husband and said, "Ben, why don't you take our guests to your study; I need to thank Jasmine and my friends. I'll be there in a few minutes."

Clovis and I duly said good night to Jasmine, who didn't seem at all annoyed to be excluded from the rest of the evening, and we followed Ben into a comfortable study off the living room. I declined a cigar, but accepted a brandy, as did Clovis, who had arranged for one of his men to drive us home.

A big desk dominated the room's center, and family pictures and mounted fish covered the walls. An iMac and a couple of unused legal pads sat on the credenza behind the desk.

Ben sunk into the chair behind his desk, waving Clovis and me into aging, but still comfortable armchairs. We'd enjoyed no more than a single swallow when Ben sat up with a start and looked toward the door. "Okay, I need to explain before she gets here. I know you're wondering about dinner. Linda got her way of doing things from her mama, and she just can't let go. She likes to be in charge of her kitchen, and she doesn't trust anyone else to cook for her guests. She and Jasmine worked this out between themselves, and I can't complain. It's her kitchen, and…" he whirled around in his chair as the door opened.

"Linda, that was a mighty fine dinner. Come on in—I was just pouring after dinner drinks." He rose and handed her a glass of bourbon, neat, no ice.

She settled into a rocking chair in the corner and put the glass on an end table. After a single appreciative sip, she reached into the corner behind the chair and retrieved a lumpy quilted bag. From there she pulled out a large ball of yarn connected to a rather small piece of work-in-progress and began to knit. I wondered how long the bag had lain in the corner.

She gave us a Yoda-like smile and said, "Now don't mind me. I'm just going to listen for a while."

I didn't believe her for a minute, but I was ready to play the game. Who could complain after such hospitality?

Ben cleared his throat. "Well…Jack, thank you for coming. After all these years, it's an honor to have you grace our home. Clovis told me you had no idea Rochelle was married. Let's not waste any time on apologies. I'm glad you're here."

"What can I do to help?" I asked. His formal tone threw me—our conversations had always been in his restaurant or on the baseball field.

"For tonight, just listen to what I have to say and ask me anything you like. Tomorrow after church we'll figure out what you can do. I want you to have time to digest what you hear."

I nodded, ready to learn if or how Ben and Linda's daughter had become an international spy.

6

BEN LOOKED AT LINDA before he began as if to ask permission—an interesting dynamic. She carefully finished her row and then dropped her work into her lap, removed her glasses, and looked at Ben with a mixture of pain and strength, as if they shared a shameful secret they didn't want to tell. She gave a slight sigh and nodded.

He cleared his throat and spoke clearly, "I was so pleased when Rochelle got in touch with Angie. She told Linda that she felt like your house was a home away from home. Angie was always there for her, and Beth was the little sister she always wanted. Linda and I were so grateful. I'm sorry we never told you how much we appreciated your family welcoming our baby girl.

"We also have two sons, Ben Jr. and Lee. Ben Jr. joined the Marines after graduating from Catholic High, did several tours in the Middle East, and now works for the U.S. Marshals Service in Tulsa. He's yet to marry.

"Lee works for the U.S. Forest Service, and his wife, Tina, is a special agent with the FBI Tina grew up in Oregon, so after they graduated from Arkansas they settled outside of Portland. Rochelle's brothers and sister-in-law live in fear that someone will connect them to Rochelle, and that such a connection could cost them their careers."

I heard a mumble from Linda's corner. "They should worry about their sister—not how it might affect them. Lee's all worried about 'poor Tina.' Poor Tina needs to have babies and quit fretting so much about her precious career. Her career isn't going anywhere out in Oregon, that's for sure."

She never looked up from her knitting, and I could tell Ben didn't appreciate her interruption.

After a long pause Ben continued, "As you know, Rochelle was our first-born. She was popular at Central High, a good basketball player, and an excellent student. Headstrong, like most teenage girls, but never got in any real trouble. She helped out at the restaurant, helped Linda care for the boys, and never gave either of us cause to worry. She earned a Nalley scholarship to the University of Virginia, a full ride—could never have gone, otherwise.

"Sure, she learned to party in Virginia, but she was active on campus and kept up her grades. But when she came home, she'd changed—didn't want to help out at the restaurant, refused to go to church, wasn't respectful of her mother. She wasn't the same girl. I blame the school."

I remained quiet, but since my own daughter had recently graduated from Davidson College, I recognized her changed attitude as a sign of normal maturation and independence—cutting the apron strings, so to speak.

Linda spoke up, not mumbling this time. "It had nothing to do with college. College may have filled her head with new ideas and made her independent, but we lost her the summer she graduated— when she went to New York and met Ira."

Ben continued, "She was a good student at Virginia. She stayed on campus during the summers working and taking classes, and graduated in four years. The summer after she graduated from UVA, she took a job with the Department of Justice in the Community Relations Service. They sent her to New York right off the bat.

"She met her future husband, Ira Goodman, on a task force trying to ease tensions between the African-American and Jewish communities in Brooklyn."

I interrupted, "Am I right that Ira was a rabbi?"

"Yes. He was also ten years older than Rochelle. She called at the end of the summer to say she was bringing someone home for us to meet. Let's say he didn't turn out to be quite the fellow I'd expected, and I wasn't prepared to hear they were getting married. I will give him this: he was polite, respectful, and asked my permission. That was something.

"I tried to talk about the obstacles they'd face, but my words fell on deaf ears. They weren't worried one bit. But what am I saying, Jack? You and Angie faced some of the same obstacles."

My late wife, Angie, was African-American, and yes, early in our relationship we faced more than a few difficulties.

"Angie's parents weren't excited about me, either, but we turned out okay," I said, smiling.

"Their reluctance had more to do with what happened at Stafford than the color of your skin, Jack," Ben said.

One particular night from hell was a distant memory that surfaced more often than I'd like to admit.

"You're right. Were Ira's parents supportive?"

"They were not. Linda and I didn't care about his skin color, or the fact that he was ten years older, or that he was Jewish. It was so sudden, so out of character. We were trying to take it all in when she announced she was converting—our little Baptist girl had decided to become a Jew—and to top it off she was changing her name to Rachel. Don't you know people talked when word got out! Preacher Barnes told Linda that Rochelle would go straight to Hell. I'm sure that man has got his own invitation waiting. It never felt right, but Linda and I stood proud and gave them our blessing."

"Sounds like you did the right thing. Did they get married in Little Rock? Did Ira's parents come?"

"No, they got married in a private ceremony in DC, witnessed by a few friends. His parents held out in their opposition to the marriage. They refused to take part, and so neither set of parents were invited. That's probably why you didn't know she was married; none of our family or friends were included. A private ceremony was their way of avoiding confrontation."

I felt for Linda, sure that she had dreamed of a different wedding for her daughter.

"I don't think I read there were any children?"

"She told me she wanted to wait until they were both 'secure professionally,' whatever that meant," Linda responded. "Their careers were more important than family. What is with young people these days? What's wrong with having children?"

Ben frowned and changed the subject. "Besides serving as a rabbi, Ira also worked for the Israeli government. Rochelle never said what he actually did for the Israelis, but it involved a lot of travel back and forth to Israel."

Linda couldn't let the children issue go. "Every time they were here, I'd ask Rochelle when she would make me a grandmother. She always said I should ask Lee's wife, Tina. She knew how to get my goat. But I knew she loved children. She was proud of what she called 'her girls' at the community center. She talked about taking them to see the Mystics play and about the time she organized a trip to the Holocaust museum for the older girls. For the life of me..."

Ben raised his hand and interrupted, "Ira and I found we had one thing in common—he liked to fish. He and I would go fishing most every morning when they visited. He knew his way around a boat, and we relaxed—he grew on me. He also spent a lot of time at the synagogue with Rabbi Strauss. I never asked what they talked about; didn't seem to be any of my business. Rochelle enjoyed spending time with her mother and a few school friends. Whenever I tried to bring up her work, she made it clear she couldn't talk about what she did for the government. They seemed happy, and we enjoyed the little time we had together."

I asked, "Did they ever talk about his parents?"

Linda answered, "Not really. His parents were not as accepting of Rochelle as we were of Ira. Sometimes they took the train to upstate New York for some family event, but Rochelle used to text me saying she couldn't wait to get home."

Ben continued, "We were resigned to the fact that our daughter had chosen to lead a separate and different life and were grateful for the time we got to see her. I'll never forget the day she called to say Ira was dead. He was killed at an open-air restaurant somewhere in Israel. A single rocket fired by Hamas killed our son-in-law and twenty other people. It was all over the news.

"We offered to come to DC, but she said she was leaving for Israel the next day. She called to let us know she was safe when she arrived and promised to come see us as soon as she got home, but she never did. We called every week to check on her, but she was always too busy at work to talk or take any time off. It's been over two years since we've seen her."

Linda spoke, "I'll never forget what she said the day she called from Israel. 'It was meant for him—they killed him, the bastards killed him.' She said it over and over."

Clovis asked, "Who did she mean? Hamas?"

"I asked her the same thing. She wouldn't say, pretty much told me to quit asking. We wanted to help, but, well, she didn't seem to want help from us, or anyone else, for that matter."

7

ROCHELLE'S BELIEF THAT HER HUSBAND was murdered might explain erratic behavior, but wouldn't be a defense to espionage. Now was not the time to discuss her defense, so I remained quiet. Ben took a healthy sip of brandy and cleared his throat.

"We had no idea she'd been arrested until the FBI showed up at the house." He continued, "Two agents knocked on the door one evening during *Jeopardy*. They were very polite, and the way they kept saying they were here as a courtesy, Linda and I thought something had happened to Tina. Then they told us that Rochelle was in custody."

"Did they tell you why?" I asked.

"They wouldn't give us any details, but said she was being questioned about documents in her possession. We didn't find out she'd been arrested for spying until we read it in the morning paper." Ben shook his head. He had stuttered and hesitated before getting out the word "spying."

Linda interrupted, "Oh, they were plenty slick. All official in those dark suits and ties. And they were real polite—asked us if we talked with her often, did she text or email us, had she sent us anything for safekeeping. I even offered them a glass of iced tea."

"Now, Linda, don't get upset again," Ben said. "We were in shock, but we didn't have anything to hide so we answered their questions. I let them take my laptop—they said they'd bring it back in a few days, but they didn't. Later they told me they couldn't return it until the case was over. That's why I have this new computer. First time

I've owned an Apple—you know, a Mac." He smiled at the computer on his desk.

I asked, "Had she sent you any attachments or strange emails?"

"Nothing like that at all," he answered.

I made a mental note to talk to Stella about Ben's emails. I didn't want government documents to show up on his computer. I have a healthy distrust for the FBI, if you haven't noticed. I felt pretty sure Ben would never see his old computer again. Several years ago the FBI had raided the home of one of Beth's college friends. They took every computer in the house, including her little brothers' Kindles. The parents were never charged, and the case is now closed, but the government kept the computers, including the boys' Kindles.

"They left me their cards, and I've called several times to see when I can talk to Rochelle. They're always polite, always say the same thing—she can't have visitors or talk to family. After a few weeks, Linda was going crazy so I decided to hire a lawyer."

Linda mumbled again, "Linda going crazy, my eye. Tell them the truth, Ben."

"Okay, Linda you're right. I was frustrated. Nobody would tell me what was going on, my business was under siege, and the boys were no help. Neither of them offered to come home, and Tina hung up whenever I called. The only person who wants to talk is Butterman— he calls almost every day. I'm sure glad you're here. That guy gives me the creeps, and he sure doesn't think much of you."

"No, he does not, and I can assure you the feeling is mutual. Let me think about what you've told me overnight, and we'll talk again tomorrow. One thing's for sure: I'll do whatever I can to help. You were there for me; now it's my turn. Let's meet back here at two o'clock tomorrow. Will church be over by then?"

Linda nodded, but Ben asked, "Thanks, but can you hear me out for a couple more minutes?"

"My time is yours," I answered.

"I have nightmares about what I saw and experienced in Vietnam, and I remember how I was greeted when I came home like it was yesterday. We knew how divided the country was over the war. Hell, most of us were dead set against it, and for good reason. But we didn't exactly have much choice, so we did our duty. Imagine how it felt to be spat upon and shunned by friends who'd avoided the draft. My best friend told me I'd risked my life for 'honky's war,' that I was no better than an Uncle Tom.

"I'm still proud of my military service. It's a lot of who I am. I saw and did things that still haunt me, but I grew up, developed discipline, and learned to focus my emotions in a positive way. So, when I hear my baby girl called a traitor it cuts me like a knife. Ben Jr. and I have talked about it; he has the same reaction. Does loyalty to country trump loyalty to family? I love my daughter, but I'm not sure how I'll handle it if it turns out if she really was a traitor. You've got to help me with this, Jack. I just don't know what to do."

Linda broke in, "Jack, I bet you're thinking Rochelle got mad about Ira's death, thought the government had a hand in it, and did whatever she's accused of doing. I know that's what is eating at Ben, but I don't believe it for a second. I talked to my daughter some after Ira died. She may have abandoned her faith and changed her name, but she's no spy. She's Ben's daughter through and through, and that's never changed.

"You asked how you could help. Find out what Rochelle is accused of doing and whether she did it. If she did I need to know why. I'll love her no matter what, and that goes for Ben, too. He'll never abandon his baby girl, no matter what she did, or what he says now."

8

CLOVIS AND I LEFT BEN sitting in his chair sipping brandy. Linda volunteered to show us out, and he didn't object. She walked us to the door and out onto the porch. I waited while she looked back to make sure Ben was out of earshot.

"Thank you again for coming. You're the only person Ben trusts to sort this thing out. It's eating him alive, and he has no outlet to keep his mind elsewhere. With the restaurant closed, he sits in that chair fretting and worrying. He reads every newspaper article and spends hours on the Internet reading what anyone is saying about Rochelle.

"I need to tell you a couple more things, but you can't tell him I told you. Promise?" she asked.

I nodded my head.

"Ben received a Bronze Star and several other commendations for his service in Vietnam. When he got off the bus in Little Rock, he was in full uniform, his medals on full display. I drove up from Dumas with his parents to meet him. I was in love with him, have been since the third grade and always will be." She allowed herself a smile.

I was picturing an idyllic scene until she continued.

"His parents and I weren't the only ones there that day. The bus was full of returning soldiers, and happy family members lined the streets to meet them. Then three pickups full of kids appeared out of nowhere. They pelted Ben and the other soldiers with eggs, paint, and excrement, calling them murderers, baby killers, and traitors."

There was nothing for me to say, and she wasn't through.

"The worst of it was that one of Ben's sisters, Maureen, was one of the kids. She'd been the one who let the group of protestors know when the bus would arrive. She got up in his face and told him she was ashamed of him, that he was a traitor to his race. Then she spit on him, right in front of her parents."

"Oh, Lord! What'd he do?"

"Nothing. He loved his sister. But I was scared what he might do to the others. Who could blame him for fighting back? Several of the other soldiers whose families were getting pelted were reacting, but instead of fighting, he shouted, 'Soldiers, it's time to go home. These people are not the enemy. Leave it be, leave it be.' Then he put his arm around me, and we left. The others followed his lead."

"What happened to the sister?" Clovis asked.

"They didn't speak for years. She tried to blame her friends, but he would have nothing to do with her. He refused to let her come to our wedding. His Mom was pretty upset about that, but he wouldn't back down. Then after his Dad died and his Mom got sick, they reconciled, sort of, but the scars are there. She's called and asked to talk to Ben about Rochelle, but I won't let that happen. I wouldn't be surprised to see her on TV soon, like she's all close and lovey-dovey with the family. She ought to know better, but she doesn't."

Such a sad and difficult story.

"It's possible the press will dig into Ben's background, discover he's a war hero, and write a piece comparing him to his daughter." I wasn't telling Linda anything she hadn't thought.

She said, "That's why I knew I had to tell you. Ben never would."

On that somber note, she walked back into the house, and we returned to the waiting Suburban. Clovis rode shotgun, and I slumped into the back seat. Not a word was said as the driver headed back to the hotel.

I noticed that both Ben and Linda continued to call their daughter "Rochelle." I expected it wasn't just the conversion to Judaism that had upset them.

I was old enough to remember the Vietnam War—my father was one of its first American victims. My mother had told me stories about soldiers returning and being greeted in a similar fashion.

She used to say, "Some people have a hard time distinguishing between the warriors and the war."

It wasn't long before the driver interrupted our thoughts. "Clovis, I'm pretty sure the guy in my mirror is a tail. Want me to lose him?"

Clovis's eyes shot to the rearview mirror, and I turned around in my seat to see a white Tundra.

"Already? Jeez, Jack—I guess I shouldn't be surprised. Jordan, you know what to do."

Jordan replied, "Right—everybody hold on."

Warned, I grabbed the handle above the window as our driver made an impossible turn on two wheels into a side street as our pursuer flew by, came to a screeching halt, and backed up.

Jordan must have earned his stripes at NASCAR because we weaved through the quiet neighborhoods at breakneck speed. The other driver didn't stand a chance. Clovis was on his phone as we tore down Broadway in downtown Little Rock. I expected to see blue lights any second.

"I need a detail at the Armitage. Tell the crews at the house and the restaurant to be on the lookout for a white Tundra."

Clovis wanted to give his detail a chance to check out the hotel, so we took a tour of downtown Little Rock. The city had opened Main Street to traffic again—the pedestrian mall idea hadn't worked after all. This day had been full of surprises; I wondered what tomorrow would bring.

SUNDAY

9

I woke up Sunday morning with no real vision of how I might help Rachel or Ben. To make matters worse, Carol Madison hadn't called or returned any of my texts.

On a whim, I checked the *Post* on my laptop—nothing at all about Harold Spencer, whoever he was. It wouldn't surprise me if Columbia had pulled some strings to keep the event out of the paper. I decided to let it go, and walked downstairs to meet Clovis.

Over breakfast, I looked through both the local paper and the *New York Times*. Both editorial pages featured opinion pieces suggesting that Rachel was America's newest traitor, comparing her to Benedict Arnold and the Rosenbergs. They had drawn these conclusions without having a clue about what she was supposed to have done or why. Prosecutors use the press to convict their targets in the court of public opinion all the time. But in Rachel's case, the slander was based on crafted hearsay and innuendo fed to the press by intelligence agencies schooled in manipulating the world media. So far, the public hadn't been given a single fact regarding her alleged crimes.

Several of my good friends work as reporters or writers for newspapers or Internet publications. They fight the rush to judgment every day, but the pressures of the twenty-four hour news cycle, Internet news coverage, and tightening budgets frustrate the best of them. Now we have an administration calling every article that casts it in an unfavorable light "fake news." Just at the time when our country needs real investigative journalism and reporters to discover and mine the truth, newsroom budgets are being cut to the bone.

Not too long ago, one friend told me we are witnessing the demise of print journalism. I hope not, but I can see why she thinks that way. My own daughter doesn't take the St. Louis newspaper— she gets all her news from the Internet.

Clovis joined me for a cup of coffee just as I was finishing the funnies. At least the *Demozette* had a good comics section. If the *Post* ever drops its comics section, it might lose me.

"Be sure and thank Jordan for me. He was as cool as they come last night," I said.

"He's been a find all right," Clovis responded. "His family's farm is near Batesville. He grew up idolizing the NASCAR Hall of Fame driver Mark Martin, who's also from Batesville, but Jordan had the good sense to get his degree. He's smart and shows good judgment."

I had to ask, "Any idea who was tailing us?"

"Not a clue. It could have been the Feds, but they aren't usually so obvious. And I've never seen them in a white Tundra; black Suburbans are more their style. You haven't made the paper yet, so who knows you're in town? Jordan's on it, but…" He shrugged.

I gave him a look, but let it go. I had to let Clovis do his job, so I could concentrate on mine.

He refilled his cup and asked, "You figured out what to tell Ben this afternoon?"

"Nope. Like you, I don't have a clue. It sounds like Linda halfway believes Rachel did something wrong. Ben will have a hard time accepting a guilty plea, if that's what's in the offing, no matter what the reason. The next few weeks won't be easy for either of them."

"Or for you," Clovis noted.

"It's further complicated because Rachel is a mature adult. She may already have counsel who won't want to cooperate with an anti-trust lawyer doing a favor for her parents. An interfering family can be a criminal lawyer's worst nightmare."

"Can you find out if she's represented?" Clovis asked.

"I'll work on that this morning. Any surprises in store when we meet Micki and Sam?"

Last time I'd asked about Micki, Clovis told me that she'd gone on a bender after finding Eric, her fiancé, in bed with one of his nurses. Sam and Clovis had intervened, and she got over the bastard. By the time she came onboard in the Billy Hopper case, Micki was seeing Larry Bradford, an artisan carpenter. I'd grown to like Larry after spending time with him. He had a calming influence on Micki, not a small accomplishment.

There was much more to Larry than met the eye. He was from an old Little Rock family whose sons have always been bankers, as have their sons, and their sons. Larry graduated from St. Albans and Princeton, but couldn't stomach the life of a banker and returned to New England to study carpentry. He became a very accomplished artisan and came to Arkansas to pursue his craft. Several of his pieces were currently on exhibit at Crystal Bridges Museum in Northwest Arkansas.

Clovis interrupted my brief musings.

"Not that I'm aware. Micki and Larry are still together. Stella and I have gone out to dinner with them several times, but you know Micki. The one thing certain is that nothing is certain when it comes to men."

Having been one of those men for a brief period, I understood what he meant.

"Sam is talking about running for the Arkansas Supreme Court—I guess that's news. I think most lawyers support him, but seats on the court have become politicized. A lot of money is pouring in from out of state to make sure the Arkansas Supremes are ultra-conservative and business friendly."

Clovis had just described the state of the judiciary all over the country. Judicial races, which used to be politically impartial and low key, were becoming expensive contests with candidates beholden to either big business or wealthy trial lawyers—Justice going to the highest bidder.

Clovis brought me up to date on Woody's mom, Helen Cole, and Judge Marshall Fitzgerald, a boyhood friend and Billy Hopper's mentor. I made a mental note to call them both before I left town.

Without even thinking, I looked down to check my messages. It had become a habit.

"You expecting a call?" Clovis frowned.

Embarrassed, I apologized. "I'm sorry. I didn't have time to talk to Carol before I left yesterday. I've been expecting a call or text."

"You sound like a teenager. If you want to talk to her, just call her. I've got a couple of things to do before brunch. Let me give you some privacy so you can get the urge out of your system." He gave me a pat on the back and left, shaking his head at my rude behavior.

Feeling foolish and rightly put in my place, I paid the bill and returned to my room. My frustration returned when I got her voice mail again. I turned to my email to get my mind off her.

I found Carol's message about ten down in the list I was deleting.

> Been busy. No time to call. Why couldn't you tell me you were going to Little Rock instead of making up a story about golfing all weekend? What's wrong? Your old girlfriend got herself in trouble again? Love, Carol.

At least she had signed off with "Love, Carol." She'd sent the message at one-thirty in the morning, not an unusual hour during her working weekends. I shot off a quick response explaining why I was in Little Rock.

> Emergency in LR—didn't come up until Saturday morning. Rachel Goodman's father is my old friend and mentor, Ben Jennings—small world. I'm here to find out how I can help. I'll be back in time for the ball game. See you there. I miss you. Jack.

I felt a rush of relief. After responding to a few work emails, I called Maggie.

"How was the symphony?" I asked.

"Fantastic. They performed Shostakovich's Fifth, one of my favorites. How's Ben?"

"He's struggling. We're meeting this afternoon to talk about how to proceed. It will be a tough conversation and is likely to last into the evening. I won't be able to leave Little Rock until tomorrow morning, and I'm supposed to meet Carol at the Nat's game tomorrow night. Hold down the fort, okay?"

"Don't I always?"

"Yes, you do," I smiled. "Try to clear Tuesday morning so we can talk. Representing Rachel is going to put a strain on the practice."

"What else is new?" Maggie laughed.

"May I ask what's got you in such a good mood? The Shostakovich couldn't have been that good," I teased.

"It was, but I have a few things to talk to you about, too. I'll clear away the whole day." She hung up with no further explanation. A secretive Maggie made me nervous.

I closed my laptop and pulled out my trusty yellow legal pad. I think best with a ballpoint and legal pad. It's how I bring order and structure to my random and disconnected thoughts.

I hardly knew where to begin. I didn't even know what charges would be brought against Rachel. Both the print and Internet articles were full of suspicion and hyperbole, but no real facts. An hour with my legal pad at least produced the tentative outline of a strategy.

I might have felt differently if I'd noticed the second email from Carol.

Rachel Goodman!! Have you lost your mind?? You'll destroy your career and mine along with it. Back off and call me. Why don't you answer your phone?

I should check my personal email more often, but I don't. I wouldn't open Carol's message until Monday.

10

WHAT I NEEDED MOST WAS INFORMATION, so I decided to call my longtime friend Peggy Fortson. She's a big dog at the Department of Justice, the Deputy Assistant Attorney General in the Criminal Division. We began our careers at Justice at the same time, but I moved over to private practice after a few years. She stayed, rising through the ranks to her current position.

"Jack Patterson calling me on a Sunday morning. Why do I think you're not calling to invite me to brunch?"

I tried to match her tone. "I wish I were, but you'd never accept such a late invitation." It wasn't the first time I'd called her on a Sunday morning.

"Okay, Jack, quit the bullshit. Why are you calling?"

"Well, it's about Rachel Goodman. You may not know this, but she's from Little Rock, and her father, Ben Jennings, is a good friend. Can you tell me if she has counsel? I'm talking to her parents, and I'd like to tell them she has a good lawyer."

I waited, long enough to think maybe she'd hung up.

"Jack, you're out of luck. I can't tell you a single thing about this case. Why are you even asking? You should know better."

"All I want to know is whether she has a lawyer. That's not too much to ask, is it? The family has resources, and she's entitled to counsel."

Peggy sighed. "She's been read her Miranda rights, but hasn't asked for counsel. Even telling you that is more than I should say, and I damn sure better not read about it in the *Post* tomorrow.

The case is being run out of the U.S. Attorney's office in Northern Virginia in consultation with relevant parties. You know, the mere fact you called must be reported to the U.S. Attorney and the appropriate intelligence agencies."

I decided not to push—I might need Peggy as a back channel. I asked the one question I knew she could answer.

"Who is the point of contact in the U.S. Attorney's office, assuming the family can find an attorney who will take the case?"

"The U.S. Attorney, Donald J. Cotton, has taken the lead."

"What can you tell me about him?" I asked.

"Why should I tell you anything about him? Surely your sources are as good as mine."

"Fair enough. I'm warned," I said with a touch of humor, hoping to diffuse her growing irritation.

We ended the call with a hollow promise to meet soon for drinks. I'd found out what I needed to know: Rachel was not represented.

I didn't mind that Peggy would report my call to the team handling Rachel's case. If Clovis was right, the government was already monitoring Ben's house.

With the Feds, you have to assume no secrets exist. Privacy rights and attorney-client privilege are a fiction one studied in law school. Reality sets in when you learn that terms such as "national security" override the attorney-client privilege and even the Bill of Rights.

*****

I strolled into Crittenden's and saw my friend Sam Pagano talking to a very tall woman I almost didn't recognize. She wore a white blouse with a soft collar, straight skirt on the long side, and—I couldn't believe it—pearls. Her sandy blonde hair was still short, but everything about her was softer than the lawyer I'd met over three years ago wearing jeans, a plaid shirt, and work boots. I even detected a hint of perfume.

Micki Lawrence looked as classy as ever; it didn't matter what she wore. Her back was turned as I approached. It must have been Sam's smile that caused her to twist around toward me.

"It's about time you got your cute ass back home. Ben's world has turned upside down, and you can't unwrap yourself from Carol Madison long enough to lend a hand?"

I gave Sam a hearty greeting, and then turned to Micki with an outstretched hand.

"Don't give me that hand." She reached up and planted a warm kiss flush on my lips. "I'm really glad to see you, but don't you get any ideas. Larry and I are very happy. You lost your chance a long time ago." Direct as ever.

"Pearls?" I asked.

She blushed. "I'm meeting Larry at his mother's after brunch. She gave me the pearls for my birthday, said something about southern women and pearls. I wasn't really listening. Our first few meetings didn't go too well, so I'm trying to make amends. Enough. We're here to figure out what we can do for Ben and his daughter. Where's Clovis?"

11

~~~

Where was Clovis? He was seldom, if ever, late. I checked my cell to see if he'd left a message, but nothing.

"He should be here," I said. "He joined me for coffee this morning, said he had something to take care of before brunch. I'm sure he'll be here soon."

"Clovis is never late," Sam offered under his breath.

While we waited, Sam told us about his decision to run for the Arkansas Supreme Court.

"I've enjoyed my work as a prosecutor, but it's time to move on. When I was first elected, the office was overwhelmed with kids who got hooked on the drugs they found in their parent's medicine cabinet and turned to crime to feed their addiction. If we hadn't done something, we'd have ended up with an entire generation unable to get work or be useful members of society. Do you realize that there are over forty-five thousand laws on the books that restrict employment of convicted persons even after they've paid their debt to society? It's one strike and you're out for life in this land of the free.

"So we spent time and effort developing a good diversion program to get them treatment rather than destroying their lives with a felony conviction. Doing that enabled us to turn our attention to the real bad guys, including sex traffickers like Jack's friend Novak."

I wouldn't characterize the Russian mobster Novak as exactly a friend. We had traded favors, but only because we needed something from each other. I thought of my relationship with Novak as dancing with the devil.

Sam continued, "Despite what we've been able to do, the job has taken its toll. Another few years, and I'll be as jaded as most prosecutors who stay in the job too long. Fresh faces, new perspectives, and turnover make a prosecutor's office responsive; too much seniority and experience fill the office with cynics and hard hearts.

"I've been a public defender or prosecutor since law school, so it's time I looked at the law from a different perspective. I've got great name recognition, the support of most lawyers in the state, and, so far, the big money people don't have another candidate. And I have a huge advantage in politics: my name ends in a vowel. Being of Italian descent has to count for something. I'm not brilliant like Marshall, but I still have a real love for law and lots of practical experience."

Sam had always been proud of his Italian heritage; felt it gave him a leg up—and why not? His ancestors had been among those who had founded Little Italy before the First World War. Today it's a tiny community near Little Rock, but in its heyday, it had boasted four wineries.

"So do you want me to support you or your opponent?"

Sam choked on his drink and then gave me a rueful grin.

"Well, I was hoping for a generous contribution from my best friend. But now that you mention it, the prospect of you supporting my opponent might guarantee a victory," he said, laughing.

I was only halfway kidding. A sizeable monetary contribution from the lawyer who defended Senator Robinson's assassin could become a campaign issue Sam didn't need.

"I'm in for the max if you want it. Just let Maggie know when and where to send the check."

I could tell Sam was appreciative, but Clovis's absence was weighing on both of us. Every minute one of us glanced toward the entrance.

We ordered brunch and discussed what each of us could do to help Ben and his daughter. Sam's public office restricted what he could do, but he could encourage the police to keep a watchful eye out over Ben and Linda and be a sounding board.

Over superb eggs benedict, jalapeno cheese grits, and fresh

banana bread we speculated on why Rachel hadn't asked for counsel.

Sam said, "If the case is as airtight as the papers make it out to be, I suspect the prosecutor has gone to great lengths to encourage Rachel to hire counsel. He doesn't want a technicality endangering his case."

Micki volunteered, "I'd bet she doesn't think a lawyer will do her any good. If she was working for Israel, Rachel has to hope she can be part of a diplomatic exchange. A criminal defense lawyer might impede an exchange from happening. Her handlers likely told her what to do if she got caught."

I tried to pay attention as Sam and Micki recalled cases they'd handled where failing to get counsel had affected an outcome one way or the other, but I couldn't help but worry about Clovis.

We had just ordered coffee when Paul, Clovis's top assistant, strode into the restaurant. He practically fell into the empty chair at our table, his face the very picture of bad news. He didn't mince words.

"Clovis went to Ben's this morning on a tip and was jumped from behind. He's still in the emergency room. The doctors say he's not critical; he'll be okay. But I'm telling you, those guys did a real number on him."

We were all stunned. Micki cleared her throat and took a deep breath, "What happened?"

"He got a call this morning about Ben's place and decided to check it out. Good thing he called the office to ask for backup."

"Turns out his premonition was correct. When he pulled up, the white Tundra was parked in the driveway. He should have known better than to go in alone, but he thought he could catch the culprits red-handed.

"He was jumped by three guys who must have been waiting for him. After a good beating, they left him unconscious and were dousing the restaurant with gasoline when the backup unit pulled into the parking lot. The culprits rushed out the back door as our guys came in the front. They got away in the Tundra while our guys were tending to Clovis."

"You sure he's okay?" Micki asked anxiously.

"He's in a good deal of pain and looks like hell. But the doc says he'll recover. He's got several broken ribs, a concussion, and bruises everywhere," Paul answered. "But even worse, he feels like a chump for getting blindsided."

"Has anyone told Stella?" I asked.

"Clovis ordered me not to, says he doesn't want her to worry."

"Bullshit. I'll take care of it."

"Better you than me, Jack. Thanks."

Sam had slipped away to call the police. He didn't have much to add when he returned. "So far no sightings of the Tundra or the bad guys. I'll do what I can to make sure the police give this top priority, but unless Clovis can identify the attackers, there's not much to go on."

"Paul, I need to see him," I said.

"That's why I'm here," he responded. "Clovis wants to talk to you before your meeting with Ben and Linda."

Micki gave me a kiss on the cheek and rose to leave, "Tell Clovis I'll drop by this afternoon, and get Stella here pronto. If she's not in charge, he'll break out of the hospital and go after those guys."

"Don't worry. I'll put Maggie on it. But I don't imagine he'll want to do much of anything right now. Broken ribs have a way of slowing even a bull like Clovis," I said, remembering my own experience with a good ass-whipping a long time ago.

We went our separate ways, worried and unnerved, but promising to keep one another informed.

Clovis was our rock and protector. How could this have happened? And who would want to kill Clovis?

12

PAUL AND I SLIPPED OUT THE BACK of the hotel and into his Sequoia. As we drove off, he warned that the press had gotten wind I was in town and had figured out I was here to meet with Ben. Three vans with satellite dishes and at least ten reporters and crew were camped out in front of Ben's house. I would have to face the music before much longer.

I called Maggie on the way to the hospital. After recovering from the initial shock, she volunteered to call Stella. I warned her that Clovis didn't want to alarm Stella, to which Maggie said something about men and their egos that's not worth repeating. Maggie and Clovis were close, and I knew her all-business tone was a mask. I expected Maggie to be on the plane with Stella when it landed.

Terry Collins, the exceptional Trauma Director at U.A.M.S., met me at the door. We'd been childhood friends, and I had kept up with her career over the years. I knew she would make sure Clovis had the best care possible, as she did with all her patients. She told me who was treating Clovis and tried to reassure me, but her words went in one ear and out the other. I needed to see him myself.

The attending nurse pulled back the curtain, and I saw my huge friend almost sitting up in bed, his massive, well-toned frame half-covered by a sheet and attached to endless numbers of tubes and wires. One eye was swollen shut, his lip was twice its normal size, and what little I could see of his body was swollen and bruised. I couldn't temper my reaction.

"Clovis, you look like shit."

He grimaced, "Please don't make me laugh, my ribs are killing me."

I took a deep breath. Most men have been trained not to show emotion. No matter what the circumstances, you hold every feeling in, at least until you're alone. Clovis was my friend, my fishing buddy—hell, he'd saved my life more than once. His obvious pain was tough to handle.

I looked at the nurse and said, "We need a little privacy, if you don't mind."

At Terry's nod, they both left, and Clovis motioned for me to come close.

"It hurts to talk. But I need to tell you something before the dope kicks in."

"Forget about business. I'll handle everything until you're up and around, and from the looks of things, that could be a while."

He frowned and said, "The guys in the Tundra weren't rednecks or thugs. They were professionals."

"What makes you think that?" I asked.

"While I was on the ground gasping for air and they were kicking the shit out of me, someone ordered them to stop. I heard him say, 'the client wants him alive when this place goes up.'"

"That's sick. Who'd you piss off this time?" I said, trying to maintain my composure.

"After I left you at breakfast, I got a text that the Tundra was at Ben's. I didn't recognize the sender's number, but like a fool I rushed out to the restaurant. The same guy who ordered them to stop kicking shouted for them to get my cell. He didn't want anyone to know about the text."

"Well, maybe they weren't amateurs, but who'd want you to burn alive? You haven't been cheating on Stella, have you?"

"I told you not to make me laugh," he tried to grin; it didn't work.

"I've racked my brain trying to figure it out, but nobody comes to mind. I've put Paul in charge of your protection. I've warned him, and I'm telling you again—these guys aren't amateurs. My gut says they're liable to come after you next. What are you going to tell Ben?"

"That's not your problem. You are no longer on the clock, my friend. You have one job and one job only: get well. You are to obey the nurses and doctors until they discharge you."

He reached out for me to come closer.

"Be careful, and listen to Paul. I didn't see this coming," he said in a whisper as his eyes closed. The drugs were doing their job.

I stood there a few minutes, just watching him breathe. It wasn't long before Terry swept the curtain back with a no-nonsense gesture. Time to leave. Paul was waiting in a chair just outside the ER.

"Where to?" he asked. I glanced at my watch.

"I need to see Ben and Linda. But, Paul, your primary job is to protect Clovis and find out who's behind this. I want someone inside his room at all times, not waiting outside the trauma unit."

13

⊰═══⊱

I'D FIRST MET PAUL during the Cole case. He was the living proof of the old adage about book covers. He wore thick glasses and looked nothing like a former college wrestler turned martial-arts expert. He stood only about five foot eight and had the wiry frame of a runner, but there was more to Paul than met the eye. Paul had been chosen to guard my daughter Beth several years ago, and Clovis's confidence in him had proven to be spot on. The only weakness I'd discovered was that he was head over heels in love with Debbie Natrova, Micki's office manager, a forgivable weakness.

As we drove to Ben's, I filled him in on what Clovis had told me. Paul didn't say a word, but I could tell he was pissed by the way he gripped the steering wheel.

I asked, "Does Clovis have any enemies?"

"Well, sure. Husbands we've followed, jerks we've restrained, and guys we've caught stealing from their employers. But those folks never strike back. This feels different—maybe it's something personal. He may have been working on a matter I don't know about, but I can't think of anyone who would want Clovis to die in such a gruesome way."

We turned onto Ben's street, and I recognized the familiar scene of satellite dishes rising from trucks and vans out of place on a quiet street. As we pulled closer, I could see reporters and cameramen set up on his front lawn.

I told Paul to wait while I spoke to the reporters.

As we exited the car he mumbled, "Your funeral."

Ben stood on his front porch staring at the trucks and people as though they were aliens. He didn't say a word as I veered toward the tent. The press didn't act surprised—they were ready with questions.

I held up my hand to stop the barrage of questions. I was used to these makeshift press conferences.

"For those of you who don't know me, my name is Jack Patterson. I'm an old friend of Ben and Linda Jennings, and, on their behalf, I ask you to please remove your equipment from their lawn."

My request resulted in a chorus of muted laughter before the questions rang out.

"Do you represent Rachel Goodman?" Two or three voices asked the same question.

"The last time I saw Mrs. Goodman she was in her mid-twenties attending graduate school. In fact, until I received a call this Saturday I had no idea that Rachel Goodman was the same young woman I knew long ago as Rochelle Jennings."

That answer didn't satisfy a soul.

"Then why on earth are you here?" came the quick follow-up.

"Ben and Linda are old friends. I grew up in their restaurant, as I'm sure several of you did. Friends comfort friends during difficult times. That's why I'm in Little Rock, and why I'm standing in this tent asking you to leave their property."

I heard a few more laughs of disbelief, then the clear, skeptical voice of a young woman. "Sure. Right. You flew here yesterday from DC, spent the evening with the Jennings, and never once talked about representing Rachel?"

"The subject of representation did not come up last night," I answered. It would come up in just a few minutes, but it did not come up last night.

Another guy tried, "Les Butterman told me that Ben wants you to represent Rachel. According to Les, that would be a big mistake."

I channeled Maggie with my answer. "Sounds as if old Les is still full of shit. Some things never change." Now I heard murmurs of approval.

"Okay. This is my last warning: if you haven't left Ben's lawn by the time I come back out of the house, I promise you will be sorry."

Nobody likes to be threatened, especially a pack of reporters. The same reporter who quoted Les snorted with derision.

"Whatcha gonna do, call the police? Haven't you heard of the First Amendment?"

I fixed a cold stare on the reporter and lowered the volume of my voice. "Contrary to what your buddy Les Butterman may have told you, I did go to law school and actually learned the rights afforded by the First Amendment. It doesn't give you the right to park a satellite truck on someone's lawn. But no, I don't need to call the police. Here's what I mean: Anyone still parked on this lawn when I come out of the house will never get a single bite of Ben's barbeque again. That I can promise."

Ben was still sitting on the porch. He laughed, nodding his head in agreement.

A seasoned reporter said, "Let's go, fellas. No story is worth that."

14

BEN WAS STILL LAUGHING when Paul and I got to the porch. Linda stood inside the door, smiling. She gave me a hug, and I introduced her to Paul. They knew what had happened to Clovis, and we brought them up to date on his condition.

"What can we do to help?" Linda asked. Her offer provided the perfect segue.

"Well, Clovis's fiancée Stella will return to Little Rock tonight, and as soon as they let Clovis out of the hospital, I bet she could use help feeding that big lug. She's not much of a cook."

"That's easy. I have plenty of leftovers, and I can organize my church circle to bring over meals for as long as they need."

I smiled my thanks and asked, "What about you, Ben?"

He looked puzzled. "What do you mean? The restaurant is closed."

"How long do you think it would take the restoration company and your insurance folks to get it open?" I asked.

"I don't know and I don't care." His voice was tight and gruff. "I closed the restaurant because my people were scared, and my suppliers wouldn't deliver. End of story."

"I understand, but hear me out, okay?" He didn't say a word.

"Let's deal with the easy part first. I have no idea how I can best help Rochelle. I'll do whatever I can, but a great deal depends on her. She's the one who has to choose a lawyer if she wants one. As soon as I get back to the District, I'll do everything in my power to meet with her and offer my services."

"Oh, Jack!" Linda grabbed Ben's hand.

The scene could have degenerated into crying and backslapping, but I held up my hand.

"Don't thank me yet. There's more."

They both looked confused, so I spoke quickly. "I can't emphasize enough that the decision regarding counsel is hers, not mine or yours. My memory of her is that of a smart and independent young woman. She may not want to have anything to do with an antitrust lawyer with no experience in espionage cases.

"And I can tell you the government will do everything they can to prevent me from talking to her. I have a plan, but I need your help."

Ben took a deep breath. "I'll do anything."

I smiled, "Be careful what you say. What I need from you is at the top of my list."

"Name it," Ben responded.

"Open your restaurant."

Linda looked down quickly, trying to hide a smile. Ben said nothing.

"Open your restaurant. Ben, I'm looking at a man who survived Vietnam, a man who overcame nearly insurmountable odds to become a successful restaurant owner. But you've let the allegations about your daughter defeat you. So far, Rochelle hasn't even been charged with a crime. If the attacks, the spray paint, and the threats had been about your race or your service in Vietnam, would you have closed the restaurant?"

"Hell, no, but we're talking about my daughter," he growled.

"Isn't she as important, if not more so? The government and the press would have everyone believe she's a spy, without having to prove a single thing. The only thing they've done so far is detain her, yet the whole world believes she's a traitor."

I emphasized the word "traitor" and saw Ben wince.

"If I have any chance of defending your daughter, I need her parents to plant that first seed of doubt as to her guilt. I need that restaurant open. Paul and his folks will make sure you and your people are protected, but I need you out front greeting people just like you did before this happened.

"Like most cities, Little Rock has its share of jerks, but lots of good folks will come around to give you their support if you give them the chance. Right now, it looks like you've turned tail, running scared."

Ben's face darkened, and I hoped I hadn't been too harsh.

Linda reached out for his hand. "You can do it, honey. Remember how much fun we had when we started the business? We put up with the city and health inspectors and suppliers jerking you around, demanding cash when we didn't have nickel. You managed then, and you can do it now."

Ben glared at me, ignoring her.

"One more thing," I continued.

"What else?" Ben asked coldly.

"I want you to turn off the computer. Quit reading every article and opinion piece about Rochelle. I'll give that job to an intern in my office, but I want you to quit obsessing over what other people are saying about your daughter."

"Did Linda ask you to say that?" He turned his glare on his wife.

"No, she didn't have to. Every high-profile client and their family thinks they need to read every single thing written about them. Before long they start believing the press clippings and think ninety percent of America is reading the same stories. Here's the reality: most people aren't paying any attention at all. Even in Little Rock, few people get past the headlines. Hell, if the Razorbacks beat Alabama this weekend no one will care if Rochelle is an axe murderer.

"People's memories are short. Don't believe Rochelle is at the center of their lives, because she isn't. And here's another reason I need you to open the restaurant and turn off your computer: your boys."

Now he looked downright angry, but he didn't budge. "What does any of this have to do with my boys?"

"Last night I heard you questioning the boys' and Tina's reaction to Rochelle's arrest. Let me tell you, their concerns are legitimate. Law enforcement is a tough environment. Other agents and their own colleagues will use their sister's arrest against your sons. I was in government myself, and I've seen what people will do to advance their own careers. But that's only part of my thinking."

Linda was silent; Ben had stuck his lower lip out.

"I know they're grown men, but they still look up to you and Linda, and they get cues about how to behave from you. Right now they see a father acting scared and ashamed, and they're following suit. All of you have bought into the idea that Rochelle is guilty. If I have any chance of convincing a jury she's not who the world thinks she is, I need her own family to believe in her and stand up for her."

Ben stared at me in silence. I was beginning to wonder if I had pushed too hard, when he pushed his chair back and rose to his feet.

"Your words are hard, Jack Patterson. You are talking about my family. What do you know about the example I set? Who are you to question the way I raised my children?"

I knew that how I responded could make or break not only my chances to help Rochelle, but a lifelong friendship. I felt a line of sweat trickling down my back.

"Who am I? What do I know about the example you set? To a great extent, I am your son."

It was hard to get the last words out of my mouth.

"You are the father I never had. My real father never made it home from Vietnam, but you did. Whether you intended to or not, you set the example that framed my life. I know my words were hard, and if I didn't love, respect, and honor you, I would've kept my mouth shut. But I owe you and your daughter my best, and if it means telling you something you don't want to hear, so be it. You never hesitated to feed me the truth, and I'm a better man for it."

Linda looked at Ben, and I waited. I thought the silence couldn't get any louder. Suddenly, Ben turned to Paul.

"Young man, you've been awful quiet. How about a beer?"

Paul glanced at me, but he was on his own.

"Um, sure, that sounds nice," he said, tripping a little over the words.

"Nice? Don't tell me Jack's poisoned you so you'd choose a glass of wine over a cold beer."

"No, sir, a beer sounds great." Paul jumped up with a relieved smile.

"Then come with me. I've got a fridge on the back porch and

the most comfortable porch swing ever. You and I have to figure out how I can run a restaurant with your men standing guard." He winked at Linda, ignoring me.

Linda took my arm and said, "Come on in the kitchen, Jack. I think we could all use a little something to eat. You can chop the onions and peppers for cheese dip."

For much of America it's called "queso," but in Arkansas it's still cheese dip. It beats "queso" every time.

15

LINDA MOTIONED ME to a stool by the kitchen counter. She handed me a glass of wine, a large knife, and the peppers and onions. Before long she was cooking the vegetables in butter in the top of a double boiler. She threw in a handful of spices and a little flour, and then added the cheese to melt. Sam's mom had always added a little beer to the mix.

"Those were tough words, Jack. Difficult to hear."

"I know. I almost lost a friend."

"No, you could never lose Ben. But you almost lost me," she smiled.

I offered to help, but Linda gave me a look, so I pulled out my phone to check my email and messages. It didn't take long to realize my phone had been on mute since I'd been on the plane. No wonder I hadn't heard from Maggie. Worse, I had three text messages from Carol to call her, and saw she'd been calling too. When would I learn?

Now wasn't the time to call Carol, so I asked Linda if she would mind if I called Maggie to check on Stella's arrival. She gave me another look.

Maggie answered on the second ring.

"Found your phone?"

"Had it with me the whole time, just on mute," I confessed.

After she quit laughing she said, "We're just about to land. We'll go straight to the hospital. I'm sure Stella will want to stay the night with Clovis. The hospital says they plan to release him tomorrow unless something shows up overnight."

"I thought I might see you in Little Rock. Is Walter with you?"

"No, he has board meetings all week. I have a room at the Armitage."

"One of Clovis's people will pick you up at the airport."

"That won't be necessary. We'll Uber."

"No, Maggie, you will not use Uber. Someone tried to kill Clovis yesterday. I'm not about to let either you or Stella go running around footloose until we figure out who's behind this and why. The same goes for Linda and Ben, even me. I don't want to hear any arguments from anyone." It felt good to let off a little steam.

I heard a rustling and then silence before Maggie whispered, "So Clovis wasn't just beat up by some thugs out to harass Ben?"

I realized Stella was in the next seat. "I'll tell you everything when I see you tonight. Paul will text you your driver's name and contact information."

She reminded me to unmute my phone and keep it with me at all times, an order I immediately disobeyed. I had a hard and fast rule—no phone calls when I was meeting with clients. The cell phone would remain muted until I left Ben and Linda's.

Linda had heard my exchange with Maggie, but said nothing. I followed her out to the back porch where Ben and Paul looked comfortable—already on their second beer. Linda placed a bowl of hot cheese dip and tortilla chips on a table we could all reach. I let Paul enjoy his beer and some cheese dip before reminding him that Maggie and Stella would need protection when they arrived.

"I want the two of them guarded 24/7 until we get to the bottom of all this, or until Clovis is ready for the job himself."

Paul grinned. "First thing he said when I got to the hospital was to work up a plan to protect Stella. Don't worry—I've already arranged for Jordan to meet them. Linda, the cheese dip is terrific! Thank you."

Paul walked out to his car to make his calls, and the three of us chattered as though nothing out of the ordinary had happened, licking gooey melted goodness off our fingers. I asked them to meet me at Micki's tomorrow morning. Her conference room would be a good place to bring everyone up to speed and to download from

Ben and Linda all the information I'd need in order to get access to Rachel.

I stood and Linda took my empty wine glass. Ben rose from his chair and smiled.

"Jack, did I ever tell you that you were stubborn and hard-headed? That it would get you in trouble one day?"

"Just about every month," I said, smiling.

"Well, it's a good thing you were too damn stubborn to pay much attention."

"Is there anything we can do for you before tomorrow?" Linda asked.

I thought about it for a minute. "Well, there is one thing."

"Name it." Ben didn't hesitate, but his face reflected his former tension.

"My friend Walter, the man who loaned me his plane, is out of your barbeque sauce. If you have any bottles left, I'd love to surprise him with a couple."

Linda laughed out loud, and Ben answered, "You'll have a case tomorrow."

16

PAUL AND I JUMPED INTO HIS CAR, and he introduced me to our new driver, Sally Halton. I found myself a bit surprised.

"So, Sally, are you a better driver than Jordan?" I asked, trying to cover my confusion.

"I can drive circles around him." She glanced in the rearview mirror, not missing a beat.

"I'm glad to hear it."

We arrived at the Armitage, and Paul excused himself to meet with the hotel's head of security. It had been a stressful day, and I headed straight to the bar. The bar at the Armitage evokes a gentler time, with dark paneling, comfortable leather chairs, and soothing music. I could almost think of it as a haven, except for having been shot there once.

The room was quiet on this late Sunday afternoon. I sat down at a corner table and ordered a martini. Truth was, it was time to call Carol, and I felt the need for a little false courage. I took a large sip and punched in her number, but once again heard only her voicemail.

I hated playing phone tag, but knew Sunday was a busy time on the Eastern Shore. I wondered why this was so hard. Why couldn't we get back to the way we were? An unexpected peck on the cheek interrupted both my frustration and reverie.

"Why am I not surprised to find you in the bar with your phone still on mute?" Maggie scolded.

"I thought you were with Clovis and Stella." I tried not to sound defensive, and Maggie gave me a break.

"Stella was a nervous wreck the whole flight, but she took charge as soon as she walked into the hospital room. It took her about a second to shoo away the nurse playing gin rummy with Clovis. Her next move was to ask if I would mind waiting outside the door for a few minutes. I don't think she realized how thin the walls are at that hospital.

"I heard her say. 'Don't you say a word, Clovis Jones. I don't want to know what excuse you have for not calling. I have only one thing to say to you.'"

"Oh, jeez. Don't tell me…"

"Don't interrupt! She said, 'Clovis Jones, I love you. Don't you ever scare me like this again.'"

"Stella opened the door ten minutes later, tucking in her shirt, and said, 'Maggie, come on in.' My presence was awkward to say the least, so after a few minutes I said you and I would see them tomorrow and left. Now, where are you taking me for dinner?"

I ordered her a glass of wine and told her about my conversations with Ben and Linda. We were about to leave for dinner when I noticed a short, bearded man wearing a skullcap walking toward our table.

"Mr. Patterson, Mrs. Matthews. Do you mind if I intrude for a few moments?" he asked.

"Please do—you must be Rabbi Strauss?" I rose and took his outstretched hand.

He nodded, and we both sat down.

"Maggie, let me introduce you to Rabbi Levi Strauss. Ben told me his son-in-law met with Rabbi Strauss frequently when he was in Little Rock."

"That and my yarmulke must have given me away," he smiled, extending his fingertips to Maggie.

He ordered a glass of wine and asked us to call him Levi, joking about being related to the blue jeans. I figured he'd used that one about a million times.

We engaged in a few minutes of light chitchat—I noticed he didn't include Maggie. So did she.

He quickly came to the point. "Mr. Patterson, I was close to Rebbe Goodman. I looked forward to his visits and sought him out every time I traveled to Washington. His death was a devastating loss to Jews everywhere. He had such a mind."

His reference to Rachel's husband as Rebbe was telling. It meant that Ira Goodman was a scholar, a leader, and a spiritual advisor.

"Mr. Patterson—may I call you Jack? Thank you, I hope you will call me Levi. Despite what you told the press today, I hope you will represent Rachel. She needs a lawyer of your caliber. But that is not my purpose for seeking you out.

"I have a message to give Rachel and her family. Your remarks this afternoon convinced me to deliver this message to you rather than the Jennings. I'm not close to them and don't think they will understand its significance. You will."

He sighed, "Israel knows Rachel will soon be charged with various crimes including conspiracy to commit espionage. In fact, she will be accused of conspiring with the Israeli government to steal military secrets. Such allegations are strongly denied by the Israeli government."

So far, he hadn't told me anything that hadn't been in the news every day.

"Because Israel values its relationship with the United States and because it denies any involvement in Rachel's activities, Israel will cooperate fully in the investigation, and has decided not to seek any sort of diplomatic resolution." He coughed, perhaps ashamed of the statement he had memorized.

No, Ben and Linda wouldn't understand the full implication of his message—in essence, Israel was throwing Rachel Goodman under the bus.

Maggie understood what it meant—her face tightened and her eyes turned to flint.

"Levi, may I ask a few questions?" I tried to keep an even tone.

"Yes, of course. I will answer if I can."

"I take it this same message has been delivered to the United States government."

"That is correct. Who said what to whom I do not know, but our denial of involvement, our willingness to cooperate, and our lack of desire to seek a diplomatic resolution was transmitted through proper channels."

"When you reference 'a diplomatic resolution,' I take it you mean any kind of spy swap or exchange is off the table?" My voice became a little firmer.

"Again, you are correct."

"Can you tell me if this decision by the Israeli government resulted from negotiation?"

"I wasn't told how Israel reached its decision. Forgive me, I'm just a messenger."

"Can you tell me whether the agreement to cooperate includes disclosure of the activities of Rachel's husband?"

"I cannot imagine how the work of Rebbe Goodman is pertinent to Rachel's recent activities." Rabbi or not, this guy was a cool customer.

I tossed a little shrug, hoping the bluff would work.

"I appreciate the courtesy. At least the Israeli position won't blindside anyone. I will do my best to convey the message to the Jennings and to Mrs. Goodman. I assume you understand what Israel's position means for Rachel?"

"Yes, I'm sorry to say, I do," he replied with a heavy sigh.

17

The Rabbi's message also meant that the U.S. government had made the decision to seek the death penalty in Rachel's case. Tomorrow, I would have to give Ben and Linda that news. I offered Levi another glass of wine, but he declined. I couldn't help but wonder who'd sent him on this errand and whether either government had sanctioned it. As he rose to leave, he offered a ray of hope.

"I come to DC quite often. Will you allow me to return your hospitality? Perhaps you know of a quiet place where we can talk. Most restaurants are so loud these days." I followed his glance to a solitary figure sitting in the corner nursing an empty glass.

After he left, Maggie and I sat in silence for a few minutes. Suddenly Maggie said, "I'm sure your Rabbi is a very nice man, but I feel like I need to wash my hands. Why don't we meet back here in, oh say fifteen minutes or so?"

A few minutes to myself sounded like a good idea, so I paid the bill and followed her upstairs. I tried to reach Carol again—still no answer. I couldn't seem to pull my thoughts together, so I threw some water on my face, changed shirts, and took the elevator down to the lobby to find Maggie chatting with Jordan, our companion for the evening. I considered asking Micki and Larry to join us, but thought better of it. Strauss's message had been a real downer. No need to spread the gloom.

Over Jordan's objection we walked the few blocks to the restaurant. The cool crisp fall air felt good. Bruno's is Little Rock's oldest Italian restaurant. My mother and I had enjoyed eating at Bruno's when we first moved to Little Rock. I had loved watching old Mr. Bruno toss pizza dough high into the air. The restaurant had moved several times and, to the dismay of all of Little Rock, had finally closed. But it had remained in the family and had now reopened in downtown Little Rock to rave reviews. The menu was more contemporary, but it still felt like the Bruno's I remembered so well.

We invited Jordan to join us for dinner, but he preferred to wait outside while on duty. I'd have to talk to that boy—he needed loosening up. From our table by the window we could see him pacing up and down the sidewalk. Maggie was unnerved, and I asked for a different table.

"Do you think we can ever come to Little Rock without needing protection?" she asked after we were reseated.

"I hope so. You're right, it is getting old, but this time there's a new wrinkle—no one has tried to kill me, only Clovis."

"Right. It isn't funny, Jack, and you still haven't told me what happened."

The waiter stepped to the table to take our order before I could respond. Rabbi Strauss's message had taken away both our appetites, so we agreed to share an appetizer portion of fresh mozzarella and Roma tomatoes and a Caesar salad.

After the waiter left, I filled Maggie in on the Tundra following us, the attack on Clovis, and the aborted attempt to torch Ben's restaurant.

If Maggie's mood had been unsettled before, the possibility of Clovis being burned alive took her over the edge.

"My God, who would do such a thing?" Her voice was shrill, and several couples turned our way.

I reached across the table to take her hand.

"It didn't happen, Maggie. It didn't happen. And you cannot mention what I just told you to Stella or anyone else, not even Walter. Clovis gets to tell her in his own good time."

She nodded, but her eyes were full of tears. Our waiter appeared with our appetizer and two glasses of Pinot Grigio, and the bustle brought us both back from the edge. Maggie cleared her throat and excused herself, returning in a few minutes, completely under control.

We tried to regain our footing with chitchat about the newly revitalized downtown. I indulged in a little reminiscing, and before long we were back on an even keel. When the waiter brought our salads, I carefully returned to the events at hand.

"It's hard to believe that just yesterday morning I was about to play golf with your husband. Less than forty-eight hours later we're here in Little Rock talking about a potential new client charged with espionage."

"Moreover, you have a second matter on your plate, one equally as difficult. Who tried to kill Clovis, and why?"

"Maggie, what's gotten into you?" I asked. "You're usually dead set against our getting involved in cases beyond the scope of our antitrust work. Now you seem ready to jump into the deep end."

She took her time, rearranging her silver and taking a healthy sip of wine before responding.

"Well, for one thing, I don't like what's happening to Rachel. I've never met her, but this doesn't seem fair. And the attack on Clovis hits even closer to home. You can't ignore that.

"I never want you to give up your antitrust practice. You know antitrust law and mergers and acquisitions inside and out, and you're one of the District's best."

She fiddled with her silverware again; I knew better than to interrupt.

"Jack, we have two great clients on retainer—the Foundation and the Los Angeles Lobos, and you give them superb advice. But you shine when you follow your heart, when you take on a case that's out of your usual bailiwick. People talk about Billy Hopper. And look what you accomplished for Liz and Doug Stewart.

"My own life experience has led me to be wary, not to take chances. But I've been wrong to fight your instincts, so I've decided to back off, within limits. Our partnership will be better served if I concentrate on a few changes in our office structure that will help accommodate those wild hairs that take you off in unexpected directions."

"What changes?" This time the other diners turned to look at me.

She smiled, looking like the cat that ate the canary.

"What changes?" I repeated, my voice now calm, but firm.

"I told you over the phone we'd talk on Tuesday. We may need to delay the conversation for a few days while we resolve the issues here in Little Rock. So let's talk about what you have planned for tomorrow. Would you like to share a dessert?"

I grumbled a little, but we ended up sharing a very creamy Tiramisu and walking back to the hotel, Jordan hovering a few steps behind. By the time I reached my room the day had caught up with me. I was asleep before my head hit the pillow.

MONDAY

18

CAROL SLEPT IN on the Mondays after her weekends at the Eastern Shore, regardless of whether she remained on the shore or drove back to DC Sunday evening. So I decided not to call her first thing, especially now that I'd read her email. Our conversation would be even more difficult, and I wanted to put it off for as long as I could.

Sam must have called in a favor with the reporters who covered the police blotter—no mention of the attempted arson. Paul texted that Clovis would be discharged later this morning. Good luck with that, I said to myself. Micki left a voicemail saying she had a court appearance at nine, but would be in her office by ten.

After breakfast and answering a few emails, I took the plunge and was relieved to hear Carol answer the phone as if it were just another day.

"I'm so glad you called. When are you coming home? I miss you."

"I miss you, too. The last couple of days have been crazy—I'm sorry we played phone tag yesterday. And I didn't see your email until this morning."

"Oh, forget that email. I sent it way too late and after a little too much wine. Why don't we skip the game, and you come here tonight—Mattie's cooking. It's been too long since I've had you all to myself. Bring your toothbrush."

Mattie was her cook and housekeeper. She lived with her husband in a small apartment near Carol in the Watergate. Carol's driver Pat and his wife lived in a similar unit. Carol owned both apartments and gave them a significant break on the rent for the convenience of having them close and on call.

The invitation sounded almost too good to be true. I was expecting a lecture about answering my phone, misplaced priorities, and being a damn fool. Instead—well, a night with Carol was just what the doctor ordered.

I took a deep breath and told her the truth. I was still in Little Rock, and wouldn't be home for at least several days.

"Well, damn. I had planned something special for tonight. It will keep, but if you don't come home soon, I may have to surprise you there."

I was at a loss. Not a word about Rachel, not a word about our earlier spat, only what sounded like a sincere wish for me to return to her waiting arms. Maybe I'd been worried about nothing.

We settled on Thursday night. Surely I wouldn't need to stay in Little Rock that long, but the attack on Clovis and his condition took first priority. Still, I walked into the hotel lobby feeling better than I had in weeks.

*****

Micki had relocated her office to a renovated ramshackle Victorian house in Little Rock's Quapaw Quarter. The renovator had taken great care to retain its original layout and charm while adding the conveniences of contemporary life. Debbie Natrova, Micki's office manager, met us at the door, happily informing us that we'd find fresh muffins, pastries, and coffee in the conference room. Linda had called to say she and Ben were running a little late.

Debbie had emigrated to the U.S. from Eastern Europe when she was a teenager. She had hoped to become a pastry chef, but her sponsor, Alexander Novak, had other plans. She and other innocent young women like her, eager for a new life in America, were robbed of their innocence when they were given hard drugs and trained how to please the men who went to their rooms night after night. Micki rescued Debbie from Novak's clutches, employing her as a receptionist so she could keep a watchful eye on her recovery. Now Debbie kept Micki's office organized and running smoothly. Her methods and manners were quirky, but no one doubted her abilities.

Another of Micki's projects was her unlikely receptionist and part-time investigator, Mongo Stankovitch. Mongo looked like he'd be more at home in a biker bar than behind a reception desk. I'll give him this—his loyalty to Micki and Debbie was unshakable. I never worried about Micki or Debbie's safety as long as Mongo was there to greet whoever walked in the door.

Debbie handed Maggie a warm muffin and a cup of hot tea already doused with milk. She had a good memory.

Munching on my muffin, I asked Paul, "How come you don't weigh three hundred pounds? Does she make these for you every morning?"

"Not every morning, but I've had to extend my morning run. What I can't understand is how she doesn't gain a pound or an inch. Neither does Micki. Mongo and I are struggling."

I sat down at the end of the table with a cup of coffee and a second muffin, waiting for the others to arrive.

On a whim, I asked Debbie if Stella had checked their offices for bugs.

"No—you know Micki doesn't worry too much about that stuff. I mean, who would want to listen?" she laughed.

Before I could answer, Micki walked into the room with Mongo in tow carrying a large box of files. She wore a bright red suit and heels.

"Jack, we only have security issues when you're in town," she said, laughing. "Give me five minutes to get out of this damn suit—itches like hell." She grabbed a muffin, kissed me on the cheek, and headed to the back office she had converted to a workout room and crash pad.

I couldn't help but grin, reminded how much fun it was to work with Micki. She kept me on my toes, never hesitated to tell me when I was wrong, and her enthusiasm and optimism were contagious.

We made small talk until Micki opened the door and sank into a chair. She'd changed into jeans and a man's white shirt, and was drying her hair with a towel.

"Sorry—I had to take a shower. I can't stand the stale cigarette smell of that old courthouse—without a shower it lingers with me all day."

We spent thirty minutes talking about what I'd learned in the last couple of days and my brief conversation with Rabbi Strauss. Suddenly concerned, I asked about Ben and Linda, but Paul told me they had gone to Ben's warehouse to pick up a case of barbecue sauce.

"What do you know about Rabbi Strauss?" I asked.

"I've defended a few of his synagogue members. He never misses a court appearance and is always there for the family, no matter what the circumstances. He's active in the community and well respected."

"I got the distinct impression he wasn't that happy to be the news bearer last night," I said.

"I expect not. I'll ask around, but from all I know, the guy's a mensch," Micki said.

"Find out what you can. Last night won't be the last time we hear from the good rabbi."

19

Mongo led Ben and Linda into the conference room. Ben carried a box crammed with jars of barbecue sauce, which he plopped down on the middle of the table. Mongo started to move it, but I stopped him mid-move.

"No, Mongo, that box deserves a place of honor. Ben, thank you—that sauce will make Walter's day.

"Ben and Linda, I promise you can trust Maggie as much as you trust me. She'll ask you for a lot of paperwork and information. You won't think most of it is relevant, but the government is a stickler for details, so I hope you'll be patient."

Linda responded, "That's okay, we're ready. I brought a file I've kept on Rochelle since she was a baby. I tried to give it to her more than once, but she always refused, said it was safer with me. It's got her birth certificate, her report cards from kindergarten through high school, her college transcripts, and even her social security card. I'm sorry, but I don't have a marriage certificate."

I knew Maggie would put her at ease in a few minutes, but I had bigger fish to fry first.

"Before I turn you over to Maggie and Debbie, I have some new information. There's no way to sugarcoat this. Maggie and I were informed last night that the federal government will seek the death penalty in Rachel's case. I'm disappointed, but not surprised. I haven't verified the accuracy of this information, but thought you should know right away."

Ben bit his lip, and Linda turned away, but neither said a word.

"I told you yesterday that I'll do everything I can to help Rochelle, and I will. Micki has agreed to help, but because of this development I want you to rethink whether you want our help or not. I can help you find a lawyer more experienced in death penalty cases."

Ben raised his hand to stop me, and I waited for him to gather his thoughts. His voice began with a quiver.

"D...Don't go there, Jack! Just don't! Woody was tried for murder, and he wanted the death penalty, did he not?"

"Yes," I answered.

"That ball player, Hopper, was accused of murder, was he not?"

"Yes, but he wasn't facing the death penalty."

Ben's voice had lost its hesitancy.

"Linda and I have talked about this more than once. If my daughter agrees, Linda and I want you to defend her no matter what the charges or the penalty. The bottom line is this, Jack: We trust you."

He turned to Micki.

"Micki, I don't know you that well, but I saw how you comple-mented Jack in both Woody's and Doug Stewart's case. If he hadn't asked you to help, I would have."

He looked back at me.

"You give Rochelle something no other lawyer can—you care. You care about Linda and me, and I know you care for Rochelle, too. In the military they stress strength, intelligence, and loyalty. But in Vietnam, I learned that leadership is most about caring about the safety of the squad and about every soldier as a person. All the rest is secondary.

"So not another word about hiring some other lawyer. You've done your duty, told us we should find a lawyer who's more qualified. Well, Linda and I have talked it over, and we want you. So that's the end of that."

Both Maggie and Micki looked at me as if to say, "We're in this now. I hope you know what you're doing." I gave myself a little shake and tried to look confident.

Maggie broke in with an offer of coffee, and the atmosphere lightened. She and Debbie took over the interview, peppering Ben and Linda with questions. I didn't need just documents—birth certificates, school transcripts, etc. I needed to learn as much as possible about the woman herself. No detail was too small, and Maggie was the perfect person to draw out Ben and Linda.

Once Ben and Linda were comfortable with Maggie and Debbie's approach, Micki and I excused ourselves to Micki's office.

"I hope you know how much you've taken on," Micki started.

"What's with the 'you,' kemosabe? You're in this with me. You heard Ben."

"I know, but it's not the same. You're the friend, the third son, and the person they trust to make things right."

I allowed myself a deep sigh. She was right, and the fact did weigh on me. But I'd made the decision, taken the job. It was too late to have second thoughts.

"So, what's next?" Micki asked, immune to my sigh.

"Our first hurdle will be to get access to Rochelle. We know from experience that won't be easy. We had a hell of a time even getting to see Doug Stewart—remember? Prosecutors can get away with most anything under the cloak of national security. From my short conversation with Peggy Fortson, I have the feeling that scheduling a meeting with our client won't be easy."

"I'll pull the research we did on the Stewart case and get my two interns to update the case law. I have a file on the DOJ procedure for getting the attorney general's approval to seek the death penalty. The rules have changed, so I'll ask them for a memo outlining those changes as well." Micki was now all business.

"If she's charged in the Northern District of Virginia things might move quickly, so give Larry a heads up. You could be in DC for some time." I was teasing, but she didn't want to play.

"Don't go there, Jack. Larry's coming, too. If you recall, he gave us the break we needed for Billy Hopper. Besides, you have Carol to keep you warm at night, remember?"

"I was only suggesting that you talk to Maggie about accommodations and let Larry know we may need you in DC on a moment's notice."

"Sure you were." She paused and turned her scowl into a slow smile.

"Jack, I look forward to working with you on this case, so let's keep it professional." She gathered up some papers into a neat stack, and then continued. "But I have to wonder if we aren't getting ahead of ourselves. Even if they let us talk to her, how are you going to convince Rachel to hire us? From all I've read, she's her own person. What her mom and dad want doesn't seem to have been a big factor in her life decisions so far."

"True, and if she decides to hire someone else, we'll turn over whatever we've found and move on," I said firmly.

"But if she does hire us, then what? If the newspapers are right, the government has her dead to rights, and Israel won't come to her rescue. The military doesn't take kindly to someone stealing information about secret weapon systems. Right now we can only speculate why she would do such a thing—anger over her husband's death? Who knows?"

Her question was rhetorical, but I gave it some thought.

"The only thing we know for sure is that nothing makes sense. Rochelle comes from a warm and giving home; she's smart, has no money problems that we know, and was a respected civil servant. Her husband's death was tragic, but our government had nothing to do with a random Hamas rocket. What am I missing?" My question was rhetorical, too, but she reached across the desk to give my hand a pat.

"Jack, have I ever mentioned that you're a good guy? Right now most lawyers would be worrying about how to get paid. They'd know that if the government has seized all her assets, she'd unable to pay any attorney's fee. They wouldn't give a hoot whether she's guilty or not."

"It hadn't crossed my mind to think about a fee. That's the least of my concerns."

She stood with a silent shrug and walked out to meet a client in the reception area. I felt a sudden pang of guilt that my lucrative antitrust practice gave me the liberty to be so cavalier about money. Micki wasn't in the same position.

20

SHERLOCK HOLMES ONCE SAID, "It is a capital mistake to theorize before one has data." I did it anyway. Why had the Israelis sent Rabbi Strauss to give me a heads-up? Whether they were complicit in her actions or not, they'd decided she was too hot to handle. Sherlock was right: I needed more information.

My thoughts turned again to Clovis. We still had no idea who had attacked him or why. Sherlock was right again: not enough information. I noticed Paul and Jordan standing on Micki's front porch, so I joined them. After a little small talk about the Razorbacks, I got to the point.

"Do either of you know who might have a grudge against Clovis?"

Paul answered. "We've pored over the company files, but so far, no luck. Clovis is well respected in the trade, and it's hard to believe anyone would pursue such a vendetta. The linkage to Ben complicates everything."

I nodded, knowing what he meant. Luring Clovis to Ben's and torching the restaurant was way too complicated for a random act of payback.

Paul continued. "No offense, Jack, but the other complicating factor is your presence. That Tundra only showed up after you arrived. We've been guarding Ben for over two weeks, and other than chasing away idiots throwing bricks and spray-painting buildings, things have been fairly calm. You come to town, and in a matter of two days we've got professional thugs trying to kill Clovis and burn down Ben's restaurant."

He had a good point, but why go after Clovis if I was the real target? Maggie and I had a tentative plan to see Clovis later today. Maybe he could provide some insight.

"Do you think Clovis will be up for company this afternoon?" I asked Paul.

He laughed, "Are you kidding? He's going nuts. He's back at home, and I'll bet the nurses are glad to see him gone. But Stella has taken away his phone, and he's bored to tears. She told me she'd kick my butt if I tried to talk business. I'm not in the habit of arguing with Stella."

Well, at least she had him under control. "Better her than me," I thought.

"Ask Stella if it's okay for Maggie and me to come by around four."

We spent the next half hour going over what I needed Paul and his people to do in the next few days. Ben and Linda had given us a list of Rachel's friends to interview. The FBI was way ahead of us; we'd have to hustle to catch up. The same went for her teachers, coaches, and her minister, although judging from what Ben told me about Preacher Barnes, I didn't think he'd be much help.

"What about Beth? Did she keep in touch with Rachel?" Paul asked.

"Good idea. Maybe she did," I replied.

I knew Beth would be unhappy to learn I was in Little Rock without her knowledge. Since Angie's death, Beth tended to act more like a mother than a daughter. I hadn't talked to her in two weeks, so I decided that at the least, she should know where I was. I dialed her number expecting to get voicemail.

"Hey, Dad! You usually call on the weekend—is everything okay?"

It took me a second to realize I was actually speaking with her rather than responding to her voicemail.

"Everything's fine—and hello to you, too. I'm in Little Rock for a few days."

"Little Rock," her light-hearted tone faded.

"No, no—don't worry," I said, and she listened as I told her about Rochelle and explained that Micki and I might end up representing her. It hadn't crossed her mind that her old friend was now the infamous Rachel Goodman, which made me feel a little better. Unfortunately, Beth hadn't heard from Rochelle in years. I also told her about the attack on Clovis.

"So you come to town to meet with Ben about Rochelle, and someone attacks Clovis and tries to burn down Ben's restaurant? That can't be a coincidence."

"No, probably not. Beth, I promise we are taking this seriously."

"Is Clovis okay?" I could hear her mind racing.

"Clovis is banged up, but he'll be all right."

"And his men are protecting you? Clovis and Stella too—right?" she asked.

"Yes, and Maggie, Ben, and Linda. You know, it would be nice, just once, to enjoy spending time with old friends with no need for protection."

She let me simmer for a minute.

"Sounds like a tough situation all around, Dad. Here's an idea. Why don't you and Maggie come through St. Louis on your way home? The only time Jeff has off is Thanksgiving, when we'll be in Charleston, but I'd love to see you and Maggie. How long will you be in Little Rock?"

It didn't escape me that she had just told me she planned to spend Thanksgiving in Charleston with Jeff's parents.

"Beth, I don't know how long we'll be here, but I need to be back in DC by Thursday. Let me talk to Maggie—we'll try."

Beth was on her way to class, so we didn't linger. As I sat idly pushing the porch swing back and forth, I wondered how on earth we could manage a side trip to St Louis. I let my thoughts wander, enjoying the small sway of the swing and the crisp fall air. At some point I became aware that Micki had sunk into the wicker armchair across from me.

"Penny for your thoughts," she said quietly.

"You know, I'm not really thinking at all, just enjoying the quiet."

"Bullshit! Something's eating at you, and it's not Rachel or Ben or the attack on Clovis. You haven't been yourself since you got here. If I didn't know better, I'd guess Carol's cut you off."

I couldn't come up with anything but a weak smile.

"Wow, no come back? No denial? C'mon, Jack. Don't tell me it's not all sweetness and light."

I took a long breath and rose from the swing.

She stretched out her hand to stop me and said, "I'm sorry, I don't know what got into me. I didn't mean that. Please don't go."

I gave her hand a squeeze and said, "It's okay. I know you didn't. It's pretty quiet right now, for me anyway, so I think I'll take a drive. I'll see if Paul or Jordan have the time."

I found Paul inside. "I need a change of scenery. Could we just drive around for a while, see what's changed in Little Rock?"

*****

We were waiting at the stoplight at the foot of Cantrell Hill, when I said, "Hey, Paul—isn't that Helen Cole's car parked in front of the Town Pump?"

The Town Pump is a greasy dive known to locals as one of the best burger joints in town.

"Sure is, that's her Mini. As I remember she has a burger at the Pump most every Monday."

"Well, pull over. It's time for a surprise."

21

WOODY COLE AND I WERE BEST FRIENDS in high school and college. No matter what the occasion, his mother Helen had welcomed us and most everyone else with open arms, plenty of home-cooked food, and no judgment.

I couldn't come to Little Rock without seeing her. I caught sight of her in a booth near the kitchen and waved. She gave a little start, and I raced over to give her a hug.

"Sit down, sit down," she said with a smile, and I slid into the booth across from her.

"I can't tell you how good it is to see you. You look terrific."

I meant it. Life had thrown her some tough curves—her husband had died early and her only son was serving time for shooting a sitting Senator. But to see her now you'd never guess it. She was well-dressed and her hair was freshly coifed. I wondered if I'd ever seen it move.

"Don't look at me that way—I always get my hair done on Mondays." She could still read my mind.

I squirmed, and she changed the subject. "Tell me about Beth. Has Jeff popped the question?"

"Helen, your guess is as good as mine. They say they have a schedule, and they seem happy, but..."

"Don't worry," she grinned. "He won't let her get away. Where do you think they'll land?"

"My bet is Charleston. He grew up there—it's home to his parents and brothers. But I worry how accepting folks will be of a biracial couple."

"Nonsense, Jack. You and Angie did just fine. Charleston is a lovely city, and times have changed. You sound like Angie's dad."

Well that stung.

"You never used to talk like that. What's going on with you?" she asked, pushing back her empty plate.

"Nothing, as far as I know," I answered quickly.

She took a sip of sweet tea, then put her glass down with a thud. "Jack, you're a bad liar. You've got bags under your eyes, you've put on more than a few pounds, and you're just plain grouchy—your friends are worried about you."

"My friends? Which friends?" I tried to keep a poker face, but my lips went tight.

"Now don't go all sensitive on me and clam up. Your friends are worried, and I don't mean just Maggie. Now that I've seen you, I am too. So, tell me what's got under your skin. I have all the time in the world."

I felt naked; I had no idea my malaise was so obvious.

"I appreciate your concerns, but I think they're overblown. I haven't played golf in a month. The extra pound or two will fall right off as soon as I get back outdoors. As far as the bags, well, both Ben and his daughter have got serious problems—it's been very stressful. I haven't slept well the last few days."

Helen smiled, calmly waiting for me to continue.

"I've been seeing a woman in DC for quite a while now—Carol Madison. She's a successful consultant and loves baseball—you'd like her. I just need to cut back on the beer and hot dogs at the games." I patted my tummy and flashed a grin.

Helen raised her brows.

I couldn't seem to quit talking, "Maggie and I have a good law practice, and our foundation is doing great work, especially Dr. Stewart's research. I have a physical every year, and I'm in good health. I don't understand why you or anyone else is worried."

She wasn't buying. "Jack, you can talk all afternoon about how great you're doing, but you're not fooling anyone but yourself. The man who came back to Little Rock to help my son and Doug Stewart was full of energy. He cracked jokes and loved every minute he was helping his friends. So don't tell me you're stressed and can't sleep on account of Ben and his daughter. You haven't done a blessed thing yet.

"You've never put on weight before because you're always going ninety to nothing. If it wasn't some sport or the other, you were off hiking or climbing mountains. You're still a handsome man, but your color is off and you look ten years older than the last time I saw you."

I tried to find a way out, but Helen was merciless. "Clovis and Maggie tell me Carol is a classy and attractive woman. You tell me she likes baseball, and that I'll like her, but not once did you say you like her, much less that you're in love. Are you?"

Okay, so maybe I'd been a little off my feed, but this was too much. I looked for the waitress, but Helen wasn't finished.

"One last thing. What's the deal with the iPhone on the table? You used to leave it at home, forget it entirely. Today you pulled out your phone as soon as you sat down, and this whole time you've been watching it like it was about to hop up and run away. What's going on with you?"

My head seemed to sink down of its own accord, and she reached across the table to take my hands into hers. "Love, we're both too old for me to mother you, and I hate having to talk to you like this. So now it's your turn—you need to tell me what this is all about."

I slouched down in the leatherette banquette, feeling both shame and irritation. Helen had me dead to rights.

"Okay, so first I'm sorry about the phone. I've picked up the habit. Not a big deal, and I am sorry.

"And you're right—too many after office hours spent with new people who seem to drink a lot and not do much of anything else— too much time in the pool chair, and not enough time in the pool.

"As for Carol, I don't know how I feel. I enjoy her company; she's all a man could want—attractive, intelligent, and fun to be with when she's not doing business. Problem is her business dominates her time, even when we're together. And then there's Angie." The lump rose in my throat.

Helen squeezed my hands. "Well, now the cat's out of the bag."

"Don't be so sure. I haven't exactly behaved like the mourning widower."

Helen dug out a little microfiber cloth from her purse and busied herself cleaning her glasses while I tried to regroup.

She filled the gap. "It's okay to move on past Angie."

"I don't want to forget Angie. She was all I've ever wanted."

"You will never forget Angie, nor should you. But your time on this earth with her is over."

Angie's words came back in a rush. "Don't be sad it's over, be glad we had the years."

"Like it or not, I have some advice for you," Helen said firmly.

"Angie's been gone five years now. You need to seek change in your life. Doing so doesn't dishonor Angie; it honors her to acknowl-edge that things can never be the same. I can't tell you what you need to do: it might involve this Carol person, it might mean changing where and how you live, or it might mean doing something else entirely. Change is a normal part of life, Jack. You need to embrace it, but make sure it's a positive change.

"The one thing you shouldn't let go is being a lawyer. All that big money law is fine—you do it well, and it pays the bills. But you're at your best when you're helping someone who probably can't pay you a dime, someone you believe in, like you believed in Woody."

I had to smile. Helen had just said what I hadn't wanted to admit. Seek change—it sounded like a book by a motivational speaker, but she was right on target.

22

$\diamond\!\!-\!\!-\!\!-\!\!-\!\!\diamond$

AT MY SMILE, both the tension and our mood lightened. She told me about her two book clubs, her bridge group, and her yoga class. She volunteered once a week at the Clinton Presidential library. I hoped I'd have half her energy when I got to be her age. Must be the weekly cheeseburger and fries at the Town Pump.

As I walked her to her car, I promised to keep her up to date on my new life plan as soon as I figured it out.

She responded, "That isn't how it works, and you know it. Help Ben and his daughter, and the rest will come. I promise."

I kissed her on the cheek and said goodbye as she sank into her bright red Mini Countryman. I looked at Paul waiting in the big Tahoe and thought it might be fun to drive a Mini, except I probably wouldn't fit.

Ben and Linda were gone by the time we got back to Micki's. Maggie told me they had shared enough information to keep Debbie, two of Micki's interns, and her busy for at least the next couple of days. "They were emotionally spent. Now Ben's gone fishing, and Linda has a baby blanket to finish."

I remembered that Linda knitted blankets for the newborns at Arkansas Children's Hospital. I could well imagine that she had once looked forward to knitting one for Rochelle.

"They agreed to come back Wednesday afternoon to tie up any loose ends. One more thing: Stella told Paul we might as well come this afternoon; she can't keep Clovis off the phone."

"Maggie, let's go over what you heard this morning, while it's fresh on your mind. I need a better understanding of Rochelle. Maybe Micki will join us if she's got time."

Micki had the time, and for the next hour we listened as Maggie, Debbie, and Micki's interns filled us in on their earlier conversation with the Jennings. It turned out to be a very useful exercise. It never failed: two or three people hear the same words and come away with different interpretations and assumptions. Differing reactions could cause confusion at first, but then clarity.

After sending the interns off for a break, Micki offered, "Why don't you and Maggie come out to the ranch tonight? You know I'm not much of a cook, but Larry can grill steaks, and I can manage a salad and baked potatoes."

About six years ago, Micki had bought a spread of two hundred acres on the outskirts of Little Rock. The ranch house was still a work in progress—she gave immediate priority to the fields and stables where she boarded her own horses and those of a few lucky friends. That's how she met Larry. He came to build new cabinets in her kitchen . . . and never left.

"Sounds great, but I know how you hate to cook. Why don't you and Larry join us at the Faded Rose after we visit Clovis? I'll ask Sam, too. We can kill two birds with one stone."

"Okay, but he won't come alone. His latest doesn't let him go anywhere without tagging along," she said.

"I didn't know Sam was dating someone new, but then again it's hard to keep up. He didn't say anything yesterday…"

"I couldn't believe she wasn't with him. I bet he didn't tell her. She's got her claws in deep. I promise you won't like her one bit."

Sam had dated a number of women since his divorce ten years ago, but I'd never known him to get serious. We were the same age, but he looked years younger. Every weekend he was running in a road race or biking. Beth had once referred to him as "a chick magnet." He'd met his match with Micki, but it didn't last. Happily, they remained good friends.

"Do I detect a little jealousy, Ms. Lawrence?"

My jibe produced a withering frown. "Her name is Kristine McElroy. Her first husband owned a bunch of car dealerships throughout Texas. They met after a Dallas Cowboys game—she was on the field at half time with the Kilgore Rangerettes. Luke McElroy was in his forties and married, for heaven's sake, but according to her it was love at first sight."

"Are you serious—a Rangerette?" Every red-blooded southern high school or college boy fantasizes about the Rangerettes, the drill team from Kilgore College who've performed at over sixty Cotton Bowls, Cowboys' games, and God knows where else. Their motto was "beauty has no pain." I wanted to know more.

Micki continued, "Luke divorced the mother of his four boys and married Kristine before she was twenty-one. Sadly, Luke suffered a massive heart attack five years later while vacationing with Kristine in Playa del Carmen. He had torn up the prenuptial agreement and executed a new will only a month earlier. Kristine inherited the entire estate. His first wife and their four sons sued, but the courts sided with Kristine.

"Her second conquest was Luke's lawyer and best friend, Butch Jones. According to Kristine, the legal hassles over the estate drew the two close," Micki said with more than a hint of sarcasm.

"This sounds like a grade-B movie. I bet the former wife and boys went through the roof," I said.

"Oh, they tried to have Butch disbarred, but they didn't stand a chance. They drew a judge who'd played football with Butch at North Texas State. Small world, huh?"

I laughed, "Right. So how did Kristine get to Arkansas?"

"Well, little Krissy tired of Butch quickly. Texas is a community property state while Arkansas doesn't include inherited assets as marital property, so she bought a lake house at Greer's Ferry, established residency, and filed for divorce as an Arkansas resident. Butch wasn't surprised. He took a modest seven-figure settlement, happy to avoid the fate of his friend Luke."

"How do you know all this? And does Sam?"

Micki gave me a knowing smile. "I represented Butch in the divorce. Sam knows because I told him what I could without violating the privilege. He wouldn't listen. You'll understand when you meet her tonight. I also represented her third husband. Remember me telling you about the securities dealer who built the ranch home I now own? The one willing to give away the farm to get rid of his wife?"

"What does she see in Sam? Sure, he's good looking, but he has no money." I shook my head in disbelief.

"Well, let's see. She's got plenty of money, no business to run, and no family. She's chaired a few charitable events, but has no real interest in philanthropy. What's left but politics? Sam may think he's running for the Supreme Court, but I bet she has other plans— Governor? Senator?"

"Well, I hope she comes tonight. I want to see what she's all about. Sam's not a fool—or at least not usually. You sure you want Larry within her reach?" I waited for her typical sharp response.

"She doesn't have a clue that Larry is old Little Rock or that his family owns a bank, so he's safe," she replied. "Jack, I wouldn't put anything past that woman. She is truly evil."

23

SAM WAS ALL FOR US HAVING DINNER. "Micki's not too keen on Kristine, but I want you to meet her—we've even talked about coming to DC.

"One problem—Kristine doesn't like The Faded Rose. She thinks it's kind of common, and the menu isn't, well… you know." He was clearly uncomfortable. Never mind that Sam and I always eat at the Rose when I'm in town. At any rate, we agreed to meet at Brave New Restaurant. Apparently, Kristine approves of its atmosphere.

Micki rolled her eyes when I told her about the change of plans. I looked forward to the dynamics of the evening almost as much as the food.

I tried to engage Maggie in conversation as we rode back to the hotel, but she remained quiet.

"What's wrong? You look like you've seen a ghost," I remarked.

She gave a start and ran her fingers through her hair, "Jack, the woman Micki described is my worst nightmare. You have no reason to know this, but my uncle Tony fell prey to the wiles of a young woman determined to get a title. She destroyed his family—my aunt committed suicide and my cousins are still in therapy. No one has seen or heard from Tony in years. I can't help but imagine some blonde gold-digger setting her sights on Walter."

"For heaven's sakes, Margaret Matthews. Your husband has eyes only for you. No Rangerette or socialite will ever get his attention as long as you're around, so stop worrying," I scolded.

"Maybe it would be best if I didn't come tonight. I'm not sure I'm up to it."

I couldn't believe my ears. "Maggie, you are coming. If Kristine is as bad as all that, I'll need your help with Sam—you'll notice things I won't. Sam is oblivious to manipulative women."

"He gets it from his best friend," Maggie said with a little smile.

"I admit I've made a few bad choices, but I'm doing better, right? Walter tells me I moved up in class with Carol. You like her, don't you?"

"Carol is an attractive and very shrewd woman." Not exactly a ringing endorsement.

The car pulled up to the hotel, and I held the door for her.

"But you do like her, right? Walter does, I know." I could hear the anxiety creep into my tone.

Maggie looked back as she walked through the lobby doors. "It's a conversation for another day. Right now I have to get ready to meet the wicked witch of the East."

The bar was busy for a weekday afternoon, so I found a stool and texted Maggie to join me when she was ready. I let my mind wander back to Helen's lecture. As usual, she was right—cocktails and sitting by Carol's pool wasn't a healthy lifestyle. Maybe I should get some advice from Stella.

I glanced around the room—no one I knew, all strangers. One guy looked a little familiar, and I realized he'd been there yesterday when Rabbi Strauss delivered his message. I thought he'd come in with the rabbi, but now there he was again, sitting in the same corner. He wore a European style leather jacket, and I could see that his face was pockmarked, the result of acne, or maybe a disease like smallpox. He sat by himself at a table for four.

It wasn't long before Maggie arrived. She looked terrific in a navy-blue silk dress, smart heels, and a gray cashmere shawl. A small set of pearls adorned her neck.

"Kristine will have nothing on you," I teased, pulling out the stool next to me. "Too bad Walter's not here."

"I have no intention of allowing Walter within a stone's throw of Kristine. You can take that to the bank."

She asked the waiter for a cup of spiced Chai and asked, "Jack, wasn't that fellow in the corner here yesterday?"

I nodded and punched a text message into my iPhone.

"Sorry—maybe Jordan can get a quick photo of him."

We chatted for a few minutes; it wasn't long before Jordan joined us, giving me a wink. I paid up, and we followed him to the Suburban, leaving the pockmarked man sitting alone with the beer he had yet to touch.

*****

The man watched them leave, knowing any attempt to find out his identity would be fruitless—he had been erased from every law enforcement and government database. He'd been called after the local contractors botched the hit on Clovis Jones. At least Jones had been taken out of play for the moment. Too much was at stake for the slightest mistake.

24

CLOVIS LOOKED A LITTLE BETTER—he was propped up in a big chair and his color had returned to normal. But between the broken rib and multiple contusions, every movement was still painful. Stella had a new look since I'd seen her last—her cropped hair was black with purple highlights, and she might have added a piercing or two. Maggie gave Clovis a careful hug before joining Stella on the front porch.

"The ride home from the hospital was almost more than I could stand," Clovis admitted, watching them leave. "I'm glad Maggie's here. Stella's been a rock, but she needs company, and I need a break. I don't mean…"

"No explanations needed, I get it. Paul has everything well in hand, so you should rest, concentrate on getting well. Time's the only thing that heals a broken rib."

"Paul's doing great, but we're spread razor thin."

He tried to shift his position, and I could see little beads of sweat break out on his forehead.

"You know Martin would be glad to help, just say the word," I offered.

Martin Wells' security firm in DC worked for all of Walter's companies. He and Clovis held each other in mutual respect and had joined forces before.

"You and Maggie will be back in DC in a day or two—Martin can take charge there. We'll be okay—I'll be back on my feet before long. Let's talk about what's really bothering you—Beth and Jeff."

"You know me well, my friend."

"Yes, I do. Our contact person in St. Louis has assured me that no one would dare come close to Beth or Jeff. He's a reliable guy, knows the ropes."

It's a long story, but thanks to Novak both Jeff and Beth were under the protection of the New Orleans syndicate and, by way of an accommodation, their counterpart in St. Louis. Funny isn't it, how fate can turn an enemy into a strange bedfellow.

"Maggie and I hope to stop in and see them on our way home—I guess we should let those guys know. I don't..."

"You'll be safe as houses," he interrupted with a grin. "Tell Maggie to send me your itinerary. Now why don't you tell me what's going on with Ben before Stella comes back."

I told him about our conversation with Rabbi Strauss and my decision to defend Rachel. I also told him about the man in the bar.

"Jordan has done a preliminary check on the man in the bar; he doesn't show up in the usual databases. If I had to guess, I'd say he's with the Israeli government, sent here to keep an eye on you and the Rabbi," he speculated.

"Well, maybe so, but the Israelis have all but said they've never heard of Rachel Goodman. Her husband..."

"Jack," he said leaning forward with a grimace. "What they say or don't say doesn't amount to a hill of beans. Every newspaper in the country believes she worked for the Israelis. Mark my words—you haven't seen the last of Rabbi Strauss. Shoot, if you take on Rachel Goodman as a client, at least half the spies in DC will be following your ass. Not to mention the FBI and the CIA."

I admit I hadn't thought about it in quite those terms. The thought of the international intelligence community following my every step was unnerving, to say the least. Then again, no sense getting all worked up. Rachel had yet to hire us—maybe she had better judgment than her parents.

Clovis leaned back again in his chair—I could tell he was tuckered out. Before long Maggie and Stella interrupted our silence.

"Okay, Jack, time's up. My man needs his rest, no matter what he may think." She paused and raised her brows. "Oh, and thanks a lot."

I looked up quickly. "Okay, what did I do now?"

"All this food—Linda sent enough to tide us over for a month, and now she's talking about daily deliveries. What am I supposed to do with three apple pies? And who is Jasmine? She's offered to sit with Clovis while I'm at the gym or running an errand."

Maggie came to the rescue. "Well, Clovis needs to eat—so do you. Please work with Linda, it gives her something to do, a way to contribute. I'm sure we can find someone to help you with the pies."

"And Jasmine?" She looked at me.

"Her name is Jasmine White," I replied. "She's a neighbor and good friend of the Jennings. She joined us for dinner the other night. I found her to be very pleasant, a good conversationalist. Her offer is generous."

I tried to keep from blushing, but Clovis and Maggie burst out laughing; even Stella couldn't keep a straight face. "Conversationalist—you are so full of shit, Jack Patterson. Don't worry—I'll work out something with Linda—without Jasmine."

"Maggie told me a little about your next case," she continued. "Besides watching over Clovis and keeping him out of trouble, how can I help?"

I was relieved to change the subject.

"Well, if we end up representing Rachel, we'll need secure computers and phones. It won't be long before hackers from all over the world try to break into our systems."

"You know how to turn a girl on, Jack," she said with a slow grin.

Clovis gave her a tired smile—it was time for us to leave. We hadn't had time to chew over who attacked him, but that could wait.

On our way to the restaurant, Maggie observed, "This case is getting complicated—international implications, secure networks—who knows what's next?" Then she threw a high, hard ball. "Good thing we're making changes at the office."

It almost blew right past me before I realized what she'd said.

"What changes? That's twice now you've mentioned changes. What are you talking about?"

Jordan stopped in front of the restaurant, and she hopped out. "We can talk about it later."

25

AN AUTUMN-ORANGE SETTING SUN reflected off the Arkansas River. Such was the view from the restaurant when we arrived, and as Maggie and I sipped on our cocktails. There was only one problem: no Kristine or Sam. Micki and Larry had bowed out at the last minute, no surprise, but at least they'd let me know.

All his life, Sam has been late. He was willing to stop and shoot the breeze with most anyone, an invaluable habit for a politician. Our waiter had no problem with the delay, noting that "Miss Kristine" was often late. They never gave away her table and always had her martini at the ready.

Like most people, I don't like being kept waiting, but the view and Maggie's company more than compensated. We were deep in conversation, and I'd just ordered a bottle of wine, when the absent couple came bustling in, an anxious waiter in tow.

Kristine stopped at every table to introduce Sam as "our next Supreme Court Justice." Sam hadn't even announced, as far as I knew.

She was quite the package: well dressed, serious makeup, too much jewelry, and way too many eyelashes for me. I couldn't picture laid-back Sam falling for her, but he looked pleased as punch. She must have qualities I couldn't see, I thought, suppressing a grin.

Sam made the introductions, and we had just sat down again when Kristine popped back up, excusing herself to powder her nose.

She was gone long enough for the three of us to catch up as old friends. I told him about meeting Helen for lunch at the Town

Pump, and he reacted with a rueful sigh—he hadn't been there for months. Sam had been a regular at the Town Pump for a decade. I wondered...

Kristine returned with a waiter in tow. She sat down with a flourish, and the waiter handed her a martini and gave Sam a local draft beer.

Kristine gave him a frown and looked at Maggie. "I've told him he needs to drink something more sophisticated. Even bourbon is better for a man in his position."

"Oh, and did Sam tell you?" she asked, turning to me. "We can't stay for dinner—we're needed at a fundraiser at the Arts Center. I'm sure you understand." She actually batted her eyelashes. "Sam has told me so much about you, Jack—I really am sorry."

Sam looked apologetic, but apparently had no say in the matter.

"Oh, no—what a shame!" I found a deep Southern accent. "But you need to finish your martini, and I need to talk shop with Sam for a minute."

Like magic, the waiter appeared with a little dish of olives and poured the rest of her martini from the shaker.

"Well..." she began, but this time Sam interrupted, "What's up?"

"I need a favor. The FBI has put Ben's home on twenty-four hour watch. They probably think Rachel gave Ben or Linda information or documents or that someone will use them to get a message to Rachel. The FBI must keep you informed. I'd like to know what you know."

"Who is Rachel?" Kristine interrupted.

"Rachel Goodman," Sam answered with a trace of irritation.

"The traitor?" Kristine's shrill voice turned a few heads.

Sam took her hand and said, "She hasn't been formally accused of anything yet, and she is Ben Jennings' daughter. Ben is a lifelong friend."

She took a deep breath, composing herself with effort. "Sam, darling, you must think of your future. I mean, you can't risk what we've planned."

She looked at me, "Jack, I'm surprised you'd ask such a favor. I thought you were Sam's friend."

To my surprise, Sam's voice was stern. "Kristine, Jack isn't asking me to do anything improper. Peggy Fortson called right before I left the office and told me that Rachel has asked to see Jack, and I am free to tell him whatever I know, which isn't much."

"What?" Our simultaneous reaction broke the tension.

Sam flashed his well-known grin. "Rachel is asking for a lawyer, and not just any lawyer, but the one and only Jack Patterson. Her father told her long ago that if she ever needed legal help, she should call you. I'll send Micki the contact at my office who's handling this first thing in the morning. Peggy said you'd understand why she didn't call you."

"Who is Peggy?" Kristine demanded.

Boy, the woman didn't let up. I wondered why she was so insecure.

"Peggy Fortson is the Deputy Assistant Attorney General for the Criminal Division of the Department of Justice. She was my contact person for the Cole case. She and Jack are very old friends," Sam smiled.

I understood why Sam emphasized the word "old," leaving out the fact that Sam and Peggy had at one point enjoyed more than a professional relationship. In fact, I wasn't sure that had changed.

Kristine pouted, but sipped on her martini as we heard her mumble, "We'll talk about this later."

Sam continued, "So far the FBI has no evidence that Ben and Linda are involved. They found no documents on Ben's computer, no strange deposits into their bank accounts, and no unusual chatter on their phones. The surveillance is to make sure that no one tries to contact Rachel through them."

"Thanks, Sam. Any leads on the attack on Clovis?"

"Nothing yet. I promise I'll call if something turns up."

Sam looked at Kristine, who threw down the remains of her martini. We all rose to say goodbye, and Sam gave Maggie both a hug and a kiss on the cheek.

Kristine said to Maggie, "So nice to meet you ...er..."

"Margaret Matthews." Maggie's tone was icy.

"Margaret. Right." Kristine smiled. I gave her upturned cheek an air kiss, and she flounced away, Sam in tow.

Maggie voiced her frustration, almost before they were out of sight. "I might as well have been a sack of potatoes. What on earth does he see in her?"

I laughed, hoping there was more to it than the obvious answer.

"Well, here's one good thing," I pointed out. "You and I don't have to spend the rest of the evening with her. The two of us can enjoy the view, a good dinner, and share a bottle of wine."

Maggie rose, still flustered. "Well, I need to wash my hands first. What an obnoxious woman. While I'm gone, order me their best single malt—neat, a double."

TUESDAY

26

I SLEPT LIKE A LOG—must have been the chocolate crème brûlée. I wondered how Maggie would feel after several single malts, but she joined me at breakfast none the worse for wear.

"I'd hoped we might go to St Louis on our way home, but I don't see how we can. I want to meet with Rachel as soon as possible before she or the government change their mind."

"Do you still need all the documents from Ben and Linda?" Maggie asked.

"Better be safe than sorry; let's assemble what we have. Depending on what the contact at Justice has to say, we still need to hand out assignments to Paul's people, update Micki and Clovis, and who knows what else."

Maggie responded as I hoped she would. "Why don't you put me in charge of the scheduling and logistics. You'll have plenty of time to get everything done. Let's finish our breakfast, and go to Micki's. She and I have a little planning to do."

*****

Micki's office was already bustling when we arrived. Micki's interns, Matt and Lauren, were cleaning up the conference room after spending most of the night on research. Debbie was busy in the kitchen baking cheese biscuits and muffins; the aroma was irresistible. Micki was in court, and Mongo suggested I use her office.

I punched in the number Sam's office had given Micki, and a deep female voice answered, "Joan Laing."

"This is Jack Patterson. Sam Pagano gave me this number to call about Rachel Goodman."

"Yes, Mr. Patterson, I've been expecting your call."

"I understand that Rachel has asked to see me," I said.

"That's correct. Maybe it would be helpful for me to explain who I am and a little bit about the process."

"Yes, please," I agreed.

"I am Joan Laing, and I am Deputy U.S. Attorney in the Northern District of Virginia. Yesterday morning Rachel Goodman requested access to an attorney and specifically asked to speak with you. If you agree to represent her, we can move forward with accommodating her request." Her tone was cool and professional.

"But, and please forgive me, I believe espionage is outside of your area of expertise. So if a lawyer's visit is just a way for her to communicate with her parents, I'm afraid that won't happen. There will be plenty of time for her to speak to her family," she said.

"Let me understand, Ms. Laing. Rachel has asked to speak to a lawyer, me in particular, but you won't let me speak to her unless I intend to represent her? That sounds like putting the cart before the horse and that you're denying her access to counsel. Please explain how that's not the case."

She wasn't at all intimidated. "Mr. Patterson, procedures must be followed in cases such as this. One of those is that her attorney must have a current security clearance."

"I already have code word clearance. I expect you know that."

"Yes, I'm familiar with that issue coming up in the Stewart case, but in this case, the interests of national security require us to follow certain procedures. Even with your level of clearance, the paperwork necessary to bring your clearance up to date will take a few days to complete. I don't want to start that process unless there is a legitimate likelihood you'll represent her."

She had a point, but so did I.

"How can I know if I want to represent her, or that she'll want me to, unless she and I discuss it?" I asked.

"Your point is valid, but there are some unusual circumstances in this case." I heard a little sigh, and she seemed to relax a bit.

"Listen, Mr. Patterson, I know you have no reason to trust me, but I am trying to speed up the process, not slow it down. Your friends at main justice assure me you're a man of your word despite your reputation for using unorthodox tactics. Tell you what—if you can assure me that you will agree to represent her unless something unforeseen happens, you'll be able to meet with her as early as Friday morning."

Her offer sounded too good to be true. I knew the barriers a hard-ass prosecutor could throw up.

"Okay, thanks. But you're right—I'm not an expert in defending espionage cases. I owe it to Rachel to explain the downsides to my representation. But if Rachel doesn't have second thoughts, I will represent her."

"That's all I need. Why don't you come by my office Thursday afternoon? We can discuss the representation meeting, and you can sign the necessary documents so it can happen."

"May I see what you want me to sign beforehand?" I asked, knowing the contents of those documents could be a problem.

"They will be delivered to your office by Thursday morning. I want to remind you that these documents are covered by the Secrets Act."

"Thanks for the heads-up. I'll make sure all the proper procedures are followed. I look forward to working with you."

I heard nothing but silence, and was about to hang up, when she finally responded.

"Please don't consider my willingness to be cooperative as anything more than a wish to get this case moving. My office has been hampered by Rachel's unwillingness to seek counsel. I must also warn you that although we've been able to keep her request for counsel out of the press, that won't last forever. There are jailers, marshals, and lay people involved. Sooner or later one of them will talk to the press."

"The press already knows I'm in Little Rock visiting the family. But let me be clear, you'll never see me quoted either on or off the record about this case. I will honor any agreement that I sign and any gag order a court issues. I have plenty of experience dancing the Texas two-step with the press."

"I hope so, Mr. Patterson; it will make working with you a lot easier."

We agreed to meet at two o'clock Thursday afternoon and ended the conversation. Ms. Laing wasn't one for small talk.

Our conversation had been awkward. I sensed she wasn't comfortable with me, and I've never been comfortable with prosecutors even when I was one. But there was something else—I couldn't put my finger on it. Maybe Peggy Fortson had warned her to be careful. One thing was certain: traveling to St. Louis was off. I had to finish things up here and get back to DC. I also wasn't about to miss my evening with Carol.

As I walked toward the conference room, I felt a little twinge of unease.

27

I HAD SENT MATT AND LAUREN home for a break, so Maggie was alone in the conference room. I brought her up to date and suggested she ask Ben and Linda to come in after lunch.

She agreed, adding, "Jack, why can't we drop in on Beth? We can wrap up matters here this afternoon and be in St. Louis in time for dinner. We can spend the night there and fly to DC tomorrow."

"You think we have time?" I asked.

"We do. I'll handle the logistics; you go see Clovis. I'm sure Stella needs a break."

I left Micki's, but not before downing two of Debbie's cheese biscuits and deciding that Clovis needed a few to help in recovery. I found Clovis sitting in a rocking chair that was much too small for him. He was on the phone, so I handed him the biscuits and walked into the kitchen to make a call of my own.

"Hey, Larry, it's Jack. I've got a favor to ask."

"Jack…um, Jack Patterson?"

I waited in silence.

"Well, sure, how can I help?"

"I'm watching Clovis try to get comfortable in a rocking chair that's way too small. Do you know where I might find a comfortable rocker for a man his size?"

I could hear the relief in his voice when he responded. I wondered what he'd expected.

"I know just what he needs. I'll have one delivered this afternoon."

"Thanks, I was sure you'd have a solution. Let me know what I owe you."

I returned to the den to find Clovis munching on Debbie's biscuits. I filled him in on the events of the day and told him that Maggie and I would leave for St. Louis late this afternoon.

"I'll give my contact a heads-up—they'll take good care of you. And Martin knows what to do in DC. Give Beth a hug for me; I couldn't right now if she were standing right here." He smiled and then turned serious.

"I don't envy you, friend. This one isn't going to be easy. Rachel is already a household name, synonymous with traitor, and it won't be long before the whole world knows you're her lawyer. Martin and I will do our best the to keep you alive—it's not like we haven't gone through this drill before. But I worry this case might not end well."

"Thanks for the reassurance, pal. But you could be right, and I'm worried, too. Something tells me another shoe is about to drop. But right now the only thing I know for sure is that Ben's daughter needs a lawyer—nothing else matters."

"Except for women, your instincts are always good. How is Carol anyway?"

I told him about playing golf instead of spending the weekend with her and missing her email about Rachel.

"She's libel to blow a gasket when you tell her you've agreed to represent Rachel."

"We have a 'don't ask, don't tell' policy. I don't ask her about her business, and she doesn't ask about mine. It's worked pretty well so far. The truth is it'll probably come out in the press before I have the chance to tell her."

He raised a skeptical eyebrow, and I knew what he was thinking—never worked for the military, why would it work for me? We both gave a start as the back door closed with a bang. Stella sailed in, kicked off her boots and gave Clovis a kiss. "How you doing, sweetie? Jack, all of Micki's systems are still secure. I'll recheck Ben's computer this afternoon, and when Maggie gets back to DC, we can check your systems remotely. How else can I help?"

"I'll know better by the end of the week. I'm scheduled to meet with the U.S. Attorney Thursday afternoon and with Rachel on Friday. I don't want the two of you to come to DC until the docs give

Clovis the okay. That's an order."

Stella smiled. "You'll get no argument from me. Say, what's the deal with Micki? She and Maggie are totally wigged out by some woman named Kristine."

"Kristine is Sam's new girlfriend," I replied. "Micki doesn't think much of her."

"For good reason," I heard Clovis mutter.

"So I gathered," she said. "Why don't you stay for lunch, Jack? I've got half a ham in the fridge, not to mention three kinds of macaroni and cheese. And my friend Marty brought two loaves of sourdough bread from Boulevard Bakery."

I wasn't in that big of a hurry, so I agreed, and we all enjoyed ham sandwiches and the South's favorite rendition of pasta.

28

THE COMINGS AND GOINGS of Micki's office appeared to reflect chaos, but no K Street office in DC was more organized, or nearly as much fun. Ben and Linda sat quietly in the corner of the reception area until Debbie appeared with coffee and cookies and shepherded them into the conference room. I waited for Micki, who greeted me with a smile and a murmured "thank you."

Confused, I asked, "Uh, for what?"

"For calling Larry. He was surprised, but appreciated you going to him and not asking me. It means a great deal to both of us."

I pretended to understand and mumbled, "You're welcome. I hope he can find the right chair. Clovis looks ridiculous in the one he has."

"He wants to design and build a rocking chair for Clovis. But he's found one that will work for the time being—it's being delivered this afternoon. When he worked near Sugarbush, Vermont, he came across an artisan who made the most magnificent rocking chairs. Your request inspired him to try his hand at his own. Clovis will be his guinea pig."

"I know Clovis will appreciate it." It was getting harder and harder not to like Larry.

We took our places at the conference table, and I began, "I'm glad you're here. I have some good news." Linda gave me a nervous smile; Ben sat still.

"Rochelle has asked to see a lawyer and according to the government she followed her father's advice and asked for me."

"Oh, thank heavens," Linda said, sighing. I could see Ben's shoulders relax and his face broke into a smile. It was a nice moment.

"What's the catch?" Micki brought us back to reality.

"I hope there isn't one. I meet with Deputy U.S. Attorney Thursday afternoon. My security clearance has to pass muster, and I'll have to sign a confidentiality agreement, but I might see Rochelle as early as Friday. The devil is in the details, but so far so good."

"They'll find something wrong with your clearance or make the confidentiality agreement so onerous you can't sign it. Don't get your hopes up," Micki warned, ever the skeptic. We both knew prosecutors love to take you down a crooked path leading to a dead end.

I ignored Micki's pessimism.

"We need to interview Rochelle's teachers and friends. Ben and Linda, you are our best resource in identifying the right folks to interview and help make introductions. I have to get back to DC tomorrow, so Micki and Paul will take the lead with the interviews. The more we can get done on this end, the better prepared we'll be.

"The Northern District of Virginia is notorious for moving their criminal cases at lightning speed, catching many a defense lawyer with their pants down, so to speak. The government takes full advantage of what is called the court's 'rocket docket.' We want to stay ahead of the game."

Ben straightened his shoulders and nodded.

I asked a few more questions about Rachel's friends, both in Little Rock and DC, but neither parent had any real knowledge. We danced around the subject of Rachel's brothers. The mere mention of them brought a new tension to the room, and I sensed we couldn't count on their cooperation. The stress of the family situation was clearly taking its toll on her parents, so I suggested we call it a day.

Maggie and I walked them to the front door and returned to Micki's office to find her reaching into a bottom drawer for a bottle of Johnnie Walker and three glasses. She poured us all a healthy shot and raised her glass in a toast.

"Here's to another lost cause. What's this make—four major cases we've worked on together? One of these days you'll learn that a criminal lawyer always talks about getting paid on the front end, not after it's all over."

This was the second time she had pointed out my lack of concern about a fee; I tried to allay her concerns.

"We don't know whether the government has seized Rachel's assets or not. My bet is they have; it's their standard operating procedure. But she may have money in her pension plan or life insurance on her husband that's still available. I don't think it's fair to have a money conversation with Ben and Linda until we know Rachel's circumstances."

"I'm just giving you a hard time, and you know it," Micki said. "I'm in whether we get paid or not, and I know you are. But it pisses me off that the government gets to take all her money before she's even officially charged, just to keep her from hiring a decent lawyer. It's not as if the system isn't weighted against the defendant already. The constitutional right to counsel is a joke unless you're richer than shit. Fuck the bastards!"

"Micki!" Maggie exclaimed, surprised by her vehemence, if not the words.

"Sorry, Maggie. It gets to me now and then. I can't tell you how many people walk through my doors, hat in hand, looking for help. I have to turn them away and send them to an overworked and underfunded public defender's office." Micki took a healthy swallow of scotch.

I tried to lighten her mood. "Speaking of richer than shit, you should have seen Clovis's face when I mentioned Kristine. I'm surprised he hasn't already called you."

"Oh, he did, the moment you left the house. Clovis was my investigator when I represented her third husband. He's the one who discovered she was having an affair with their marriage counselor in Miami. Don't worry. Maggie and I have a plan."

"It's better you don't know," Maggie interrupted before I could ask.

"Okay, have it your way, but I hope you know what you're doing."

29

THE FLIGHT TO ST. LOUIS WAS PERFECT: smooth and uneventful. Despite my repeated attempts, Maggie refused to elaborate on the plans for Kristine. I let it go. We had touched down and were taxiing to the private hanger that Walter's pilots used when I received a text from my client, Red Shaw, owner of the NFL franchise the Los Angeles Lobos. I had a retainer agreement with the Lobos to give antitrust advice, and Red sought my counsel in other aspects of his corporate empire.

Red and I had an unusual friendship and attorney-client relationship. He was engaged to Senator Lucy Robinson, the widow of the former Senator from Arkansas who was shot by my client, Woody Cole. Lucy wasn't a fan of mine, and not just because I represented her husband's assassin. Our tenuous relationship began in college when she was a friend of my then-future wife, Angie. To complicate things further, I first met Carol Madison at Red and Lucy's engagement party. Did I say our relationship was unusual?

Red's text read:

> Looks like you're in deep shit again. Rachel Goodman? And I ran into Carol at the Nats' game with former Congressman Eric Hartman. He's an asshole! Call me when you get back. We need to do damage control.

How did Red know I'd agreed to represent Rachel? Carol's "date" was equally disturbing. Yes, Carol was in the business of gathering information, and Eric Hartman was one of the most powerful lobbyists in DC, but only two days ago she had planned to meet me at that ball game.

All thoughts about Red and Carol disappeared when we walked down the plane's steps to find my daughter Beth waiting on the tarmac. She was the spitting image of her mother, with short, black hair, dark brown eyes, and honey colored skin. She wasn't as tall as Angie, but she had the same quick wit and temperament. We embraced for a long moment before she turned to hug Maggie.

"Jeff will meet us at the restaurant, but he may be a few minutes late. His shift just ended, and he wants to clean up before dinner. Let's drop your bags off at the hotel first."

We had barely settled into her car before she began to pepper us with questions.

"How's Clovis? Are Micki and Larry engaged? Did you have time to see Helen? What color is Stella's hair this week?"

Beth knew all the Little Rock characters; she and Jeff had been involved in two of my more interesting cases. I let Maggie answer her rapid-fire questions. I was content to listen from the back seat. Beth seemed a little older, a little more mature, as well she should. Still, I couldn't help but miss the little girl who was long gone.

I interrupted, "Where are we having dinner?"

"I Fratellini in Clayton, Jeff's favorite. We were lucky to get a table. I promise you'll love it."

Both the décor and the aroma at the restaurant brought back memories of Italy, and the menu certainly didn't disappoint. Maggie and Beth opted for grilled trout, Jeff ordered the filet of beef with porcini mushrooms, and I went with one of my favorites, linguine with clams. Beth knew how to make her father happy.

Beth and Jeff talked non-stop about their lives, their schools, and their plans for the future. The only response expected from either Maggie or me was the occasional nod of approval. As I expected, their goal was to settle in Charleston, but were also giving thought to spending a year or two in Charlotte before making a final decision. I shouldn't have been surprised—they were both Davidson grads and knew Charlotte well.

I tried to remain neutral, knowing any real enthusiasm on my part about Charlotte would ring the death knell for that idea. I parried a few questions about Rachel, thankful when Maggie changed the subject to her recent trip to Scandinavia with Walter.

Beth said "Dad, you said you wanted to talk. We can order after-dinner drinks here, although I'm sure the restaurant would love to turn the table, or we can go back to your hotel. The bar at the Cheshire Inn is nice. Let's get a Lyft—I can pick up my car tomorrow."

We agreed and were soon back at the hotel and settled into the comfortable pub.

"Okay, Dad, out with it. Is it about Carol? Are you two getting married?" Beth demanded.

I choked, almost spilling my glass of port. "That's a question a father's supposed to ask his daughter, not the other way around."

Beth smiled. "Don't worry, Dad—Jeff and I won't keep you in suspense much longer." She looked at Jeff and squeezed his hand. "Come on, Dad, this is about you. What's up?"

"No, it is not about Carol and frankly, Beth, I'd rather not talk about her. As you know, we've become close and I like her a lot, but there are issues we need to overcome before we could ever get serious." I couldn't believe the stiff, formal voice I heard was my own.

Beth looked at Maggie, who raised her eyebrows. Her eyebrows could be very expressive.

"Okay, Dad, I'm sorry. What is it then?"

I paused, taking a healthy sip. "I had lunch with Helen the other day in Little Rock. Without going into all the details, she ended by giving me a lecture about seeking positive change, change that's good for me. Her advice got me thinking. Remember how I let people think I was selling our house during Billy's case? I came close to actually selling, but couldn't go through with it. I told myself I didn't want a case strategy to dictate such a decision, that I wasn't ready to let go of the memories yet."

"Dad, the memories never go away."

"You're right, but somehow I couldn't do it. I've given it a lot of thought the last few days, and I've decided that selling the house might be the nudge I need to step out of the past. But I want to talk to you first. Your memories are in that house, too."

Beth glanced toward Maggie. "Dad, the memories have never

been in the house, but in our hearts. The house is great, but it's way too big for one person. Maggie and I have been telling you that for some time; you weren't ready to listen. New digs will be good for you—just be sure whatever you buy has at least two bedrooms. Jeff and I can't afford DC hotels."

Well, that wasn't so hard, I thought.

"I wasn't asking your permission, you know. I was putting you on notice that all your clothes and stuff in the basement will have to go, including that trunk you took to camp every summer. You haven't been to camp in seven years, and you still won't let me throw it away." Her camp trunk had been a bone of contention for a long time.

She laughed. "My trunk won't be a problem—you can just put it in the extra bedroom in the new place," she laughed.

I shook my head. Beth will bury me in that trunk.

"You're okay with my decision?" I asked.

"Dad, I'm ready to agree to most anything you want to do, as long as it's not marrying Carol!"

"I thought you liked Carol." The vehemence and obvious relief of her reaction caught me off-guard.

Maggie's eyebrows shot up again, and Beth responded carefully. "She's very nice, Dad. But let's get you moved first."

The two of then talked about neighborhoods and the relative merits of condominium life or town homes, ignoring me. So while the women in my life were deciding my future, Jeff and I discussed the possibility that the Razorbacks could upset Alabama. Jeff gave the Razorbacks a slim chance, a little higher than any chance I had in deciding where I would live. The eternal optimist, I predicted that this would be the year.

We stayed up too late enjoying each other's company. The bar was dark, but as we got up to leave, I thought I saw a familiar man sitting in the corner. Then again, it could have been my imagination.

WEDNESDAY

30

MAGGIE AND I WORKED on our schedules during the flight home to DC.

"I'm not sure I need protection," I groused while still in the air. "But Martin should know that things are likely to get a little crazy once the press discovers we're defending Rachel."

Maggie shook her head. "A man with a disfigured face follows us all the way to St. Louis, and you don't think we need protection? How in the world did he know where we were, and how did he get to St. Louis so quickly?"

"He *was* in the bar, wasn't he? I thought it was my imagination. Remind me to call Clovis when we land."

Thinking to change the subject, I asked, "You want to tell me about these 'changes' you have in mind? Don't you think I should have some say in any changes?"

"Okay. Why don't we go straight to the office, order in sandwiches, and talk about the changes I have in mind? Rose is taking a few days off to help her sister move into assisted living, so it will be just us and the temp manning the phones."

"Perfect. While you're thinking about changes, what do you think about bringing in a young associate or a paralegal? We have plenty of business to justify the hire."

No response. Okay, we'd wait for the office.

The Falcon glided into the airport without a hitch, and Martin loaded our bags into his big Tahoe. We briefed him on what we had been up to, what had happened to Clovis, and the recurring presence of the man with the pockmarked face.

Martin was a man of few words. "I'll call Paul as soon as I drop you off. One of my men will stay with you at the office. We'll have a short-term plan in place by tonight. We should meet soon to discuss long-term staffing. I'll try not to bug Clovis, but if I know him, he'll be calling me."

"Speaking of that, I need to call him and tell him about St. Louis," I said as I pulled my phone out.

"How is Beth?' Clovis asked without preliminaries.

"She and Jeff are great. We had a wonderful time, but we had company. The same man who was at the bar in Little Rock showed up at the hotel bar after we got back from dinner last night."

"Are you alone now?" he asked.

"Maggie and I are with Martin, on our way into DC." I knew why he was asking. Maggie didn't know about the protection arrangement I had arranged for Beth.

"I'll be brief. I know you had company. My contact called me last night. His people spotted the man and tailed him to your hotel, but you were in no danger. He offered to have the man questioned, but I declined. Whoever he is, the guy took a hell of a chance following you to St. Louis. Tell Martin to call me after he drops you off. You and I can talk later."

"Sure thing, but I have an idea. Micki plans to meet with Rabbi Strauss. Maybe he can help with identification."

"Do you want the Israelis to know you're being followed?" he asked.

"He might be one of theirs, and if not, I bet they already know," I shot back.

"I don't like this. You be careful and listen to Martin. Thanks for the chair, by the way. It has really made a difference."

I smiled. My having once had broken ribs had proven to be of some use.

*****

The office door was open, and I found a young man who I presumed to be the temp, sitting at Rose's desk. He rose and introduced himself as Brian Hattoy. He appeared to be in his early thirties, lean, and well dressed in a sport coat and tie.

I was about to respond when Maggie interrupted, asking him to pick up the sandwiches she had ordered from Bub and Pop's.

"I've asked Brian to fill in for Rose," she explained after he closed the door.

"Well, please tell him he doesn't need to wear a coat and tie. Where did you find him?" I asked.

"We might as well get this out of the way," she sighed. "Brian comes courtesy of Red Shaw, who asked if we could use some help. He's Red's nephew. He served one term of duty in Iraq, and a second term with the JAG Corps as a paralegal. As a favor to his sister, Red offered to help his nephew find a job." She looked nervous, a rare occurrence.

I pretended to be annoyed. "Tell Red absolutely not, his nephew is his problem not ours. If he needs a job, let him work for the Lobos. When were you going to tell me about this?"

"He was awarded both the Purple Heart and the Silver Star, and he has wonderful references from the JAG Corps, just the sort of help we need. Moreover, Red offered to increase his retainer to cover part of his salary. Why would you object when less than an hour ago you suggested adding someone?"

"What's the catch? Why is he having such a hard time finding work?" I already knew, but it was fun to mess with her a little—I seldom got the opportunity.

"Despite having fought the enemy and served with distinction, Brian was encouraged to seek a career outside the military. He was told that he didn't fit in." Maggie blushed, and I relented.

"You mean he's gay," I stated as Brian walked in carrying a sack of sandwiches.

There was an awkward silence, which only I could fill.

"Brian, I'm not sorry you walked in and heard me. Maggie was telling me what damn fools the military were to let you go, and I was trying to understand. I thought those days were long gone. I still don't understand, but the military's loss is our gain. If you're willing to work your butt off and put up with my tendency to stick my foot in my mouth, you're hired—and not as a temp either. You keep Maggie happy, and I'll be happy."

I extended my hand, and he took it. "Thank you, Mr. Patterson." He looked a little dazed, but his grip put mine to shame.

"Let's eat in my office."

After we had settled in I asked, "So, you're from Texas? Longhorn fan or do you root for the Aggies?"

"Yes, sir, not far from Longview. And, actually, neither; I'm not much into American football. I enjoy watching soccer, but my game is tennis."

"That's heresy in Texas. Good thing you moved east. Let's get a couple of things straight. First, we trade off getting coffee or any-thing else we want—not much hierarchy here. Next, unless we're going to court or meeting a new client, there's no need to wear a coat and tie. We're business casual every day. We're about to take on the defense of Rachel Goodman—I expect you've read about her. With your background, I'll understand if you don't want to be involved. We have plenty of other work."

Both Brian and Maggie were still in shock. I didn't want either of them to know that Gina Halep, the Executive VP for the Lobos, had already given me a heads-up about Brian. She had met him through Red and thought the world of him.

"Sure he's gay, but so what?" she'd said. "Why on earth would anyone care? He's smart, witty, and his military record is exemplary. I'd hire him in a minute, but he wants to live on the East Coast. Red's old military, but it bugs the heck out of him that the military drummed a war hero out of the service."

I enjoyed working with Gina. She was truthful and direct with everyone she dealt with—she called a spade a spade. Red had told me that one day she'd be the president of his NFL club, and I didn't doubt him.

She cared about both the players and the coaches. She did her best to be sure players weren't getting ripped off by agents, family, or their so-called friends. She implemented a creative program that enabled the players to complete their college degrees during the off-season and made use of the talent that worked with movie stars in L.A. to offer players and coaches media and public relations advice. More than a few players and assistant coaches had landed endorsement deals and opportunities for speaking engagements during the off-season thanks to her program. Word was getting out that the Lobos organization was a player's team.

Gina maintained a tough, professional image in public, but outside the office she was a lot of fun. She loved good food and a nice bottle of wine. Whenever I was in L.A., she and her husband took me to their favorite new restaurant. I trusted her judgment, so her ringing endorsement of Brian sealed the deal even before I met him.

"All right, Brian, if you don't mind manning the phones for the next few hours, Maggie and I have a couple of things to discuss, including your salary. Please call me Jack."

He left the room, and Maggie gave me a sheepish grin.

"Okay, Ms. Matthews, what other surprises do you have for me today?"

31

"I AM GLAD YOU THINK Brian is a good idea," she said avoiding my question.

"I hope Brian will be just what the doctor ordered. We've both been working too much, and I worry every day you'll decide that your life as Mrs. Walter Matthews should take priority."

I kept my tone light, but this was a constant and real fear. Maggie and I had worked together hand and glove for many years. I worried I might lose her when she married Walter, but it didn't turn out that way.

Maggie responded, "Well, my marriage does take priority, but it hasn't conflicted up until now."

"What do you mean until now?" An uneasy feeling settled in the pit of my stomach.

"Well, if you'd attended the Foundation Board meeting last month instead of spending the weekend with Carol, or if you'd bothered to read the minutes, you'd know that Susan Sandler at Evers found the perfect location in eastern Maryland for Walter's new corporate headquarters, an office and conference center for the foundation, a retreat center, and my dream home.

"We plan to create paths for walking, biking, and horseback riding, and facilities for recreation on the river. If the federal government removes its restrictions on marijuana medical research, we can move Dr. Stewart's research lab and farm onto the property. We still have plenty of land for the home and stables that Walter and I have always wanted."

"That's great." I knew how much Maggie and Walter loved to ride. Maggie still limped from a jumping accident incurred when she was a young girl in England. "But what does it have to do with our work together?" My voice sounded hollow, couldn't help it.

"The existing home on the property is quite large and with a few modifications can serve as a welcome center and staff headquarters. In the meantime, Walter and I have decided to live there so I can oversee the construction of our new home and the stables. Susan is putting our home in Virginia on the market next month."

The bottom had just dropped out of my life, and she wasn't even finished.

"I'll still come in to the office, but, Jack, the practice of law is changing. We can handle at least seventy-five percent of our work on the computer and through the Internet. These days we can work from most anywhere. Besides, our plans for Maryland include a satellite office for the law firm. I'm trying to keep us ahead of the game."

"Fine, I can't argue with that. But I've finally decided to ask Susan to sell my house. Now she'll be too busy to handle mine." I heard the whine—change didn't come easy for me.

"Don't you even go there, Jack Patterson. Susan can juggle more than one ball at a time. Women multitask, have you not noticed? Shoot, she'll be tickled pink. Beth and I already have some idea about where you should move."

"I should take a vacation to the south of France. You and Beth can handle the sale of the old place, close on a new place, and have the dishes unpacked by the time I return."

Maggie refused to rise to the bait. "You're a might touchy today, don't you think? You've been talking about selling the house for years. Have you forgotten last night's conversation?

"Let's get back to business—what do you want to pay Brian and how much do you want to add to Red's retainer?"

"You mean I have a say?" Maggie's face showed her opinion of my sarcasm. "What's the going rate for paralegals these days?"

She told me, and I whistled. Beth should switch to paralegal school.

"Okay," I said, gulping. "Pay him that and tell him he'll get a raise in six months if he proves his worth. As for Red, don't increase the retainer, but tell Gina we'll bill Brian's time outside the retainer when he works on Lobos' business. She'll be okay, and I don't want Red to think he can dictate how we do business. If Brian proves worth his salt, we'll all get a bargain. What do you think?"

"I think you're being generous, but I don't disagree. Our old law firm made obscene money billing me out hourly. It's none of my business, but I wonder why he hasn't applied to law school."

"I'm sure you'll know in a matter of days," I teased.

I'd had enough change and rethinking for one day, so I suggested we call it quits, go home, and unpack.

32

BIG MIKE, a new addition to Martin's team, drove me home and then back to the office in the afternoon. I invited him inside the office to get familiar with where and how Maggie and I worked. I gave him a brief explanation of our security, phone, and computer systems, then asked Brian to join us in my office. I got right to the point.

"You're both former military. Any reservations about our potential engagement on behalf of Rachel Goodman?"

Brian spoke up quickly. "No, sir, none. Everyone's entitled to a defense. When I was in the JAG, we defended deserters, guys accused of terrible atrocities, and guys who just lost it. That's not to say I'm a fan. If she spied for Israel or any another country and put American soldiers at risk, I'd have no qualms seeing her hang. But until she's found guilty, she's innocent in my book."

Big Mike nodded his head in agreement.

I didn't respond immediately. I was dead set against the death penalty in any circumstance, but I understood how Brian and Mike felt given their background.

After a moment, though, I said, "Mike, how long have you been with Martin?"

"Only three months, Mr. Patterson. Before that I served in Iraq, like Sergeant Hattoy."

Brian looked startled. "You know who I am?"

"You bet I do. It's an honor to be working with you, Master Sergeant. I mean that. You are and always will be a hero in my book."

Brian stared at his shoes, and neither man said another word about their service—a common trait of many vets who served in combat. Mike cleared his throat, said he had another appointment, but would be back at six o'clock unless I needed him earlier.

I asked Brian to update Maggie's research on Rachel while I concentrated on other clients' needs—it might be a while before I could give them attention. I was knee-deep in a Lobos issue when Mike texted that he was on his way back.

Stretching my stiff back, I called out, "Hey, Brian, I'm famished. How about joining me for crab cakes? Black Salt isn't Cantler's, but it's on the way home."

"I'm new in town. Never heard of Cantler's or Black Salt—I'm at your mercy." He shut down his computer, and we walked out into the late afternoon sunshine. September had turned into October, and I could feel just a whisper of chill in the air. Traffic was light, so it only took Big Mike ten minutes to pull up to the restaurant on MacArthur Boulevard just outside of Georgetown.

I ordered a dozen Wellfleet oysters. For a Texan, Brian was surprisingly comfortable with an oyster fork. I brought him up to date on what little we knew about the charges against Rachel and my scheduled meeting with Joan Laing.

"I've met Ms. Laing. Our JAG office had frequent interaction with the Northern District. She's a no-nonsense prosecutor who takes the lead on any sensitive cases out of the Pentagon. So far, the U.S. Attorney, Donald Cotton, has been smart enough to leave her alone. Cotton's ambitious—he's preparing a run for Virginia's Attorney General. You won't see him unless the press is near."

"That's very helpful." I smiled. "Does Ms. Laing have any glaring weaknesses?"

"None that I know. She seems to have good relationships with the judges in the Northern District and, generally speaking, the respect of the defense lawyers she faces. If she makes a deal, she keeps her part of the bargain. At least, that's her reputation."

We finished our oysters in silence, and I thought about Joan Laing. I knew I couldn't call Peggy Fortson, but my friend Phil had practiced both criminal and civil rights law for many years in Northern Virginia. I felt sure he could add to Brian's assessment.

"So, Brian, I'd like you to come with me to meet with Joan tomorrow. You ready to get your feet wet?" I asked.

"Really?" he asked. "I thought I'd be answering the phones while you and Mrs. Matthews met with Ms. Laing."

"Maggie's always with me in court, but to meet a prosecutor, no. Ms. Laing referred to my first interview with Rachel as a 'representation meeting.' That's a new one on me—any ideas?"

"Yes, sir. Defense lawyers complain about the process, but it's standard in national security cases. The government wants to be sure the attorney is on the up and up, not the tool of another country or a terrorist group. An FBI field agent will be present during your first meeting with Ms. Goodman. You must go through a background check before they'll let you meet with her alone."

"But I already have a top-level security clearance," I protested.

"Doesn't matter—it's the price of playing ball. The FBI has to bring a clearance up to date no matter how current. I hope they've already started the process."

"Oh, shit, what if the FBI knocked on Carol's door?" I thought to myself.

"What would they be looking for?" I asked. "I mean, most of the time I'm just a mild-mannered corporate attorney."

"Affiliations with the country or organization with which Rachel was working."

"Well, that shouldn't be a problem. Anything else I should know?"

"Rachel won't be in an ordinary jail—the FBI will drive you to a secret location, probably out in the Virginia countryside. You can't bring a phone or any recording device. Be prepared for a thorough search."

Oh, joy. I knew what that meant.

"What have I gotten myself into?" I lamented.

"I'm sorry, sir, but I've been through this routine before, and you did ask."

He looked a little anxious, and I smiled my encouragement. "No, no—go on. And please drop the 'sir.'"

"Okay. I won't kid you—it will be tough at first. But if you play by the rules, things will get easier."

"I've dealt with searches before—I can handle it. But I am worried about Micki."

"Maggie told me about Ms. Lawrence. She represents criminals regularly. She knows what's coming."

I'd never thought about that aspect of Micki's work.

"Micki's tough—you're right, she'll be okay. I think you'll like working with her. I do."

"That's what Maggie told me." His smile caused me to wonder what else she'd told him.

The waiter arrived with our entrees, and we tucked into excellent crab cakes and fries. It wasn't long before Brian broke our companionable silence.

"Mr. Pat… sorry, Jack—you've been thoughtful enough to ask if I have a problem working on the Goodman case, and I appreciate that. So I feel obligated to ask if you have any problem working with me."

"No, why should I?"

"Well, some people do. My superiors in the military decided I didn't fit in. My family back home in Texas knows I'm gay, but they still refer to gay as 'a condition' or 'that thing you have.' Uncle Red has been very generous with my mother and me, but he's uncomfortable with my sexual orientation. He says you and he are a lot alike. So I can't help but wonder how you feel about working with me."

Red thought he and I were alike? No way—but the thought gave me pause. I took a deep breath.

"Brian, your personal life is none of my business. We're a small office—we know each other pretty well, maybe too well sometimes. Maggie knows me better than I know myself, and it won't be long before she knows you that well, too. I could care less about your sexual orientation, and I'm confident Maggie doesn't either. Listen, work hard and pitch in no matter what the task, that's all I ask. We're taking on a tough case—jump in the deep end."

"That's fine, but…" he began, but I interrupted, looking at my watch.

"Look, we should make it an early night. Ms. Laing promised to send me some documents to sign. If they come in tonight, I'll email them to you for review."

"Sure, but I'm only a paralegal. I have no formal training in the law or reviewing documents."

"Right. So now you begin your training."

33

I turned on the ball game and sank into my favorite chair with my laptop. The only new message was from Red. "I'll see you tomorrow morning at ten—we need to talk." I wasn't surprised—Red was a defense contractor, and Rachel could well be a spy.

Phil was a night owl, so I had no hesitancy calling him. After a few minutes of catching up, I got to the point.

"What do you know about Joan Laing?"

"Saint Joan? What you need to know is she always wins. If you cross swords with her, I can promise you'll lose," he warned.

"That good, huh?"

"She's better than good. Looks as innocent as St. Joan, hence the nickname—but her razor wit and intelligence have cut many a witness to shreds. She'll kill you with kindness, but don't be fooled. The woman's a hard ass prosecutor to the core."

"Sounds as if you've run into her more than once."

"I have, and so far none of my tricks have worked. My advice is to ignore her blue eyes and innocent looks."

"Does she have a flaw I can exploit? Quick temper? Oversized ego? What about her personal life?"

"Forget it, Jack. Your charm will not work with Laing. Her husband writes science fiction novels, works out of their old townhouse in Alexandria. I've invited them over for a few parties—they always come as a couple, not a hint of trouble at home. You may have met her at Keith's wedding."

Phil knew better than to ask about a pending case, so we chatted for a few moments and agreed to get together for lunch. I made a mental note not to forget this time. It occurred to me that maybe my mental notes rather than written ones were part of the problem.

With the difference in time zones I didn't feel bad about calling Clovis. He picked up on the second ring.

"Micki has an appointment with the rabbi tomorrow morning, and Ben met with the insurance representative today. He's taken your direction to heart. If his suppliers cooperate, the restaurant will be open in a couple of weeks. Paul's put together a good plan for protecting the place. He had ideas I hadn't thought about."

"You okay?" I asked.

"Ribs hurt like hell. I can't sleep because I have to sit up, but this rocking chair has made the world of difference. Don't worry, I'm on the mend."

"Has Stella found anything on our computers?"

"Well, yes and no. The computers are clean, but she found something strange on Maggie's phone, something she's never seen. Someone may be using a signal from her phone to trace your location. Just to be safe, you'll both have new phones tomorrow. Don't worry—she'll figure it out—that woman loves a challenge."

"You're Exhibit One," I kidded. "By the way, I guess you've heard we've taken on a paralegal—can Stella get him a phone, too?"

"Sure, not a problem, but..." I heard him take a deep breath. "Look Jack, I've got a bad feeling about this case. I can't put my finger on it, but something's got me worried. Promise me, as a friend, you'll be careful."

"I'll be careful. And you need to get well—I might need you soon."

I put the phone down wondering why Clovis was so worried. The truth was I was uneasy, too. Who had been behind the brutal attack on him? Who was this guy who kept appearing out of the blue? Had Rachel Goodman really become a spy, and if so, why? As I walked upstairs, my thoughts wandered from Rochelle to Harold Spencer, the man who been found dead on the eighteenth green. I wondered idly if the police had made any progress in solving his murder.

THURSDAY

34

I'd asked Mike to pick me up at eight o'clock the next morning, and he was right on time. Rush hour was in full swing, so we decided to stop at Bourbon Coffee until the traffic died down. In DC, traffic dying down means you can get somewhere faster in a car than on foot. We enjoyed a cup of coffee and spent the time talking football.

We arrived at the office before Maggie, an unusual occurrence. Brian had already picked up on office protocol: first one in made the coffee and put Maggie's kettle on to boil—she would have nothing to do with the microwave. A package of documents arrived from the U.S. Attorney's office, and I tossed them onto Brian's desk.

"Um, do you think I can handle this?" he asked.

I smiled and said, "Well, Brian, we're about to find out. We're supposed to be at Laing's office at two o'clock, so let me know by noon if you see a problem."

Maggie bustled in before long, and we sat down in my office over coffee and tea to review the day's schedule. She asked me to join her and Walter for dinner, but I declined, reminding her I had plans with Carol. I told her I expected Red most any minute, and she asked if she should join us.

"No, I don't think so. He knows about Rachel, but he didn't sound too concerned. You need to be somewhere?"

"It's a good time for me to pop over to the Apple store in Georgetown to get the new phones Stella ordered and ship her my old one. Cellphones don't appear like magic, you know. How was dinner?"

"The crab cakes were excellent," I responded mildly.

"I don't give a fig about the crab cakes," she scowled. "How was Brian? What do you think?"

"I think he might work out. His experience with JAG has already come in handy," I smiled. "I know you have a raft of employment forms for him, but don't give them to him until he finishes the project I gave him. Tell him what he will get paid. He didn't ask last night."

"You worried he'll quit when he finds out?"

"If he does, I'll take his job, and he can have mine. Did I tell you what I made at Justice when I graduated from law school?"

She laughed. "Only a hundred times."

I would miss this daily banter if she and Walter left for the Eastern Shore. Sure, lots of lawyers managed their practice from a computer in their pajamas and socks, but there's no substitute to the give and take between human beings.

I heard a commotion and knew Red Shaw had arrived. Maggie rose and disappeared into her office. She respected Red, but didn't enjoy his company.

"Red, good to see you," I said as he strode into my office. "Coffee? How about something extra in it?" Red enjoyed a little brandy added to his coffee, even at ten in the morning.

"Not this morning. I'm meeting Lucy for lunch." He flashed a rueful smile. "I see my nephew has already started. How much is that going to cost me?"

"Not a dime, unless he works on one of your matters, then you'll be billed at a healthy rate." I got a kick out of surprising him. "He's got great experience and has already contributed. Looks like I may owe you."

Red couldn't hide his skepticism. "Did he tell you the army as much as discharged him, said he didn't fit in despite winning the Silver Star?"

"He did. I also met an Iraqi vet last night who considers him a hero. The army's loss is my gain. He'll do a good job for us both." Red still looked uncomfortable.

"Well, thanks for taking him. His mother will be pleased."

"No problem," I responded. "So, what's up?"

Red was happy to get to the business at hand.

"Jack, Lucy was right. I'm already leaning on you for more than the Lobos' business. So far you've always steered me right."

"I appreciate that. And I don't mind telling you I've enjoyed our arrangement," I said, wondering where this was going.

"I was dead wrong about Billy Hopper. You believed in him, and you were right. You not only saved a fine young man, you saved me a boatload of money." There had to be a catch, I'd never known Red to admit he was wrong.

"My top advisors want me to cancel your retainer and drop our business relationship."

I doubted that advice had come from Lynn and Guy, the advisors who seldom left his side. But I could imagine his fiancée, Lucy Robinson, might have had some say in the matter.

"I take it they object to my potential representation of Rachel Goodman; they feel your association with me might be detrimental to your business. Your advisors don't want you to lose government contracts on my account."

"Well, something like that. How can we minimize the damage?"

"Here's an idea I bet one of your advisors will love. I haven't taken the case yet, but if I do, get Lucy to condemn me on the Senate floor. She can say I'm nothing more than a publicity hound and talk about how much pain I caused her family when I represented her husband's killer."

"You serious?" Red looked confused.

"Lucy and I have a unique relationship. No one will doubt her, and up to a point, I feel I owe her."

"Well, I don't know," he began. "That may satisfy that press, but I need you for the Moss merger."

"That's six months away. The FTC isn't about to let you complete that merger until they know how the Bass deal affects competition. By then, the outcome of Rachel's case will be known."

"Okay, but what about the Lobos? The team knows you, knows what you did for Billy, but the sports press can be vicious."

"Dodge the sports press, but tell Gina to speak to one reporter she likes off the record. Have her tell him that you're trying to cancel our retainer, but the contract has a hefty penalty clause, which it does."

Red smiled. I had solved his problem, but I wanted him to know one more thing.

"Red, if our association becomes a problem, I'll tear up the retainer and hand over the work to any lawyer you choose. I don't want to be a problem for either you or Lucy."

Red smiled. "I knew you'd say that. You'd walk away from hundreds of thousands of dollars for Rachel, wouldn't you?"

"Yep—not for Rachel, but out of friendship with her father and loyalty to you. That's how I hang."

Red understood loyalty. He was quiet for a moment.

"Your sense of loyalty will be your downfall one of these days, but not with me. I'll take your advice. Lucy will be thrilled with your suggestion, though you misunderstand her. She's the one who told me to ask you how to get around the problem."

"You think the fallout will be that bad?" I asked.

"I'm afraid so. People say everyone has a right to counsel, but they don't really mean it when it comes to traitors. You know how this town works. Don't be surprised if your oldest and closest friends forget who you are. Have you told Carol yet?"

"No. She wasn't pleased to learn I was talking to Rachel's father, and she doesn't know I intend to represent Rachel if she will have me."

"When do you see her next?" he asked.

"Tonight. We're having dinner at her place, but we never talk about each other's business. It's a ground rule she set when we first started."

"Should be an interesting evening," he observed dryly.

As we walked to the elevator, he left me with a piece of advice.

"Jack, if you represent Rachel, more power to you. But a word of caution?"

"Your advice is always welcome."

"This time you'll be on your own. The government will make your life miserable, and you can expect every politician, business, and the media to line up against you. Even Walter Matthews will come under intense pressure to distance himself. I hope you're prepared for a rough ride."

I smiled. "I appreciate the warning, but surely it won't be that bad."

He turned to enter the elevator with a frown. "Don't be naïve. And remember, you've been warned."

35

DESPITE THE WARNINGS I'd received about Joan Laing, I still didn't know what to expect when Brian and I arrived at the U.S. Attorney's office. A middle-aged woman wearing a cream pantsuit greeted Brian and me with a cool smile. She wore her light blond hair pulled back at the neck. Her fair complexion and lack of makeup conveyed a school girls' image. With a start, I realized her pale blue eyes were assessing me, as I was her. Looking amused, she introduced herself and led us into a small, windowless conference room. I gave her my card and introduced Brian.

She waved for us to sit and said, "I apologize for the accommodations. I scheduled a nicer room, but got bumped by the U.S. Attorney."

She wasted no time with small talk.

"I hope you received the documents I sent. Were they satisfactory?" she asked.

Brian had gone over them with a fine-tooth comb, noting several trouble spots, but nothing I couldn't live with. I wanted nothing to impede my meeting with Rachel.

I reached into my briefcase and handed her the documents, signed and notarized.

She placed them on the table and said, "Thank you. Now we can talk about tomorrow.

"Meet me outside the courthouse in Alexandria at eight o'clock. Two marshals will drive us to Ms. Goodman's location. You may talk to her for an hour in my presence. That should be plenty of time for you to agree about representation. We should be able to return to the courthouse by two o'clock."

A quick calculation showed a location about two hours from Alexandria. Or she could be just around the corner—I knew my Sherlock Holmes well. I pushed just a little.

"Mr. Hattoy has explained the rules: no papers, no computers, no cell phone. He mentioned a thorough personal search. Is that necessary?" I asked, letting annoyance creep into my voice.

"Master Sergeant Hattoy is correct on all points." Her voice contained no hint of apology.

"You may have missed that I will ride with you to her location. I will sit in on your first interview, along with an FBI agent. If it makes you feel any better, I will be searched as well. Nor will I be allowed to carry a cell phone. The rules are specific."

"Well, I appreciate the company; I'm sure we'll find lots to talk about. But is all this necessary? I have an upper-level security clearance, and I've signed all your forms—seems more theater than necessity. And what is the reason for your presence at this interview? We can't be candid with you and the FBI in the room."

She gave Brian a quick glance before responding.

"Mr. Patterson, I know of your reputation and appreciate your belief in your potential client, but to the rest of the government she presents an enormous security risk. She is a traitor, a spy who handled sensitive military information that would be very dangerous in the hands of our enemies. Only a very few people know where Rachel is being held, and I am not one of them.

"I understand the importance of confidentiality between an attorney and his client, but the Department of Justice is not the only government agency involved. I hope you will cooperate with these initial security requirements so your client can have access to counsel, and I can have someone with whom I can discuss her future in a rational way."

"What do you mean 'her future?'" I asked.

"Our office will seek the death penalty in this case. I'm sure you are aware that the procedures necessary to get the Attorney General's permission to seek the death penalty have been changed. Once that permission has been obtained, it's very difficult for a U.S. Attorney to back away even if he or she wants."

I interrupted, "You're saying that if I want to discuss a plea, I need to get on board damn quick. Once you start the process, Rachel won't have a chance in hell." I'd already lost my cool—maybe Phil was right.

She kept hers. "Let's not get ahead of ourselves, but I'm glad you understand."

She'd given me fair warning: the window of opportunity to craft an agreement that would save Rachel's life wouldn't be open for long.

"You may as well get the ball rolling on my associates' clearances. Micki Lawrence from Little Rock will be my co-counsel, and Mr. Hattoy has joined my firm as a paralegal and will work on this case."

For the first time she looked uncomfortable. "Ms. Lawrence's clearance will not be a problem. Uh… Mr. Hattoy might be another matter."

She blushed when she looked at Brian, and I felt the blood rush to my neck.

"Ms. Laing. Let me explain something. I believe in getting along with opposing counsel, but if your problem with Mr. Hattoy has a thing to do with his sexual orientation, you and I have a big problem, one you don't want. I expect Mr. Hattoy's security clearance to be approved post haste—no ifs, buts, or ands about it. I hope I've made myself clear."

"Mr. Patterson, you know security clearances are not issued by me or my office. I'm not involved in such decisions." Her face had resumed its normal color.

"Then I suggest you get involved, because this is not a matter that's open to negotiation. I'll see you tomorrow morning."

36

BRIAN AND I WALKED to the elevator and out of the building in silence. The tension lifted as we walked into the fresh air. I motioned to a bench on the sidewalk.

"I hope I didn't embarrass you, but I'm not about to let a prosecutor dictate who works for me or for my client. Unless you can give me a good reason otherwise, I'll stand my ground. Imagine a desk jockey deciding a war hero is a security risk because he's gay. I thought that way of thinking was long gone."

He smiled. "I appreciate your standing firm, thank you. Both my uncle and Maggie told me you'd be full of surprises. I didn't expect them to come so soon."

Mike dropped Brian off at the office and took me home to pack an overnight bag. He wasn't happy with the idea I planned to spend the night at Carol's, but I told him my plans weren't negotiable. The last time I planned to stay the night at Carol's it didn't work out so well; I was optimistic tonight would be different.

I told Mike to pick me up in the morning, that I needed to be in Alexandria a little before eight tomorrow, and that if my plans changed, I'd take a cab home and let him know.

My high spirits dropped when Mattie, Carol's cook and housekeeper, greeted me at the door telling me she was running late. I poured myself a drink and joined Mattie in the kitchen. She'd made one of my favorites, King Ranch Casserole—it was still in the oven. She told me it needed to bake a little longer and then rest a few minutes. There was a salad in the fridge and a key lime pie. Usually she stayed until after the dishes were done, but not tonight. She said Carol wanted tonight to be just the two of us. I grinned, sure I could handle the rest of dinner.

I wandered around the flat, examining photos and admiring art. Carol had explained that her home was her oasis from work—she never entertained clients here. Her place on the Eastern Shore was filled with pictures of Carol with politicians and other luminaries, but her home was adorned only with art and a few museum worthy photographs.

The minutes stretched on, and I grew a little uncomfortable, feeling almost like a voyeur. I turned off the oven and checked to be sure I hadn't missed a message. I was just about to resort to the television when I heard the clatter of heels in the hallway. Carol burst into the room, out of breath and looking a little disheveled.

"Sorry to be so late, couldn't help it." She tossed her heels into the corner and said, "I'll be right back. I need to freshen. Pour me a glass of wine, will you?"

I found a bottle of a French Chablis in the fridge and was trying to figure out the electric corkscrew when she appeared in jeans and a crisp white shirt that looked terrific with her dark full hair. This time she greeted me with a long kiss.

"Why don't we skip dinner?" I asked pulling her toward me.

"What? And miss Mattie's casserole?" she asked with a grin. "We have all night, Jack. You pour the wine, and I'll get the food on the table."

We were soon enjoying the spicy casserole. Looking across the table I wondered how I deserved someone as special as Carol and told her so.

Her brows furrowed, as though bothered by my compliment, but only for a moment.

"How was Arkansas?" she asked.

I concentrated on Clovis, whom she knew.

"Who would want to harm Clovis?" she asked.

"No one seems to know, but you can bet he's got people trying to find out." I didn't mention the possibility it might have something to do with me.

She told me about the weekend I'd missed, and I told her about the man found on the eighteenth green at Columbia. She hadn't heard about his murder, and shrugged it off when I couldn't give her any real details.

We finished, and I cleared the table as she sliced the pie. She handed me a plate, we both sat down, and she gave me a long look.

"Jack, we need to hash something out before we get comfortable."

"Okay," I said, dreading what was next. I didn't want to talk about her weekends or my desire to play golf.

"One of the many things I love about you is your loyalty to your friends. Sometimes you carry friendship and loyalty too far, but it's who you are, and I never want to change that." She reached across the table and took my hand.

"I know we agreed not to discuss each other's business, but if it's even crossed your mind to represent Rachel Goodman, please forget about it. It would be a career-ending mistake.

"You make your living representing clients who need the approval of the government for their mergers. If you represent a traitor, people will think you've become a radical anti-government lawyer, not the well-respected antitrust expert you are. How can you represent their business interests if the government thinks you're a kook?"

I gave her hand a reassuring squeeze. I understood her point of view, but I didn't agree.

"Besides, we'd never see each other. My weekends at the Shore include defense contractors, lobbyists, and members of both the administration and Congress. None of those people will want to be seen with you if you choose to represent Rachel Goodman. The same goes for all the events on the Hill during the week."

I couldn't argue with her points, so I kept quiet, knowing I'd need time to figure this one out. I didn't want to lose her.

"Now enough about business," she said. "I've said my piece. Put the dishes in the sink and open another bottle of wine. I'll turn on the ball game and meet you in the den in a few minutes."

I put two glasses and the bottle on the table beside the oversized sofa in her den. I sank into it and saw that the Redskins were playing the Giants. Carol came in as I was getting settled. I took a quick breath—she was wearing a Stafford State Cardinals baseball jersey bearing my old number and name.

"Where in the world did you find that?" I asked.

"I've been waiting for the perfect occasion. You like?" she asked as she vamped a sexy pose.

She curled in beside me, and it didn't take me long to realize the Jersey was all she was wearing. We sipped on the wine and pretended to watch the game, but it wasn't long before I pulled her closer and ran my hands under the jersey. She pulled a soft wool blanket from the back of the sofa over us and kissed me with a passion unusual for her. My jeans came off, and we came together with a sudden urgency, like first-time lovers. We parted when she rose, pulling me up with her.

"Take me to bed, Jack Patterson. I want you again. And this time, let's take our time."

FRIDAY

37

CAROL WOKE ME with a soft kiss on the neck. To my disappointment, she'd already showered and was dressed in butternut colored pants and a cream silk blouse. A quick glance at the clock reassured me it was only six-thirty.

"I've got a breakfast meeting, so roll over and go back to sleep. Mattie's already here and will cook breakfast whenever you're ready." She gave me a quick kiss and was out the door before I could even say good morning.

I found and pulled on my pajamas, stumbled into the kitchen, and poured myself a cup of coffee. Mattie wasn't surprised either by my presence or by my apparel. She smiled and asked when and how I'd like my eggs.

"I'll hop in the shower. Give me a few minutes, okay?" I asked.

"No problem, Mr. Patterson. You have time for your favorite?" she asked.

Mattie made a special egg dish for breakfast that included spicy sausage, onions, and peppers. It was too spicy for most of Carol's guests at the shore, but Mattie knew I loved it.

"I wish I could, but not this morning," I sighed, unsure how long I'd be locked up in the back of a van. "Just Grape-nuts or whatever cereal you've got handy."

By seven-thirty Mike and I were headed across the Potomac to meet Joan Laing at the Alexandria Federal Courthouse. Traffic patterns in the DC area fascinated me. Every weekday morning from about five-thirty until nine-thirty tens of thousands of cars poured into the nation's capital. The process reversed beginning at about three in the afternoon. For the commuters who lived in towns like Manassas or Burke, it could take a couple of hours to make the trip, another good reason to live in Chevy Chase.

I found Ms. Laing waiting for me on the courthouse steps. She wore a different beige pantsuit, and I wondered how many she owned. She greeted me and waved me into a room where a U.S. marshal patted me down, a little too hard for my taste. I soon faced her in the rear of a windowless van that contained nothing except benches attached to each wall.

She said nothing, so I tried a little humor. "I'm surprised we're not blindfolded and handcuffed to the seat." There were U-bolts in the floor intended for that purpose.

Without a smile she deadpanned, "It was discussed."

"Really?' I asked with a frown.

She allowed herself a smile. "Just kidding."

That broke the ice, and as we bounced along over what I thought must be rural roads, we talked about where she had attended school—McGill and Boston College Law—her husband's science fiction novels, and several mutual friends at main justice. I got up the nerve to ask her to call me Jack, and she agreed, returning the favor. The van slowed, backed up, and came to a stop.

The van had backed into a closed and windowless garage, and we were escorted from the garage into an attached cinder block building. I had no idea how long we'd been driving or where we were. Joan and I were separated, and a marshal escorted me to a small room and told me to remove my clothes. As I stood there shivering, he passed a wand over the clothes I'd piled on the table, and then passed the wand over my body. I'll spare you the indignity of the rest of the search, except to say he was very thorough.

After I dressed, he led me to another room, this one fitted with a steel table and two chairs in its center. Joan and another woman sat next to a smaller table against a wall. Cameras were situated in each corner. So much for private conversation.

The other woman, Agent Hudson, handed me her card in silence, and I apologized for not having a card on me. She failed to notice the irony. A marshal led Rachel into the room. She wore a blue jumpsuit and was hampered by leg shackles connected by a chain to handcuffs. At my request the leg shackles were removed, but the handcuffs remained.

I hadn't seen her since her college days, but I recognized her immediately. She was slender, of average height with very dark skin, with her hair in a short afro. She was the spitting image of Ben.

Joan introduced everyone and reminded Rachel of her rights. Rachel responded that she understood her rights. It was my turn.

"Rochelle, it's been a long time. I don't know if you remember, but we met when you were in DC to see Angie and Beth. I understand you asked to speak about hiring me to be your lawyer, but before we discuss that matter I caution you not to say anything about the case. This discussion is not protected by the attorney-client privilege. Agent Hudson is taking notes, and I suspect those TV cameras in the corners are recording this conversation."

My eyes went to the camera across from me, and Rachel glanced at the one in front of her before she spoke.

"Okay, thanks. But I need to ask a favor right off the bat. I changed my name to Rachel when Ira and I married, and I prefer you to use it, if you don't mind."

"Of course—you must remind me if I slip up." I was glad to see she wasn't daunted by the circumstances.

"I remember meeting you, and you're right, it was many years ago," she continued. "But my father always said if I were ever to need a lawyer, I should call you—he thinks the world of you. I followed the Hopper case, and I loved your wife and daughter, so I feel like I know you more than a little. Ms. Laing continues to tell me I need a lawyer, so I asked her to contact you. I hope you don't mind."

"No, I'm glad you did. In fact, I was in Little Rock talking to your parents about helping you when I learned you'd asked to see me."

"You've seen Mom and Dad?" She interrupted. "How are they? I wish…" I raised my hand, and she halted.

"They're concerned, and I won't kid you—it's been tough. But they're strong and are holding up well. Your message was welcome."

"My main concern is the effect it will have on them and my

brothers." I stopped her again before she could continue.

"Rachel, we can talk about your family later. We'll have plenty of time to talk about what happened, your concerns, and the charges against you after I've been hired and we can meet in private. But Ms. Laing insists we talk about representation first."

"What do I need to do? I have money put aside, but I don't know if it's enough for a lawyer of your reputation," she said.

"We'll work something out, don't worry. Your dad has offered to help, but I'd rather not discuss money today. I'll bring an engagement letter when we're able to meet in private. Money isn't going to a problem, I promise."

I noticed out of the corner of my eye that Agent Hudson had stopped writing and was looking at Joan. I suspect they were wondering if someone else had agreed to pay my fee. I'd deal with that issue later.

"Then what do I need to do?" Rachel asked.

"Listen for a few minutes while I tell you why I may not be the best lawyer for you. I'm an antitrust lawyer—I've never represented anyone charged with espionage."

Now Rachel interrupted. "Don't waste your breath. Dad said you are the best—you represented Billy Hopper, and I know all about what you did for Woody Cole. I don't need an espionage expert, that's not what's going on here at all. When we talk in private I will explain."

I reached across the table and stopped her from saying anymore. I was dying to know what she meant by "that's not what's going on," but now was not the time.

"Okay, then look over to Ms. Laing and tell her you want me to represent you. We'll do the paperwork, talk about your family, and talk about other issues when we meet in private," I responded.

Rachel did as I instructed, and I asked, "Now that this charade is over, may I meet with my client in private, please."

Joan didn't budge.

"I'll report her decision to the appropriate individuals, and we'll do our best to speed up your clearance. I see no reason why you shouldn't be able to have an attorney-client meeting by mid-week."

She rose from her seat and added, "I'll call the guard."

"No. You promised me an hour," I said firmly. She looked annoyed, but resumed her seat.

I turned to Rachel. "How have they been treating you? Are you getting enough to eat? Are you comfortable?"

For the next thirty minutes I tried to garner as much information as I could about her treatment, her health, and anything else that didn't involve the case. I received permission to enter her apartment, and she told me who had a spare key. I was confident the FBI had ransacked it, but at least I could see what was left.

I knew I was over my time limit, irritating agent Hudson, but I continued to chat until Joan broke in.

"Mr. Patterson, you've used up your time and then some. I'm calling the guard to take Ms. Goodman back to her cell. Say your goodbyes."

Rachel said, "Please give my parents my love and tell them everything will be all right. It's not what it seems."

The guard came in and reattached the shackles and chain, so I said, "Try not to worry too much, Rachel, everything will be okay. You and I will get to the bottom of this. This nightmare will be over soon."

"Thank you, Mr. Patterson—with your help I know it will, too. Tell Mom and Dad I'll see them soon." She smiled Ben's smile, a smile of confidence.

"I will," I said, trying to return that same confident smile. I couldn't help but think, "Thank God she hasn't seen the newspapers."

38

THE SECOND STRIP-SEARCH came as a surprise. My holding Rachel's hands raised concerns that we might have exchanged something, which was ridiculous. Say what they want, it was about power and humiliation.

I dressed and returned to the van, but Joan wasn't there. Maybe they had searched her again. I waited on the hard bench for what seemed a long time before she appeared and returned to her spot across from me.

"I don't know how you did that. I'm impressed," she said with what seemed to be an honest admiration.

"Did what? I couldn't say a thing."

"You gave your client the impression you think she's innocent and you will get her off. You exude confidence and it's contagious. So, I'm serious, I'm impressed." She smiled pleasantly.

"She is innocent. You're familiar with the phrase, innocent until proven guilty? I believe in it. Right now, this case is a blank slate, and I've not seen a shred of evidence establishing her guilt. So it wasn't an act; she's innocent in my book. That fact that you've detained her and are about to charge her doesn't mean a thing. I've seen too many men and women prosecuted for crimes they didn't commit." Joan's smile faded.

"You don't know me, but I assure you I don't prosecute someone, much less ask for the death penalty, unless the evidence is overwhelming. Don't worry—before long you'll have plenty of evidence. I'll be interested to see if you still exhibit that same confidence when you've seen the proof."

She exuded confidence herself, and although I wanted to change the subject, I didn't want to leave it on that note. "I'll keep an open mind, as I hope you will." I reached across the van to shake her hand, and she extended hers. I didn't trust her one bit.

She changed the subject, but not with good news.

"She told you she had money put away. I'm sorry, but my office has seized all her bank and brokerage accounts. I'm sure you're not surprised," she said.

"Surprised no, disappointed yes," I answered with a tone that didn't disguise my displeasure. "I suspect you have a warrant to check Rachel's parent's accounts to make sure no one tries to funnel money for a lawyer through them."

"We do. You will receive a copy of the warrant soon. I can also tell you that so far there's no evidence that any money was funneled to Rachel by way of her parents' accounts."

"Thanks for the information—now I'll give you some. No matter how little money is available, I will represent her—not only in the criminal case, but also in the asset forfeiture matters. I'm in for the long haul, money or no."

"Well, that is your prerogative," she said. "You may have noticed that I was late in returning to the van. I'm sorry to tell you we've had a leak. The press has gotten word you were visiting Rachel and has assumed you represent her. I don't know the source of the leak—I can promise you that my office has been airtight."

I had no reason not to believe her. "How is your office handling the press right now?"

"You might have noticed that our U.S. Attorney, Donald J. Cotton, is a bit of a press hound. When he was asked about the rumor at his usual Friday press conference, he said he could neither confirm nor deny the story. The press interpreted that answer as a confirmation. I'm sorry.

"Another thing. I don't like having to bring this up, but I've been asked to remind you of the confidentiality agreement you signed yesterday." Her pale face took on a ruddy hue.

I smiled, as much at her embarrassment as at how silly all this was:

gag orders, leaks, and confidentiality. Everyone in DC made a big deal about confidentiality and secrecy, but the whole town leaks like a sieve. Law enforcement leaked whatever they wanted and always got away with it. I felt bad for Maggie, who was having to field press calls with no guidance.

"Joan, I honor my agreements, so please tell whoever is concerned that I intend to follow not only the letter of my agreement but the spirit as well. I can't speak for anyone else. For example, if the press corners Ben Jennings before I can give him guidance, I don't know what he might say. But no one on my legal team will say a word other than what was agreed. The agreement allows me to confirm I've been hired, so I'll issue a press release to that effect, just to keep the wolves at bay. I'll email you a copy. I'll also speak with Ben as soon as I can."

"Again, I'm sorry."

I smiled. "That's okay. I'll forgive you, if you complete the clearances so I can see Rachel in private sooner rather than later."

"I'll work on it. The only problem I'll have is with Brian," she said.

"If there's a problem, I will make it a bigger problem. I'm adamant. Brian has joined my office staff, and he will work on this case."

I might have said more, but the van came to a stop and the rear door opened. It felt like the return trip didn't take as long as the trip out, but isn't that always the case?

Joan and I agreed to stay in touch, and we went our separate ways. So far, so good, but Phil's warnings lingered in my ears. I wouldn't let down my guard. As I watched her walk away, I wondered what it would take to get past her guard.

39

I CROSSED THE STREET to the waiting Big Mike who mouthed "Maggie," and handed me my phone.

"I'm so sorry..." I began.

"Jack, the calls have been non-stop for at least an hour—they even have my cell number. Why didn't you warn me?"

"I had no idea. I was locked in a van without a phone when Joan told me about the leak. How bad is it?"

"Well, it's calmed down a bit since Brian and I decided to ignore the phones and lock the office doors. Martin's men are outside, shooing people away."

"Listen, send out an email that I'm about to dictate to our media list, then close the office, and have one of Martin's people drive you to... oh, how about the Boathouse on MacArthur. It's out of the way, and your driver should be able to get out of the garage without being followed. Bring Brian with you. We need to talk strategy."

I dictated a short statement for the email:

> As part of my representation of Rachel Goodman, a confidentiality agreement was reached yesterday between the U.S. Attorney's Office for the Northern District of Virginia and our office. All media inquiries and requests for interviews should be directed to Donald J. Cotton, U.S. Attorney for the Northern District.

Cotton liked publicity—I'd just given him plenty.

I got in the back seat and told Mike I needed to make a couple of calls on the way to the Boathouse.

The first call was to Ben.

"Ben, I saw Rachel this morning, and I'm on board as her lawyer. We couldn't talk privately, but she looks good, misses you both, and is in good spirits."

"Tell me what happened."

There would be time later to explain the parameters of the attorney-client privilege. I gave him an abbreviated version of the morning's events, omitting the strip search and shackles.

"I don't know how to thank you, Jack," he said with obvious relief.

"Barbeque," I kidded. "Tell me how the reopening is coming."

"We're still getting rid of the gasoline fumes. Don't worry—I'll keep my end of the bargain. We haven't talked about money, but I've got money put aside, and I have an idea that should bring in a bunch more."

I cut him off. "Let me talk about money with Rachel first. She said she had money saved, but the government has seized her bank accounts. Let's not worry about money now—we've got work to do first."

"What do you mean, the government seized her bank accounts? They can't do that, can they?"

"They can, but not forever. Listen, Ben. The press found out I've been to see her. You'll get calls. They can be aggressive. It's okay to confirm I represent her. But please say nothing else, just hang up the phone. Same for Linda."

"What can I tell her brothers?" he asked.

"Tell them she's doing well and I am representing her, but nothing else. I know it will be hard, and at some point, either Micki or I will talk with them to set boundaries."

Neither of us was quite sure what I meant by boundaries, but Ben promised to do as told. I was struck by our changing dynamic. I used to go to Ben for advice; now the tables had turned.

Next I called Micki to give her a quick report.

"Don't get sucked in by some blue-eyed prosecutor, Jack," she cautioned. "Remember, she's seeking the death penalty."

I was momentarily offended, but she had a point.

"Do you need me up there?" she asked.

"Not yet. She hasn't been charged, I've seen none of the evidence against her, and I haven't had a chance to talk to her in private.

They'll slow walk our clearances. That's not all bad. I suspect that when we do get cleared, the case will move quickly. I'm off to meet with Maggie and talk about the press. Maggie says they don't know about your involvement. How do you want to handle it?" I asked.

"I'd prefer not to have the local press follow me around while I interview people and gather information. If it's possible, keep me out of it for now. But at some point, the prosecutor will leak that you and I are working together. The news will break first in DC, so give me a heads-up."

"I'll do my best. How's Clovis?" I asked.

"Driving Stella and everyone else crazy. The rocking chair helped for a while, but now he can't sit still. I can't wait for you to see the chair Larry's building. It's a work of art."

"I look forward to it. I'll fly down next week for a day. You and I need some time together to figure out a communications strategy that doesn't run afoul of the gag order. I'm sure Ben and Linda will want to be part of the discussion. I'm worried that whatever I tell them will go straight to the FBI through the boys or Tina."

"Well, life is always livelier when you're here," she said with a laugh, and rang off.

Maggie and Brian hadn't made it to the Boathouse yet, so I scanned the menu and quickly found exactly what I wanted: for my money, the best French Dip sandwich in DC.

Maggie and Brian arrived, and I apologized again.

Maggie pretended to be in a huff. "The office is locked, my cell phone is on mute, and yes, I will have a glass of wine."

Brian asked for a beer and a burger while Maggie ordered the fish and chips. It had been a tough morning, and we were all hungry. I was relating the day's events when Maggie interrupted.

"I've got an idea. Why don't we all meet tomorrow at the site of the new offices and retreat center? I'll pack a lunch, and we can tour the grounds. The weather should be perfect! We can spend the afternoon planning, and Walter can grill steaks for dinner."

Brian said he was free, so we agreed to meet the next morning.

"Good idea, Mags. I'm a little done in right now—that van ride took something out of me."

Maggie teased, "You sure it wasn't last night at Carol's?"

I feigned shock and surprise. "Maggie, that's unworthy of you. I'll have you know we had a nice dinner and watched the ball game." I hoped she wouldn't ask who won.

"Oh, I forgot. A courier left a package for you at the office." She reached into her carryall and brought out a package marked "personal."

She put out a restraining hand as I started to open it. "You sure you want to open it right now?"

I frowned and reached inside to find the Stafford State jersey Carol had worn last night. A note fell to the floor, and I picked it up.

I thought we had an understanding! Bastard!

I tried to hide my surprise and confusion, but Maggie reached for the note. She gave it a glance and stuffed it back into the package.

Brian looked uncomfortable. "Maybe I should get a cab back to town."

"No need. I've been dating a consultant by the name of Carol Madison for, well, for a while. Last night over dinner she suggested that I was a damn fool to consider representing Rachel. She was adamant it would ruin my career and could damage hers. I didn't tell her I was meeting with Rachel this morning."

Maggie frowned. "You didn't tell her?"

"I know it sounds bad, but she and I have an agreement that we don't talk about each other's business. And I didn't agree to anything last night—I simply chose not to discuss the issue. Besides, we had a game to watch," I said. Maggie gave me a dirty look, and Brian intervened.

"You know, she wouldn't remember, but I met Ms. Madison at one of Red's parties. She sure can work a room. Sounds like you might have fences to mend."

"No shit," I responded without thinking. "Sorry, Maggie."

"Unnecessary," she laughed. "Shall I put your apology on the agenda for tomorrow?"

"No, thanks. I think I can handle it by myself."

"And how are you going to do that?" Maggie continued, enjoying my misery.

"I don't know, but I'm sure some serious groveling will be in order."

40

WE FINISHED OUR LATE LUNCH, and Maggie agreed to coordinate tomorrow's logistics with Martin. Big Mike waited for instructions, and I hesitated—I wasn't ready to go home to an empty house. I glanced at my watch, and was surprised to find it was almost cocktail hour. What did any red-blooded golfer do on a Friday afternoon when he was alone? He headed to the golf course, or at least to the nineteenth hole, otherwise known as the club grill. It used to be called the men's grill, but time and the need for revenue have removed both the exclusivity and the gender-tagged name.

We were on our way to Columbia when my phone rang. The number was familiar.

"Hello, Red."

"Well, you did it, and Lucy's headed to the Senate floor to damn you and the horse you rode in on. But she wanted me to tell you she still loves you—it's strictly business."

I felt sure that Lucy didn't give a rat's ass about me, but if she kept Red on an even keel, and I was able to keep the Lobos as a client, I was fine with whatever she said.

Red continued, "My office will send you a copy of the press release the company just issued. Hurry and get that girl off. I need you."

"I'll do my best," I replied with a smile.

"You headed to Carol's tonight?" he asked. Red was a frequent invitee to Carol's place in Maryland for the weekend, but since his engagement to Lucy, he seldom went. Lucy kept him on a tight leash.

"No, I've got work this weekend."

"You didn't tell her, did you?" he asked. I assumed he was asking about representing Rachel.

"I didn't mention it." This was getting old.

He whistled. "Boy, I bet she's pissed. Carol doesn't like surprises."

"I've got some major sucking up to do, that's for sure. If you're going, you can run interference."

"Lucy has me going to some damn fundraiser. As to running interference, you're on your own, my friend. My advice is stay out of the line of fire for a week and send lots of flowers."

"Good advice, and for once I'll follow it," I joked.

"Yeah, right." He paused and his voice lowered. "Jack, let me ask you something. Any chance your client isn't guilty?"

"All my clients are innocent, as you ought to know. Why do you ask?"

"I was in a meeting with a group of defense contractors and military procurement officers this morning when word hit that you had agreed to represent Rachel. Most of them seemed surprised, but I got the impression a few weren't. Nothing I could put my finger on, a few exchanged glances, a couple of knowing smiles and huddled conversations, that's all. I'll keep my eyes and ears open."

He hung up before I could question him further. I was mulling over how I might make use of his information when we pulled into Columbia's parking lot.

"Mike, I'd like you to come in. I know you can't drink on duty, but I'd appreciate it if you would sit and let me bounce a few ideas off you, help me get organized for tomorrow."

Mike shrugged his acceptance and parked the car. We found a table, and I took a few moments to enjoy the familiar scene: golfers checking their scorecards to see who owed whom, older guys playing backgammon, and a few fellows watching football highlights at the bar. The room felt comfortable in the same way as did a corner bar in a blue-collar neighborhood after work—different games and drinks, but the same camaraderie.

I broke the ice. "Well, Mike, any thoughts? You bored to death by now?"

"I'm not bored, that's for sure. We've been followed almost

everywhere. Martin wasn't surprised, but this is my first experience having a tail."

"Really?" I asked. "Even last night?"

"Oh yeah. Two guys followed us to the Watergate, parked at the edge of the circle. I waited until one of our guys drove up to relieve me. They spotted us and drove off, but this morning the same car was back on our tail. Funny thing, though… as soon as you and Ms. Laing got in the van, they drove off. I thought for sure they'd follow the van."

"Seems odd. Have they come back?"

"I'm not sure it's the same guys, but it's the same car. They're sitting out in the parking lot right now."

"Do we have an idea who they are?"

"The other unit took photographs and got their tags, but I haven't heard if Martin has identified them yet. They haven't tried to disguise their presence. It's like they want you to know you're being followed."

"Huh." I was about to dig deeper when I saw the club pro and motioned for him to join us. He sat down and called the barkeep for a gin and tonic. Buying the pro a drink was the price of his company, and it was well worth it.

"How you doing, Junior? Let me introduce you to Mike Fendler. I've been out of town since Saturday. Any idea yet what happened to Harold Spencer?"

Junior took a sip of his drink and spoke in a whisper as if he were sharing the secret to lowering your handicap by three strokes.

"I'm fine, thanks, and no, not a clue. The police interviewed everyone who played poker that night; nobody even remembers him getting up from the table. That's no big surprise—a lot of those gentlemen don't remember getting home, if you know what I mean. Couldn't have been one of them—some of them have a hard time lifting their cards, much less a rake."

"Any clues? Did he have any enemies?" I asked.

"Not that I've heard. He wasn't a big golfer. I gave him a few lessons, but he hit the golf ball like he had a tennis racket in his hands. I couldn't get him to quit rolling his wrists. His wife is pretty

shaken up. A delegation from the club paid her a visit, but it didn't
go too well."

"What do you mean?" I asked.

"You'd have to ask one of them. What I heard was that she
slammed the door in their faces." He downed the rest of his gin and
left the table to find another.

I explained to Mike what had happened a week ago—I couldn't
believe it had only been a week. Mike wouldn't join me in a beer,
but ordered a burger and fries at my insistence. I ordered a second
beer and munched on popcorn. I was still full from lunch at the
Boathouse. I liked Mike and wanted to know more about my new
driver/bodyguard.

By the time Mike had finished his burger and I finished my beer,
I was spent. I told Mike it was time to go home. He drove in silence,
and I mulled over the events of the past week. Carol and I had our
first real tiff, Harold Spencer was murdered, and Clovis had been
attacked. I'd met with Ben's daughter and agreed to represent her
against charges of espionage. Espionage! Now Carol had dumped
me, maybe for good. Yes, quite a week.

"No telling what next week might bring," I thought as we pulled
into the driveway of my dark house. Remembering my promise
to Clovis to be careful and the fact two guys had been tailing us, I
looked around, but I didn't see anything unusual. Mike was also
cautious. He said he was going to walk around the house, and would
stay with the car until his relief showed. We both got out, and I
walked up the sidewalk to the front door. I had just pulled my keys
out when I noticed the door was slightly ajar. I backed off a bit and
motioned to Mike.

He walked quickly up the walk, drawing his gun from under his
jacket. He motioned me to stand aside and kicked the door open,
arm raised. The umbrella stand fell over with a crash, and I nearly
jumped out of my skin. But the old house remained silent. Mike
motioned me to turn on the hall lights, and he slowly advanced into
the house, turning on lights room by room. It was totally empty,
and we both sighed with relief. My bedroom had been rifled, and
my office was a mess, drawers emptied, files scattered everywhere,

but that seemed to be the extent of the damage. According to Mike, someone had tampered with the security system and the back door was jimmied open. Great, now what?

"Jack, Martin would have my hide if I let you stay here tonight even if we post guards inside and out. The house will have to be swept before you can stay here. Why don't you spend the night at Barker's? Martin told me you've stayed there before. I'll make the arrangements while you get a bag together. Tomorrow we'll have the security system stabilized, and we will upgrade our surveillance."

Barker's is an oddly exclusive Washington institution, a very secure private club whose members are carefully screened by Barker himself. It's modeled after the gentlemen's clubs in London—very private and very secure. I'd spent a good deal of time there when I was working on the Hopper case.

I knew he was right, so I packed a bag and before long found myself nursing a third Scotch at the bar in Barker's basement. I felt totally unsettled—surely this hadn't been a normal robbery attempt; nothing of value had been taken as far as I could tell. What had the intruder been looking for? Had he found it? Or were there more than one? Exhausted, I ordered another Scotch and took it upstairs.

SATURDAY

41

I HAD TO DRAG MYSELF out of bed the next morning. An empty glass that had contained good Scotch betrayed the source of my misery. Now I was in the car with Mike and Brian, trying not to reveal the extent of my hangover. I needed a real Coke. And maybe a greasy cheeseburger.

Mike answered his cell phone, listened for a second, and handed it to me without a word.

Clovis was on a tear. "Jack, didn't I tell you to be careful? What were you thinking, walking into an empty house by yourself? You could have been killed. Of all the boneheaded…"

"Wait a minute. I didn't walk into an empty house. I called Mike and he did. What would you have had us do?" I was in no mood for a lecture.

"All right, all right. Mike says they didn't take anything. What were they after?"

"Darned if I know…."

"Well, someone is clearly trying to spook you. Martin will have your security system upgraded today. Don't take any chances, Jack. These guys might try to do more than scare you next time." With that, he hung up.

Now my head really hurt. I tried to shake it off—it was time to figure out how we might defend Rachel Goodman, alleged traitor and spy. The first thing might be to come up with a different descriptor for our client.

Mike's voice interrupted my thoughts. "You gonna answer that?"

I saw the caller unknown tag, but picked it up without thinking.

"Jack, this is Peggy. Are you somewhere where we can talk?"

"Why do I think this is not about brunch?" I repeated her oft-used response to my calls.

"No, it's not. Can you talk? If not, get where you can and call me back."

From the tone of her voice I knew something was wrong. I told Mike to pull over and in less than a minute I was outside the car standing on the road's shoulder.

"What's wrong, Peggy?"

"Are you sitting down?" she asked.

"No, I'm standing on the shoulder of a highway in Maryland. Tell me what's wrong."

Nothing for a few seconds, then a deep intake of breath.

"Rachel Goodman committed suicide last night."

I sank to my knees, hardly able to breathe.

"Jack, are you okay?" Her voice sounded far away, and I tried to get myself under control.

"No, I'm not okay. Are you sure? What happened?" I got to my feet, but my shaking hand could barely hold the phone. Mike had gotten out of the car, motioning Brian to stay put.

"Yes, I'm sure. Rachel Goodman committed suicide sometime last night. She was found in her cell at count time this morning, hanging from a bed sheet."

How could that be? She'd seemed so unconcerned yesterday, almost dismissive of the circumstances. My thoughts went quickly to Ben and Linda.

"Have her parents been notified?"

"The FBI is knocking on their door as we speak. I'm meeting with the AG and all affected agencies in about thirty minutes. Burt decided you should be notified, over several agencies' objections, I might add."

I bet they'd objected. The accustomed procedure is to get your story straight and cover your ass before the press begins to dig.

"Can I attend that meeting?" I asked.

"Sorry, Jack, but you know the answer to that one,"

"Well, will you let me see her body and the cell?" I asked.

"Rachel's body has been sent to the medical examiner for an autopsy, but I would think a family representative will be needed for the formal identification. I assume that will be you. As to seeing the cell, an internal investigation will take place before anyone on the outside is allowed in." She sounded apologetic.

"Any way I can be the one to break it to Ben and Linda?"

"I'm sorry, but the answer is no. Law enforcement is trained for the job. I know the family will have a thousand questions. The AG will appoint someone this morning to be your point person—the person you can contact with questions and information. He'll make sure you aren't shut out of the process, I promise."

"I have to take you at your word, Peggy. I already have a million questions. Any chance that point person can be you?" I asked.

"Sorry, no. Everyone knows we're friends. The AG would be okay with it, but there's no way the other agencies would agree."

Right. I should have known.

"Listen, Peggy. I met with Rachel yesterday. She was in good spirits, eager to talk. There is just no way she committed suicide. Ask Joan—she and some FBI agent were there with us."

"We already have, and her reaction was the same as yours. She's pretty shaken; so are the rest of us. Nobody saw this coming, but hindsight is twenty-twenty, as you well know. The whole world will wonder how this could have happened."

"You sound like they've already ruled out foul play. I'm telling you Rachel didn't kill herself, and you're trying to figure out how to defend her jailers. If you don't believe Joan or me, watch the damn tapes. She was murdered, I'm telling you."

"Calm down Jack. No one has come to any conclusions. There will be a full investigation, of that I can assure you. Let us do our job. You will have your hands full with the family and the press."

"Speaking of the press, do they know yet?" I asked dreading her response.

"Not yet, but it's only a matter of time. Too many people and agencies are involved. She was being held at a military base in central Virginia. How to deal with press inquiries is on this morning's agenda."

I took a deep breath, trying to calm down. No sense killing the messenger.

"Jack, I've told you everything I know. I promise you'll have a contact this afternoon, but I have to warn you—don't expect to learn much in the next few days. Please be patient." She knew how impatient I could get and how quickly.

"I know I owe you for making sure I was notified. Please give my thanks to the Attorney General. I'm sure the intelligence agencies want this all to go away. Now at least I have a little time to prepare. Anything else you can tell me?"

"I feel sure you will be interviewed as part of the investigation. As far as we know, you and Joan were the last people to speak with her. We must know what you talked about."

"Well, that shouldn't be too tough. The interview was taped and an agent Hudson took notes."

She didn't respond—something else was wrong.

"Peggy, what aren't you telling me?"

"Well, I guess you'll find out. Things got a little crazy when they found Rachel. The guards didn't know how to handle it or who to call. Too many people got involved. Both the tapes and the agent's notes are now missing. But they're bound to turn up."

I almost shouted in the phone. "Missing? You have got to be kidding me."

"Please don't jump to any conclusions and get all conspiratorial. The tapes will be found, and either the autopsy will confirm suicide or it won't. Patience, Jack. Remember it's a virtue."

Her snippy comment was the last straw. I threw the phone into the brush and allowed myself a few obscenities, not giving a damn who heard. I saw Mike rustling around in the grass to find my phone, and I apologized, struggling to regain my composure.

42

MIKE AND BRIAN WERE SHOCKED when I told them what had happened, but there wasn't much they could offer. As Mike sped us toward the office, I called Clovis.

"Are you sitting down?" I asked, repeating Peggy's question.

"I am. I've calmed down and am sitting in a comfortable rocking chair designed and built by Larry. You'll want one of your own."

"Clovis, Peggy Fortson just called—Rachel is dead." I paused to let the words sink in. "They claim she hanged herself with a bed sheet last night. I don't have any details, but the FBI is at Ben's house now. Can you send an extra detail over there? I'll call Micki as soon as I hang up with you; maybe she can get there before the press."

"Look, you've got your hands full. I'll call Micki. We'll take care of everything here. Anything more you can tell me?"

"I met with her yesterday; she was in good spirits. I can't believe she committed suicide. I don't believe it. The AG is convening a meeting of all the affected agencies, and Peggy assures me there will be a complete investigation. I wish I could believe her. Her body was taken to the Virginia's medical examiner's office for an autopsy, but when or if we'll get a report is anybody's guess.

"Ben and Linda will be devastated. Get their family doctor over to the house—Jasmine will know who he is. I wish I could take the next plane down, but someone has to identify the body and...."

"Jack, Ben and Linda have good friends who will support them, but they have no one in DC. Stay where you can do the most good. Micki and I will do what we can and keep you up to date."

In times of crisis we jump ahead—what about funeral arrangements, where are the insurance papers, who will take care of the cat,
that kind of thing. It's a natural reaction—humans like to believe
they're in control of events over which they have no real control.

Mike and Brian remained silent, absorbed by their own emotions.
My thoughts went to Rachel and her family. Family and friends never
recover from the suicide of a loved one. The question is always, "why?"
Guilt hovers just beneath conscious thought, haunting your life like a
recurring virus. You should have known, you should have been able
to do something, you should have done something. Again, it seems to
boil down to our need to control, if not ourselves, then others.

In that vein, I couldn't help but second-guess. Maybe it had been
suicide. Had I said something to bring her to such despair? I thought
I'd lifted her spirits, even Joan had commented on it, but...? On an
intellectual level, I realize and believe that depression is a disease
and that suicides occur more often than society likes to admit. But
at this moment I couldn't help but feel a bit responsible.

I tried to imagine the impending meeting with the Attorney
General. I could well imagine fingers pointing, each person trying
to cover his respective ass. I supposed that because it was a military
facility, the guards and jailers were military police. The FBI and
at least two intelligence agencies were knee-deep in her arrest and
detention. One had to believe that the White House and the National
Security Council were already in damage-control mode.

I had no choice but to hope that a complete investigation was in
the works. But my instinct told me not to expect much of anything.
Both press and public interest would wane, and eventually a bland
report confirming her unfortunate suicide would be released. I was
convinced that her death couldn't have been suicide, but what could
have happened? Why should someone need to kill her? The government already intended to do that.

Brian's voice brought me back to reality. I heard "yes, ma'am"
and "got it" a few times, and realized he was talking, or rather listening, to Maggie. I had asked him to call her while I called Clovis.
"We'll meet you at the office in half an hour. Yes, ma'am, I will." He
looked a little uncertain, but forged ahead.

"Maggie says you should quit feeling responsible and get to work on a press statement. She said to remind you about the confidentiality agreement, and whether it has any restrictions covering what you can or can't say under these circumstances."

I smiled. I could always count on Maggie to keep a level head. I found a notepad and began to jot down a list of things I needed to do before leaving for Little Rock. I couldn't concentrate and soon gave up, allowing my thoughts to drift where they would.

In the space of a few minutes, I'd gone from starting to strategize Rachel's defense in one of the biggest espionage cases since the Rosenbergs to dealing with the press and handling clean up matters for her parents. No wonder I felt such a void. Whether or why she had downloaded military secrets had become a moot point. A complete investigation might decide if she had committed suicide, but a venue to litigate her guilt or innocence no longer existed.

I couldn't help but think about the time I had spent with her yesterday. Should I have been more confident, more reassuring? Her own words kept pushing through my muddled thoughts.

"It's not what it seems."

43

WORKING IN DOWNTOWN DC on the weekends is eerie. No noise, no bumper-to-bumper traffic, no sirens—the streets are empty except for tourists. There were no satellite trucks or waiting reporters in front of our office building, thank heavens.

Brian quickly went to work on the long list of items Maggie had given him. Mike made coffee and, at my request, went across the street to buy doughnuts, Tylenol, and a Coke. My headache had returned. I found the confidentiality agreement and read through it. It was hard to determine what was or was not covered given the circumstances.

I turned on the TV and muted the sound, expecting regular programming to be interrupted any second. I took up a pencil and my trusty yellow pad and began to draft a statement that said absolutely nothing. I was good at saying nothing. My cell phone rang—it was Maggie.

"I should be there in five minutes. We just drove by the Justice Building. There must be five satellite trucks outside, and it looks like they're setting up a bank of microphones on the steps. Do you want me to stop and listen or come on in?"

"Come on in. We can watch it together. It's bound to be carried live. I'll ask Brian to record it," I responded, handing Brian the remote.

"Have you heard anything from Clovis or Micki?" she asked.

"Not yet. I'm sure they've got their hands full. They'll call if they need me." Every part of me wanted to call Ben, but I knew he must have his hands full, too.

I went back to my statement, and it wasn't long before Maggie rushed through the door. Her presence and long hug were exactly what I needed.

She looked up to the TV and asked. "Anything on the telly yet?

"Not yet," I answered, and she left to put the kettle on for her tea.

The TV flashed breaking news and the next thing we saw were the steps of the Justice Building. What looked to be about twenty people were emerging from the large double doors. I didn't see Peggy or the Attorney General. The only person I recognized was Donald Cotton, the U.S. Attorney from Virginia, who walked up to the microphone and began to speak.

"I will read a short statement and then take a few questions. I appreciate your coming here this morning on such short notice. I am saddened to report that at four o'clock this morning, Mrs. Rachel Goodman was found dead in her cell at Mullins Army Base, the cause of death an apparent suicide. Ms. Goodman was housed at the base while being questioned about her involvement in the theft of highly sensitive government documents. A full investigation of the circumstances surrounding her death is already underway. My office in the Northern District of Virginia will take the lead in coordinating all aspects of the investigation. Any questions should be directed to our press office. Questions?"

There was a brief silence. I don't think anyone in the press was expecting this news. After a shocked silence, Cotton nodded to a raised hand.

"You said apparent suicide—can you give us any details?" the reporter asked.

"This is preliminary, but it appears that Mrs. Goodman hanged herself with a bed sheet."

The press took a collective gulp, and another reporter jumped in.

"Was she depressed? Was she being watched?" Good question.

"I would rather wait on the report to answer that question, but she was about to be charged with espionage, having been caught red-handed downloading military secrets."

"Bastard," I mumbled.

Next question. "Will there be an autopsy?"

"Yes, it is being performed by the Virginia Medical Examiner's office. We should have the results soon."

I muttered, "Rush to judgment, why don't you." I really didn't like this guy.

He continued, "I'd like to answer all your questions, but I really can't say much more. I assure you the investigation into the cause of her death will be thorough and complete, but sadly I'm afraid most of the answers as to why she killed herself will never be known.

"This entire matter has been a tragedy. For reasons unknown, this woman stole highly sensitive documents from her country, putting us all at risk. A plea agreement might have provided us some answers, but now we'll never know."

I hoped Ben and Linda weren't watching.

"One last question," was shouted, and Cotton nodded.

"You mentioned a plea agreement. Was that in the offing?" My ears perked up.

"My understanding is that Deputy U.S. Attorney Laing and Ms. Goodman's attorney, Jack Patterson, traveled to the Army base yesterday to meet with Ms. Goodman. I haven't had an opportunity to speak with Ms. Laing, but I'd be surprised if a plea deal wasn't discussed."

"You lying sack of shit!" I screamed at the TV. Expletives continued to fly until I noticed that Maggie was wincing. I quickly apologized. He hadn't actually lied, but he'd done his best to give the impression that Rachel was about to admit she was a traitor.

I quickly called Clovis.

"Please tell me Ben and Linda didn't watch the press conference," I begged.

"Sorry, but they did. You can imagine how upset they are." I suspected that the whole room watching thought that I'd sold Rachel down the river.

"Clovis, believe me. That bastard is lying through his teeth. May I speak to Ben?"

Clovis put Ben on the phone. I had calmed down only a little.

"Ben, please don't believe a word that man said. I don't know why he's lying, but he is."

Ben's voice was calm, almost devoid of emotion.

"I know he is, so does Linda. His words hurt, but we both know Rochelle didn't commit suicide and wasn't about to plead guilty to something she didn't do. Jack, right now I have to bury my child, and that's all I can think about. The government can't hurt me any worse than they've already done. I could care less what they say."

I felt better—and worse. "Ben, the press will be outside my office before long. I'll try to set the record straight."

"We trust you, Jack. We know you'll do what's right; her defense is completely in your hands as far as we're concerned. Do whatever you think you should do."

"I'll get there as soon as I can," I said and hung up.

I immediately thought about Ben's comment, "her defense is in your hands." Now was not the time, but before too long I would have to break it to him that there would be no defense. Rachel was dead, and the government would use leaks and innuendo to convince the world of her guilt. Suicide never made anything better; it just made matters worse for those who were left.

The phones started ringing before Maggie and I could think through a strategy. I told her to tell the press I would make a brief statement and answer a few questions outside our building within the hour. I needed at least fifteen minutes to revise my statement, and, frankly, to calm down.

I asked Mike to notify Martin. Brian and Maggie dealt with the phones while I revised my statement. There were several people I needed to call, but I had to concentrate on the task at hand: doing my best for Rachel in perhaps the last forum I would ever have.

44

I LOOKED OUT over the makeshift podium of microphones. Maggie, Brian, and Big Mike stood behind me, a visual Brian had suggested would bolster the appearance of my conviction. I looked out over a sea of reporters and took a deep breath.

"I've been informed that Rachel Goodman was found dead in her cell in the early hours of this morning, around four o'clock. The FBI has notified her parents. This terrible news comes as a complete surprise and shock to us all. On behalf or her family, I ask that you respect their privacy. Please direct any inquiries to my office until further notice."

I stepped back from the microphones to the puzzlement of the reporters.

"Is that it?" one reporter called out.

"What else can I say? The Justice Department has promised her family a complete and thorough investigation into the circumstances of her death. I take them at their word and hope the report will tell us what happened. I refuse to jump to conclusions, and ask that you do the same. False conclusions could prove very embarrassing."

"Are you suggesting she didn't commit suicide?"

"Personally, I don't believe she committed suicide, but I'm suggesting nothing because I don't have any facts. I hope to get more information over the next few days, but as of now the only thing I know is that Rachel is dead. That fact in itself is hard enough to accept, much less the notion that she committed suicide."

"Mr. Cotton says you met with Ms. Goodman yesterday to discuss a plea deal. Is that true?" I looked at a young reporter who was wearing horn-rimmed glasses.

"I did meet with her yesterday, but Mr. Cotton is completely wrong if he suggested that the purpose of our meeting was to discuss a plea deal. He was not present, but I was, and the possibility of a plea agreement was not mentioned. Deputy U.S. Attorney Laing and Agent Hudson from the FBI were present the entire time. I am confident they will confirm that the subject of a plea never came up. The meeting was also video recorded."

I wanted to call attention to the fact that our meeting was recorded. I didn't want Joan or Agent Hudson to fudge on the purpose of the meeting, and I was convinced that anyone who saw the tapes would have serious doubts about suicide. The murmurs from the press indicated I'd succeeded.

"What was the purpose of the meeting?" another reporter called out.

"Ms. Goodman asked if I would act as her attorney, and I agreed. Normally such a meeting would be confidential, but because of certain national security protocols, this initial meeting had to be witnessed—thus the presence of Ms. Laing and Agent Hudson. I might add that Ms. Goodman was in good spirits when I left."

I saw a few ears prick up, and a few note pads emerge. I nodded to a young woman who was probably about Beth's age. "Mr. Patterson, you're not suggesting that Ms. Goodman was innocent, are you? For weeks we've been told that she stole highly sensitive military information about top-secret weapon systems. We've heard that the government would seek the death penalty. Why wouldn't you try to make a plea deal? Do you have any evidence at all that she wasn't guilty?" The woman's tone was indignant.

I took another deep breath. "Whatever you may have been told, no charges were ever brought against Rachel Goodman. Under the law and our system of justice, she was and is innocent, just like every other citizen. I hope each of you remember that when you write your stories. A young, intelligent American citizen has died while in federal custody. Surely that is story enough."

I figured that would raise a few hackles. The horn-rimmed reporter raised his hand.

"Mr. Patterson, you're presenting a very different picture. Contrary to what Mr. Cotton said at his press conference, would you have us believe that Ms. Goodman was not depressed and that no plea deal was in the offing?"

I paused before I answered.

"I had just been hired and had been given no facts regarding the potential charges. I can assure you that when I left the room yesterday morning, Rachel was in good spirits, and neither of us had any intention of asking for a plea arrangement. To the contrary, I left the room planning to wage a vigorous defense that would confirm her innocence."

Someone said, "Too bad that opportunity is gone."

That should have put a final stamp on the press conference, but I couldn't resist.

"I wouldn't be so sure about that. I have every confidence in the Department of Justice, and I believe that a full and complete investigation will conclude that Rachel did not commit suicide. I also hope that the truth will come out and that Rachel will be completely exonerated."

The formerly indignant young woman asked, "Mr. Patterson, Ms. Goodman is dead; there can no longer be a criminal case against her. How do you think her exoneration might come about?"

She clearly thought I was nuts.

"I don't know, but you can bet I'm going to try."

I stepped off the podium, and the reporters began to drift away, some running to catch cabs, others talking among themselves. The reporter with the horn-rimmed glasses spoke my name quietly, and I turned toward him. He handed me his card and said, "After Rachel is buried and the suicide investigation is complete, we should talk." With that he walked away, leaving me with the impression that he had known her. His name was Ken Chandler.

As I walked back to my office I wondered how the press would react to my comments. I'd done my best to plant seeds of doubt about the government's accusations, but the young woman reporter was right. Where could I go from here? Clovis called before we reached the office.

"We watched the whole thing. Ben and Linda are pleased. I'm worried, though, that your comments about her possible innocence could be dangerous. If there's a remote chance she didn't commit suicide, whoever did kill her isn't going to want you snooping around."

He had a point. "You're probably right, but the U.S. Attorney really pissed me off. I said what I did for Ben and Linda. Truth is there isn't much I can do if the government decides to sweep the truth under the rug."

We talked a little bit about my coming down for the funeral, and he handed the phone to Micki.

"You know the Feds aren't going to let you near their investigation or any evidence that might exonerate Rachel, don't you?"

"Yeah, but that won't keep me from trying. Too bad, I was excited about working with you again." I meant it.

"Me, too. Hurry up and get here. I need one of your hugs."

"What about Larry?"

She laughed. "When Larry and I hug it leads to sex. Hugging you is more like hugging my brother."

Maggie suggested we close the office and reconvene at her house.

"Walter will make you one of his special martinis. I expect you could use one or two right now. I've sent Mike to your house to repack your bag from Barker's with extra clothes. The guesthouse is all ready for you. None of us need to be alone tonight. I invited Brian, but he declined, and I didn't push it. We'll wake up fresh tomorrow and decide what we need to do here, and when you and I need to go to Little Rock."

It was a relief to have Maggie take charge—I was running on empty. I expected a similar dynamic was going on in Little Rock. Ben and a few of his friends were sipping on bourbon on his back porch while Linda's kitchen was full of her friends, everyone carefully trying to avoid talking about what had just happened. I wouldn't be surprised if soon Clovis, Stella, Micki, and Larry were together at Micki's ranch grilling steaks and enjoying a few beers.

Maggie and Walter would try to keep my mind off the young woman who just yesterday had asked me to call her Rachel. That was going to be hard to do, but I knew one thing. From now on, I would honor her request and do my best to give her chosen name the dignity and reputation it deserved.

SUNDAY

45

THE EVENING WAS PLEASANT ENOUGH. The martinis were cold and dry, and Walter had a way with steaks. We avoided discussing Rachel, and spent the evening discussing Walter and Maggie's plans for the new corporate headquarters, foundation offices, and retreat center. I was tempted to let them build a house on the grounds for me. I could abandon DC entirely. I excused myself to the guesthouse right after dinner, poured myself a nightcap, and made the mistake of turning on the Nationals game. As the cameras focused on a fan who'd caught a foul ball behind first base, I caught sight of Carol. She was with Eric Hartman. I turned off the TV, and tried to go to sleep.

I tossed and turned for most of the night, desperate for sleep. Around five o'clock I decided to chuck it and got up. I'd made a decision. My life was falling apart, but I had no time or right to throw a pity party. The next few days would be difficult—identifying the body, attending the funeral, reviewing the suicide investigation, and probably having to tell Ben I'd done all I could do. I could continue to knock on doors, but I knew the words "national security" would be invoked to keep me from finding out anything useful.

I decided that after the funeral I would take a real vacation, the kind where you do a lot of nothing. I needed to get my head straight. Helen's words had made an impression: I needed to seek change rather than allow life to change me. I didn't really want Beth and Maggie to decide where I might live. And I needed to make a decision about Carol. Should I try to reconnect, repair our relationship? Did I even want to? It was time to fish or cut bait.

I searched VRBO and the website of a real estate company that specialized in properties on Pawleys Island, South Carolina. A house I'd rented before was available beginning Friday, and I booked it online immediately for three weeks. It would be too cold to swim in the ocean, but I hoped long walks on the beach and fresh seafood would give me a new lease on life.

I ran through the pictures on the website again and began to feel better. I went to the kitchen, made coffee, and decided to treat Walter and Maggie to my own version of the perfect breakfast. Maggie might prefer tea and toast, but I knew Walter would be happy with my efforts. I scoured their refrigerator and determined they had all I needed to make my southern version of eggs benedict using sausage and gravy rather than Canadian bacon and hollandaise. Besides, they didn't have any Canadian bacon and I never could make a decent hollandaise.

I couldn't find any English muffins, so I decided to further improvise with the Hungry Jack buttermilk biscuits I found in the cheese drawer. Maggie did have some late season fresh tomatoes, so I threw the sausage in a pan and went to work.

It wasn't long before Maggie joined me. I was surprised to see her pour a cup of coffee.

"I allow myself one cup in the morning, then I switch to tea," she explained. "My kitchen smells quite wonderful, but what got you up so early? I told Walter I thought you might sleep all morning. I hope the guest bed wasn't uncomfortable."

"The bed was perfect, but my brain wouldn't cooperate. Maggie, when we get through this week I'm going to take a few weeks off."

"Have you arranged a trip with Carol?" she asked.

"No, I'm afraid Carol may have gone the way of all my love interests—into someone else's arms."

Maggie's eyebrows rose slightly, but she said nothing. She seemed neither surprised nor disappointed.

"No, I need to spend some time with just me. I've rented a place on Pawleys. If you need me, I'll have my phone and Internet access, but I'm spent, and I'll be no good to anyone until I figure some things out."

"I'm glad," she said. "In fact, I was going to suggest something of the sort—the beach is a fine idea. Brian and I can handle anything that comes up, and like you said, there's always the phone and the Internet."

It wasn't long before Walter joined us, woken, he said, by the smell of sausage and baking biscuits. Maggie was many things, but she wasn't much of a breakfast cook. A slice of buttered toast was the extent of her breakfast repertoire.

Each biscuit, split in two, received a generous blanket of sausage gravy, accompanied by an egg over easy on one half of the biscuit, and a slice of grilled tomato and a sausage patty on the other half. We ate at the counter, eating more than we should, but who cared? The easy morning meal freed us from the sadness of yesterday, giving us a renewed feeling of well-being. Walter volunteered to deal with the dishes while Maggie and I went over our priorities for the next few days.

The weather was warm for October, and they asked me to join them on a horseback ride through their newly acquired estate. It was a tempting invitation, but I declined. I was ready to go home and relax, watch a little mindless football. The Chicago Bears were undefeated so far, but I doubted they could beat the Falcons.

I called an Uber before anyone objected and was soon on my way back across the river. When we pulled up to my house, I found the security guys talking with one of Martin's guys. I pushed past them, figuring somebody would explain the new system to me later. I had just dropped my bag in the front hall when my cell phone began to vibrate. I wanted to ignore it, but recognized the Department of Justice number.

"Peggy—I just finished breakfast, but I'll be happy to join you for a mimosa."

No response. The brunch gag had obviously played itself out. I sank into a chair in the den, waiting for a response.

"Mimosas with a good friend sounds really good right now. But I'm calling to inform you that the investigation into the death of Rachel Goodman is complete. A copy of the report is being emailed to you as we speak."

"The conclusion?" I asked.

"Suicide."

"Well, I can't say I'm surprised. Are you my contact person after all?"

"No. The investigation is complete. If you have questions you can go through normal channels. Your press conference wasn't well received, Jack. Several people are in favor of prosecuting you for violating the confidentiality agreement." Her voice faded.

"You think I violated the agreement? I took my lead from Cotton. She'd never been charged—how could he presume her guilt? It was pure bullshit, designed to make your guy look good for his next election, nothing more."

"Jack, be careful what you say. Read the report before you go flying off the handle. The report is definitive that the cause of death was suicide. For your information, cooler heads spoke up for you, including the AG. Cotton is a fool. But you need to be reasonable."

I did as she suggested. "Okay, let's talk about something else. How does Ben get her body back to Arkansas?"

"The family was informed this morning how to make arrangements. I believe that process has already begun," she said matter-of-factly.

"Peggy, I should have been called. What's going on? Has there been a deliberate decision to cut me out? She was my client."

"I'm sorry, Jack, but your press conference put nails in the coffin. There's no longer a criminal case, and you no longer have a client. Why shouldn't the agencies involved be able to go straight to the Jennings?"

"Don't you think I should have been consulted on that decision?" I asked.

"What I thought did not carry the day. Don't make this conversation any harder than it already is, Jack. The limb I'm out on is already pretty short."

Wow. I wondered who had the power to overrule both Peggy and the Attorney General.

I gave it a moment's thought and asked, "Peggy, tell me this. Did the investigation conclude that Rachel was depressed?"

"It did," she answered.

"Did they look at the tapes of our meeting?"

"Jack, the investigation has determined that her death was a suicide. And no, the tapes have not been found. If it's any consolation, the report says she should have been watched more carefully."

"Thanks, but, no, it isn't."

"Jack, I'm really sorry your client died, but it's over now, and you've got to let it go. The case is closed."

There was no sense beating up Peggy any further. I wondered exactly how far her limb extended. I knew that Attorney General Bertram Sharp was out of favor with the administration because he had investigated the President's Chief of Staff for bribery and campaign finance violations. The *Post* still carried op-eds questioning whether Sharp should continue to hold office. I'd never met the man personally, but I knew Peggy thought he was terrific—honest, forthright, and seemingly immune to White House pressure. Certainly, he was a surprise appointee in this administration.

"Thank you, Peggy. I really do appreciate the call. Better to hear the information from you than from a reporter."

46

WHATEVER ENERGY I'D GAINED from breakfast was gone. I managed to call Clovis, who verified that the U.S. Attorney's office had called Ben to inform him that Rachel's body had been released and was ready for transport to Little Rock. He suspected the funeral would be on Tuesday. I reminded myself to ask Maggie to handle our travel arrangements.

The security guys wanted to explain the new system, but I wasn't interested and told them I'd call if I had any problems. Truth was I was worn out, ready to "let it go" as Peggy suggested, except I couldn't. The "full and complete investigation" that came by way of email was bullshit, a total whitewash. Rachel had been found hanging by a bed sheet, no other marks on the body—that was it. Oh, and an admonition to the military that she should have been more closely watched. There was not one lick of evidence in the report indicating Rachel had been depressed. The author simply assumed she must have been suicidal since she was about to be charged.

I tried to concentrate on the Falcons, who were being demolished by the best defense the Bears had fielded in years. I should have been in Seattle with Red, whose Lobos were playing the Seahawks on Monday night. I'd turned in my tickets because I thought I'd be defending Rachel. I had just dozed off when my cell rang. It was Red.

"Jack, I'm sorry to hear about your client. I really am. Are you okay?"

"Thanks, Red—I'm...well, I'm okay. Think we have a chance tomorrow?"

"Yeah, we do—at least I hope so. Listen, just a heads up and something to think about."

"Okay," I said.

"You raised a lot of eyebrows at your press conference yesterday. You said your work for Rachel wasn't over—that you were going to try to prove her innocence."

"I did, but to be honest it was mostly bluff, an unsuccessful attempt to get the government to do a thorough investigation of her death. They've already ruled it a suicide—after less than a day. It was made clear this morning that the matter is closed, that I should drop it."

Red lowered his voice to almost a whisper. "I'm getting some pressure—the military types I do business with are very unhappy with you. You might want to issue a statement that the case is closed."

"And who might they be?" I asked.

"You know I can't tell you that. But the sooner I know this case is closed, that you're ready to move on, the better I'll feel. Shoot, Jack—just let it go. You can still hop a plane and join us for the game. Might be good for you to get away."

"Red, I don't know quite what I'm going to do about Rachel. Right now I'm just trying to deal with what's happened. But I am going to Little Rock for her funeral, and then I'm going to get away, for a few weeks."

"You and Carol going somewhere special?" he asked.

"No, just yours truly. I don't know where I stand with Carol—I think I may have some competition."

"Eric Hartman?" he asked.

"They looked pretty cozy at the Nats' game last night."

"Aw, geez. I hate to hear she's taken up with Hartman again. He's a jerk, has the moral code of a snake. Carol really does believe she can provide information without knowing or caring how it's used. Hartman will use her and spit her out. I don't know why, but whenever Carol gets close to someone, she runs for the hills. I'd hoped you would be different. It's too bad, but for her, business always comes first. I'll say something to her, but I doubt it will do any good. I've warned her about Hartman before."

This conversation wasn't helping either my ego or my mood.

"Please don't. I need to deal with this one myself. It will either work out or it won't. Thanks for calling, Red."

Maggie called to say we were scheduled to take off at ten o'clock the next morning. She asked if we should issue a press release before we left town. I thought of Red's advice, but decided against it. I might not be able to do much, but I wasn't quite ready to throw in the towel.

"Do I need to help you pack?" she asked. I smiled, knowing she meant well.

"Thanks, but no, I think I can manage. I'll take the Metro—see you tomorrow morning."

"No, you won't. Mike will pick you up at eight-thirty. Neither Clovis or Martin think we should let our guard down yet."

"Why? The case is closed." I was tired of having a bodyguard. I sure didn't want one following me around in Pawleys. "I don't know how you and Walter stand round-the-clock protection every day of the year."

"That's not what you told the press. Besides, the guard posted in your house monitored two men in a gray Camry watching your house last night. It's almost a question of who's zooming who. So do as you're told."

I caught the humor, wanted to argue, but was just too tired to care.

MONDAY

47

THE NEXT FEW DAYS WERE A BLUR. We landed in Little Rock mid-day and drove directly to Ben and Linda's. Beth was due in on Southwest that afternoon. As expected, the funeral had been scheduled for ten in the morning on Tuesday. Ben's house was filled with well-wishers and mourners, and his kitchen was full of food: peppered hams, casseroles, deviled eggs, grits, biscuits, salads, cakes, and pies—all the food you'd expect for a Southern funeral.

Despite Preacher Barnes' glowering presence, a full bar had been set up in Ben's den, and a keg and ice chests full of soft drinks were on the back porch. Children were everywhere, running and playing in their Sunday best. Ben's friends were clustered in small groups, talking about kids, sports, their various ailments, most anything but Rachel. Feeling a little lost, Maggie and I were content to settle into a corner of the living room until Jasmine caught sight of us. She rushed over and guided us through the crowded room to Ben's office where he and Linda sat on a small sofa.

We all hugged and he said, "Thank you for coming. I have so much to thank you for. But not now—there'll be time to talk later."

We slipped out a few minutes later, feeling a little guilty and more than a little relieved.

Jordan and I picked up Beth at the airport that afternoon, and after a brief stop at the Armitage, we joined the others for dinner at Micki's. Sam appeared sans Kristine. An ailing aunt had unexpectedly called Kristine to Florida. When asked, Sam admitted he didn't know she had an aunt. We spent the evening cozied up around the fireplace in Micki's great room, talking about old times, good times, bad times—anything but Rachel.

The next morning Helen Cole joined us for the funeral. An usher guided us to a designated pew, and for the next hour Preacher Barnes lectured us about the perils of too much education and big city life. I can't think his words provided much solace for her grieving parents—or hope for anyone else, for that matter.

We followed the crowd back to the house, but didn't stay long. Ben and Linda were always surrounded, and their sons were nowhere to be seen.

Jasmine tugged on Maggie's sleeve just as we were leaving. "Can y'all come back around six tonight? Ben wants some time alone with you. Hopefully things will have calmed down by then."

I glanced at Maggie and said, "Of course we can." We had planned to join Clovis and Stella for dinner before we left town, but surely we could spend a little time with Ben beforehand.

It seemed to me that the more sensational a death is, or the younger the departed, the longer folks wanted to stay—whether to be a part of the history or maybe witness a little drama, I can't say. Late that afternoon, Maggie and I slipped in through the back door.

Ben greeted us with an exhausted smile. "I'm sorry we haven't found time to talk. Maybe that's the point of these things—you put one foot in front of the other till you're plum worn out. But at least for a while you don't have to make decisions or think about much of anything."

I had no answer to that—and I was sure he didn't expect one.

"Linda and I owe you so much. We'll get to that later. Right now we have a favor to ask." Linda nodded in agreement. I noticed the knitting lying in her lap. It reminded me of a child's "lovey."

"Anything," I responded.

"Can we talk again in a few weeks' time? We will have put our daughter to rest and comforted everyone who needs comforting. I'll need to come to DC. Her landlord called to tell me he'd give us an extra month, but we need to clean out her apartment.

"That's perfect. I'm going away for a few weeks myself. You don't need to come to DC. We can take care of her apartment, unless it's something you want to do. We'll make an inventory and send it to you. You and Linda can decide what can be pitched and what you want sent home. I may need to get some kind of authorization from you first. Do you know if she had a will?" I asked.

"I almost forgot," he said, rising to rummage in his desk. "The FBI gave me her will along with some other personal effects. She left everything she had to Linda and me. I was going to give it to you, but I plum forgot. The FBI said the government has already seized all her bank and brokerage accounts, so I don't know if it's worth anyone's time to do anything." He pulled the will from beneath some other papers and handed it to me. His eyes were swollen and he looked miserable.

"Aw, Ben, I wish I could have done more. Of course I can come back, whenever you're ready. In the meantime, I'll keep Rochelle's will in a safe place. If you don't mind, I'm going to talk to an estate lawyer to make sure I'm right about what you should do."

I assured them that Maggie would be able to reach me if they needed anything. They gave me the keys to Rachel's apartment and car, and we said our goodbyes. On the way out, I pulled Jasmine aside to emphasize that if something came up she should call Maggie immediately.

On the way to Stella's, Maggie commented, "Jasmine is very attractive. Stella is right to keep her away from Clovis."

I laughed. "What does Bonnie Raitt sing? 'Don't advertise your man?' Both you and Stella really are protective."

Without a hint of a smile, she replied, "Damn straight."

I wondered if Carol, or for that matter, any other woman would ever feel that way about me.

"Maybe you should introduce Jasmine to Sam," I offered.

Now her face widened into a slow, satisfied smile. "Jack Patterson, you are a genius."

When we arrived, Maggie quickly cornered Micki and Stella. Jordan had pulled Clovis and Paul aside, leaving Beth and me alone in the living room. As usual, Sam was late.

I handed Beth a glass of wine and said, "Beth, I need a break. I'm going to Pawleys for three weeks. You still okay with my selling the house?"

"If you don't, I might come to DC and hire Susan for you. Dad, it's time, it's time for change. I hope that's what Pawleys is about."

"It is. Now tell me about school and Jeff."

Soon everyone broke up from their private conversations and joined us in the living room. Larry and Sam arrived, and we all relaxed into easy conversation while we tucked into take-out Chinese.

After dinner, I pulled Micki aside and gave her the will, asking her to make a copy and send the original to Janis Harold, probably the best tax and estate lawyer I'd ever run across.

"Tell her I'll call her in a few days," I said.

"I thought you were getting away for a few weeks?"

"I am, but it doesn't mean I won't be thinking. In fact, that's exactly what I want to do—walk the beach and think."

"You okay, Jack? You haven't flirted with me once—a girl might get her feelings hurt," she smiled.

"I've got a lot on my mind, but as to flirting, well—I've grown to like Larry. He's good for you, and I'm not."

Her blush caught me by surprise—I hadn't seen Micki blush very often. "He is good for me, very good, but..."

"Trouble in paradise?"

"Not between Larry and me. We're great, but his mom is not my biggest fan. She thinks he can do a lot better, and that he's wasting his time designing and building furniture."

"She's wrong on both counts. Give her time to adjust to a future she hadn't imagined for her son; she'll come around. Speaking of furniture, the chair he built for Clovis is perfect. You think he'd build another for me?"

"There's already a waiting list, but I'll see what I can do. After all, I am sleeping with the carpenter," she said with a laugh.

"Your sacrifice is greatly appreciated," I said with a little bow.

She took my hand and gave it a squeeze. "God, Jack, it's fun working with you. Hurry up and find us another case."

I smiled, but didn't say anything, wondering if I should.

SATURDAY

48

I spent the next few days clearing the decks at the office so I could be gone without Maggie having to call me every five minutes. We both stayed in the office late the two nights before I left, and it was well worth the effort. Martin had insisted on a security detail at my house, but they didn't see a soul except the neighbors walking their dog and a couple of kids out for a lark. No men in a grey Camry followed me. I issued a press statement saying all questions about Rachel should be referred to Micki, counsel for the family. Micki was okay with this while I was gone.

By Thursday, I was ready to leave, in fact chomping at the bit. Clovis had finally given me the okay to spend my vacation without a bodyguard. I was frankly surprised when he relented and wondered if Maggie and Clovis hadn't conspired behind my back to have me watched by somebody locally. As long as they left me alone, I frankly didn't care.

Walter offered his plane, and I accepted, glad to avoid the commercial flight into Myrtle Beach. We landed at the Georgetown County Airport, where, thanks to Maggie, the rental car was waiting. After a trip to the new Lowes grocery for provisions, I was driving across the north causeway onto Pawleys an hour later.

Now my toes were wiggling in the wet sand of the Atlantic Ocean. The weather was a little warm for October, but the wind still required a jacket as I ventured out on my first walk to the fishing pier and back. The home I had rented was perfect. With a large kitchen, family room, and master bedroom on the first floor, I had no reason to go upstairs at all. I wasn't expecting company.

I quickly fell into a routine, getting up early in the morning to walk the beach from one end to the other just after sunrise, a distance of about three and a half miles round trip. I then cleaned up and went across the causeway to a little place I'd found off Highway Seventeen that served breakfast. I figured that after a three-mile walk, I deserved a good breakfast.

I picked up both the *New York Times* and the local Myrtle Beach paper at the Food Lion and returned home to settle in. After reading the papers, I picked up one of the many books I'd been meaning to read, keeping my vow not to turn on the TV until after dinner. I took a second walk around noon or rode a rented bike around the island, then ate a light lunch. My afternoon reading session usually resulted in a nap. The length of these afternoon naps revealed the extent of both my mental and physical exhaustion.

I'd told Maggie I wouldn't read any emails or answer the phone for the first week, unless she or Beth needed me. So far neither had called. I took a final short walk every evening at sunset, made myself a cocktail, and then took an Uber back across the causeway for an early dinner at one of the excellent mainland restaurants. Frank's was my favorite.

I never stayed out late, and usually ended up watching a ball game or finishing a book before an early bedtime. Sounds boring, but I've left one factor out of my daily routine, and she wasn't the least bit boring.

Every morning at breakfast the same employee greeted me from behind the cash register. Her face was covered with freckles, and her long red hair looked like it hadn't seen a comb in weeks. She wore it piled on top of her head, held up with a variety of combs, pins, and pencils. She always wore the same outfit—a plaid snap-pocket shirt with the sleeves rolled up, blue jeans, and cowboy boots.

She appeared to be in her early thirties, and at first I thought she might be the owner's daughter. She was always in motion, seemingly willing to do most everything—combination hostess, waitress, busboy, and cashier. She flirted outrageously with every man or boy who walked through the door. I later learned she was the owner, and that her name was Jo Ellen Murphy.

Everyone seemed to enjoy her shtick—it was so over-the-top not even the wives or mothers could object. She wore a diamond ring and wedding band on her left hand, and any guy who got out of line got the back side of that hand as well a firm nudge out the door. I hadn't been to Pawleys often since Angie's death, but she greeted me each time like I'd been there just the day before.

On Monday night, I was watching the game between the Saints and the Redskins when I heard a knock and the front door flew open. I have to admit I nearly jumped out of my skin. When I could focus, I saw Jo Ellen walk in like she owned the place. She'd changed into a blue dress shirt and had pulled her hair into a ponytail, but the jeans and boots were the same. I thought I detected a hint of perfume.

"I thought you might want some company for the game. Who's winning?"

Somewhat taken aback I said, "Uh, the Saints so far. Can I fix you something to drink, uh, Ms. Murphy?"

"It's Jo, and no, I brought my own, hope you don't mind," she said, pointing to the large leather bag at her side. "I'm sure you have a blender. Just give me a couple of glasses and some ice."

I found the blender in the cabinet above the fridge and watched as she made a concoction she called a redneck margarita— frozen limeade, Sprite, Bud Light with Lime, and lots of tequila. I chose to stick with my glass of Cabernet. Unfazed, she carried the frothy mixture into the family room, and sank into the sofa, and asked, "What's the score?"

The first thing I learned about my unexpected guest was that she knew one hell of a lot about football. She also knew a good deal more about me than I knew about her, which was basically nothing. I asked about the wedding rings, and she told me she'd gotten married fresh out of high school, but in her words, "it ended badly." She still wore the rings to avoid complications at work, although she'd "upgraded the diamond quite a bit." She was closer to my age than I'd guessed and didn't mind admitting it. She was easy to talk to, had definite political opinions, and made no bones about them.

The game was a blowout, Saints ahead by 28 to zip at halftime, so we took our drinks out on the deck to enjoy the rising moon. She was very different from the people I knew in DC or had met at Carol's. She seemed utterly authentic, both a product and part of her environment. Then again, I had to admit maybe my DC friends were exactly the same: I just didn't like the environment. But why was she here?

"I am so glad you dropped by tonight." I began, but she quickly interrupted me.

"Hold that thought, Jack, I gotta pee. I think I'll switch to wine—do you have any white? Great, pour me a glass, and let's continue this conversation inside. I'm getting cold."

I followed her through the screen door and pulled a bottle of Sauvignon Blanc from the fridge. I'd just rinsed out a wine glass when she walked in wearing only her white shirt and panties. Gone were the boots, jeans, and her ponytail. Her hair was a beautiful, tangled mess. She kissed me softly on the lips.

"You were about to ask me why I came over tonight. Well, the answer is sex. I want to use you for sex. Now let's take our wine into the family room, and I'll explain the rules."

I was dumbfounded, but followed her like an eager puppy, and we sank into the couch facing each other. She leaned in and gave me a long, slow kiss.

"Jo's rules: If you come for breakfast tomorrow morning there will be no hint about tonight. No wink, no comment, not a word. I have a reputation to keep. No self-respecting off-island girl ever sleeps with a tourist. Agreed?"

"This tourist off-island girl thing doesn't make any sense to me, but agreed," I said. Why would I argue?

"Next. I like spontaneous. No dates, no dinners. I show up if and when I want. If you have company, I'll disappear. But when I come over is totally up to me."

"You won't even let me take you to dinner?" I asked.

"I told you I have a reputation to keep," she said sternly. She also began to trace the back of my hand softly with her nail.

"They're your rules, but I'd still like to take you out. How about a beach walk and dinner here?" Her hand was now working its way up my arm.

She took a long sip of wine before she answered. "Well, maybe. I don't normally take beach walks because I'm on my feet twelve hours every day. But dinner here might be nice if I don't have to cook." She reached over and kissed my neck.

"Finally, this is about sex, not some love affair that always ends badly. When you leave it's over between us, plain and simple. No phone call, no flowers, and no cards. Deal?"

She rose, taking my hand and pulling me toward the bedroom. How could I argue with her rules? Just then, I might have agreed to most anything.

49

JO WAS GONE WHEN I WOKE UP: no surprise, as she opened the restaurant at six o'clock sharp every morning. I wondered if her visit last night had been a dream. I mean surely this sort of thing doesn't happen often; at least it didn't to me. I did my best to avoid her at breakfast that morning, and she did the same, although I thought I caught a glance now and then. I finished my country-fried steak, gravy, and eggs and walked over to the counter to pay. Without looking up she commented, "You seemed hungry this morning." I tipped my baseball cap and walked out, trying not to grin.

She didn't appear that evening or the next. I was tempted to push it at breakfast on Thursday, but her rules had been clear. Maybe it had been a one-night fling after all. That night I decided to try a new Italian restaurant in Litchfield. It was pretty good, but all in all, not worth the drive.

When I opened the front door I was startled to find Jo lounging on the great room couch, sipping a glass of wine, and wearing nothing but my best blue dress shirt.

"About time you got back. I almost gave up on you. Pour yourself a glass of wine and come on over. I want you to teach me to play chess." She had laid out the board on the coffee table in front of the couch.

I did as ordered and said, "I like the outfit, but what if I'd brought someone home?"

"You weren't going to pick up anybody at that Italian place. Only snowbird couples go there. I mean do you really expect to find Little

Italy on the beach?" She laughed and added, "I've been right here waiting."

I decided to ignore her jibes and began to arrange the pieces on the wooden chessboard that had been left behind by a previous guest. She was a quick learner, and the evening passed quickly. Jo was easy and uncomplicated, a nice change for me.

Once more she was gone before I woke, and so a routine began. For me, a wonderful night, easy sleep, and a healthy morning walk. Did I mention uncomplicated? Most evenings I'd come home after dinner to find her curled up on my couch watching a ball game, a movie, or simply ready to talk over a game of chess.

Conversation was effortless—no masks, no pretense. Raised by her mother and stepfather, she had begun working at the restaurant when she was fourteen, mainly to get away from home and the stepfather. Her early marriage had soured quickly, so she never left the restaurant. The owner and his wife appreciated her hard work and agreed to sell it to her when they retired. It now belonged to her free and clear.

She was like a woodland sprite—I never knew when she might appear. It was a kick to let someone else be in control. And she certainly was in control—of when and where she appeared, of what we did that night, and definitely of the sex. I was okay with that, too. Some nights it was wild and glorious, some nights we simply spooned and fell asleep.

I felt better as the days passed—there's nothing like regular sex to lift one's spirits. I even added the occasional jog to my morning walk. And my thoughts began to return to Rachel.

At first my walks had been just mind-clearing exercise, but I couldn't forget what Ben had told me about handling her defense. Nor could I forget Rachel's words to me, "it's not as it seems." So the walks had also served as incubators, helping me hatch out the beginnings of a strategy. First I spoke with Maggie. She wasn't surprised by either my ideas or the list of requests I had for Brian. I spoke with Janis Harold about probating Rachel's will. Each morning I spent phone time with both Micki and Maggie vetting ideas and our options.

Bottom line: I didn't believe Rachel had committed suicide, and I didn't think she was guilty of espionage. But it would take lots of digging, lots of work to get to the truth, and who knew where the chickens would come home to roost. I needed more information before I brought my proposal to Ben and Linda—after all, whether to proceed would be their decision.

My fledgling plan was risky. I could be wrong—Rachel could be proven guilty without a doubt, a bitter pill for all of us.

I also hadn't forgotten about the rest of my life. It turns out that productive change requires more than good intentions. I called Susan Sandler at Evers to re-start the conversation about selling my house.

"Really, Jack? Are you sure this time?" She sounded skeptical, and who could blame her? She'd been down this road before.

We talked about various neighborhoods and property types. Her probing questions led me to think about issues I hadn't considered. I had no idea where I wanted to end up, but she was patient, and every day I received a new set of listings in various neighborhoods. I asked her to copy everything to Beth, who knew the DC area as well as I did. I valued Beth's opinion and hoped we could have some fun in the process.

Most of my clients left me alone during this three-week period, but I emailed back and forth with a few of the needier ones. Maggie told me Carol had called the office several times asking where I was. I got the impression that Maggie enjoyed telling her that she "wasn't at liberty to tell, but she'd be happy to convey a message."

She also texted me directly a few times and left a couple of voicemails, all of which I deleted. I wasn't ready to muddy my vacation with Carol. I honestly didn't know what I would say. She would have to wait.

Jo and I fell into another game. I ate dinner at one obscure restaurant after the other, but each night she knew exactly where I'd been. If I didn't know better I'd say she was having me followed. After a few bad meals I gave up trying to win—I enjoyed a good dinner too much.

No matter how long, beach vacations always end too soon. When

I woke up on the last Friday morning, I found her sitting on the deck with a cup of coffee.

"Not at the restaurant this morning, Ms. Murphy?"

"I feel like a walk on the beach. Yvette can handle the restaurant this once."

An easy response, but a serious tone. We walked down the path through the dunes to the quiet beach. It was still early, and I saw only a few determined fishermen. I tried a little tease. "What about your reputation?"

"See for yourself—the shell seekers have already gone inside for breakfast. We have the beach almost to ourselves."

She took my hand and we walked for a while in silence. I noticed someone on a deck looking out at the ocean through binoculars, but I assumed he was looking for dolphins or sharks. For some reason he looked out of place, but I didn't say anything to Jo.

She finally turned and said, "Jack, I have a favor to ask."

"Sure—most anything," I responded.

She gave me a quick kiss. "How did I know that would be your response? I've decided to break my own rule. I would like you to take me out to dinner tonight."

"Like a date?" I kidded.

She smiled. "Like a date. Get us two chairs at the bar at Frank's tonight at seven."

Definitely an unexpected request, but I was happy to comply.

"Just one question," I asked. "Do you kiss on the first date?"

Her eyes twinkled, and she changed her tone to match mine.

"I don't normally, but just for you I might. I've had enough of this beach walking. I don't get the point—besides I'm suddenly horny. You think you can help me with that, Mr. Patterson?" She took my hand and we ran back to the house.

50

I WANTED TO SAVOR THE MORNING and anticipate the evening, but knew I needed to keep to my routine, so I sat down with a cup of tea and called Brian and then Micki and Maggie to catch up on what had happened at home. I asked Maggie to check flights to Little Rock for Tuesday so I could meet with Ben and Linda. I was glad to be through with business in time to walk and occasionally jog the whole length of beach at noon. I kept to my usual schedule of afternoon reading—I didn't want to skimp on the last day. After a final sunset walk I took an Uber across the causeway to meet Jo.

Frank's was always busy, whatever the time of year, but I caught sight of Jo almost immediately. She was seated at the bar, wearing a very short black dress and heels, red hair more or less controlled by a twist of black fabric.

She looked uneasy, and I walked over quickly, kissing her lightly on the cheek. She moved her purse from my chair, and the guy sitting next to her moved away abruptly. She was sipping a martini, so I ordered the same.

She turned to me in confusion. "I'm glad you're here—that guy…. I don't know how people drink this stuff. It's basically straight Gin and a little olive oil. What should I have ordered?"

I suggested a Manhattan and ordered her one, which she liked much better.

"Why the bar instead of a table?" I asked. "I'm fine with either, just curious."

She seemed reluctant to answer, but finally said, "Well, I've lived on Pawleys all my life, but I've never been here. My girlfriends come here whenever they can; they love the food and tell me the bar is the place to be. Now that I know what they're talking about, they can keep it."

It occurred to me that working twelve to fourteen hours seven days a week couldn't be conducive to a social life. I took her hand and said, "Jo, I'm sorry to have kept you waiting. You look fabulous. I love the dress, your hair, the whole look. Right now, every man in this room is envious. Let me ask for a table."

She wore very little make-up, just a bit of mascara, so her sudden blush highlighted her freckles. I felt like the king of the mountain. She, on the other hand, had a complaint.

"You may love the look, but these damn shoes are killing me. I don't know how why in the world I ever bought them. I miss my boots!"

I laughed, "Cowboy boots with that dress would definitely draw a crowd."

"Well, are you going to just sit there, or are you going to feed me? I'm starving, and I want the most expensive item on the menu."

A few words with the owner got us a table and over she-crab soup, deviled eggs with jalapenos, and cornmeal-crusted grouper we talked about her restaurant, football, and where she liked to vacation. Turns out she closed the restaurant for the first two weeks of every year and vacationed in Key West, where she was a complete unknown and could "let her hair down." I couldn't help but wonder how much further down it could get.

"How about some dessert?" I asked after the waiter had cleared our plates.

"Thanks, but I'd rather have some ice cream at your place. Tonight you are finally going down in chess," she challenged. "Besides, if I don't take these shoes off soon, I won't be able to walk tomorrow."

So we returned to the beach house. She looked much more comfortable, sitting barefoot, Indian style, studying the chessboard. She was close to putting me in checkmate, when she turned serious.

"Jack, you leave tomorrow, and I need to remind you of my rule.

No emails, no calls, no flowers, and no contact for at least a year. You're an easy man to get used to, but you and I both know we live completely different lives. If we don't back off, it will end badly, and all our good memories will turn sour. Okay?"

I wanted to argue, but I didn't want to make the leave taking harder on either of us. I thought for a moment, trying to get the words right.

"Jo, these three weeks will stay with me forever. You are special, and I want so much to say no to your silly rule. But no matter how much I want to stay here with you, I have to leave, at least for a while. But a year? I want to negotiate." I smiled, she didn't.

"One year's a minimum, probably should be two, but my bet is it will be never. Some lucky woman will realize what a find you are, that she needs to grab ahold of you and not let go. A few years earlier and I might have been the one."

"What's wrong with now?" I asked as I moved my chess piece. I admit the black dress interfered with my concentration.

"Checkmate!" she squealed as she stood up. "Now it's your turn to have your way with me." As I stood up, she threw her arms around my neck and kissed me flush on the lips as her dress fell to the floor.

SATURDAY

51

HER SMELL LINGERED on my pillow the next morning, but of course she was gone. Pondering whether I could possibly practice law from the beach, I went into the kitchen to start the coffee, only to discover it was already brewing. My heart jumped—maybe she hadn't left after all.

"Mornin', Jack—sleep well?" Clovis was sitting at the kitchen table.

"No offense, but what the hell are you doing here? Aren't you supposed to be home recuperating in a rocking chair?" Disappointment had made me snarky.

"Sorry, but your vacation is over—it's past time for you to come back to the real world. Maggie's with the plane at the airport; we're going to Little Rock so you can meet with Ben and Linda. We'll bring Micki and Stella back to DC with us."

Maggie was always a step or two ahead of me, but I needed a couple of days to recover from the beach, not to mention Jo.

"Oh, jeez, Clovis, I'm sorry but—wait a minute," I said realizing something wasn't right. "Why is Maggie with the plane? Why didn't she ride in to pick me up? What's the rush? I could easily have flown back commercial. And why are you here?"

"Let's close up the house. I'll tell you everything on the way to the airport."

I finished packing, loaded the dishwasher, and put out the linens. I took a few minutes to watch the ocean from the deck, wondering when I'd see it again. Finally, Clovis and I drove away. After we'd cleared the causeway, I turned to him and asked, "Okay, Clovis, what's up?"

"Jack, you were followed almost every second you were in Little Rock for the funeral. Your pockmarked friend even attended the service. Martin and I decided one of his men should come to Pawleys."

I started to object, but Clovis silenced me. "I know it was an invasion of your privacy, but you seem to be oblivious to reality—it's as simple as that. Stella discovered that both your phone and computer were being monitored, and sure enough you had a tail the first week you were here.

"We wanted to tell you, but Maggie insisted we should leave you alone unless it became absolutely necessary. Fortunately, whoever it was lost interest after a few days. Your regular schedule and those long walks on the beach convinced the bad guys you really were on vacation—they packed up and left."

"What about Martin's guy? Did he leave, too?" I knew I sounded churlish, but damn!

"Well, no, but he kept a discreet distance. And, yes, we were also concerned about Ms. Murphy. Your bad judgment has almost got you killed twice before."

I sighed, ready for the worst. "Well, give me the bad news."

Clovis laughed. "Ms. Murphy is exactly who she appears to be—born and raised in Pawleys, hardworking—the only thing she's ever done wrong is to get involved with you. Quit worrying, Jack, there's not a phony bone in that woman's body. I'm impressed—for once your choice in women was flawless."

Well, that felt good, even though Jo had done the choosing, not me.

"How much does Maggie know about, uh, our relationship?"

"She told me that unless Ms. Murphy turned out to be an international assassin, for which you have a strange affinity, she didn't want to know. She said you've been a different person these last two weeks, and whether it was the beach or Ms. Murphy, she doesn't care."

"It was definitely the beach," I lied.

His tone changed. "Hard to leave?"

"More than you can imagine." He knew I wasn't talking about the beach.

Maggie was waiting in the little office associated with the private airport when we pulled up. I pretended to be annoyed. "When were you going to tell me I had company? Don't you trust me to stay out of trouble on a three-week vacation?"

She replied in the same tone. "No, I don't. You seem to find trouble most anywhere. I hope you had a good time while the rest of us have been working ourselves to the bone."

"I've been working, too. Just in between beach walks."

She relaxed and said, "You look good, Jack. Whoever she was, she was good for you, and I'm glad. The tan and dropping ten pounds also help."

"I have no idea what you mean, but I accept the compliment. Now let's get to work. What's the rush? Why do we need to go to Little Rock today?"

"The guys who inventoried Rachel's apartment found the asset forfeiture notice—it was sent weeks ago. If we want to object to the seizure, we're almost out of time, and we need to get Ben's permission to proceed. Of course, we could handle it by phone and Internet, but I knew you'd want to explain the process to the Jennings in person." She handed me the government's filing.

Part of my strategy to discover what had happened to Rachel was to resist the government's claim to Rachel's bank accounts and assets. The government had sent the notice to her home while she was locked up in a military prison, an old and dirty trick. If we hadn't gone into that apartment all her money, life insurance, and the assets in her pension plan would belong to the government by default.

Normally a lawsuit against someone who has died must be revived with sufficient notice to the heirs: in Rachel's case, her parents. But a forfeiture proceeding is technically against the property itself, which, of course, has no heirs.

Maggie enjoyed sitting up front, so Clovis and I had the rear seats to ourselves. Nonetheless, I leaned over and spoke quietly.

"Assuming Ben and Linda give us the go-ahead, whoever was responsible for Rachel's death is going to be pissed."

"We're ready," he answered.

"I know you are, and Beth should be okay in St. Louis, but whoever was following me at Pawleys may know about Jo."

My conclusion was met with silence.

"Look, Clovis, it was only a beach fling. We agreed not so see each other for at least a year—her stipulation, not mine. But I sure don't want her to be in any danger."

"Jack, what is it with you? You finally find someone who has no pretenses and isn't trying to murder you, and you agree not to see her for a year. What were you thinking?"

"Well, when she first knocked on my door I wasn't thinking about much. How would you have reacted?"

"I know what you were thinking about," he grinned.

"Jack, from what I've learned, Jo is as tough as nails. She has to be to run that restaurant. I admit I hadn't thought about it, but, don't worry—we'll keep her safe. What about Carol?"

"Well, we're not as close as we used to be. I think she's moved on to greener pastures." I tried to keep my voice even.

Clovis raised his eyebrows. "You think she could be involved?"

"No, at least not in the way you're thinking. She's been very public recently with Eric Hartman—he's a top-dollar DC lobbyist. The fact is our relationship has gone south. I'm confident she's not in any danger. I don't have that same confidence about Jo."

Clovis teased, "You know it would be helpful if you stuck to one girl at a time. Protecting your girlfriends is spreading my folks thin."

"Maybe it would be better if I quit getting involved in cases where the opposition's solution is to threaten my girlfriend or kill me," I laughed.

"You got that," Clovis finished.

52

We landed smoothly, taxied to Hodges Air, and drove straight to the Jennings' home. I'd practiced my words for the last two weeks. Most people think lawyers are like surgeons: surgeons like to cut, lawyers like to sue. A good lawyer knows that a lawsuit should be a last resort, never brought before the lawyer has carefully laid out the downsides. Truth to tell, by itself, my proposed strategy had little chance of changing hearts or minds about either Rachel's actions or supposed suicide. What it did provide was a vehicle for investigation and time. Problem was, I might end up proving she was indeed a spy.

Micki met us at Ben's house, and, after accepting iced tea and cookies, we all sat at the dining room table. I was about to start my rehearsed speech when Ben interrupted.

"Before you begin, Jack, I've got something to say. The restaurant will be open for business next Monday just like I promised. I've only made one change—I've increased the price of every item by exactly one quarter. Those quarters are for you and your legal team. It could take many a year, but I'll pay off every penny I owe you and Micki. It may not seem like much, but believe it or not, I sell a lot of sandwiches," he smiled.

I had never planned on charging Ben a fee. I started to protest, but he wasn't finished.

"No arguments. You'll receive a check once a month, but in exchange, I'm going to hold you to your promise. We want you to find out whether and why our daughter did what she was accused of doing. Will you keep your end of the bargain?"

I thought for a minute and looked at Linda.

"I did make that promise, and I'm prepared to keep it, but I have to warn you, the answers may not be what you want to hear. I may spend a lot of time and effort only to discover that the allegations are true and are for the reasons the government alleges. Are you prepared for that result?"

Linda answered quickly, "Jack, I can live with any answer, but Ben and I need to know the truth, whatever it might be. I know you and Micki came here today to explain why we should let it go, but save your breath. Nothing you can say will change our minds. Please tell me you'll do it."

"Jack, you know we have complete trust in you," Ben added.

A lawyer seldom hears the words "we trust you completely," but I knew they meant it. Still, so much trust was also a huge responsibility. Had it been anyone else, I probably would have turned them down. But I couldn't deny my gut feeling that Rachel had been made the scapegoat for somebody else's misdeeds.

"Oh, Linda, Micki and I have no intention of giving up now. Why else would we be here? I didn't know your daughter well, but the government's story about her just doesn't ring true. I sure would feel better, though, if you'd let Micki explain what we need you to sign and why."

Micki spent the next few minutes explaining the process. She'd clearly spent a good deal of time working with Janis Harold preparing the probate papers for Rachel's estate and drafting our response to the asset forfeiture. They listened politely and signed without a single question.

We were scheduled to leave for DC in a couple of hours, so Micki and Clovis left to pick up their respective sweethearts. Maggie and I wanted to spend a little more time with Ben and Linda. The four of us gravitated to the porch so Ben could enjoy a cigar.

Linda offered us all more tea and said, "We have a little bit of good news. Ben Jr. has decided to resign from the U.S. Marshals Service and move back home to help Ben with the restaurant."

"That is good news," I said. "I'm sure you can use the help."

"Ben's not so sure. He's worried that Ben Jr. will start telling him how to run the business, and they'll fight and argue," Linda said, looking nervously at Ben, who remained silent.

"They will, and it will be good for them both. What have you heard from Lee and his wife?" I asked.

"Not a word. Our relationship with Tina has never been easy. Now she won't even speak to us, and apparently pitches a hissy fit whenever Lee calls." Her tone left no doubt about her opinion of Tina.

"Give them time—they'll come around," I predicted.

Ben took a long pull on his cigar and exhaled. "Well, maybe and maybe not—I'm not going to spend good time worrying about it. And neither should you." He turned to look directly at Linda.

"Jack, what I haven't mentioned yet is how grateful I am. Only a fool wouldn't realize that both you and your team will raise some hackles once you start digging around. Whoever killed her may decide to come after you."

"You're right, they might do exactly that," I said, reminded of the attack on Clovis. "But sometimes the truth is worth a little trouble. We've discussed the potential dangers as a group and have decided we're willing to take the risk."

Linda began to tear up, and Maggie absently handed her a tissue. "You could always count on Maggie to remember the tissues," I thought, and continued.

"You know, a month ago I might not have felt this way. But I had the opportunity to speak with and listen to your daughter. Her strength and confidence were immediately obvious to everyone in the room. She certainly didn't act or sound like a depressed traitor. She was in good spirits, ready to explain what she had done and why, and excited about her prospects and future.

"If she was murdered, the facts are worth discovering. Think about it—someone was able to sneak onto a military base, murder your daughter, and make it look like suicide. That person or persons must have had particular skills and must have had a very good reason to take such a risk. The implications are very troubling."

I paused to let my conclusions sink in. "There's one more thing, and it won't be easy. You have two sons and a daughter-in-law, as well as various friends and support groups here in Little Rock. You can't discuss what we've said or agreed to today or what I may report to you in the future with any of them. Not a single word."

"You mean I can't tell Ben Jr. or Lee anything?" Linda's voice rose sharply.

"No, Linda, you can't. You'll probably see news or articles in the paper or on the Internet about the investigation. Your family and friends will, too. We'll try our best to let you know what's true and what isn't, but you can't say a word to anyone."

"Not even that we met?" Linda was incredulous.

"Of course people know we're good friends, and it's fine for you to tell them I'm your lawyer, but that's it. Not a word about what you signed, and certainly not what Micki or I have said. No matter how bad the press may get, absolutely nothing." My tone left no room for doubt.

Ben frowned. "Are you worried the government will use our children to spy on us? Just because they work for the government doesn't mean they're disloyal."

That possibility was exactly why we were having this conversation, but I knew I needed to tread lightly.

"Do I think either of your boys or your friends for that matter would breach a confidence on purpose? No, I don't. But let me give you a hypothetical: Lee calls you about something he's read in the paper and you explain how it's part of my strategy. He feels better and agrees to keep what you tell him in confidence. Then Tina asks him what he's been talking to you about and he relates the confidence to her—after all, she is his wife. The next day she's asked about the newspaper article at work, and she repeats our strategy to her coworker at the FBI. She hasn't meant to, but a leak can destroy our strategy."

They both nodded, seeming to understand. What I wanted to say was, "Damn yes!" At the very least the government would try to enlist Tina. This was the same government that pitted mother against son in minor drug cases.

"Listen, if anybody starts bugging you, especially your children, have them call me. If I can answer their questions, I will."

Ben spoke firmly, "We'll do what you ask, but don't drag this out. I don't like the idea of keeping my boys in the dark. Rochelle was their sister."

"I promise to move as fast as we can. In fact, my biggest fear is that this will play out faster that we can handle."

53

JORDAN PULLED INTO THE DRIVEWAY, and Maggie and I hugged Ben and Linda, promising to keep them up to date when we could. On the flight home, I learned that Maggie had indeed handled all the logistics. Our entire operation had been moved out to the property in Eastern Maryland. Maggie had said the house was large, but I had no idea how large. The original owner had built it to be a small inn, thinking to offset the mortgage with paying guests. The house had nine bedrooms, three on the first floor and six laid out dormitory style on the second. With an apartment above the garage, it was large enough to accommodate all of us during the course of the investigation.

Martin and Clovis wanted to house us under one roof for security reasons. It reminded me of the times we had used Micki's ranch house during the Stewart and Cole cases. Stella was happy to have only one location to protect from cyber threats. Maggie had arranged for a caterer to bring out food once a day, and both the pantry and the bar were more than adequately stocked.

When the plane landed I was surprised to see my daughter Beth leaning against the waiting car. I turned to Maggie. "What the…?"

"Hush, Jack," Maggie chided. "Let her explain." Beth ran out to greet us.

"Hey, Dad—while y'all are working on Rochelle's case, I'm going to make sure Susan Sandler finds you a new home and get the old place ready for the market. If you wait until you have time, it will never happen. I can also run errands and help with research or whatever you need."

"What about school and Jeff?" I asked.

"Classes are over, and I've finished my exams. I've got a couple of papers to write, but I can easily do them here. As for Jeff, he's either at the hospital or asleep. He was feeling guilty about me sitting all alone at our apartment every night."

"Well, of course I'm glad to have you. Has anyone told Clovis? Will you be ..."

"I cleared it with him as soon as Beth told me she wanted to come," Maggie interrupted. "Jack, we're going to need all the help we can get. I'm glad Beth is willing to help." Beth beamed, and I gave in. I loved the thought of having her here.

It was about an hour's drive to Maggie and Walter's new property on the Western Shore of the Chesapeake. The driveway meandered first through some woods, then through open pastures to the house on the banks of the West River. Walter had made a shrewd invest-ment: the property was stunning. The house itself had been built in the mid-sixties, so it was a bit of a relic. Frankly, as long as the toilets flushed and the stove worked, I didn't much care. After we had unpacked and settled in, the whole team gathered in the big family room. We chatted easily about this and that for a few minutes before I cleared my throat.

"Well, we all know why we're here—it's time to get going. For the last week you've all been searching for puzzle pieces. Now we need to bring the pieces together, see if they make sense. Let's begin with you, Stella. Are these conversations private? Are our phones and computers secure?"

"We have a digital safety net covering this facility with a perimeter of approximately one mile. If you're outside the perimeter anything goes. The phones and computers are secure, and to tell you the truth there have been no attempts to access any of our electronics in at least a week," she reported.

"That will change in the next few hours," I said.

No one said a word.

Stella continued, "I can monitor everything from here. We should talk about how you want me to handle any intrusion. You also asked me if I could discover who Rachel might have recently called or emailed before she was picked up. It would help if we could get her computer or her cellphone, but I'm also looking at other resources."

Micki grumbled, "Fat chance of getting her phone or computer."

She was right, but I responded, "Patience, Micki, you're next. What have you been up to?"

Micki laughed, "You know damn well what I've been up to, but, okay, I'll report. Janis Harold has probated Rachel's will. It leaves everything to the Jennings, thus giving Ben, who is the executor, the obligation and right to assemble all of Rachel's assets. Ben has employed Jack and me to do just that, including all the assets that the government has seized.

"On Monday morning we'll enter an appearance in federal court objecting to the government's seizure of assets, including her bank accounts, her pension plan, her government life insurance, and anything else they may have seized."

"Including her computer and cell phone," I added, which made Stella smile.

"Yup, her cell phone and computer. I hadn't thought of that."

Big Mike spoke up, "We might be able to help. When we inventoried her apartment we found a large stack of mail by the front door. I'll bet we find her phone bill somewhere between the insurance ads and the Wal-Mart circulars."

"What else did you find?" I asked.

"I've got a complete inventory, except for the rotten vegetables in the fridge." Mike passed copies around the room. "I have to admit the apartment was pretty bare. No telling what the FBI took," he commented.

Micki said, "At some point we should be able to get a complete inventory of what they seized, one way or the other."

I agreed. "Mike, I'd like to see the apartment myself. Do you think we could go tomorrow?"

Mike looked to Martin who nodded his okay.

We spent the next hour or so letting everyone report on the tasks I had given them. Most of them were dead ends, but even dead ends gave us information. Maggie looked pointedly at her watch and then at me.

"Good job, everyone. Time for a drink of something before dinner, don't you think? Go ahead—I have a couple of phone calls to make, and I want you all to know to whom and why. The first is to Carol Madison and the second to Red Shaw."

"Why? I mean, why do you need to tell us? Isn't that private?" Beth asked, seemingly perplexed.

"Not anymore. I'm telling you because once I've made these two calls the cat will be out of the bag. I'm going to tell Carol that Micki and I now represent Rachel's estate, which I believe will end my relationship with her forever. I'm going to call Red because he's my friend and client, and I owe him. I don't want either him or the Lobos to be blindsided Monday morning. Both Carol and Red probably think Rachel's death means the case was closed but they're wrong."

Beth replied with a bit of a frown, "Okay, Dad, that's your business, certainly Carol is. But why are you making such a big deal out of it?"

"Because once the cat is out of the bag, there'll be no going back. We'll have to be ready for the consequences, come what may."

54

No one had much to say to that. Micki gave me a thumbs-up as she and Larry left the room. I knew they were both itching to explore the property. Maggie left to check on dinner. Beth caught me as I sat fiddling with my phone.

"Dad, I don't understand. You know I'm not a big fan of Carol, although she is a step up from the other women you've dated. Maggie told me that Carol didn't want you to represent Rachel, but how could telling her be dangerous?"

"Let's deal with this in private," I suggested.

She followed me to my room, and I sank into an overstuffed chair while she perched on the edge of the desk.

"My relationship with Carol has always been complicated because we both deal with confidential information. We came to an agreement when we first got together. She would never ask me about my clients, but if I ever volunteered information she would be free to use that information however she wanted. The moment I tell her I represent Rachel's estate, she is free to tell her clients, and I believe one or more one of them won't be pleased."

Beth asked a logical question, "Then why call her? You two seem to be on the outs anyway."

"Well, again, it gets complicated. She tried very hard to convince me to drop Rachel like a hot potato. She made no bones about it—my career would be kaput if I didn't let it go. In the moment, it seemed better to let her think she'd won the argument." I tried not to squirm, and Beth pretended not to notice.

"As a result, she may have reported to a client what I'd led her to believe—that based on her encouragement I'd decided not to represent Rachel. When it became clear that I was still pursuing the case, she must have been angry and embarrassed. She's tried to reach me several times since Rachel's death, I suspect at the behest of a client.

"I like to think Carol's an innocent pawn, but I feel sure her client used her to try to get me to back off and will use her again if he can. I can't continue to dodge her calls and texts, and I won't deceive her again," I said with a touch of remorse.

"Dad, I think you really care about Carol. The two of you had a special relationship. It may have run its course, but maybe not. Can't you just steer clear of the subject?"

"Thanks, Beth, but it's too late for that," I said.

"Why? You're an expert at dodging questions."

I smiled at her backhanded compliment. "Because I can't think of any other way to flush out the quarry. Carol may not realize her client is using her, but I know damn well I'm using her to send a message. That's not the way to treat someone you love. I feel guilty and sad and relieved all at the same time."

I hadn't even told Maggie how I felt. In fact, I still wasn't quite sure how I felt, and I wondered if Beth would be able to understand. She watched me in silence for a few moments, and then gave a little sigh.

"Dad, I didn't mean to pry, and maybe I shouldn't have, but I'm glad you told me what you did. You used to tell me that things aren't always black or white, and you were right, and Maggie was right, too."

"What does Maggie have to do with it?" I asked warily.

"She told me your time at Pawleys had done wonders for you." With that she said, "Make your calls, and come to dinner. We can talk some more later."

I phoned Carol as soon as she closed the door. This time she answered after the second ring.

"I was beginning to believe I'd never hear from you. I admit I was mad and hurt, but why didn't you return my calls? When Rachel died, I thought you might want my company."

"You had every right to be mad and hurt. I misled you, and I'm sorry."

"Apology accepted." That was quick. "Where have you been? Maggie wouldn't tell me a thing."

"After the funeral I decided to spend some time at the beach to clear my head. Just got back yesterday."

"Okay, fair enough. But you're back now, so when am I going to see you? Why don't you come to my place tonight? They say make-up sex is the best."

I paused. Both her cajoling tone and quick acceptance of my apology were out of character. I wondered what, or who, was behind the change.

"I'd love to see you, but I can't. I'm knee deep in representing a new client."

"Surely you're not working all night. Come on over. I'll ask Mattie to make you something special." Her voice was warm and inviting— so was her offer. I took a deep breath.

"I'm tempted, but we're getting ready to fight the federal government."

"Now you're hurting my feelings. You can't be that busy. What are you not telling me? Is there someone else?"

I had been fairly direct. The Carol I knew would have thrown me out on my ear by now. It was time to end the dance.

"Okay, here it is. Ben Jennings has asked Micki and me to represent Rachel Goodman's estate. It will be public information by Monday, if not sooner. We are filing objections to the government's seizure of her assets. Those assets won't mean much to the government, but they mean a lot to her father and mother. The time to object is about to run out."

There was a long pause on the other end. "I...I thought that since Rachel was dead, the case was over. Now you're representing the estate?"

"Yes, Rachel's father is the executor of the estate, and he and his wife are the prime beneficiaries."

"Are you insane?" Her voice was suddenly shrill. "Jack, listen to me. Everyone might understand you meeting with her as a favor to an old friend. But suing the government on her behalf? You'll lose every client you have! Lucy won't let Red have anything to do with you. Please come over and let me talk some sense into you," she begged.

I almost said, "I've already done that." Instead I tried to correct her assumption, "I'm not suing the government. They seized her assets, and I'm simply objecting to the seizure."

"Well, don't they have that right? She was a spy, she stole military secrets. Isn't that grounds for seizure?"

"It would be if she were guilty, but she wasn't." I was emphatic.

"Of course she was guilty. Why else did she commit suicide?" Carol asked.

Sadly, most people who'd thought about Rachel's death were of the same opinion as Carol. The only way to change that opinion was to prove her innocence.

"Why else indeed?"

I could almost hear her silence. Finally she asked, "Is there nothing I can say or do to talk you out of this death wish?"

"No, there isn't," I replied.

"This will be the end of us. You know that, don't you?"

I gave it one more shot, couldn't help myself. "It doesn't have to be. When this is…"

"No, Jack," she interrupted. "You are making the choice now."

She was right, and at this moment it hurt. Part of me wanted to try to put our relationship back together. But the fact was that no matter how good we were together, our respective careers made us a bad fit. She had used me to further her career, and I was using her to reach her client.

"Carol, you're right. I have made a choice, and I can't take it back. We were very happy, and I wanted it to work, but it didn't. I'm …" I heard a loud click. If you can slam down a cell phone, she certainly had.

55

GREAT. I'd just given up any chance with one of the classiest women I'd ever met. How would I feel in a couple of months when we lost in court? My thoughts drifted to our first meeting at Red's, her swimming pool on the Eastern Shore, and the two weeks we spent in St. Lucia right after the Hopper case. I was an idiot.

But after a few laps in the pool of self-doubt, I toweled off and called Red.

"Jack Patterson. I wondered when you'd get bored with the beach and come back to work. Were you enchanted by a blond mermaid?" he kidded.

"Nope, a redhead," I bantered back.

"Really—I can't wait to hear more, but I'm sure she's not why you called. What can I do for you?"

"Well, Red, I need you to give a message to your fiancée."

"Be careful now, Jack. You know better than anyone that Lucy doesn't take kindly to directions from anyone, including me. But go ahead."

"Lucy did us both a favor when she took me to task for representing Rachel. It was the correct reaction. Micki and I now represent her estate. We'll file papers in court Monday objecting to the government's seizure of Rachel's assets."

"Good Lord, man! The woman is dead, the case is over. Are you nuts? You know Lucy will have to give you what for—she has no choice."

"No, I'm not nuts, at least I don't think so. And Lucy might want to hold her cards until the game is over. Red, tell her to play it cool. The same goes for you and the Lobos. I'll call Gina and explain. I promise that when the smoke clears you'll understand why silence is the right course."

Red didn't appreciate my subtlety, so I gave him the basic outline of our plan, asking him to keep the information confidential: that we would object to the seizure, that the government would have to prove that Rachel was guilty in order to retain the assets, and that we would fight those efforts.

"You mean you think you can prove Rachel was framed and murdered," he stated flatly. Red never minced words.

"Exactly," I responded.

"And if you fall on your ass?"

"Well, as Carol implied a little while ago, I may need to find a new career."

"And if you're successful, you're likely to get shot or worse." He wasn't laughing.

"I like to think there are other options." I sure didn't like the word 'worse.'

"Okay, Jack, I'll warn Lucy. You've always been one independent cuss, and so far you've had your way. But this time, take my advice: go back to your red-haired mermaid and let Rachel go. Do you realize what you're up against?"

"The same federal government I've been fighting most of my adult life," I answered.

"The federal government doesn't frame and murder analysts. They may fire them on occasion, or send them to prison if they screw up too bad. But if you're right, she stepped on the powerful toes of someone who won't hesitate to prevent whatever she discovered from seeing the light of day. You be careful, my friend."

I remained in the armchair for some time. The conversation with Carol had taken a lot out of me, and Red's warnings had made an impression. If I was right, someone had known where Rachel was being held and was able to break into the military brig and murder her without being discovered. Surely that person or persons could easily find his way into our little enclave in the Maryland countryside.

It was time to talk to Clovis and Martin.

I walked into the big family room where everybody was eating fried chicken and biscuits with cream gravy, perfect comfort food. I filled a plate and motioned for Clovis, Martin, and Big Mike to join me.

"This is your bailiwick, but my conversation with Red has got me a little spooked. Someone must have infiltrated the military complex where Rachel was being held. If they could do that, getting into this place would be a piece of cake. Any thoughts?"

Clovis smiled, "Martin and I are way ahead of you, as is Stella. For the last few days we've been building an electronic fence she designed. Neither of us have seen a system quite like it."

"Let's discuss this with everyone," I said.

We joined the others just as Maggie was bringing in a large platter of brownies. One thing was certain: whatever else happened, we would never starve. Martin and Stella described the electronic fence and how it worked.

"My compliments, Stella. If your system is as good as we all hope, I want to introduce you to my client, Red Shaw. He's just the man to help you patent and market it."

She shrugged off both the compliment and my offer. "Well, part of my work at IBM was developing security systems for military bases. Both the technology and my expertise have evolved since then, so it's better than good. It's not perfect, no system is, but it's better than you might expect. And, thanks, but I'm not sure I want to get involved with another of your clients. I'll stick with my gym."

I noticed that Mike had sort of halfway raised his hand.

"Mike, we're not in school. You don't have to raise your hand. What's on your mind?"

"Well, if you think someone might try to breach this place, I'd ask Master Sergeant Hattoy what he thinks. I bet he's already spotted holes."

We all turned to Brian.

He looked uncomfortable, but spoke right up. "Well, first it would be fairly easy to find this location. Haven't you told people that Ms. Lawrence will be in court Monday? If it were me, I'd wait until she arrived at the courtroom and attach an electronic tracking device to her car. Once the group's location is known, I'd set up surveillance. Within a matter of days, I'd know exactly when the caterer arrives and leaves every day. Then it's only a matter of how to hitch a ride or substitute caterers with a team of my own men. I can think of better methods, but that's the first one that came to me."

No one said a word. Brian had just breached our security in a matter of seconds.

Clovis broke the silence. "Well, young man, since you figured out how to get past our preparations, maybe you can come up with a plan to prevent it from happening. How about first thing tomorrow morning? Jack, okay if we borrow your paralegal tomorrow?"

I smiled, "He's all yours. Brian and Mike, my thanks to both of you. You were right to speak up; please don't hesitate. One more question, Brian—how easy is it to secure a tracking device to a car or van?"

"Pretty damn easy, and you would have no idea it was there."

Maybe Rachel's killers had made a mistake. It was unlikely, but worth checking.

56

IT HAD BEEN A LONG DAY, and I felt pretty sure the next few days wouldn't be any easier. We all needed a good night's rest. I caught up with Larry and Micki as they rose to leave.

"Larry, I'm afraid you'll be bored for the next few days while we get this train out of the station, but I meant what I said a while ago: Speak up if you have a question or an idea. To some extent you're an outsider; you may see things the rest of us don't," I said.

Micki frowned, but Larry smiled easily and said, "Maggie has asked me to give her my thoughts on the new conference and retreat center. She wants the entire complex to blend in with the natural surroundings. I've already started making sketches, so I won't be bored. If you don't mind, I'd like to sit in on the security meeting tomorrow. I think I might be able to contribute a thing or two."

"I'm sure Clovis will appreciate your input. You should know that this crew gets up early. I wouldn't be surprised if Stella has them tossing tires at sunrise."

I found Maggie sorting out cups and glasses, and offered to help.

"Thanks, I'm just tidying up for tomorrow. Won't take long."

"Okay, but a penny for your thoughts," I replied, taking a full tray from her hands.

"I miss my husband. Martin suggested this would be a good time for Walter to travel, so he's off on one of his 'listening tours,' checking in with his top agents and other insurance executives. Walter has his suspicions, but if he thought we could be in any real danger, he would never have left me here. It's scary, Jack. We don't know what kind of risk we face or even who the enemy is."

"Oh, Maggie, I'm so sorry. This isn't fair to you or anyone else. Maybe we should just call it quits, walk away this time," I said, meaning every word.

"No, no—that wouldn't be right either. We can't abandon... look, I'm sorry, I don't mean to be a crybaby." She resumed her no-nonsense face and said, "Now bring that tray into the kitchen and help me with these dishes."

When the last of the dishes were put away, she asked, "You have time for a nightcap?"

"With you, always," I answered. I poured her a single malt and myself a port, and we sat down on the sofa.

"Were you able to reach Carol? How did it go?" She couldn't relax about Carol, even in conversation.

"Not well. I'm using her in the same way she inadvertently used me. Carol and I were good together, but in the end, it just didn't work. She loves her work, and I love my independence. Neither of us showed any willingness to compromise, end of story." Apparently, I couldn't relax either.

"Oh, Jack—the right woman is just around the corner. What about the woman at Pawleys."

"What do you mean? What woman?" I feigned surprise.

"I haven't seen you in such a good mood for a long time. Everyone's noticed. You've paid attention; you're polite and inclu-sive. Take tonight. You made everyone feel they're part of a team. I know you—there had to be a woman."

I didn't want to discuss Jo. I'd promised not to contact her for a year, and it didn't feel right to talk about her. But at least I'd sought change, or should I say, change had found me.

"How about you? This complex is a very large project to take on, not to mention building a new home. I thought you and Walter wanted to travel more. When will you find the time?" I asked.

"Well, I hope Brian will work out so I can spend less time at the office." She averted her eyes.

"And I wouldn't be much of a friend if I got in your way, right? But damn, Maggie. I know I'm supposed to seek change, but losing you might be more change than I can handle. We need to find a way to work this out."

"Jack, you know I won't leave you. Forgive me, but you'd be lost, even with Brian. And I wouldn't be happy either. So for now, let's agree to find ways for me to spend less time in the office, less time on your routine antitrust business, and a lot less time involved in dangerous, off-the-wall cases. Maybe you should think about that, too."

She was right. An antitrust lawyer is supposed to get his kicks from reading economic analyses, not from dodging bullets. And she was also right that having no idea what to expect or who the bad guys were made it even worse.

"Maggie, I'll take however much of your time and attention you can give. You and Walter are my best friends. If my work impinges on that friendship, then work has to go. It's that simple."

We both wiped away a few tears, and before long Maggie said she was ready for bed. It had been an exhausting day, but I wanted to be alone with my thoughts for a little while.

I sank into one of the big arm chairs in the big family room. The springs were loose and the fabric was worn, but it was still comfortable. The room was totally silent, and my mind wandered to my first encounter with Maggie. She was employed as a part-time receptionist at my old law firm. I had no idea that she even existed until she volunteered to help organize documents for my first trial. We worked so well together she became my paralegal, then my partner in our own law firm, always my best friend.

It wasn't long before she married my good friend and golfing buddy Walter Matthews. Our working arrangement had served us well so far, but it was time for it to evolve into something new or we ran the risk of losing it altogether.

It seemed that so much had changed, or was about to change, so quickly. A new house—Beth seemed determined to make that a reality. A new paralegal—Brian was bright, and so far had proved himself competent. Carol—I wondered if she was alone tonight or had sought solace with Eric Hartman. My grandmother would have said it didn't do to think about.

Had I really changed so much in three weeks that people

noticed? Had I changed so much before? Had the beach made the difference, or had it been the time spent with Jo?

It didn't matter. Jo was out of my life for the moment, and for the time being I needed to focus all my attention on Rachel. If my suspicions were correct, it shouldn't take long. I turned out the lights and walked toward my bedroom. There was no redhead waiting under the sheets, so I took a couple of Advil and went to sleep.

SUNDAY

57

I WOKE TO THE SOUNDS of Stella putting Brian, Big Mike, Martin, and a few of Martin's men through their paces outside my window. I threw on my sweats, not to join them, but to get a cup of coffee and watch from the porch. Clovis and Larry were already there, giving the guys various words of encouragement and grief. The men looked exhausted: Drill Sergeant Stella was clearly in her element.

"Why aren't you out there, Larry?" I asked, gesturing toward the workout.

He laughed, "I couldn't leave poor Clovis all alone. Micki, Beth, and Maggie are on a walk."

"How are the ribs?" I asked Clovis.

"Well, I can still feel them, that's for sure. But I'm moving better every day—Stella never cuts me an inch of slack. How about you? Still on that beach high?"

"I'd be lying if I didn't admit I'd rather be at the beach, but it's time to get to work. The sooner we do our jobs, the sooner we can get back to normal," I answered.

"Exactly what is normal in your world, Jack?" Larry asked.

"Good point," I laughed. "What are the plans for breakfast?"

Clovis looked pleased as punch. "I've got sausage and egg casserole cooking in the oven and sweet rolls in the warming drawer. Can you believe this place has a warming drawer? If you want healthy, Stella made a batch of vegetable smoothies."

"Sorry, but I never do green before lunch," Larry deadpanned. "Or after, for that matter."

Clovis laughed, and the three of us headed to the kitchen and dug into the savory casserole and sweet rolls. There are some benefits to not exercising.

Micki, Maggie, and Brian soon joined us, and after breakfast we cleaned up and gathered in the great room.

Micki began, "I've scheduled our first meeting with Rabbi Strauss at the Willard Hotel at eleven o'clock. He didn't seem surprised by my request and has reserved a conference room, which we can use as long as we need. After that, I thought you and I could revisit your vision for the press conference after the filing tomorrow."

"I understand why you're reluctant to hold a press conference, but we're trying to smoke out a few rats," I responded. "A press conference on the courthouse steps will surely get their attention." She didn't look convinced.

"Our next meeting is with Ken Chandler. Sucking up to the press hasn't been your style so far—what's up?"

"I'm not sucking up," I said, frowning. "Ken has an excellent reputation as an investigative reporter. And I believe he actually met Rachel. We need to be careful, but I have a hunch."

"You're the boss," Micki shrugged.

"No, Micki—that won't do. No bosses—we're partners. If you disagree with any part of my strategy, you need to speak up." She had far more experience with criminal cases than I, but we always had to have this conversation.

"I hear you, Jack. Just be sure to use the press, not get in bed with them. The *Post* is a bastion of the fourth estate, not some talk news host or Internet blogger who's satisfied with innuendo and fake news," Micki warned.

"And what if we're wrong? What if it turns out Rachel was a spy? What if she did commit suicide?" Her point was valid; we'd be way out on that limb.

"Micki, we need the press this time. Ken Chandler will keep us grounded. He'll ask reasonable questions and point out any flaws in our suppositions. Ken can ask questions we shouldn't, go where we can't. If it turns out to be a dead end, we go home and try to find other work."

She continued, without even a hint of a smile. "After we meet with Ken, we meet Mike and Brian at Rachel's apartment."

"You have the inventory—what's the point?" Maggie asked me.

"I only had an hour with her, under extremely difficult circumstances. After her husband was killed, she lived alone for over two years. I hope maybe her apartment can give me a better sense of who she was.

"The Rachel I interviewed at the military base didn't seem to be worried at all. She certainly didn't act depressed, but impressions can be wrong. Lawyers like to think they can represent anyone, but if you don't believe in your client, your doubt becomes evident in every action you take. I'd love to have you come with us, Maggie, but Clovis told me you had work to do here?"

"With the change in catering because of security issues, I need to figure out how to feed us, not to mention prepping all the paperwork for tomorrow morning. Beth wants me to meet with Susan Sandler after lunch, and," she smiled broadly, "the Redskins are playing the Panthers tonight in Landover. Someone needs to organize the watch party. No sense in this compound becoming all work and no play."

Micki shook her head in amazement and said, "Maggie, I don't know how on earth you manage to do so much in one day. You take multi-tasking to a new level, and I mean that as a compliment!"

With that, they all left to get started on the business of the day, so I wandered back into the kitchen to find Beth nursing another cup of coffee.

"Sleep well?" I asked.

"Not really. You know— first night away, plus I miss Jeff."

"Thanks for working with Susan. I'd take the first one she showed me just to avoid the hassle of shopping."

Beth scolded, "This isn't buying a golf shirt, Dad, and I can't choose a house for you."

I laughed and gave her a quick hug. "You should step into our discussions, too. Everyone values your opinion."

"So far I'm content to just listen. I am glad you hired Brian, and not for Maggie's sake alone. He's quiet, but I can tell he has good instincts."

"I'm glad he's on board, too. After today, I'll know if we're on the right track or if we should close up shop. My own instincts certainly aren't perfect. My love for Ben may have clouded my vision."

"There's nothing wrong with your instincts, except for women. When are you going to tell me about the new girlfriend in Pawleys? It's only about an hour from Charleston. Maybe I could meet her for lunch?" she teased.

Beth lunching with Jo? No thanks.

Micki rescued me. "You ready to roll?"

I grabbed a jacket and was about to jump into the back seat of the Jeep when I noticed shoulder-length blond hair and hesitated.

She turned, handed me her ID, and said, "My name is Lisa Eckenrod, I work for Martin, and I'll be your driver this week." Her tone was pleasant, but no-nonsense, and we were soon off. I tried to quell a nagging feeling that I'd forgotten something or left something undone. It was as if I was searching for a golf ball in the woods, while it was lying in the fairway. Maybe my subconscious just needed a round of golf.

58

THE WILLARD HOTEL has hosted almost every U.S. president since Franklin Pierce. Notable guests have included Charles Dickens, Buffalo Bill, P.T. Barnum, Martin Luther King, and countless others. People sit in the lobby just to see who walks through. I wondered idly why Rabbi Strauss had chosen to stay in such a public place.

Sure enough, we found him seated in a very visible chair in the lobby, calmly reading the *Post*. We all shook hands, and he escorted us to a small conference room equipped with a pot of fresh coffee, hot water, and an assortment of teas and soft drinks. Stella had warned me that our conversation would likely be monitored and videoed.

Rabbi Strauss waited until we were all comfortably seated. He got right to the business at hand. "Let me begin with Ms. Lawrence's request for information about the man who observed us at the bar in the Armitage. He does not appear in any of our databases, which is most unusual. We are trying to ascertain his identity; the fact that he observed us is of concern. Should we learn his identity we will share that information."

Not a single unnecessary word—this conversation could be like pulling teeth.

"I take it he does not work for any of the Israeli government's intelligence agencies or the military?" I asked.

"Most assuredly not," he replied with a frown.

"Well, you can report that the same man not only followed me to St. Louis, but also attended Rachel Goodman's funeral."

"That is indeed interesting, and I'm sure most disturbing to you," he replied in the same stilted language.

"Most disturbing, but let's move on. What can you tell me about Ira Goodman, Rachel's husband?"

He finally relaxed a bit. "You are perceptive, Mr. Patterson. Do you know the word Tzaddik?"

"I believe it means 'righteous one,' a very spiritual man. It is identified with Hasidism. Ira wasn't Hasidic, was he?" I asked.

"No, but had he lived, he would have been a Tzaddik for millions of Jews, especially those living in Israel. He worked tirelessly to bring peace to that region, and through his thoughtful intelligence and charisma was able to accomplish a great deal. Israel lost one of its brightest lights when he died."

"Was he employed by the Israeli government?"

He pursed his lips and thought for a minute, "Before I answer your question, I'd like to know why you ask."

I'd clearly struck a nerve, and I didn't want to piss him off. I needed information. I decided it was time to give him a little.

"Rabbi, Micki and I represent the estate of Rachel Goodman. In that capacity, we must locate all sources of income she might have had. I have a hunch that Rabbi Goodman received money from the Israeli government. The discovery of deposits from the Israeli government led the Feds to believe that Rachel was a spy for Israel. I believe they later discovered the truth, yet chose to leak the story that she had been paid by Israel. That story gave them cover to prevent the media from discovering the real reason Rachel had chosen to download military secrets." He said nothing, and I decided to push.

"Well?" I asked.

"You live up to your reputation, Mr. Patterson," Strauss smiled. I waited patiently while he added some raw sugar to his coffee and took a careful sip. Having gathered his thoughts, he finally responded.

"Rabbi Goodman received what you might call a salary from a branch of Israeli intelligence. As the widow of a man who died in the service of Israel, Rachel received a widow's pension as well as payment on a life insurance policy. Those deposits into her bank account did indeed prompt inquiries by your State Department. The

Israeli government answered these inquiries to the government's satisfaction, but was asked not to disclose the existence or nature of these payments. In a spirit of cooperation, Israel agreed to your government's request."

"Do you know the monthly amount, the amount of life insurance, and the bank's name?" Micki inquired.

"The life insurance payment was for two hundred thousand dollars. Her pension amount was four thousand dollars per month. I apologize, I do not know the name of the bank." Turning to me, he asked, "Won't your government give you this information?"

"Under normal circumstances, yes, it would. But this case is sensitive, to say the least. Can you please find out the name of the bank? Did she receive any other benefits?"

"The bank's name should not be a problem. I am not aware of any other benefits she received," he answered.

Micki continued, "Who will receive the pension payments now that his wife has died?"

Strauss answered, "They will probably end, since they had no children. I will confirm that supposition as well."

"Please. Did you speak with Rachel after her husband's death?" I asked.

"Unfortunately, no, not substantively. I tried, but after she returned from Israel she kept to herself. I always called when I was in town, but she begged off meeting for a drink or dinner." He shrugged his shoulders.

"Did she ever tell you she thought her husband had been murdered?" Micki asked bluntly.

"No, she did not. But a rocket fired into a café by Hamas killed him. If that's not murder, I don't know what is."

"What type of rocket?" I asked.

He looked uncomfortable again. "I don't think I'm at liberty to answer that question. What difference does it make?"

I wondered how much I should tell him. I decided to light the first match.

"It could make a great deal of difference. I understand that Israel may not want to divulge that information. Perhaps you could check

with your sources?" This conversation was beginning to remind me
of my occasional conversations with Novak.

He seemed to think about it, but didn't respond.

"Rabbi, you admired and respected Ira Goodman. What did you
think of Rachel? I understand that Ira's family did not approve of
the marriage."

"Ira's family was wrong about Rachel. Their son loved her very
much, and she him. He considered her a partner—she comple-
mented the work he did to bring peace to Israel and the Middle East.
She was also a superb student who understood both the historical
and contemporary basis of the regional conflict." He hesitated just
a little before continuing.

"She was sincere in her conversion to Judaism. When they came
to Little Rock she sat in on meetings I had with Ira about issues of
faith. I found her to be as articulate and intelligent as her husband."

He glanced at his watch, and I realized it was time for us to leave.
I tried one more question.

"Rabbi, is the Israeli government conducting its own investigation
into Rachel's death?"

"Why… why should it? According to the papers, she committed
suicide." His surprise was authentic.

"Doesn't Israel find it troubling that Rabbi Goodman was killed by
a rocket attack? That his wife was accused of spying for Israel, which
your government knows is untrue? Finally, that Rachel committed
suicide the day she hired a lawyer and was eager to explain her
innocence? If I were in your government's shoes, I'd be concerned
that these two deaths were not a coincidence. Did you ever once
consider that Rachel could be a spy? Did you ever imagine that she
would commit suicide?"

He sat in stony silence, but I wasn't about to let him off the hook.

"Tell me, Rabbi, do you believe Rachel was a spy?"

He sighed, "No, Mr. Patterson, Rachel was not a spy."

"Then I'll ask again. If the Israeli government isn't willing to
carry out its own investigation, why hasn't it asked the U.S. government to undertake one? You told me that Rebbe Goodman was one
of Israel's brightest lights and that Rachel was his partner as well as

his wife. Why would the Israeli government allow these two murders to be swept under the rug?"

I hoped the people listening in on the microphone heard my message.

Clearly shaken, Rabbi Strauss responded, "That, I cannot tell you. When Rachel committed suicide, as we were led to believe, I assumed that any interest in their deaths would be over, forgotten."

"No, Rabbi, nothing is over. It is just the beginning."

Blinking back honest tears, he pushed back his chair and quickly left the room.

59

I WAS STARVING, so Micki and I walked around the corner to the Old Ebbitt Grill across from the Treasury building. We spent a little time talking over the Strauss interview, agreeing that we had definitely lit a flame. Over coffee we turned to what Micki might expect at tomorrow's press conference.

"They'll push you on the suicide being proof of guilt. Without giving away the farm, we have to hold to our story that the government hasn't satisfied the family that her death was suicide. The government has to prove the money was the fruit of her illegal activity, and since we contend she was innocent, the government must meet its burden of proof or has to turn her assets back to the family."

"I'm more worried that now we look greedy. You know, 'Shouldn't the family be mourning rather than trying to retrieve her bank accounts?'" Her reproachful tone was right on the mark.

"What's your comeback?" I asked.

"I knew you'd ask," she snapped. "Why don't you cut me some slack and suggest an answer?"

"Micki, the answer has to sound sincere, as if the question is catching you unprepared, and it must be in your voice."

"Okay." She thought for a few seconds before responding. "I'll say the questioner is right. This is a time to grieve, but the government froze her assets before she had any chance to plead not guilty to the charges. Their precipitous action forced the family to hire a lawyer to try to block their money grab before time ran out."

I laughed, "No more preparation. You'll do great. Let's pay

the bill and walk back to the office. We should have plenty of time before Ken arrives."

I was wrong. He was pacing back and forth outside my office. I apologized and said I hoped he hadn't been waiting long. After unlocking the doors and turning off the security, I went to make a pot of coffee while Micki tried to put him at ease in the conference room.

While the coffee was brewing, we played the game of who do you know, idle chat before combat began. Micki brought in the coffee and cups, and we began.

"Tell me, Ken, was Rachel a spy?"

After he had recovered, he said, "I'm used to asking the questions."

I responded, "Right, but I'm the person who asked for the meeting, so we play by my rules."

"Which are?" he asked without a blink.

"First, when I preface a subject or sentence with 'off the record,' and you don't object, then it's off the record. If you object, we'll discuss it. Second, I expect you to be candid with me, and I will be candid with you. You are sitting on a big story, but you need me, and I need you. Third, if you tell either Micki or me something in confidence, it will never leave the room without your permission."

"Sounds fair enough."

"So I ask again: Was Rachel a spy?"

"What does it matter? After all, she's dead," he answered, clearly uninterested.

"Well, if that's what you think, we have nothing to discuss. Good day, Mr. Chandler." Disappointed, I rose to see him out, but he caught my sleeve.

"Not so fast, Patterson. My turn: Why do you think it matters?" he asked. He remained seated, so I returned to my chair.

"Okay, I'll tell you why. Tomorrow morning, Ms. Lawrence is going into federal court to object to the government's seizure of Rachel's assets. The government has two choices: they can release her assets, thus tacitly admitting that Rachel was innocent, or they can fight us, claiming the seizure was proper because she committed espionage. That gives us a forum to prove she wasn't guilty.

"I'm looking for a friend in the press who will do his or her own honest investigative reporting, but will give our effort credibility to those who will try to write us off as greedy lawyers or publicity hounds."

"So you want me to be your shill," he said flatly.

"No, not a shill. Just a reporter who's willing to keep an open mind. But don't worry, you're off the hook; it won't work. I thought you might have met Rachel, or have doubts about her guilt. No harm, and I wish you the best." I watched him weigh what I had said, unsure how to proceed.

"Under your rules, I could report the substance of this meeting in tomorrow's *Post*, blow your strategy wide open."

"You could, but you won't," I said.

"And why is that?"

I was ready to end the cat and mouse routine.

"Because you did speak with Rachel, more than once, before her death. When I'm able to verify this, I will use the facts to make you look like—you used the word—a 'shill,' for the government.

"Ken, this story could win you the Pulitzer, but I can't help you if you believe Rachel was a spy. I won't ask what she told you; I'm content to read about it in the *Post* someday. But I won't travel the road with you unless you work with me. Did you meet with Rachel?"

Ken was on the spot. He couldn't very well call his editor, he had to act on his instincts. He sat quietly for a few minutes; neither Micki nor I filled the silence.

"Off the record?" he asked.

"We will never use what you tell us without your permission."

"Rachel wasn't a spy any more than you are, and I have sincere doubts about her suicide. Rachel contacted me over six months ago. She was very cautious, obviously concerned about confidentiality. She talked in hypotheticals. What if this and could this—asking about defense contractors, arms dealers, and government programs that had failed. She was as smart as a whip, obviously knew a lot already, and gave me almost nothing. I was hesitant to say much, so it was a slow dance. We had just begun to establish a degree of trust when the government took her into custody."

"Any specific contractor or program?" I asked.

"No, I tried to probe, but she would have none of it."

Micki asked, "Did she give you any idea what she had uncovered?"

"She was very careful. My impression was that she had unearthed evidence of a government contractor defrauding the government, and she was sure that her superiors either didn't want to know or were party to it. But that's only an assumption. I can't begin to tell you how careful she was. Our meetings were random, and she always chose where and when."

Micki asked, "Why you? No offense."

He blushed. "Good question. I was working on the international desk when her husband died. I wrote an article about him that she liked. At least that's the reason she gave me."

"One of our sources refers to Ira Goodman as 'a shining light.'"

"That's not the half of it. I'll send you what I wrote, not what the *Post* published. I'm not exaggerating when I say that if Ira Goodman had lived, the situation in Palestine would be much different today."

"Okay, so now that we've got the lay of the land, how do we move forward? Can we expect you at Micki's press conference tomorrow? It would be helpful if you brought a few friends." I smiled, ready to cement the partnership.

"I wouldn't miss her press conference for the world, and I promise you that when other reporters hear I'm going, they'll be there. We're like a children's soccer game. We congregate wherever the ball is. What can you can give me today?" he asked.

"Off the record?"

"You can be sure my senior editor is the only other person who will know."

"Rachel received a widow's pension and life insurance payment from Israel after her husband's death. When our government discovered the money wasn't payment for secrets, they asked Israel to keep that information quiet." I repeated what we had learned from Rabbi Strauss.

"Holy shit! Can you verify that?" I finally had his attention.

"Our source is impeccable, and when we find her bank records we'll be able prove it," I answered.

"A Pentagon source told me she was receiving large sums from Israel in exchange for intelligence. If he was deceiving me, the game has changed." His voice took on an angry tone. "When my editor hears this, he'll be all over this story."

"As I said, my source is excellent, but we haven't found the records yet. I'll get the information to you as soon as I can. At the right time, you'll be able to publish the government's lies in bold print."

He was excited, but I had to make sure he understood the danger.

"Ken, we both need to be careful. Either Micki or I will text you with the time and place when we need to meet. You're not to share that information with anyone. And you should have your phone checked out by an expert. At Micki's press conference, you are free to ask her whatever you want. Just don't put her in a spot based on information we've fed you."

"Deal," he said.

"I hope the paper provides you protection," I said.

He raised his eyebrows. "No one goes after a member of the press."

I looked at him for a long time before speaking. "Ira and Rachel Goodman are dead, my good friend and bodyguard was almost burned alive, and I have been followed every day since I took Rachel's case. Don't underestimate the people involved. The minute they find out you've been talking with me, you will be at risk."

I hoped I had disabused him of the notion that reporters in the United States are immune from danger.

This time we both rose, and he walked out the door in silence, looking a little less cocky than when he had arrived.

"You scared the shit out of him," Micki said, with a rueful laugh.

"I meant to," I answered. "We are counting on the legitimacy of the press to further our theory. Our opponents are no dummies. They will realize the same thing."

Micki nodded and asked, "Are you okay? Maggie says this case feels different, that you're worried we'll all be in danger again. I haven't been involved enough yet to know."

"I'm okay, but she's darn right I'm worried. I haven't been able to sleep for the last couple of nights. Don't you feel it?"

"No. Larry and I have sex, and I sleep like a baby." She laughed and poked me in the ribs. "Come on, let's go to Rachel's apartment. Who knows? We might find the very clue that breaks open this whole case."

"Do I have to hear about Larry and you in bed?" I poked back, remembering how well I had slept at Pawleys.

60

BRIAN AND MIKE were waiting for us when we arrived at Rachel's building. Her apartment was in one of those cool mid-century buildings where you walked either up or down a floor from a small landing to a large space with two-story ceilings and a killer view. Her bedroom and bath were off the main room, as were the kitchen and dining area.

The furnishings were spare and contemporary, a style totally different from her parents'. Good for her. A small study contained shelves crammed with books and a desk that had once hosted a computer. Brian and Big Mike had conducted an inventory and a thorough search of the books.

Micki volunteered, "I'll go through her drawers and clothes closet. My mother's biggest fear was that after she died, a stranger would go through her underwear drawer. She made me promise I'd get there first and throw it all away."

"Thanks, Micki. But before you get started let me just walk around the apartment for a few minutes."

"Go ahead, I'll read a magazine," she said with a smirk, sinking into an oversized sofa.

I wandered through each room, opened every closet, trying to imagine Rachel's life here, trying to get the sense of the woman herself. The study was full of scholarly works; a few appeared to be in Hebrew. I found a library copy of the latest Louise Penny mystery on her bedside table. I flipped through it, recognizing the familiar characters, and made a mental note to get a list of the books she had checked out from the library over the last couple of years.

I opened the fridge and realized it hadn't been cleaned since the day of her arrest. I found a trash bag under the sink and began tossing spoiled food, just about everything except the condiments.

I opened the freezer and called out to Brian and Mike. "Hey, you guys want a bowl of ice cream? She's got a pint of Ben & Jerry's Chunky Monkey."

Brian and Mike came running into the kitchen.

"It's been here quite a while—are you that hungry?"

Brian put on plastic gloves and said, "It's not that I'm hungry. I can't believe I overlooked the freezer when we did the inventory."

"What are you talking about? There's not much in here—Bagel Bites, frozen veggie burgers, and a pint of ice cream."

Brian took the ice cream from me, worked the frozen container open, and put the contents in a plastic storage bag which he placed in a large bowl. He put the bowl in the sink and ran hot water over the plastic bag.

"What are you doing? Why ruin the ice cream?" I asked, bewildered by his actions.

Hearing the commotion Micki rushed into the kitchen.

"I love Chunky Monkey—what are you doing?" Micki cried.

"Softening it up," Brian stated the obvious.

"It will melt faster if you put it in the microwave," I offered.

Brian laughed, "A Captain I knew did just that. He fried the zip drive."

"What on earth? What zip drive?" I stopped, suddenly getting the picture.

Brian opened the bag, dug a spoon into the ice cream, and pulled out a zip drive wrapped in plastic wrap that had been hidden in the middle of a pint of now melting Chunky Monkey.

"This zip drive. If I had put the ice cream in the microwave, we might have lost every bit of its data." He held up the small device with a grin. "What should I do with it?"

I didn't want to admit it, but I was stunned.

"Make sure it's secure and Micki and I will get it to Stella right away. I don't think we need to turn it over to the government yet.

Now tell me what made you look in the ice cream."

Brian answered, "Israeli intelligence has been known to hide valuable items in frozen foods. I bet Rachel chose Chunky Monkey because of the attention it might draw. She hoped Israeli intelligence would search her apartment if something were to happen to her."

"Smart girl. No telling what's on it," I said.

Micki looked concerned. "I don't like this. If we discover Rachel put military secrets on that drive, shouldn't we turn it over to the government sooner rather than later?"

"I understand your concern, Micki. But you're assuming that Rachel put that zip drive in the ice cream. What if Israeli intelligence put the ice cream in her freezer? What if the FBI planted it? That's happened to us before," I reminded her.

Brian intervened, "I doubt it was the FBI. The different intelligence agencies don't share information. And I can't imagine the Israelis sharing their techniques with anyone. I only learned about it by accident."

"Well, if Rachel kept her father's recipe for barbeque sauce in her ice cream, we're going to have a good laugh. Let's get this zip drive to Stella before the ball game starts." I was suddenly anxious to leave.

Micki and I found Lisa waiting outside and were soon on our way back to Maryland. We had just exited the Beltway onto Highway 50, when Mike called. "You have company. They probably trailed you from the office to Rachel's. Let me speak to Lisa. We've got your back, but I want her to lose him before we get to the compound."

"Okay, but tell Martin to keep an eye on Rachel's apartment tonight."

"Done. We'll be ready."

Micki squeezed my hand and said, "I hope you know what we're doing."

"And I hope you don't get carsick," I whispered in return.

61

THANKFULLY, Lisa lost our tail after a few easy turns—for whatever reason, he'd clearly lost interest. It was a relief to turn into the long drive of Maggie's new home. I found Stella at her computer tweaking the electronic security system. I tossed her the zip drive, remarking that Brian had found it in a pint of ice cream. She laughed and turned the still sticky plastic over a few times before responding.

"Jack, I know you are excited, but this zip drive may contain a virus or worse. It will take at least an hour to check it out before I can tell you what's on it."

That was okay with me. I'd remembered what had been nagging at me earlier. I pulled out my laptop and composed an email to Joan Laing with a copy to Peggy Fortson. It read:

> Joan, please check out the van that took us to the military base. You
> may find a tracking device attached to its underside. If it's still there,
> can you let me know the manufacturer? Jack P.

Maggie came up behind me. "Are you sure that's wise?" she asked.

"Elvis has left the building," I replied with cocky, uplifted arms. I followed with a full report on our day: Strauss, Chandler, and finding the zip drive.

"Zip drives in the ice cream," she laughed. "You sure it wasn't in a box of Cracker Jacks? When do you think Stella will finish?"

Micki and Larry walked in just ahead of Stella. We turned in unison, waiting for her to speak.

"The good news is the drive doesn't contain a virus," she said.

I couldn't contain myself, "Great, but what's the bad news. Don't tell me there's nothing on it."

"Calm down—there's plenty of data on it, but it's encrypted. If I had access to the NSA's computer, I could break her code in a few minutes, but since that's not an option, it will take a good while. I assume the government won't give us her computer, so I'll have to go after it the old-fashioned way. My guess is it will take me at least twenty-four hours."

We were all disappointed; the delay was a real downer. I tried to recover. "Stella's report is a hidden gift. Until we find out what's on the drive, we don't have to give it to the government. We can go forward with our plans without distraction. If we had to turn over the drive now, and if it contained military secrets, the game would be over in short order."

There was one other bit of good news. Brian had helped fix the holes in the security system. That also meant no caterer, so Maggie and Martin had decided to bring in a cook to join our team. I wondered where she would put him, but she didn't seem worried, so I let it go. Martin told me that Larry had suggested moving several electronic outposts. Now the outposts were almost invisible.

I was startled by the sound of my phone chirping, but not by the number I saw calling. "Peggy, I bet you aren't calling for brunch. It's dinner time."

"The possibility of us ever having brunch again is getting more remote by the day. What in the hell did your email mean?" Peggy Fortson was not in a good mood.

"No more than it stated. I asked Joan to check the van that drove us to the military base for a tracking device."

"What does it matter? Rachel committed suicide, case closed."

Should I let the cat out of the bag? I'd been doing so all day. Besides, I would need Peggy's support before long.

"You're right—there is no criminal case, but the government's seizure of her assets is still pending. We will file our objections to the asset forfeiture tomorrow morning."

"I told the Attorney General you wouldn't quit. You want to know what he said?" she asked.

"I'm all ears."

"He said, 'good.' Now how in the hell am I supposed to know what that means? Your email will have to go to the intelligence working group of which I'm not a part."

"That's okay. I copied you as a matter of courtesy. I was simply asking Joan to check out the van."

"Sure you were." Her voice rose unpleasantly. "Well, here's some more news for you. Joan is no longer involved in this case. The entire matter has been sent to intelligence to try to prevent this sort of theft from happening again."

"You mean there will be no further investigation into her death, no determination of her guilt?" I already knew the answer.

"Correct. Her death was a suicide, and the investigation into the alleged espionage is being handled by the affected agencies." I detected a note of melancholy in Peggy's voice.

"Peggy, do yourself and the AG a favor—check out the van. I'm convinced a tracking device was placed underneath the van before we left Alexandria for the military base."

"Let it go, Jack. There is no forum where you can litigate her guilt or innocence. Nor is there any way you can convince the military to investigate Rachel's death."

"You're wrong Peggy. Tomorrow we file objections to the seizure. If the government wants her assets, they must prove her guilt, and I will fight them with everything I've got."

"Jack, calm down. I'm sure the U.S. Attorney's office will propose a reasonable settlement. Don't blow this out of proportion, okay?"

I took a deep breath. She had always been a good friend; it wasn't fair for me to take out my frustrations on her.

"Peggy, I apologize, but I'm emotional about Rachel's death. I fear my interview led her killers right to her, and my willingness to defend her necessitated her murder. I'm willing to bet that if you speak with Joan, she feels the same way. She was with me for that interview. If you remember, neither the recordings nor the agent's notes have been found. Or if they have, no one's told me. I know she will confirm that Rachel wasn't depressed."

Peggy took a second before answering, "Jack, you haven't asked, but my advice is don't let any misguided guilt over Rachel's suicide consume you. You didn't cause it, and you couldn't have prevented it. Settle the forfeiture case and go back to practicing antitrust law. You are out of your element."

She was giving me good advice, but I'd already gone too far.

"Maybe so, and thanks for the advice. But, Peggy, do us all a favor—check the underside of that van before someone beats you to it. Here's another thing you are free to convey to the intelligence community."

"What now, Jack?" she sighed in frustration.

"I'm not settling, no how and no way. They either fold their tents and go home, or we go to trial."

MONDAY

62

THAT EVENING, while Stella worked to decode the encrypted files, the rest of us had watched the Carolina Panthers destroy the Redskins. Luke Kuechly was a beast on defense with fourteen solo tackles, two sacks, and one interception. This morning we would file our objections to the seizure, and Micki would hold a press conference. We had agreed that Micki should take the lead in the civil litigation, mainly because I had been one of the last persons to see Rachel alive. Her state of mind could become an issue, and if the government responded the way we expected, I could be called as a witness.

Over breakfast we talked about the issues that had come up yesterday.

"Until we get their inventory, don't mention the money from Israel," I said.

She smiled. "Don't worry. My biggest worry now is your reporter friend. What if he doesn't keep his promises?"

"Then you'll handle it. I have every confidence in you. Ken won't pull any punches. He'll act as if he's never met you and ask you tough questions, but he won't betray our confidence. I'm not worried."

The press conference was to take place immediately after the court filing, around ten-thirty or eleven. We'd made several calls to the local DC news outlets last night to give them a heads-up, but had no way of knowing if any of them would be there. Rachel's story was already becoming old news.

I cleaned up the breakfast dishes and decided to check on Stella. She had worked late into the night, but I'd noticed her outside before breakfast, giving anyone willing a morning workout. She was now seated at her computer, drinking her green concoction, which she told me included kale, collards, and other stuff that was good for me.

"Try it, Jack. It has a good flavor," she offered.

"No thanks—I have real trouble drinking anything green."

"You sure? It will flush out all the impurities in your body and pump you full of vitamins," she urged.

"How's the decoding coming?" I asked, choosing to keep my impurities.

"More slowly than I expected, but I made good progress last night. Either Rachel was super smart, or she had help with this. Any chance your source in Israel knows how to break this code?"

"Maybe, but we can't afford to let a soul know we have this. If they did, we'd have helicopters landing on the front lawn in a matter of minutes. Did you back up the drive before you started working on it?"

She gave me a sidelong glare. "I forget that what I do is foreign to you. Of course I did. I've made two back-ups, in case I make a mistake and fry the drive. I'm now working off a copy. The original is secure. Now, go away, if you don't mind. I work better with no distractions."

I did just that, wandering back into to the family room. While we waited to hear from Micki and Brian, I called Ben to give him an update and to remind Paul that the local press might descend on Ben's house when news of the filing hit. Clovis and I were talking football when my phone rang.

Red was direct. "Well, Jack, if it was your intention to stir up a hornet's nest, you've succeeded. Word's out that your associate is at the courthouse filing objections to the asset forfeiture. Several high-powered lobbyists ambushed Lucy outside her office this morning demanding that she denounce your obvious perversion of justice and demand an investigation. They insisted that the government was right to claim any monies Rachel received as a result of her treasonous activities. It wasn't a chance encounter."

I could have told them that demands weren't the way to Lucy's heart.

"I wish I could have been a fly on the wall," Red continued. "She said, 'Thank you very much, but I'm late for a meeting with the delegation from the Arkansas garden clubs over their concerns with the Department of the Interior. My assistant will be glad to take note of your concerns.' Can you imagine?" he chortled.

"She said the look on their faces when she mentioned the Arkansas garden clubs was worth the money she lost in campaign contributions. I do love that woman."

"She should know they'll find another senator to take up their cause," I warned.

"That's the good part. The lobbyists have been working both sides of the aisle, trying to stir up bipartisan indignation. Hasn't worked so far. Lucy hasn't shown much interest, and other senators worry she might know something they don't."

His laughter quickly faded when I asked, "Okay, Red, what else have you heard?"

"Our friendship and business ties are well known, so for the most part my sources in the military community have dried up. But what I hear is that no one understands why the government is pushing the asset forfeiture or why you continue to pursue the matter. My bet is the government will settle."

"Oh, they'll try," I answered.

"Son of a bitch, I'm glad you're representing me and not my competition. You be careful, Jack. This thing feels like it could get out of control."

"Red, we're doing the best we can, and I'll let you know whatever I can. If you get a chance, catch Micki's press conference."

"I'll do that," he said, abruptly ending the call.

I'd barely put the phone down when Brian called.

"We filed the motion without a lot of hoopla, but were met by none other than U.S. Attorney Cotton before we could leave. He sucked up to Micki for a couple of minutes, asked if they could meet in private. I wish you could have heard her. She looked him up and down and said she didn't meet in private with any man who wasn't her lover.

"Cotton about wet his pants, but managed to convince Micki to meet with him and Carl Clifford, the head of their Civil Forfeiture Division, in an empty conference room down the hall. Cotton said I could sit in, despite my lack of a security clearance."

"What a jerk, you don't need a security clearance to talk about asset forfeiture. What did they want?"

"They wanted to talk settlement. They offered to exchange Rachel's account at the credit union, for the estate's claim to her Pentagon pension. Micki didn't budge an inch. 'There will be no settlement until we have a full inventory of seized assets, and we expect to receive that inventory post haste or we'll file a motion with the court.'" His tone was perfect mimic of Micki's.

"No mention of her widow's pension or the life insurance proceeds from Israel?" I asked.

"Not a word," he confirmed.

"You can give me a full report this afternoon, but were there any surprises?"

"They asked Micki to hold a joint press conference with them to confirm that the filing was a formality. She was almost polite, but basically told Cotton where he could shove it. Then she asked him to release Rachel's cell phone, computer, and her personal effects 'as a demonstration of goodwill.' Cotton's face turned beet red, and Deputy Clifford's mouth dropped open."

"What was that about?" I asked.

"I'm not sure, but they all agreed to keep the lines of communication open and got up to leave. Cotton sort of shoved his way past Micki and ran down the steps to the podium, Clifford in tow. Micki just laughed, told me not to worry, she'd have her turn. The press is here waiting, and I can see a couple of satellite trucks."

"Thanks, we'll try to find it on TV," I said motioning to Maggie. "If we can't find a local station covering it, I may call you back for a play-by-play."

Maggie, of course, went directly to the right station.

Their off-screen reporter had just begun to speak: "We are coming to you live from the Federal Courthouse in Alexandria, where U.S. Attorney Donald J. Cotton is answering questions raised today in a court filing by the estate of Rachel Goodman. Her estate asks the court to set aside the government's seizure and to return the assets she gained as part of her illegal activities to her estate. We go live."

I muttered, "Illegal activities—what does that guy know?"

Maggie shushed me, and I heard Cotton say, "We are disappointed at this attempt by Mrs. Goodman's lawyers to pervert justice in a greedy attempt to obtain monies that are the fruits of her criminal activity. But in order to put this chapter in our country's history behind us, our office will look for ways to resolve this matter quickly and fairly."

"How much money is involved?" a reporter called out.

Cotton responded, "If we can't reach an agreement, the government will file a complete inventory in a few days."

Hmmm... he clearly didn't want to file a public inventory.

Cotton continued, "Next question."

"Ken Chandler, *Washington Post*. Mr. Cotton, what happens if there isn't a settlement? Are you prepared to prove that Ms. Goodman committed espionage, which I believe is a prerequisite to your right to seize her assets?"

Cotton looked to Clifford, obviously unprepared for the question. He'd figured the entire press corps would buy his bull. "If it comes to that, we are prepared to prove her crimes by a preponderance of the evidence. But I say again, let's hope for the sake of the country we won't have to air this dirty laundry. Our intelligence community is working hard to remedy the holes in our national security exposed by her activities.

"But let me be clear. My office will consider settling this civil matter only because Mrs. Goodman is dead, and our county is better served by giving her estate a few dollars to protect our national security. Had Mrs. Goodman not taken her own life, our office was fully prepared to prove her guilt and would have sought the death penalty."

"Son-of-a-bitch," I muttered.

Cotton had turned away from the microphone when Ken Chandler followed with, "What if Mrs. Goodman didn't commit suicide?"

He turned back with a bored sigh. "Mrs. Goodman's death was a suicide. Virginia's Office of the Medical Examiner reached that conclusion, and there's no evidence to think otherwise." Without another word Cotton and his entourage hurried back into the courthouse.

We had to put up with a few minutes of comment and an eternity of commercials before the camera returned to Micki stepping up to the podium. I know I'm prejudiced, but she looked fantastic in a navy jacket and slim skirt. She was already taller than Cotton, even more so in heels. I laughed as she took her time adjusting the microphone.

She nodded to the reporters. "Thank you. Y'all don't know me, but if you check with the reporters back home, they'll tell you I don't normally hold press conferences. First, let me thank Mr. Cotton for his opening remarks—saved me the explanation." She waited for the laughter to die down.

"So now that you've heard his opinion, let me try to give you a different perspective. Questions?" Micki's southern accent was deliberately thick, and achieved the desired effect.

"Ken Chandler, *Washington Post.* Ms. Lawrence, the U.S. Attorney has described your objections to the government's seizure of Mrs. Goodman's assets as a greedy attempt to grab monies that are the fruits of her illegal conduct. Any comment?"

Micki paused to give a slow smile before responding.

"Well, Mr. Chandler, I guess my reaction is that Mrs. Goodman's estate has never grabbed anything. The federal government seized Rachel's bank and brokerage accounts even though she was never charged with a crime. The family believes that if she were alive, she'd fight the government's money grab, so we will do so on her behalf."

The same reporter who had asked Cotton how much money was in play repeated his question, "How much money is involved?"

Micki smiled again. "Fair question, but I can't give you a good answer. As of yet the family hasn't received an inventory of exactly what the government seized. We know for sure she had a bank account, a car, a computer, and a few personal effects, including her wedding and engagement rings, but your guess about how much we're talking about is as good as mine."

Linda had complained that Rachel's body had been returned to Little Rock without her rings. I was sure they were in a personal effects locker somewhere, but it didn't hurt to imply that the government had taken her wedding rings.

A young woman called out, "Mr. Cotton intimated that the government wants to resolve the civil forfeiture case. Are settlement negotiations ongoing?"

This was a tougher question.

"I've told Mr. Cotton that once we receive an inventory and determine that it's complete and accurate, we're more than willing to discuss a settlement. I asked him earlier today to return Mrs. Goodman's wedding rings, computer, and other personal effects as a show of good faith. Surely the engagement ring and wedding band given to her by her late husband weren't the fruit of any crime.

"But to repeat Mr. Cotton's words, let me be clear: the government has produced no evidence of criminal wrongdoing. Rachel is and always will be innocent. We're not asking the government to give the family something Rachel owed her employer or that belonged to the government. We only ask that the government return to the estate what once belonged to Rachel Goodman."

From my perspective, Micki hit that one out of the park. She got in another dig over the rings, told the press we wanted her computer and cellphone as well, and she had laid down the gauntlet by asserting the case was about innocence, not money.

It was Ken Chandler's turn to make Micki uncomfortable.

"Ms. Lawrence—same question I asked Mr. Cotton. What if Mrs. Goodman's death wasn't a suicide? And as a follow-up, what happens if a settlement isn't reached over her assets?"

By now the other reporters were sensing more of a story. I saw a few more cellphones and recorders emerge from pockets.

"Your first question is difficult for me to answer. At this point, Rachel's family doesn't believe she committed suicide; neither does her legal team. There are just too many unanswered questions.

"And if Rachel was indeed murdered, then it is incumbent on the press, the authorities, and Congress to do everything possible to find and apprehend her murderer. I know Mrs. Goodman's legal team will do everything in its power to discover who was behind such a tragedy.

"You also asked what will happen if the government doesn't settle." She looked at Ken, and he nodded his head in agreement.

"Well, that's easy. We go to court and litigate the issues of whether Rachel committed a crime and whether any of her assets resulted from criminal activity. The burden of proof lies with the government. In the course of this litigation and with the subpoena power the case gives us, we will discover the truth behind a heartbreaking story. We believe our government arrested a fine young woman and wrongly accused her of committing crimes against her country, and that she was killed to prevent her exposing separate criminal conduct."

You could hear a pin drop in the family room, but not at the courthouse steps. The reporters were throwing out question after question, and finally Micki raised her hand and smiled. "I'm sorry, I told y'all I'm not any good at this. No more questions for now. The next time we meet I hope to tell you that Mr. Cotton has agreed to return Rachel's wedding rings and her other assets to her family. Thank you for coming."

I waited a few minutes before I called Brian.

"Are you in the car yet?" I asked.

"Getting in right now," he answered. "Just let me get the doors closed. Here she is."

"Fantastic!" I said, forgetting about hello. "You are our permanent spokesperson from now on."

"Oh, no you don't. I almost peed in my pants. You don't think I went too far?"

"You got out there, but that's what we wanted. I love how you reminded them of the wedding rings. I bet Cotton didn't have a clue."

"I'm not so sure. I might have forced them up against a wall. Cotton may think he has no choice but to litigate."

"You wait. I'll bet they've already been told to settle and are trying to figure out how to save face."

"Well, I've done my bit for now. As soon as I get back, I'm going to put on some jeans and ride one of Maggie's horses 'til we're both worn out. I need some fresh air. What about you?"

"I'm about to turn up the heat. Delay and time is on their side. We have to increase the pressure and hope the bad guys make a mistake."

"Either that or they put a stop to both of us," she said.

"Yeah, that's certainly a possibility." A chill went up my spine.

63

As soon as the press conference was over, Maggie and Beth left to meet with Susan Sandler. I appreciated their efforts, but my brain was too full to think about house hunting today. Sitting alone in the family room, I mulled over Cotton's comments, trying to anticipate how the government might react. One worry kept niggling at me, so I called Matt and Lauren, Micki's interns, to ask them to help with some research. The few minutes of silence felt good—I knew they wouldn't last. Sure enough, the first caller was Red.

"If Rachel was murdered, what makes you think they won't come after your ass next?" he shouted. I wondered idly if Caller ID had made a polite "hello" almost completely unnecessary.

"If she committed suicide, I have no worries. If she didn't, I guess I'd better start worrying," I responded, doing my best to keep it light.

"Yeah, right. Look, if you do turn out to be right, which I doubt, who do you think was behind it?" he asked.

"No good leads yet, but I'm working on it. Who knows, you might find out before I do. Tell Lucy to hold her fire a while longer. There's more to come."

"If you live that long," he said gruffly.

I decided to call Rabbi Strauss. He answered his cell immediately.

"Mr. Patterson—I watched your partner's press conference. Friends think you've pinned a target on your back."

"Any idea who might want to take target practice?" I asked.

"No, but we've identified your pockmarked man. His name is Bart Stone, former Special Forces, now an independent contractor working for companies that sell weapons. His military record was wiped clean, and our people say he goes by several aliases."

"What exactly does he do for these companies?" I asked.

"Whatever they want him to do, at least that's his reputation. He's not someone you want to cross, nor are his associates."

"Don't keep me in suspense. Who does he work for?"

"He freelances now, but used to work for Rouss Military Systems." I jotted down the company's name as he continued.

"I related the facts of our previous discussion to my sources in Israel. Their eyes are now open to the possibility that Rachel's death might not have been suicide. Please keep us informed, and I will do the same."

"Rabbi, please tell your friends that Rachel was a victim, as was her husband. Encourage them to search the site where he was killed again."

"You think Ira's death was something other than a random attack?"

"If I were in Israeli intelligence, I'd check out that site, and ask who might want Ira dead."

"I'm not sure I can do that. I'm only a poor rabbi from central Arkansas." I could hear his smile and wondered how a "poor rabbi from central Arkansas" had the money to stay at the Willard, or knew the identity of a contractor who'd gone off the grid.

Micki and Brian returned from the courthouse just as I put down the phone. True to her word, Micki walked directly to the barn to saddle a horse and look for Larry, who was out exploring the property. I told Brian what I had learned from Red and Rabbi Strauss. He was familiar with Rouss Military Systems. "Who in the military isn't?" he asked.

I asked Brian to pull up whatever information he could on Rouss, including their Washington lobbyists. It only took me a couple of seconds to realize Red might have some answers.

"Twice in one day, yet I never hear from you when you're working on my matters," he jabbed, clearly in a better frame of mind.

"What can you tell me about Rouss Military Systems?"

The pause before his response was telling. "Is your question covered by the attorney-client privilege?"

"Maybe they're looking for a merger partner?"

Red laughed, sounding more like himself. "Patterson, you're like a good coon dog. When you want to find something, you find a way. There's no way they're looking for a merger partner. They're bigger than God. My company may be worth several billion, but I'm small potatoes in comparison."

"Well, what can you tell me that I can't find on Google?"

"They're involved in the designing and building of a third of the weapons systems built for our government. Did Rachel steal one of their designs?"

I swallowed a testy comeback and let it go. "Are they involved in the design of rocket systems?"

"Sure they are. They've designed a version of most every system in the world today. If they didn't design it, they tested it. And if they didn't design or test it, and it doesn't work, they're in charge of dismantling and disposing of it."

"What does that mean, exactly?" I asked.

"Jack, lots of weapons either don't pan out or are outdated by the time testing is complete. The Pentagon won't allow the designer or the testing company to dismantle and dispose a failed system—too many opportunities for double-dealing. Let me give you an example."

"I'm all ears."

"Remember that stealth submarine that sank after its launch last year? My company was well paid to recover the sub and figure out why it sunk. A different company, probably Rouss, will get the contract to dismantle the submarine, making sure the plans and the electronics are destroyed in a way that preserves secrets."

"Fascinating," I responded. "I've never thought about what happens to airplanes or ships that don't work."

"Dismantle and dispose is handled by only a few companies; Rouss gets a lot of the work. They also design and sell systems that do work, and not just for our government, but for many other countries as well."

"Who runs Rouss?" I asked.

"Rouss himself is no longer with us. He was a former admiral, one

tough son-of-a-bitch. Plenty of former generals and admirals sit on
their advisory board, but family members and a few select senior officers own the company. The current chairman of the board is Rouss's
grandson, Preston Rouss III, but he's a figurehead, more interested
in Formula One racing than government contracts. The real force
in the company is the COO, Dennis Maxwell. He runs the company
with an iron fist, makes the family boatloads of money. He pays his
employees well and treats them fairly. In return, they're incredibly
loyal. As far as I know he's on the up and up."

His tone had become just a bit defensive, so I didn't push. I'd
learned enough for now, but he chose to continue.

"Jack, there's a guy at Rouss who can tell you a lot more than I
can. He's the head of their testing division, great guy. I've tried to
hire him, but he won't budge."

"Who's that?" I asked.

"Harold Spencer. I'll text you his information. Feel free to use
my name."

"I'll do that," I said, and then my memory kicked in.

"Don't bother with the phone number, Red."

"What? Why not? Just give—"

"Because Harold Spencer is dead—murdered on the eighteenth
green of Columbia over three weeks ago."

I heard his quick intake of breath, almost like a hiccup. "You
sure it was Harold? Maybe it was a different Spencer."

"I was at Columbia the day his body was found."

"Jack, I'll get back to you. But, listen to me—whatever security
you have—double it."

64

RED WAS USUALLY UNFLAPPABLE. I was taken aback by how upset he was to learn of Spencer's death. I thought about it for a few minutes and went in search of Clovis. He and Martin were in deep conversation with three other men in the small office where they'd set up temporary headquarters.

Clovis looked up, but didn't invite me to join them.

"Martin and I will be through in a minute—give us a sec," he said tersely and turned back to the others.

I'd worked with Clovis long enough not to get my feelings hurt. Stella was still working on the encrypted zip drive, and Brian wasn't working at his usual table. I poured a cup of coffee and sat down with my laptop to check my email.

The quiet was interrupted by sudden chaos. Micki and Brian came storming in, followed by Larry. Brian held Micki's elbow—she was clearly furious. Larry had wisely chosen to bring up the rear.

"I can take care of myself. Who told you to track me down? Let go!" she demanded, jerking her arm away.

"I did." Clovis's voice conveyed control and authority. Micki's protests came to a halt.

"Brian came to find you and Larry because we located a sniper on the property—and he wasn't here to shoot skeet. Micki, please get a cup of coffee or something stronger and sit down. That goes for everyone. Maggie and Beth are on their way back from the city. House hunting is on hold."

I did as I was told, and the others followed suit. Clovis turned to

Martin, who took the lead.

"Last night a man tried to break into Rachel's apartment. We were waiting, and he's now in custody at the military base where Rachel died a few weeks ago."

I frowned, "The same military base? Why?"

Clovis spoke, "I think you already know part of the answer. Before you went to Pawleys, Brian told you that while he was with the JAG Corps, he met a Captain Morrison, head of military police at the facility where Rachel died. You asked him to find out if Morrison had concerns about the suicide findings and the lack of any investigation. While you were gone, he and Martin met the Captain at a bar near the base. Morrison doesn't believe for a minute that Rachel killed herself, but he has no evidence. The base commander put the kibosh on any investigation, told him the case was closed. Morrison said if we could give him any hard evidence he'd open an investigation in a heartbeat, orders be damned.

"Martin and I have been worried about what we should do if we caught an unauthorized person on the property. We surely couldn't give him or her to the local police. Morrison gave us our answer, and he has proven true to his word. When I told him we'd caught someone trying to break into Rachel's apartment he said, 'Bring him in. We can hold him for a while.' His response was the same when we told him about the sniper."

"You actually caught him? I thought you just scared someone away." I was dumbfounded.

"Thanks to Stella's warning system, and Brian and Larry's modifications, it wasn't that difficult. We knew the moment he came onto the property and easily found where he'd set up shop. A professional sniper isn't someone to mess with, but Big Mike and his team were on top of him like ducks on a June bug. He's on his way to the military base right now. I think he might have a headache, but, honestly, who cares."

"Won't both guys be screaming for lawyers?" I asked.

"Morrison has assured me he can hold them for at least three days without telling a soul. At that point he'll tell the base commander and open an investigation into Rachel's death, holding our prisoners as long as he can."

Brian added, "Morrison is one of the good guys. His unit has egg on its face over Rachel's death, so if anyone has a reason to find out what happened, he does."

"Thanks for taking the initiative with Morrison. You've given me a great deal to think about. Let's take a break until Maggie and Beth get here."

As we broke up, I pulled Larry aside and asked, "Do you mind if Micki and I walk and talk for a few minutes?"

He raised an eyebrow, but said, "Of course not."

"Clovis, will we be safe in the great outdoors?"

He finally smiled, "Just don't wander off the beaten path."

We hadn't stepped off the porch before she asked, "What's up, Jack?"

"Truth is, I'm having a hard time with you and Larry together."

Her reaction was immediate, her voice shrill. "Jack, you promised. How could you?"

I laughed, "Sorry, that came out wrong. As you never let me forget, the past is over. No, the fact is that I've really come to like Larry. He's smart and I appreciate what he brings to our team. The more I get to know him, the more I wonder if he's too good for you."

She punched me in the arm. "Thanks. You sound just like his mother." She took my arm, and we continued to walk down the path toward the river.

"Now, come on, what's bothering you?" she asked. I stopped and guided her toward a convenient bench. I didn't want to get too far from the house.

"Well, there's the likelihood of criminal and civil liability when Cotton or anyone else finds out what Clovis and Martin pulled off," I said. "After all, they didn't exactly ask those guys if they'd like to be driven to an unknown location in Virginia."

"Oh, c'mon—what would you have them do? They found someone on our property armed with a high-powered rifle. Would you rather they had called, let's see—the local sheriff?"

"No, of course not. But, think about what you just said. They actually found a guy on Maggie's property with a high-powered rifle!

What have I gotten us into? I have no right to put any of you in this kind of situation. Fencing with Cotton is one thing, but snipers are way beyond what any of us bargained for."

"We've been there before, and we survived, remember?" She said gently.

"I know, but this is different. If I'm right, we may have uncovered an illegal scheme that has international implications."

"If you're right, it was Rachel who uncovered it. We're only continuing the work she began."

"Right, and Rachel is dead."

"That's exactly why you can't let it go. If you're right, Rachel Goodman didn't deserve to die. She deserves to have her good name restored."

"Yes, she does, and I'm not going to let go. But I can't justify putting the rest of you—"

She interrupted roughly, "Jack Patterson, if you think you dragged us blindly into this mess, you need to get a grip. We volunteered. Do you hear anyone whining to go home? You're not the only person on the side of truth, justice, and the American way. Besides, you and I are partners, remember?" She gave me a gentle kiss on the lips. "Now, don't let that go to your head. I'm just reminding you of what you gave up a long time ago."

Micki and I had once enjoyed a brief, passionate affair that had evolved into a wonderful friendship full of teasing and banter, but nothing more. We were too much alike. Micki had found Larry, and I . . . well, I was still looking.

Our conversation was interrupted suddenly when Clovis called out, "Micki, Jack, come inside. Stella wants you."

We hurried inside to the small library where Stella had set up shop.

She looked up and said sternly, "Jack and Micki get behind me, everyone else out of the room. I don't have any idea what we'll find. At least for now we need to keep it on a need to know basis."

Clovis tried to linger, but after a sharp glare from Stella, he quietly closed the door. Micki and I stood behind her as she explained.

"It appears that Rachel uncovered a plan by Rouss Military

Systems to get paid twice to design and develop weapons systems over the last few years—once by the United States and a second time by another country. The amounts of money involved are incredible."

"Are you sure it's a case of being paid twice? Contractors build aircraft all the time for the U.S., and then sell the same or similarly designed aircraft to other countries—with the Pentagon's approval, of course," I countered.

"Not if the weapons are supposed to have been dismantled and destroyed," she replied.

"Show me." I was skeptical. We turned to Stella's computer screen.

"First, you will see the layers of encryption I had to peel back. I was able to bypass the twenty-eight bit encryption on the password, pretty simple, but the file protocols are pretty next level; it took me longer than expected." It all looked like gobbledygook to me—she might as well have been speaking in Portuguese.

"Okay, so now you'll see an Excel spreadsheet with the heading: *Rouss Military Systems Inc.* Got it so far?"

My eyes jumped to the next set of headings on the page—project, cost of development, cost of testing, and cost of dismantling. The project column contained a list of Rouss's projects for the Pentagon. The first project was the Logmod Project, and under the column titled "cost of testing" was the number thirty-seven million dollars. I figured that meant Rouss had tested whatever the Logmod Project was and been paid thirty-seven million dollars.

As I scanned the list, I noticed five projects Rachel had high-lighted in yellow. For those five projects Rouss had not only been paid for design and development, but also for dismantling, which, according to Red, violated the Pentagon's policy. The amounts of money involved were indeed staggering.

Stella clicked to page two of the spreadsheet. Now the heading read: *Rouss Hired by Pentagon for Both Development and Termination.* Listed were the five projects she had highlighted on the previous page in yellow, including one called—Specific Target Missile System (STMS). Rouss was paid two-hundred-and-seventy million dollars to develop STMS, and another fifty-seven million to dispose of the same system.

The third page of the spreadsheet consisted of an analysis of the sales of a weapons system called the Pinpoint Missile System, by one company, Surplus Systems, Ltd. It cited the number of systems sold, the delivery date, and the purchasing country. Rachel had written on the spreadsheet:

> All the sales of the Pinpoint systems occurred after the disposal contract for STMS had been completed. Israel was the sole purchaser.

Each of the next four pages contained a similar analysis for four other systems. In each case the seller was Surplus Systems. The only obvious difference I could see was that these systems had been purchased by different countries.

Stella looked back at me. "Are you following this?"

"So far so good. But the only thing that seems wrong is that Rouss was paid to both design and then later dismantle five weapons. It may be a violation of Pentagon policy, but it's not fraud. As far as the sales of weapons by Surplus Systems, I don't see her point. Different company, different weapons."

She smiled and pulled up the next page without a word. It contained just two paragraphs. The first gave a description and the specifications for STMS The second included a description and the specifications for the Pinpoint Missile System. The descriptions and specifications of the two systems were identical. For all appearances, STMS and Pinpoint were one and the same. But how could that be? Rouss had dismantled STMS and been paid a cool fifty-seven million dollars for the work.

The next four pages contained the descriptions and specifications of the other four weapons Rouss had designed and later dismantled. Each description was followed by the description of a weapon sold by Surplus Systems. In all four cases, the systems were the same.

I quickly googled Surplus Systems, but found only a couple of West Coast companies dealing in home goods and electronics. Yet Rachel's Excel spreadsheet showed that Surplus Systems had sold almost two billion dollars of product all over the world for these five systems alone. *Two billion dollars.*

The answers came on the next pages labeled Report to the I.G. Rachel had developed a glossary in which every fact and figure was explained in minute detail, followed by her conclusion:

> In at least five instances, Rouss both developed and was later paid to dismantle a weapons system that didn't pass rigorous testing. After the dismantling was complete, a product identical to the one developed and discarded appeared on the secondary market, manufactured and sold by a company called Surplus Systems, Ltd. The likelihood of this happening out of coincidence or happenstance defies credibility.

I let out a low whistle. "Well, what do you know?"

"Great work, Stella. No part of Rachel's report is confidential except for the specifications of the systems, but let's be careful. Make several copies, give me one to read tonight, and keep the rest with the original zip drive."

Stella wasn't finished. "You need to keep reading, Jack. Rachel has also included a set of notes, explaining how she discovered what she describes in so much detail. It all makes sense now—what she was doing for the last two years."

I assured her I would read everything very carefully and asked her to find out whatever she could about Surplus Systems, Ltd.

"If this is what I think it is, what happens next?" Micki asked. Her voice betrayed her unease.

"It's exactly what you think it is, a ticking time bomb. I wish I knew how much time is left on the fuse. I need to speak with one more person before we decide what to do next."

"And who is that?" Micki inquired.

"Harold Spencer's widow."

65

I HAD FINALLY REMEMBERED why Harold Spencer sounded familiar. Angie and I had played Harold and his wife in a club mixed doubles tennis tournament many years ago. They won and that was the end of it—handshakes, off to dinner with friends. I gave up tennis when Angie died, and our paths hadn't crossed again.

But would she agree to see me? My first thought was to show up at her front door and hope to catch her by surprise. But I knew this plan was neither fair to her nor likely to succeed.

I wandered into the kitchen and sat down at the table. After a bit of thought, I called Red.

"I need a favor," I demanded, mimicking his blunt style.

"Who works for whom in this relationship?" he chuckled. "What now?"

"I need to speak with Harold Spencer's widow. Will you call her? Give me an intro?"

"Won't be necessary. She's already expecting your call," he said, reciting her number.

"Why should she expect my call?" I asked, jotting the number down on the back of someone's grocery list.

"For a couple of reasons. After you told me about Harold's death, I drove out to see her. I was close to both Harold and Judy—her name is Judy. I hadn't heard about Harold and felt the only way to make amends was to see her in person." His lengthy explanation was unexpected.

I couldn't help but wonder how close they had been, but kept my wondering to myself.

"The other reason is that Harold gave her a sealed envelope with instructions to give the envelope to you if something happened to him. I have no idea why. I told her that you are one of my attorneys as well as my friend and that she could trust you. You should make the trip soon, she's leaving town."

"I'm on my way," I told him.

"Better call first, Jack. Her son and some of his buddies are guarding the house—they're all Navy SEALs. Now it's your turn to do me a favor. If you learn something from Judy that you need to tell Lucy, leave me out of it. Okay?"

"I never disclose my client's confidences, even to a fiancée."

"Good man, and good luck," he signed off.

I punched in the number I'd jotted down. A male voice answered with a curt "Yes."

"Hello, my name is Jack Patterson…"

"Say no more. When can we expect you, and who will accompany you?" the voice asked.

"We should be there in about an hour and a half. My driver is Mike Fendler and my paralegal is Brian Hattoy."

The stately colonial was set on about half an acre, a large lot for Somerset. Normally a leafy oasis, it now bore a harsh resemblance to a scene from *The Godfather:* men patrolling the grounds, dogs straining at their leashes, and the house lighted as though for Christmas. Checkpoints had been set up on both driveways. I shuddered to imagine what the neighbors thought.

We were waved through and directed to a small parking area. A very polite young man escorted us to the back door, where a muscular young man greeted us. "Mr. Patterson, please come in, but Fendler and Hattoy will need to be searched."

To my surprise Big Mike replied in a threatening tone, "By you and who else?"

I was about to say something about not feeding the lions, when several guys rushed up to give Mike and Brian those clenched-fist man hugs that must hurt.

The man who had greeted us said, "Okay, men, back to your stations," and extended his hand.

"Welcome, Mr. Patterson. Mike and Brian are old friends, so forgive the little scene—I'm John Robert Spencer." He turned to Brian and said, "Master Sergeant, it's an honor to have you in my home. My mother doesn't know you're here."

We had to dodge several large cardboard boxes on the way to the family room: someone was packing up.

"Mom will be down in a minute. Can I get you a drink?" he asked.

I started to decline, but was interrupted by a clear voice from the stairwell.

"Please, Jack, join me for a cocktail or a glass of wine. My mother taught me that a lady never drinks alone, and I could use a scotch. Do you still play tennis?"

I turned to face the voice and understood why Red didn't want Lucy to know about Judy Spencer. She wasn't beauty-queen gorgeous, but she exuded class and self-confidence. I recognized her, but only just.

I waited until she reached the bottom step before replying.

"I'm surprised you remember; I gave up tennis a long time ago."

"You and your wife were charming and worthy opponents, as I recall." She paused and added softly, "I'm sorry for your loss."

"Thank you. It's kind of you to remember. I am sorry for your own recent loss. I hope…"

"Please forgive my attire. I've been packing all day so I must look a fright," she interrupted, flashing a tired smile.

She wore jeans, tennis shoes, and an oversized polo, but certainly didn't look a fright. She looked ten years younger than I, although I suspected we were at least fairly close in age given that her son had to be at least thirty.

"Lucy had better watch her back," I thought.

Her son John Robert introduced her to Mike and Brian. "Mother, meet Mike Fendler; he and I served together in Iraq." She greeted Mike with an extension of her hand and a "pleased to meet you." John Robert turned and continued, "And Mom, let me introduce you to Master Sergeant Brian Hattoy."

She gave a little start. "You're kidding!"

"No, he works for Mr. Patterson now."

Judy walked up to Brian, threw her arms around him, and said through sudden tears, "Thank you, thank you."

Brian returned her hug, but looked more than a little uncomfortable. John Robert responded to my puzzled expression.

"Sergeant Hattoy saved my life in Iraq, along with several of the men you met outside. Small world, isn't it?"

I agreed, feeling a little misty-eyed myself.

Judy stepped back, totally in control again. "I'm so pleased to finally meet you, but Mr. Patterson and I have a little business to conduct. John Robert, please bring me a scotch and whatever Jack wants, then you men leave us alone. I'm sure you have lots of catching up to do."

We were soon seated in two large armchairs with our drinks and, after a few minutes of chitchat, she turned to the business at hand.

"Did you know Harold well?"

"No. In fact our tennis game was the only time I met him, either of you for that matter. I gave up tennis when my wife died. Since then, I've limited myself to golf," I answered.

"You're right. Our paths haven't crossed since, but I've kept up with you in the papers. You've had quite an interesting career lately. But back to Harold—he was club champion for several years, and he and I won the mixed doubles until I tired of the competition. Several of the women were downright nasty about our winning every year. Now, I only play with my group for fun, not blood," she laughed.

"He was also a very good poker player; a mathematician by education, and he had a photographic memory. He seldom missed the Friday night poker game at the club. Did you know the guys he played with that last night tried to call on me after the funeral? I told them to keep the hell away. None of them cares a hoot about me. I'm sure all they wanted to know was if I still had their IOUs. I most certainly do have them, and I'll call every one of them, but not now, not before you do your job, Jack."

"My job?" I asked uneasily.

"I want you to send those bastards that murdered my husband and your client straight to prison." I was taken aback by her sudden vehemence.

"Do you know who murdered your husband?"

"No, not specifically, but I have a good idea. That's why John Robert and his friends are outside standing guard. I'm leaving town as soon as possible."

"Aren't you worried they'll find you? Your son can't guard you forever, and a moving truck is easy to follow."

"Oh, you mean the boxes. They're all going into storage, as is the furniture. If you're successful, I will come back to Bethesda one day." She gave me a wry smile.

"My son has chosen the spot for my exile, somewhere warm and exotic, where no one can find me. Thanks to sweet Red, we leave tomorrow. He's offered his jet to take me wherever we like."

I tried again, deciding not to rise to the bait. "So who do you think murdered your husband?"

She allowed herself a touch of irritation.

"Again, Jack, I don't know. But I'll tell you what I do know. Harold was shaken to the core by Rachel's arrest. He'd told me she was a colleague, and I thought he was simply concerned about a friend. But one day he gave me an envelope and said, 'If something happens to me, get this envelope to Jack Patterson, the lawyer.'

"I was frightened, but he assured me it was just a precaution. He made me promise not to open it and said to be sure to get it to you."

"Why me?" I tried to keep my voice steady.

"He said you were a friend of Rachel's father, that he trusted you to get it into the right hands."

"Did you open it?" I hated to ask.

She wasn't offended. "I wanted to, but didn't. I was afraid what might be in it. Harold was, well…let's just say he wasn't perfect. I put it under the silver trays in the buffet and tried to forget about it. Harold's death was such a shock—nothing seemed real. One day life was normal; the next day it was hell. For the first few days the police were all over the house, searching and asking questions. But I had no answers, and neither did they. I was trying to figure out what to do next when I heard about Rachel. Her suicide was just too much—it couldn't have been a coincidence. That's when John Robert and I got really worried."

"Does he know about the envelope?"

"No, and I'd prefer he didn't. Other than one tennis match, I don't know you at all. But Red says he trusts you, and Red doesn't trust many people. So I'll do exactly what my husband asked and let you decide what to do with the contents."

She reached under her seat cushion and handed me a manila envelope. "Please don't open it here. Now, do me one more favor, please."

"Name it," I said gripping the envelope.

"Ask John Robert to freshen our drinks, and let me spend a little time with the man who saved my son's life. This may be my only opportunity."

66

I LISTENED as Judy, John Robert, and Brian spent a nice half hour reminiscing about the happy personal outcome of a conflict that had proved fatal for so many. When I sensed the conversation was dying down, we wished her and her young protectors well and sped off toward the Western Shore. I made myself wait until we were out of DC traffic to tear open the envelope.

Dear Mr. Patterson:

If you are reading this letter, it means that I am dead, likely murdered for what Rachel and I discovered. I can only hope that Rachel is still alive—she is a courageous young woman. We were colleagues of a sort. She was an analyst at the Pentagon and I am, or should I say was, the head of the testing division for Rouss Military Systems.

Rachel approached me almost two years ago. She said it was possible that a missile system developed by Rouss, tested, and eventually discarded, had not been dismantled or destroyed, but in fact, had been retained and sold to a third party. She also told me that contrary to the Pentagon's policy, my company had been given the contract to dismantle the system. I told her that her conclusion was nuts, couldn't have happened under Pentagon policy. But she was able to produce other such instances, and over time I came to believe that she was correct: Rouss had been given the contract to dismantle systems that it had developed and tested.

As my wife may have told you, I am good with numbers. But one doesn't have to be a genius to realize that the revenues from each of the five projects Rachel identified make no sense. The revenues far exceed the dollar amounts of the government contracts and so do the profit margins. See the attached Exhibit A.

For over a year, I have been working, without success, to prove that these numbers were the result of accounting errors. I have come to agree with Rachel that Rouss has developed a plan to remedy the defects in a discarded system and sell it on the international market; whether the Pentagon condoned this scheme remains to be seen.

It took some careful digging, but I found that lobbyists paid by Rouss had managed to bury language in an agriculture appropriations bill granting a waiver to the Pentagon's long-standing policy. How such a waiver could benefit the country is beyond my understanding. I doubt anyone on the agriculture subcommittee even noticed it.

We were very careful to keep our collaboration secret—no texts or emails, just the occasional meeting at a local coffee shop. We were almost ready to send our report to the Inspector General of Defense when Rachel was arrested. Nothing she or I did or wrote compromised the government in any way. And it was certainly never meant for or sent to the Israelis or any other foreign government.

I have entrusted our analysis to this envelope, and thus to you. I cannot confirm that weapon systems were sold rather than dismantled as per Rouss's contracts with the government, but I also cannot explain the increased revenues and profits far above Rouss's norms.

Please tell my wife and son I love them. I was not a perfect father and husband, far from it, but I loved them both very much.

Harold Spencer

September 12, 2016

The summary and exhibits supported the conclusions stated in the letter. They were much more detailed than the Excel spread-sheets I'd seen only hours before on Rachel's zip drive. I found myself wishing he'd left out the part about not being a perfect hus-band or father.

Rouss was up to no good, but so far nothing linked them to either death. My mind wandered for a few minutes—what had Judy said about poker? I punched in her cell number.

"Judy, I'm sorry to bother you, but did your husband carry his cell phone with him when he played poker?" I asked.

"He did, but the police never found it. It belonged to Rouss anyway."

"Did he have his own computer at home?" I asked.

"We have a Mac, but Harold never used it except to pay the bills. He always used Rouss's laptop for work."

"Do you still have it?" I asked.

"Their HR person took it away. He came by to explain my husband's life insurance, how to move his 401K, that kind of thing. He was very helpful."

Another dead end, I thought. But Judy wasn't quite ready to let go. "Did you open the envelope?"

I couldn't lie, so I answered. "I did. He told me to tell you and your son he loved you both very much."

After an unexpectedly long silence, she said, "I suppose he did, in his own way. Thank you, Jack. Maybe our paths will cross one day, but please don't try to reach me. Be careful—surely you know they'll come after you next."

I didn't acknowledge her concern, but said goodbye and wished her well. Who could blame her for skipping town? I wondered what she meant by "he did in his own way."

The phone buzzed almost immediately—it was Micki. "Our pal Donald Cotton wants to settle the asset forfeiture case. Says he'll give us Rachel's Defense Department pension and bank account. He'll also give us all her personal effects, the rings, her phone, and computer—but the phone and computer will be scrubbed."

"And how did we respond?" I asked.

"'We' told him I wanted him to file an inventory with the court before I'd consider any settlement. He said he had already done so under seal; he left my copy with the court clerk—jerk. One of Martin's men will pick it up first thing tomorrow morning. Stella would love to get the computer and phone before they are scrubbed, but I think we'd lose that one if we fought it."

"No mention of the insurance and pension money from Israel?" I knew the answer.

"Not a word. That's why I want the inventory. And Jack, we need to find that money from Israel," she said.

"I'm on it. Listen, we should be back at Maggie's in about twenty minutes: assemble the troops—it may be a late night."

After a little thought, I called Rabbi Strauss.

"Sorry to call so late, but were you able to find out the name of the bank where the pension checks were deposited?"

He hesitated, and I pushed. "Rabbi, the name of the bank is not a state secret."

"No, no, of course not. My mind was elsewhere. The monthly deposits go to Parra Bank in Alexandria. I also verified that the widow's pension goes to her parents during their lifetimes. The embassy will send you the correct paperwork for the Jennings to fill out." He sounded apologetic.

"Okay, and did anyone check the site where Ira was killed?"

He laughed, "Nothing gets past you, Mr. Patterson, does it? I'm sorry, but if shell fragments were found at the scene, and if their origin could have been identified, it would not be in the interest of the state of Israel to reveal such information."

I had never mentioned shell fragments, and he had just given me some very interesting information.

"Do you have any idea how Hamas obtained the weapon in question?" I asked.

"Surely you know I have no answer to that question," he answered, with almost no inflection.

"Rabbi, let me be clear. Two wonderful, young American Jews are dead. So far the only response from either American or Israeli authorities has been a blank stare and evasion. Oh, and that old shibboleth—national security.

"If someone doesn't kill me first, I will find out who murdered them and why, and you can tell the Israeli government that I won't hide behind the words 'national security.' I will tell the whole world."

67

I CAUGHT MIKE AND BRIAN exchanging glances in the rearview mirror. They quickly looked away, and I realized I needed to be a little less dramatic. And what about Harold Spencer? He'd been a blip in my life. Now, he was dead and he'd left me the keys to the kingdom.

My thoughts were all in a jumble. A few weeks ago my best friend and I had sat at the bar at Columbia wondering who Harold Spencer was and how he'd come to be murdered. Now his death was at the very center of a probable illegal international arms sale, and he'd been working with Rachel Goodman. "Small world" seemed a bit inadequate.

We pulled into the compound's grounds and quickly joined the others in the big family room.

Micki stood and saluted. "All your troops are present and accounted for, waiting your guidance and direction, Sir!"

"Ha, ha, very funny." I tried to smile—I knew she was teasing. "First, I need to fill you all in on what's happened today. There's been quite a lot. Then we can try to figure out what to do next."

Micki and I spent the next half hour explaining the events of the day. I ended with my conversation with Strauss.

"We need to check and double check both our facts and our conclusions before we can go much further. And I need to go over everything Rachel included on that zip drive." I finished.

Maggie immediately asked, "How can we help? We're all ready, just tell us what to do."

Maggie was always the good soldier, and her quick grasp of the situation came as a relief. I saw heads nod in agreement, so I pressed forward.

"Beth, Maggie, since house hunting is off for the time being, Stella will give you the names of the five weapons systems that Rachel identified. She won't give you any confidential information about their specifications. I want you to find out everything you can—who built them, what they were designed to do, any sales, whatever you can dig up. We'll crosscheck the public information against the information on Rachel's spreadsheets. For example, her spreadsheet states that Israel purchased a missile system called the Pinpoint Missile System from Surplus Systems. See if you can find out if that's true, and try to get me more info on Surplus Systems."

Beth asked, "What do you want us to do with what we find?"

"Put it in a format I can understand," I answered.

"A one-pager," Maggie said, and everyone laughed.

"Exactly," I smiled.

I turned to Micki. "You're my partner, so this is only a suggestion."

"Can it, Jack. Tell me what you need me to do, and if I don't like it, I won't do it." Straight from the hip, as usual.

"Before you get back to Cotton about his settlement offer, go to the Parra Bank, get copies of Rachel's bank statements, and if the government froze the account, get written evidence of that fact. I don't want to deal with the settlement offer until we know if Rabbi Strauss was telling me the truth."

"Do you think he just made it up?" Maggie frowned.

"No, I don't, but the more we can document now, the less chance anyone will be able to change the facts."

"You sound like you don't trust anyone."

"Well, I trust the people in this room, but that's about as far as it goes. Speaking of that, Brian, I'd like you to go with Micki tomorrow, and please, Micki, don't argue. Martin and Clovis, these next few days will be tense. If the bad guys find out what we have, they'll stop at nothing to get at it."

Martin didn't smile this time. "We'll do our best, but from now on no one leaves the grounds without a driver and another of my men riding shotgun."

"Clovis, same goes for Ben and Linda." He nodded, and I knew he took my words to mean to check in with Jeff's protection in St. Louis, too. I made a mental note to call Red.

"Okay, let's talk about phase two. Let's assume Micki verifies that the Israeli money is sitting in a Parra Bank account that has been frozen by the government, and that Cotton's inventory fails to mention the account. What do we do?" I asked.

Everyone had an opinion: We could seek contempt of court charges in federal court for a false filing, we could give the information to the *Post*, or maybe we could ask the Department of Justice's Office of Professional Responsibility to launch an investigation. Micki remained uncharacteristically silent.

"Micki, what do you think?"

She smiled, "I know you're trying to be inclusive, but you really are the boss here—the general, since we're knee deep in the military. None of us has any idea how to prove Rachel's innocence and bring her murderer to justice. That's your job.

"I can't wait to see how you want to play this, because for the life of me I don't see how we can pull it off without getting killed. So Jack, please give up this new act of yours. Order us all around, and for God's sake quit being so damn nice. It doesn't suit you." Maggie and Beth's laughter infected the whole group, and I got a kick out of their hilarity.

It took a while for us to settle down again.

"I take it that Micki speaks for the lot of you. Okay, then you need to get busy—first thing tomorrow morning. I have a few loose ends to tie up and then it's on to phase two. Right now, I think we could all use a break."

As we all rose to find snacks and drinks, Clovis pulled me aside.

"I'm leaving early tomorrow morning, should be back tomorrow night. I want to check in with my guys in Little Rock and St. Louis. Martin has everything under control here."

"You think they'd go after Ben or Jeff?" I asked.

"We know they murdered Spencer and Rachel. Nobody's safe," he said. Clovis was never what you'd call expressive, but when he worried, everyone should worry.

"What about Carol? Pat keeps a close eye on her, and now that I'm out of the picture, she should be safe. What do you think—should I call Red?"

Clovis said tersely, "Call him."

I found an empty corner. Red answered on the first ring, almost as though he'd been waiting. I could hear the tension in his voice as he tersely asked what was wrong.

"Sorry to call so late, but Clovis is concerned about Carol. I know she's seeing someone else, but the next few days could get a little rough."

"I'll take care of it."

"No questions?" I asked.

"No. I'll take care of it. I owe you," he said.

"You don't owe me, I owe you."

"I'll explain later. Just, thank you." Red was seldom vague—one more thing to worry about.

The phone interrupted my thoughts again. I saw that it was Ken Chandler with the *Post,* and picked up quickly, determined at least to get in "Hello."

"Um, hello to you, too," he sounded a bit confused. "I just emailed you tomorrow's headline. It's not above the fold, but I figured you might like a head's up. It's not what I'd like it to be."

"Thanks, I'll check it out. If tomorrow morning works out, we should talk. You available after lunch?"

"I think I can manage coffee somewhere. Listen, despite Micki's press conference getting Cotton's goat, my sources tell me he's willing to settle to get you off his back."

"Your sources are correct, but it's not me he should worry about," I answered.

"For the record?" he asked.

"No, not yet."

"Okay, but not for much longer. I'll need a real story before long. Anything else?"

"Tomorrow," I answered, and the phone call ended without a goodbye. I felt like a spy.

I checked the email. Tomorrow's headline read:

GOODMAN'S LAWYER CLAIMS SHE'S INNOCENT

The second line, in slightly smaller type, read:

ALLEGES WRONGFUL SEIZURE OF ASSETS

Game on!

TUESDAY

68

STELLA BARKING ORDERS to her sweating acolytes interrupted my dreams the next morning. The ranks of participants had grown. I recognized John Robert Spencer among those going through their paces. I poured a cup of coffee and joined Martin to watch from the porch.

"Looks like Stella has some new recruits. What's going on?"

"Mike told the guys about Stella's morning workout yesterday, bet them they couldn't keep up. He cleared it with me last night. Can't hurt to have a few SEALs hanging around for the next few days."

"Do they know this could be hazardous duty?" I asked.

He smiled. "That's why they're here."

He was right; a few Navy SEALs might be the perfect deterrent.

Beth stumbled toward the coffee pot, still groggy with sleep, her eyes widening as she took in the scene outside. "I wish my girlfriends could see this."

"That's all we need—your girlfriends. Besides what are you going to tell Jeff?" I teased.

"That I'm surrounded by a bunch of ripped guys every day, and he needs to get in better shape."

Micki joined us and whistled, "I could get used to this kind of scenery." She and Beth traded a few more comments before she turned to me.

"Cotton's already called. He's ready to cave. The *Post* ran an online piece about the press conference and reports we're close to reaching a deal. He all but accused me of leaking that part of the story to the press."

"What did you say?" I asked.

"I told him when I talk to the press it will be for attribution, not some quote from an 'anonymous source.' Of course, I wasn't speaking for you."

"Good, because if I'm right, we might need that reporter this afternoon," I replied.

"So soon?"

"Listen, Micki—before you go to the bank this morning, take a look at Cotton's inventory of the assets seized. I bet he fails to mention the account at Parra Bank. If you find that the Israeli pension and the life insurance money actually exists, and that the account has been frozen, we'll know that Cotton is hiding assets and has committed fraud on the court. Go straight to Cotton's office and get the release of the assets he listed on the inventory. Brian has all the information he needs to get the money wired to our trust account."

"And if the assets aren't at Parra Bank?"

"Then Strauss was lying, and we'll have opened a whole new can of worms. But why would he lie? He could easily have chosen to ignore me. I'm willing to bet you'll find that money exactly where he said it would be. I'll leave it to your judgment as to how and when you demand the Israeli money."

"You trust me with that decision?"

"Yeah, I do. I trust your instincts, and besides, I'm likely to lose my temper. For the life of me, I can't understand what in the world is behind this money grab when there's so much more at stake. Matt and Lauren just sent me a memo outlining why the seizure of an Israeli widow's pension payment violates several international treaties. Maybe that's why they don't want to admit its existence."

"Hmm—did I ask for such a memo? My instincts must have been really good." She laughed.

"Must have slipped your mind. I'll email it to you so you can read it on the way to the bank."

"Any more surprises?" she asked.

"I feel sure we'll have plenty more surprises. If I knew what they were, they wouldn't be surprises."

Stella's training broke up, and Micki and Brian left soon there-after. John Robert and his buddies volunteered to accompany Larry onto the property so he could work on his plans for the conference and retreat center. They also wanted to check out Stella's design of the electronic fence and warning system.

Beth and Maggie were putting together my one-pagers with back-ups, so I decided to call Red to ask how Lucy had reacted to this morning's article in the *Post,* but got his voicemail. The phone buzzed almost before I could put it down.

"Jack, this is Pat," the voice said.

"Well, Pat, this is a surprise. What can I do for you?" I asked. Pat was Carol's driver slash bodyguard. We'd gotten to know each other fairly well during those weekends on the Eastern Shore.

"I have a message from Carol, but she wants you to keep it private."

"Whatever Carol tells me through you is confidential unless you tell me otherwise," I answered.

"No matter what?" he asked, and I wondered if Carol was with him.

"No matter what."

"First, she appreciates your calling Red. She's about to leave the country for an extended vacation, but I'm allowed to tell you where she is if you ask."

"Tell her it's tempting, but I have to pass. Duty calls." I tried to sound disappointed, but these games were getting a little old. What exactly did she hope to accomplish?

"That's what she thought you'd say. She also hopes you under-stand why she can't tell you why she's leaving or why she's concerned for your safety. And she says to tell you she's very sorry." Wow! Pat was reading from a script full of hidden messages.

"Tell her I understand, and to use plenty of sunscreen," I responded lightly. I could hear Pat chuckling.

"Is there anything else you can tell me? I promise no one will ever know my source."

He hesitated for a moment, and then said, "Eric Hartman used her, plain and simple. She knows it; she's embarrassed and plenty mad. I was already getting worried about her, so your call to Red couldn't have come at a better time. Carol made a big mistake putting her career ahead of you. When this is all over, I hope she'll swallow her pride, and you two can pick up where you left off—that is, if you're still alive."

"Still alive? That doesn't sound too promising—what do you know, Pat?" These predictions of imminent doom were beginning to get old.

"I know that you're in way over your head. Hartman's clients would like nothing better than for you to disappear."

"And who might those clients be?" I asked.

"Jack, you already know the answer to that question." He laughed, and our conversation ended.

He was right. Now how did I prove it, and to whom?

This thorny little problem had been simmering in the back of my mind for days. Unless I could prove that Rouss had committed an actual crime of some significance, who would care about Rachel's discoveries or her death? No lobbyist was more influential in DC than those representing the defense industry; more than a few members of Congress depended on their money for their existence and reelection. Countless decisions were made, deals cut, under the table or behind closed doors, well protected from public scrutiny. Why rock the boat? It was far more likely that all parties, including the government, would close ranks to protect the golden goose.

The most seasoned politicians fear the military-industrial complex's influence and power. Defense issues were complicated, and the media had no interest in covering stories they couldn't explain. Moreover, wars and international peacekeeping were the bread and butter of mainstream media. Why would they risk losing a major source of news by reporting on corruption or influence peddling inside the Pentagon?

Even presidents feared the military-industrial complex, so why on earth should a young reporter be willing to go where presidents and career politicians feared to tread? Many reporters learned the hard way that if they criticized the military, their career would soon end up in the deep freeze.

The next bit of news came just moments later, from an unlikely source: an email from Joan Laing's personal email account:

Jack, by now, you know I'm no longer involved with any part of Rachel Goodman's case. I have requested a transfer to the U.S. Attorney's office in Fayetteville, Arkansas. My husband's family is from the little town of Elm City, and we've decided it would be a nice place to raise our children. So you will understand why I've not looked into the matter you asked me to check out.

I enjoyed the little time we worked together, even though we were representing different interests. Please keep in touch; I look forward to following your career. I know I will be in good company with others who keep track of your efforts to pursue justice. You attract attention and followers in every case you take on.

Again, I wish you the best of luck.

Joan Laing

Joan had been very careful in her response; not only by using her personal email, but also by using language only I would understand. A tracking device must have been found underneath the van. Maybe she had been more direct in discussing the matter with Peggy Fortson. I sent an innocuous email back wishing her luck in Arkansas.

Still nothing from Micki or Brian. My phone rang yet again, and I was surprised to see Lucy Robinson on the caller ID.

"Jack, from what I read the papers this morning, I think you're blowing smoke. You don't have one lick of evidence to support your claim that Goodman was innocent or that she was killed."

"And good morning to you, Lucy. How are you?"

"I don't have time for your bull. Give me one good reason why I shouldn't tell the whole world that you're full of it?"

"Because I'm not. Keep Hartman and Rouss and whoever else off my back for one more day, two at the most. If I can't produce the goods, you have my permission to crucify me on the floor of the Senate or anywhere else."

After a long pause she asked quietly, "How did you know Eric and Rouss are leading the charge?"

"Lucy, I can't tell you that, but I can assure you I'm not bluffing."

"Damn you. You'd better deliver. Eric is threatening me with a primary opponent if I don't play ball. He controls enormous sums of campaign money."

"One more day?" I asked. "Should I call you or Red?"

"I thought you knew. Red left the country for a few days. Call this number. But Jack, don't bullshit me. Do you really have something?"

She needed reassurance. Her fellow senators were turning the screws, wondering why Lucy was keeping her powder dry. It wasn't her style.

"I've got a big something on the line, that's for sure. Problem is I haven't figured out quite what I've caught."

"One more day, Jack," she said.

"One more day."

69

I COULDN'T HELP BUT WONDER where Red had gone—had he gone off with Judy Spencer? Was he with Carol at a beach resort? Maybe he was out of the country on business. Why wouldn't he have told me? My phone beeped again; at last it was Micki.

"You were right. The money from Israel was deposited in Parra Bank. She set up the account with the life insurance money—two hundred thousand dollars. She has received a little over four thousand dollars a month for the last two years. I have copies of the account statements and the paperwork. The funny thing is, she never withdrew a dime," Micki reported.

"Any possibility she didn't know it was there?" I asked.

"No way. She had to sign a number of forms to receive the pension money. I have copies. Besides, the branch manager told me he advised her several times to invest the money. She said she might one day, but that for now it was fine where it was. He said she seemed very sure of herself."

"Hmmm… anything else? I know you're probably already on your way to Cotton's office."

"It's okay—I have time. At first the branch manager didn't want to cooperate, but he changed his tune when I mentioned delivering a subpoena with the press in tow. He produced the paperwork for the government's seizure order, all duly signed by the deputy who's in charge of asset forfeiture. Think it's possible Cotton doesn't know about the account?" Micki asked.

"It's unlikely. At the time of her arrest, all the newspaper accounts

suggested she was spying for Israel. He had to know what the forfeiture division was doing. How could he know about one account and
not the other? I'd love to see his reaction when you ask him about
the Parra account."

"There's one more complication."

"What's that? Don't tell me the branch manager called Cotton.
That would definitely spoil our plans."

"No, I put the fear of God in him. I showed him the accounting
the government filed that doesn't include the Parra Bank account on
the list of assets seized. I told him if he contacted the U.S. Attorney's
office, he risked being charged with conspiracy to defraud. No, he
wants nothing more to do with this matter.

"The complication is that a little over a month ago over a million
dollars was wired from offshore into the account."

That was a problem. Why would anyone wire that much money
to Rachel Goodman? "Any idea who sent the money?"

"No, but I have all the routing information. I hope Stella can run
down the source."

"Good idea. When did the money hit the account?"

"September 23, 2016," she answered.

It took a moment for the date to register. I couldn't hold back
a chortle.

Micki voiced her displeasure. "This isn't a joke Jack. No wonder
the government thinks she was a spy."

"I'm laughing, my dear Micki, because Rachel was taken into custody weeks earlier; her assets were frozen the very day she was arrested.
Check the paperwork the banker gave you. Now we know why someone
is desperate to keep this account secret. In their effort to frame
Rachel, they transferred big bucks into her account, but it arrived
after the government had taken her into custody. What a blunder!"

"Cotton's office will have to tell us about the account eventually,"
Micki pointed out.

"Why? Think about it. The bad guys thought she would plead
guilty to espionage to avoid the death penalty. Most lawyers would
negotiate a plea in a heartbeat to avoid lethal injection. With a guilty
plea, all the frozen assets would go to the government, and what she

had discovered about Rouss would be locked away forever. Even if she had lived to tell her story, Rachel would have had no credibility. But she was made of sterner stuff, so they tried her in the press and then killed her. When we contested the forfeiture and made noises about proving her innocence, they knew that if they disclosed the Parra account we'd discover the deposit and its date and there would be hell to pay. Your meeting with Cotton should be interesting."

"That means that Cotton or someone in his office has to be part of the conspiracy. You sure you trust me to handle this on my own?"

"My presence might raise a red flag. If you show up with just Brian, seemingly ready to settle, they may screw up even more. And, yes, I trust you, Micki."

She was quiet for a minute. "Okay, but if I'm the one who screws up, it's on your head. So, while I'm out freelancing, what's your next move?"

"Well, I think I'll call Peggy Fortson and ask to meet with the Attorney General. I'm sure she'll tell me I'm nuts and refuse."

"Why would you do that? If you already know it won't work, why should we give away our strategy to anyone else?"

We had discussed this before; Micki raised a good point. Maybe it was because I trusted Peggy, or maybe it was because I had worked for the Department of Justice. Whatever the reason, I had to give them the chance to do the right thing before I did what so many others do—bypass regular channels.

"I understand, and you may be right. But like I trust you, please trust me."

"You know I do," she answered. That trust was a big part of what made us a good team.

She and Brian left for their confrontation with Cotton, and I decided to stretch my legs and clear my head. I really missed my long walks on the beach; for now a quick jog to the lake and back did the trick.

I tried to check on Stella's progress with the routing number, but she told me to bug off, so I returned to my comfy chair in the family room. Hoping to avoid the office run-around, I left a message on Peggy's cell. She called back almost immediately.

"Jack. How nice to hear from you." Her tone belied the words.

"Thank you. Listen, I heard you found a tracking device under the van," I fudged.

"Who on earth told you that?" she responded after a bit of a pause. "Are you sure of your information?" Her hollow tone confirmed that she did indeed know about the device. I knew she must be worried about Joan, so I tried to help.

"Since you won't tell me a damn thing, I have to get my information where I can. By the way, I got an email from Joan Laing today. She tells me she's no longer involved in the case, and that she and her husband have decided to move to northwest Arkansas. A less stressful lifestyle, for sure."

"That's good to know. I wish her well." She sounded relieved. "But, Jack, if you're not going to ask me out for dinner, why exactly did you call?

"To ask to meet with the Attorney General about Rachel's case," I replied.

She made no attempt to hide either a heavy sigh or her irritation. "Give it up, Jack. There is no case against Rachel. She is dead, and as I understand it, the asset forfeiture case will soon settle. Why in the world would the AG want to meet with you about a resolved matter?" she asked, adding, "Her alleged theft of military secrets is no longer in our portfolio, it belongs to the intelligence community. We'll be lucky to get a copy of their final report."

I thought about chucking it—let the chips fall, so to speak. But she was a friend, so I gave her another chance.

"Then maybe the Attorney General should alter his portfolio. Peggy, I'm trying, but y'all need to help. Otherwise, I will go somewhere else with my story."

I waited through the silence, before she finally responded. "Can you hold a minute?"

Thank goodness the Department of Justice doesn't pipe in music while you're on hold. After several minutes, Peggy came back on the line.

"The Attorney General wants to know if you're about to raise a stink."

I could only imagine where she was and with whom. "I sure am, a big stink," I confirmed.

I could tell she had put her hand over the phone, but I could hear a muffled "Really?"

Her voice was clear again. "Are we off the record?"

"Of course," I said, wondering whose record we would be on.

"Well, the AG's response to your threat to raise a stink is, 'Good!'"

I thought for a minute. "Let me understand; the AG won't meet with me, but he doesn't mind if I raise holy hell?"

"That seems to be the general idea. If it were up to me, I'd tell you to go to hell, but he doesn't think you're as crazy as I do. When do you expect to begin? I think I'll take a few vacation days."

"It's already too late for that, but call in sick tomorrow."

70

THE POCKMARKED MAN, Bart Stone, eased himself into a reclining position behind a large stone boulder. He had a perfect view of the house. The computer console that housed the rocket launch system rested by his side, already programmed to launch the rocket that would finally rid the world of Jack Patterson. The order to kill had been given—this time he'd do the job himself. Two of his men were missing, and he was not about to leave this job to chance.

He had doubts about the mission—not its execution, but its aftermath. He didn't think the murder of Patterson and a few Navy SEALs could be explained away as a "gas explosion." Well, it wasn't his problem. As soon as he got the text confirming that Micki Lawrence had signed the release of claims, he was to fire the rocket and then leave the country; others would handle the rest.

Getting past the electronic fence had been more difficult than he thought. He had never seen anything quite like it, and despite all his training he had come close to tripping it more than once. No wonder his sniper had gone missing. Once he settled behind the rock he texted his contact a brief description of the fencing system and suggested that its design should be acquired.

If it were up to him, he would wait until Lawrence returned from the courthouse. He had seen her perform, and he doubted that she would go away. The same went for Jones, who had disappeared this morning, although his girlfriend was still at the house. In his estimation, Lawrence and Jones would make a very dangerous combination, but Patterson had to be eliminated. All attempts to scare him off or encourage him to walk away had failed. Too bad Jones's murder had been botched—that would have been the perfect way to cripple Patterson without casting suspicion.

This new Pinpoint Missile System was one heck of a weapon. The rocket itself was smaller than some bottle rockets, but had the firepower to destroy a single building and everyone in it. He remembered the first time he programmed the rocket. It had destroyed a small open-air restaurant in Israel and everyone inside with amazing force and accuracy. The coordinates for the Matthews property had been entered, he was ready. His cell phone would vibrate, he would enter the coded text, then sit back and enjoy the show. It was time for Jack Patterson to join Spencer and Goodman.

In a matter of minutes he'd be on his way to Canada and then on to Guatemala. A smile crossed his lips as he thought of the woman who waited at his hideaway in Central America. She had been a gift from an Afghan warlord for a job well done.

"Take your hands off the keyboard and raise them into the air. Now." The words were spoken with calm authority.

He was shocked to the core, but didn't move a muscle. Then the voice shouted, "Now!" and he knew it was over.

He lifted his hands and raised them into the air. Turning slowly, he recognized four Navy SEALs with HK Mark 23's aimed directly at his head. Someone was standing behind them, but he couldn't see who. For a second, he thought to touch the launch override button on the keyboard, but he knew his life would end the moment he moved. Spencer's team meant business. Better to wait for his contractor to get him out on bail, then flee to Guatemala.

"I want to speak to my attorney," he stated.

Spencer's son spoke. "You mistake us for law enforcement. We are private contractors protecting our employer. No attorney for you, I'm afraid. It's time to go."

"Where are you taking me? I tell you I want a lawyer!"

"If it were up to me, we'd take you off in the woods and beat the holy shit out of you until you admitted you murdered my father. Then I might go after you with a rake. So if I were you, Mr. Stone, I'd keep my mouth shut and be thankful for wherever we take you."

The SEALs soon had him bound and gagged. They dismantled the rocket launcher and turned to Larry Bradford, the man who had led them to Bart Stone.

Larry shook Spencer's hand and asked, "What next?"

"We'll take Stone and the weapon in different cars to the military base where the others are being held. Tell Jack that the weapon is the same as the Pinpoint System and has American markings. I'm sure Rouss designed it and supervised its manufacture. I wish my Dad were alive—he would know in a heartbeat."

He started to choke up, but caught himself. "It's a good thing you spotted this guy—a few moments later and, well, it wouldn't have been a pretty picture. He's good—I'd like to know how he got past Stella's system. Tell Jack that weapon is a game changer. I doubt the commanding officer will be able to keep this quiet for more than a day or two." Spencer and his men left, and Larry hurried back to tell Jack what almost happened.

*****

Needless to say, I was dumbfounded by Larry's account of the incident. Martin and I thanked him profusely for spotting the guy, trying not to think about what might have been. I have to admit I was pretty shaken up. Here I'd been calmly reviewing our strategy while some guy had come within seconds of blowing me and everyone else to smithereens. Martin started to suggest that perhaps Larry shouldn't have been wandering the grounds, but I stopped him. We were all damned lucky he'd been out there today. I asked Martin to try to track down Clovis. I missed him, and as things were getting dicier, we needed his steadying hand.

No word from Micki, which I took as a good sign, so I called Ken Chandler at the *Post*.

"We should meet," I began.

"Why bother? You've already sold Rachel down the river."

"What are you talking about?" I asked, trying to remain calm.

"Cotton just had a press conference to announce the settlement of the asset forfeiture case."

"Why is that a problem? It's proof that Rachel is innocent," I said.

"Cotton insisted that she was guilty, but because she's no longer alive, it would be a waste of the government's assets to continue to fight over such a paltry amount of money. His magnanimity was overwhelming."

I didn't think Micki would be able to get Cotton to back off Rachel's guilt. The reference to "a paltry amount of money" meant Micki had decided not to mention the million dollars. I couldn't wait to find out what had happened.

Ken continued, "My editor has told me to drop the story. Rachel is dead, the civil suit settled. There's nothing to write about."

It was time to put a few cards on the table. "Ken, Micki and I would like to meet with you and your editor this afternoon. After that meeting, if he still thinks you should drop the story, so be it. But he owes it to you and Rachel to hear me out."

"Can't you give me something right now?" he asked.

"Cotton said we were only fighting over a 'paltry' amount of money. Did Micki say or do anything to confirm that statement?" I asked.

"No, she didn't have to. The inventory is a now public filing; Cotton removed the seal," he answered.

"What if I were to tell you that the inventory fails to list a bank account belonging to Rachel containing over a million dollars? I wish to remind you we are still off the record." I emphasized the latter.

He took a moment to gather his thoughts. "Where would she have gotten that kind of money?" he asked.

"Maybe a better question is why would the government, without so much as a whimper, return more than a million dollars that came from an off-shore account to the estate of an alleged spy?"

"I can't run with this without some kind of documentation," he said.

"I wouldn't expect you to. That's why I want to meet with both you and your editor. It's time I told you what I know." I figured Micki and I would have plenty of time to backtrack, if she disagreed with my strategy.

"I'll call you back if he agrees," he said, hanging up without another word.

Stella walked into the family room, and I said, "I miss your boyfriend."

She laughed, "I do, too. I told him he better come back soon; those SEALs are looking better every day. I finally managed to track down that wire transfer. It originated in Malta, and I traced the funds to an off-shore account belonging to a subsidiary of Rouss Military Systems. They're turning up a lot these days."

"They sure are," I said. "Do you have any documentation? Do you have a name for the subsidiary?"

She smiled. "I gave the documentation to Maggie and Beth who are putting together your exhibits. The subsidiary is none other than Surplus Systems, Ltd. What do you hear from Micki?"

Micki and Brian walked into the room before I could respond. Micki was in a snit. She'd found out that Larry had discovered the sniper and had gone with the SEALs to capture him.

"I may kill him myself," she said, fuming. "Imagine wandering around without clearing it with Martin or anyone."

"He saved our lives," I reminded her, quick to come to his defense.

"I know, I know, but he shouldn't be taking chances. Where is he?"

"The last time I saw him he said he was going for a long shower," I joked. With Micki, showers carried a special message. "Why don't you go talk to him? Brian can tell me what happened with Cotton."

She looked angry for about a second and then smiled. "He saved your lives?"

"Sure did. Maybe yours, too. Now go check on him before we need to get back to work," I ordered.

"Whatever you say, sir." She saluted and sauntered out of the room.

"Okay, Brian, pour yourself a coffee. I'll get Maggie and Beth— we all want to hear what happened with Cotton."

We settled in, and he began. "Cotton and his deputy, Carl Clifford, agreed to return everything in her regular bank account and her Pentagon pension. They brought her computer and phone with them, as well as her rings and other personal effects.

"All Micki had to do was approve the dismissal of the lawsuit and sign a release from any liability for wrongful forfeiture."

"The release was limited only to the wrongful seizure of her assets, right? Nothing else?"

"Nothing else. Micki and I went over it word by word," he answered. "She was worried that referencing another potential asset might raise a red flag, but we decided we had to chance it."

"And?" I pressed.

"She told them she was concerned that another asset might turn up after the release had been signed, giving as an example a second car or a timeshare no one knew about."

"Cotton's deputy argued that since no assets had been seized other than those on the inventory, a newly discovered asset wouldn't be subject to the seizure complaint.

"But Micki continued to talk about her 'fiduciary duty,' just wouldn't let go. Even I was getting exasperated when Cotton suggested a solution. They would change the language of the release and dismissal to release any government claim from any of Rachel's assets, known or unknown."

"Known or unknown?" I asked, hardly able to believe our good fortune.

"Known or unknown. Micki is convinced Cotton doesn't know about the Parra Bank account; she's not so sure about Clifford. He was drumming his fingers on the table when Cotton wrote out the language and gave it to his assistant to prepare, but he was in a box."

"Micki couldn't get him to back off having a press conference, and he wasn't about to say Rachel was innocent, but I suspect she let him get away with his moment because we got we wanted," Brian finished.

"Good work, both of you," I said as Micki and Larry entered the room. He looked a little sheepish, and Micki's hair was damp. Any anger about Larry's walk-about had evaporated.

I filled them in on my calls to Peggy Fortson and Ken Chandler, then figured it was time to give out instructions.

"Brian, you're in charge of getting the funds at Parra Bank moved into my trust account. If you need any help, ask Maggie."

"Martin and Stella, if that rocket had hit the building our evidence would have gone up with it. Please find another place to store the originals of the zip drive, Spencer's letter, and the other documentation."

"Beth and Maggie," I said turning to them. "After Micki and I meet with the *Post* this afternoon, we should know whether phase two will work or we have to go to phase three. If they don't take the meeting, all bets are off. We need all the documents organized. Maggie, you know what I need, and Beth can help.

"Martin, Larry, our intruder got past our system. By the way, thanks again Larry, I—we all—owe you one." His only response was a barely perceptible nod. "Is there anything else we can do to keep intruders out? I sure hope our SEALs decide to stay for a few more days."

I looked at Beth. She was chewing on her lower lip, a childhood habit I had failed to break. "Do you think the bad guys will try something again?" she asked.

"I do. By now they've surely figured out that we have three of their people in custody. I'm afraid they'll bring an army next time." I hated to be so blunt.

"Stella, I doubt you'll find much of anything on Rachel's computer or phone, but will you check them out, please."

Everyone went off to do his or her tasks, including Martin and Larry, who wanted to do another tour of the property, which left me alone with Micki.

"Good job today," I offered.

"We got lucky, thanks to Cotton's eagerness to settle. You know you've boxed the bad guys in a corner. They're bound to come out clawing and biting."

"I know, and it's driving me crazy that we still don't know exactly who they are. That sniper guy will never talk, and the other two are just stooges. I have a feeling there's another layer we haven't uncovered, someone we haven't reached yet. But we've gotten this far, maybe our luck will hold."

"Right," she said with a laugh. "And maybe the bad guys are out of rocket launchers."

71

KEN CALLED TO ASK if we could meet with his editor at one-thirty. That gave us time to get downtown, but we'd have to work on our tactics on the way. I said a few encouraging words to the team, and we left.

When Micki and I arrived at the offices of *The Washington Post,* I admit to feeling queasy with self-doubts. An intern escorted us to a small conference room, no coffee and no pastries. After waiting more than a few minutes, Micki gathered up her papers in irritation. "This isn't worth it. We can figure out a better way to get the story out."

"Calm down. They're just playing games, trying to look reluctant so we agree to give them more information. Patience is a virtue, Ms. Lawrence."

She smiled, "I'm sorry. I'm not known for my virtue."

Fortunately, Ken and his editor, T. J. Henry, arrived before she got really pissed off. T. J. was a trim man who looked to be about sixty. His hairline was beginning to recede, and the round wire-rimmed glasses he wore gave him an owlish appearance.

After the usual introductions, Ken pulled out a tape recorder and turned it on—the opening gambit.

"Come on, Ken. You and I had an agreement. Off the record first— don't play games. You've worked hard on this, don't screw it up now. Micki and I are here to fill in the gaps in your story."

T.J. growled, "What gaps? How would you know about any gaps?"

"This morning Ken told me I had sold Rachel Goodman down the river, and that you were taking him off the story. Now, only a few hours later, we find ourselves sitting in this nice conference room.

Why? Because he discovered there's way more at issue than thirty pieces of silver."

T.J. tugged at his lower lip and said, "You're right. We're meeting because Ken told me that Rachel received a large sum of money from an off-shore account. What I don't understand is why you would present such clear evidence of your client's guilt."

"Simple. You don't know the details of the transfer yet, and the details establish the fact that my client was framed. The money wasn't deposited into Rachel's account until weeks after her arrest. To avoid anyone from discovering this clumsy mistake, the government hid the deposit's existence from us, the court, and the public at large.

"But don't assume we settled in order to obtain the million dollars. That money never belonged to Rachel, and we make no claim to it. We have what we wanted from the get go: Rachel's computer and cell phone."

"What good are her computer and phone? The government has assured us they've both been wiped clean," asked Ken, looking confused.

"We have one of the foremost forensic computer experts in the country on board. For example, Ken, would you like to know how many times you talked to Rachel? For how long, and on what days?"

Micki kicked me under the chair, but Ken gave the game away with a stutter. "Th-those conversations were confidential."

Time to tone it down. "Listen, your conversations weren't recorded, but I hope to read about them in the articles you write. I have no intention of putting anyone else's life in danger, especially yours. Who would write the story?"

T.J. asked, "Then why are you here?"

"To give you the documentation about the bank account, and to let you interview Micki off the record about the Cotton negotiations. You'll need both before you call Cotton to get his version of the facts. My bet is Cotton will deny knowing anything about the account, which may be true. But someone in his office had to know. Otherwise how could the government have seized the account? You might also ask why it wasn't included in the inventory. I wonder when it will dawn on him that Micki tricked him into giving up over a million dollars?"

"I'm more interested in asking him where the money came from," Ken said.

"I will tell you what we've discovered, but it has to be off the record. Any problems with that?"

T.J. nodded his agreement, so I answered.

"Two hundred thousand dollars of the money has been in the account for two years. This money was a lump-sum life insurance payment Rachel received after her husband died. Another hundred thousand accumulated by installments of four thousand dollars a month, a widow's pension from her husband's employer. That employer was an arm of the Israeli government."

"So she did receive money from Israel," T.J. stated flatly.

"Yes, and I'll bet some anonymous source told your paper the money was payment by Israel for Rachel's spying. In fact, they were legitimate payments—a widow's pension, and by international treaty pension money is not subject to tax or seizure. What's more, the Israeli government explained the life insurance and pension payments to our government to absolve themselves, and our government asked them to keep quiet." I handed him a copy of Lauren and Matt's research.

T.J. was asking the questions now. "Let's say we were told that payments from Israel were made into this account to the tune of four thousand dollars each month. You're saying these payments were a widow's pension, not money for spying?"

"I am, and I have the documentation to prove it."

"Yet the government seized that money, along with her life insurance money, but didn't list the bank account on the inventory? I know we're off the record, but I want to be sure to get it right."

"Yes, and a few weeks after her arrest, a million dollars hit her account. I think it was to bolster the story that she was a spy, but the source of the money knows better why it was wired and why it came in after the arrest. For all I know, it might have been a payment to the U. S. Attorney's office."

"I assume the source of the money was Israel." T.J. relaxed until I answered.

"No, the source wasn't the state of Israel or anyone affiliated with Israel."

Ken almost shouted, "Then who?"

"I think you know," I answered.

"How would Ken know?" T.J. interrupted.

"Because he was working with Rachel and a man named Harold Spencer. I don't know the extent of their communications because Spencer's phone was taken from him when he was killed. Ask Ken who has the resources to wire that kind of money into her account."

T.J. looked to Ken, who answered quietly, "The money came from Rouss Military Systems."

"Technically, it came from an off-shore subsidiary of Rouss. I'll give you the information we uncovered, and you can make your own determination," I told them.

T.J. responded, "You've put yourself in a pretty dangerous position, don't you think? Two people are already dead."

I remained silent, trying to look unconcerned. He frowned at my silence, and I finally responded.

"Yes, and as a matter of fact, there have been at least two attempts on our lives, but I will not turn belly up. Rachel and Harold deserve more. My hope is that once Ken reports that my client was framed, by whom and why, the bad guys will lawyer up and back off. See how helpful we can be to each other?"

T.J. smiled for the first time. "It sounds like you have more to tell us, and I bet you'd like a little help from *The Post*. Let's get that out on the table."

"You're right, I do. But for the next eight hours, your plate is full. You need to interview Micki, verify the information we've given you, and get to the bottom of why your source lied about the payments to Rachel. Ken needs to write his story about the wire transfer, and the *Post* might want to write an apology to the state of Israel.

"Add to that, the moment Ken calls Rouss to ask about payments into Rachel's bank account, both your publisher and editor-in-chief will receive calls demanding that Ken's story be killed. Am I right?" I asked.

"I suspect you are right. But, once more, what do you want?"

"At the least, I want Ken to call Cotton and Rouss. I want you to book the National Press Club tomorrow afternoon for a briefing where I will lay out what we have discovered to date—on the record. You may assemble as many *Post* reporters as you want, and I leave to your judgment whether you wish to invite other members of the press. I do plan to invite a few guests who are either public officials or employees of Rouss. I'd also like to meet with Ken again tomorrow morning, off the record, so he can tell me if any of the information I have is inconsistent with what he's discovered. And, finally, I want the *Post* to publish a piece in tomorrow's paper outlining the facts of the million-dollar deposit, even if you have to say Micki duped Cotton."

T.J. had taken off his wire-rims and was rubbing his eyes. At last he sighed and said, "Okay, you've got it. If we can't get the Press Club, I'll find another suitable venue. I'll email you within the hour to tell you where and when. I'll talk to the higher-ups about inviting other members of the media. It might help the credibility of our stories, but I bet my editor-in-chief will want an exclusive. We'll run a story under Ken's byline in tomorrow's paper. No guarantees about placement or content, but if the documentation pans out it won't be just about Ms. Lawrence duping Cotton.

"But I'm curious, why meet with Ken off the record first tomorrow?" he asked.

"Because like you, I expect the subjects of my investigation will stop at nothing to prevent the press conference. If they should succeed, I want Ken to have all the information we've uncovered. But I don't want to be its source if I have to go to our back-up plan," I answered.

"You have a back-up plan?" T.J. asked.

"I always have a back-up plan."

72

WHILE KEN INTERVIEWED Micki, T.J. and I talked in hypotheticals about what else I'd discovered. I wanted him to realize that I hadn't showed all my cards. Micki and Ken emerged from a small office after about an hour, and we left immediately.

Big Mike was waiting in the Tahoe, and I called Maggie as soon as we were settled in the back seat. "The meeting at the *Post* went better than I expected; we're on our way back. Can you get everybody in the family room in about an hour? The press conference is on for tomorrow, and I'll need everyone's help preparing. We should probably have a run-through tonight."

"We'll be ready. You'll be glad to know that our SEALs are back and working with Martin on security, expecting the worst. John Robert told us that the C.O. at the military base gave them twenty-four hours before he has to report the prisoners' existence and the missile system. Clovis should be back soon. His plane is in the air."

I hung up and asked Micki, "How'd the interview go?"

"Good, I think. Ken's done a lot of leg work and seems to have his facts straight. He doesn't think Cotton has any idea there's a separate bank account not listed on the inventory, much less that it contains more than a million dollars. Ken told me Cotton may be ambitious, but he's a straight shooter. He expects Cotton to go nuclear."

"Good. Learn anything else?"

"Right now, he believes Rachel was set up, but not murdered. Her death is the biggest unknown in what we have, that is unless Bart Stone confesses. My bet is that Rachel told Ken a lot more than he's admitted, but he lacks the hard evidence that we have in the zip drive. His focus is on Rouss, and he doesn't see any broader conspiracy. I have to tell you I have my doubts about that, too,

"That's not surprising. Rachel thought she'd uncovered a scheme for Rouss to make more money. I have a feeling that the scheme goes way beyond greed, but I could be wrong. God knows I have been before."

"Well, if you are wrong, then it's on to phase three, that back-up plan you haven't yet shared with your partner," she teased.

"What make you think I've got a back-up plan?" I asked.

"Because you told T.J. you always have a back-up plan," she reminded me.

"Oh that. Did I ever tell you I can run a mean bluff at poker?" We both laughed.

"Speaking of bluffs, what if Ken had called yours about Stella cracking a scrubbed cell phone?"

I shrugged my shoulders.

Micki turned serious. "What's your biggest worry about tomorrow?"

"If the chips don't fall right, my back-up plan will take a while. There's no way we can all live under this intense scrutiny for any length of time."

"So you have a back-up plan, but it won't work." She laughed and punched me on the arm.

"In a nutshell, yes," I laughed. "Hell of a mess I've gotten you into, once again." I smiled, and we were both quiet. Micki unbuckled her seat belt and scooted over to rest her head on my arm.

"Hell of a mess," she whispered, and we rode the rest of the way home in silence.

*****

Maggie met us at the car.

"At this rate we'll need to hire another cook. John Robert brought along a few more buddies who don't believe what the guys are saying about Stella's workouts. She's had to add an afternoon session."

Micki went inside quickly to search for Larry. I noticed John

Robert sitting on the porch, so I said to Maggie, "Come on, I'd like you to sit in."

I sat down on the swing and asked, "How's your mom?"

"She sounds happy, and relieved to be away," he responded. "She's a strong woman, but she was pretty spooked by all that's happened."

"She should be—I'm a little spooked myself. Listen, John Robert, I appreciate you guys being here, but this post could be hazardous duty for the next few days. You might want to reconsider."

"We'll leave when we are no longer needed. You're trying to find out who killed my father, something I can't do. The least we can do is offer a little protection. Stella is getting us in better shape than we thought possible, and protecting your perimeter is valuable training. The danger is real, but there isn't a man or woman who doesn't want to be here."

I couldn't have talked him out of putting his life on the line if I'd wanted to, which I didn't. So I figured I might as well give him the rest of it.

"I need to tell you it's likely that whoever is behind all this will try to destroy your father's reputation. I'll do everything in power to stop it from happening, but I can't promise—the press can be brutal."

The confident smile on his young face faded. "I told you Dad wasn't the best of husbands or fathers, but I loved him, and so did my mother."

He took a deep breath before continuing. "He spent a week in Vegas four times a year, and he didn't just play poker. He took full advantage of the perks Vegas offers high rollers. I won't go into the other things he did to make both my mother's and my life miserable, but we made it past his outbursts and remained a family. It wasn't exactly a secret, so I'm not worried about his reputation. Do your best, Mr. Patterson, and let the chips fall where they may."

Maggie put her hand on his shoulder, and I thanked him for the confidence.

Ken called to confirm that we were on for tomorrow afternoon at two o'clock at the National Press Club. I assembled our group and handed out assignments: phone calls to invitees, exhibit books ready to go, security logistics. All those little details needed to be in place.

So far, Stella had been unable to coax any further information from Rachel's computer, but she was still trying. I was about to call Lucy when she called me.

"Jack, I owe it to you to let you know I've accepted the chairmanship of the Senate Armed Services Subcommittee on Readiness and Management Support."

"Congratulations! I take it the quid pro quo for this appointment is for you to attack me for being a greedy, shyster of a lawyer who's made outrageous accusations about my client's innocence and murder."

"I also intend to ask the government to revoke your security clearance—I hope you understand."

I didn't, but throwing me under the bus was pure Lucy. At least she'd been rewarded with more than thirty pieces of silver.

"Lucy, do yourself a favor. Lock up the chairmanship today, but wait until you've read tomorrow's *Post* to go after me. And you might want to send one of your best staffers to a press briefing scheduled for two o'clock at the National Press Club."

I could hear her fingernails clicking on the wood of her desk. "A press briefing. Yours, Jack? And what about the *Post?* They're not writing about *me*, are they?"

"No, it won't be about you, Lucy, so relax. But I'm pretty sure it will cast new light on the Goodman matter. I'm very sure it would be a mistake for you to speak out against me or my team before the press briefing."

"Come on, Jack, tell me what this is all about!" she demanded shrilly. This was the old, insecure Lucy, not the newly polished senator.

"And spoil all the fun? Hope to see you tomorrow. Good night, Lucy."

I heard, "Damn you, Jack,' before the line went dead. I heard an odd, snuffling noise and realized that Maggie was trying to control her laughter.

Still laughing, she escaped to the kitchen, and I got up to stretch my legs and collect my thoughts before calling Peggy Fortson. I wasn't at all sure she would take my call.

This time I went through proper channels, so it was some time before I got through to her.

"Jack, I'm sick of your lunch, brunch, dinner routine. What do you want now?" Okay, forget friendship, time to play it straight.

"Peggy, I'm calling to invite you to a press briefing tomorrow afternoon at the National Press Club. I think you may find it worth your while."

Her comeback hurt. "I never thought you'd become a media hound. What's wrong, Jack, can't get anyone to listen to your off-the-wall theories?"

I felt a slow burn. She knew exactly which buttons to push. I struggled to keep an even tone.

"Something like that, yeah. The Attorney General won't meet with me, and the U.S. Attorney still insists Rachel was a spy, so the *Post* was kind enough to invite a few folks to hear my story. You know—the one where I explain why Rachel was framed and murdered."

"C'mon, Jack, that's not fair. A meeting with the AG would be useless. You know as well as I do that we've been excluded from any investigation into how Rachel stole military secrets, or why she committed suicide for that matter."

"Yeah, so you told me. That's really too bad. Because if you'd listened, if you had been at the table, you'd know there hasn't been any investigation, nor will there ever be. Peggy, I'm trying to protect you, but events are moving fast. You are running out of time. Tomorrow morning the *Post* will run a piece that will probably ruin Donald Cotton's political ambitions, and tomorrow afternoon we will go public with the rest of the story.

"The DOJ won't give me an audience, so I have no choice but to make my findings public. I chose the National Press Club because I want the invited guests to know that I am confident, that this is a serious issue, and that I have real evidence that Rachel wasn't a spy. Nothing I say will implicate the AG, but I'm about to hand you a mess of dramatic proportions. If I'm wrong, you'll have a front row seat to see me fall flat on my face."

"Who else is coming? Or will you be talking to the walls?" Tough words, but I could hear a note of anxiety creep into her voice.

"I hope not. I've extended invitations to Rouss Military Systems, the Israeli ambassador and several other ambassadors, the director of the CIA, the head of the NSC, the Intelligence Czar, and several senior deputies at the Pentagon, for starters."

"You didn't include the Secretary of State?" I ignored her sarcasm.

"No, I believe he's in India. But we have invited his deputy as well as the Chairman of the Senate Foreign Relations Committee and his counterpart on the House side. Oh—I've also invited Senator Lucy Robinson whose committee has an interest in what I'm up to these days."

"You expect these people to show up to listen to a DC antitrust lawyer who's lost his marbles?"

No anxiety now. She was clearly trying to piss me off.

"No, I don't expect the big dogs to show, but I think that after tomorrow's article in the *Post* we might get a staffer or two."

We were getting nowhere, and I could feel my patience waning. I couldn't figure out her hostility; maybe she just needed some time to think and the opportunity to brief the AG.

"Peggy, just drop by tomorrow. It'll be fun," I pleaded.

"You have a warped sense of humor, Jack Patterson. What is it that you want?"

A good question, and I didn't hesitate in answering.

"Justice, Peggy. Justice for Rachel Goodman, but in one word: Justice."

73

MOST OF THE TEAM reported similar results from their phone calls: polite comments that the invitation would be "conveyed to the right person." At least no one could say they hadn't been forewarned. Micki volunteered to call Cotton.

"He clearly hadn't heard from Ken yet, because butter wouldn't melt in his mouth. When I extended the invitation, he said, 'Why in the world would I want to hear Jack Patterson whine about Rachel Goodman's innocence?'"

Maggie complained, "Why do you give me the assholes? I managed to get through to Dennis Maxwell at Rouss. He told me in short order that hell would freeze over before he attended one of 'Jack Patterson's circus shows.' I got the impression you aren't on his A list. The ambassadors were what we expected. I was routed to a staff member who took the information and promised to pass on the invitation. We'll be lucky to get an intern to show."

"I almost forgot. Micki, please call Rabbi Strauss. I bet somebody higher than an intern shows up from Israel. How did you guys do with the military types?"

"We had a little better luck," Brian replied. "I expect the under-Secretary of Defense for Acquisitions and Technology to send several staffers. The CIA pretended they didn't know who Rachel was, but they'll send someone. I also contacted a friend at JAG. After all, Rachel's murder did occur on a military base. They're sending a senior JAG officer."

"Good thinking. Sounds like we might have a crowd," I said.

Micki brought me back to reality. "A crowd of junior staffers and interns."

"The *Post* article should gin up a bit of interest," I said.

Maggie said, "You're putting a lot of faith in Ken and T.J. What if tomorrow's piece is a hatchet job?"

"Then we'll adjust accordingly. We will not panic, and no matter what the *Post* reports, we will proceed. Thank you everyone. After dinner, which Maggie tells me is about ready, I want to have a dress rehearsal of tomorrow's events."

John Robert asked to skip the rehearsal. "It's not because of my dad. If something happens, it's likely to be tonight. My men want to deploy throughout the grounds tonight."

I walked him to the front door, and stood there a few minutes, wondering where Clovis was. I needed him for the dress rehearsal. He'd find the weaknesses in our plans. I admit I was also getting a little worried.

I had just turned to go inside when I heard the noise of tires on the gravel driveway. Clovis jumped out of the front seat, flashing an easy grin. Thank God.

"What are you grinning about?" I smiled in return.

"Well, this place hasn't burned down, and I made it back in time for both tonight's briefing and tomorrow's fireworks. Stella and Maggie have been keeping me up to date. Sounds like you're way out on a limb. You sure you know what you're doing?"

"No, but I know you can plug the holes. How was Ben?"

"Anxious, but the restaurant is open and he's selling more barbecue than ever before. You were right: he had to get back on the horse. One bit of good news is that Ben Jr. has moved back to Little Rock. Linda says they're already bickering. She's thrilled to have one of her children back home."

"It won't surprise me if Lee comes home, too," I mused. "The accusations and allegations are pulling the family together. Who knows? Maybe even the daughter-in-law will change her tune. How's Jeff? And was a trip to St. Louis really necessary?"

"Ask him yourself—he flew back with me."

"He did? Where is he?" I turned back toward the door.

"Calm down. He and Beth are reintroducing themselves. They'll join us later. Let me tell you what I know, and they don't."

"Oh, great—more secrets. What now?" I asked.

"Well, you know I've been worried the bad guys might go after Ben, so I used Walter's plane to go to Little Rock. While I was there, I got a call from our friends in St. Louis. Someone was following Jeff, and they wanted to make sure it wasn't one of mine before they picked him up.

"Paul had everything under control, so I hightailed it to St. Louis. Our friends had the fellow in custody. He's clearly former military. Jeff doesn't have a clue, but if our friends hadn't stepped in, Jeff might have been kidnapped or worse.

"This guy must not have enjoyed his time with our St. Louis friends. By the time I got there, he was scared shitless, ready to do most anything to get out of St. Louis. So I bundled him into the plane and delivered him to the Montgomery County Police. We had a nice talk on the flight home. He swears he didn't kill Spencer, but has a good idea who did. He also knew all about the attempt on my life. Sam is working with the Maryland County prosecutor; as soon as they know anything definitive they'll let me know."

"Seems you've been busy," I deadpanned.

"You could say that. I decided it might be a good idea for Jeff to come for a visit, although I'm not sure he's safer here. Beth told him about the sniper and Stone—he didn't take much convincing."

I wasn't hungry. While everyone else ate I walked to the porch, took a seat on the porch swing, and tried to gather my thoughts and emotions. The sun was setting across the fields, and the sky was a vivid red, reminding me of Jo's hair.

She was as open and transparent as Carol was closed and secretive. My mind went to that first night when Jo showed up at the house with all the fixings for redneck margaritas. What wouldn't I give to be on Pawleys right now?

"Penny for your thoughts," Maggie said softly, handing me a glass of cabernet. "You worried about tomorrow?" She joined me on the swing.

"To tell you the truth I'm trying to figure out what happened to that simple life you and I once enjoyed. We had a nice law practice, you and Walter planned to travel, and Beth and Jeff had a great future. Now I'm in the fight of my life with people willing to launch a rocket to kill us all. Is telling Rachel's story worth it?"

"It was worth it to Rachel and Harold Spencer, and, despite the risk, it's worth it to those Navy SEALs who volunteered to guard us. Micki and Larry, Clovis and Stella aren't in this because they're loyal to you. We don't often encounter an injustice of this scope, nor do we often have the opportunity to influence the outcome. It's our responsibility to give it all we have." Maggie smiled and took a sip of her wine.

"As to a simple life, our life was never that simple, and it never will be. You attract complexity and danger, like a magnet attracts iron shavings. Simplicity sounds good, but you'd be bored to tears with a simple life—so would I, that's why we're such a good fit.

"Now I think it's time for you to come inside and tell us what tomorrow will bring. It's time for the big picture."

WEDNESDAY

74

THE *POST* was lying on the kitchen table when I got up the next morning. Micki and I had spent almost two hours last night going over our presentation for today. The group peppered us with questions, both ones we expected and some that were off-the-wall. Jeff was the most vocal, since he was brand new to the story.

I had made it a point to review the information on Rachel's zip drive again before I went to sleep. Rachel had downloaded all her notes, beginning with her trip to Israel to bury her husband's remains. They revealed an intelligent young woman whose love for her husband had driven her to spend the last two years pursuing Rouss. I went to bed with Clovis's final words spinning in my head.

"Some way, somehow, they'll stop you."

I picked up the *Post*, scanned the front page and found the headline just below the fold:

U.S. ATTORNEY ACCUSES PATTERSON OF FRAUD

FEDS RELEASE OVER $1M TO GOODMAN'S ESTATE

The article that carried Ken Chandler's byline was much better than the headline. It verified that Rachel's bank account at Parra Bank and her other assets had been seized on the same day as her arrest, and that the Parra Bank account held funds from a life insurance policy and pension money owed to her by the Israeli government after her husband died. It went on to state that the account wasn't listed on the government's inventory of seized assets, and that a million dollars from an off-shore account had been deposited in the account two weeks after Rachel's arrest.

The article failed to mention that the money had come from a subsidiary of Rouss. I wondered how difficult Ken's editors had been and whether he'd tried to argue about the headline. In the old days, before budget cuts and the proliferation of online news, reporters seldom wrote their own headlines. I felt sure Ken hadn't written this one either. The article continued with a brief description of the negotiations to settle the forfeiture case, describing how we had discovered the account while searching for her widow's pension.

The article gave equal treatment to Cotton's explanation. Cotton claimed he had no knowledge of the account, and that since the inventory didn't show the account's existence, he had agreed to close the case by settling the forfeiture case for "peanuts." When Ken pressed him that someone in his office must have been aware of the account, he blamed the "oversight" on an overworked staff.

Cotton was adamant that Micki and I had committed fraud. "They knew I would never give up a million dollars to the estate of America's Mata Hari," he blustered and vowed to be in court this morning to set aside the settlement and to get a court order ordering me to return all of Rachel's assets. He probably wanted her wedding rings back, too.

We expected this maneuver and were ready should he follow through with his threat. He couldn't vacate the settlement without a hearing, and a hearing would allow me to discover what and when his office knew about the account. It would also allow me to file a counterclaim against his office for seizing Rachel's widow's pension despite a number of international treaties prohibiting such tactics. Moreover, if he did manage to reinstate the seizure, we'd get our chance to prove her innocence in court.

The last line of the article mentioned that I would hold a briefing at the National Press Club this afternoon at two o'clock. The *Post* had decided to open the event to other media. Fine with me.

Micki walked in, looking for coffee, and I handed her the paper just as my phone rang. It was Lucy.

"You commit fraud, yet you want me to hold my fire until you make a bigger fool of yourself?"

"I didn't commit fraud. Cotton and his staff did by hiding the account and failing to tell the court of its existence. As far as making a fool of myself, why don't you come watch?"

"I have much better things to do, thank you very much," she snapped.

"I'm sure you do, but you might ask the Chairman of the Foreign Relations Committee if he's going."

"Senator Benton? What in the hell are you up to, Jack?"

"Making a fool of myself," I said, and clicked off. I'd spent too much time and energy trying to keep Lucy from making a fool of herself.

Micki wasn't happy with the headline, but we both knew that the fact the *Post* had published anything was helpful, and the article itself wasn't too bad. The next call was from Ken.

"I'm sorry about the headline." I shrugged it off, and he continued. "My editors are being cautious. They're scared to death of Rouss, scared of getting sued."

"I would expect nothing less. Sounds like Cotton was ready for your call."

"When I called to ask him about the account, he denied its existence. Who did I take him for, et cetera, and hung up. A few minutes later he called back to apologize, saying he'd accidentally dropped his phone. He talked about his overworked staff and spouted his fraud theory. I wanted to write about the conversation, but my editors made me play it safe."

"When and where do you want to meet?" I asked.

"You still going forward? After the headline, I figured my name was mud."

"I don't write newspaper articles or headlines—that's your job. My job is to get out the truth, and right now you're my best chance of doing so. Why don't we meet at Barker's, say about eleven?"

"Cotton's holding a press briefing at ten; let's make it eleven-thirty. Does that give you enough time?" Ken asked.

"Eleven-thirty at Barker's. See you there."

I hung up and told Micki about Cotton's briefing.

She shook her head. "I thought he'd have better sense."

"Me too, but we'd better send Brian. Whatever he says, we'll need to deal with it this afternoon. We're meeting Ken at Barker's at eleven-thirty."

"Barker's! I thought your club was for men only. Clovis and Judge Fitzgerald have been, but you've never taken me," she teased.

"That's because you and Larry were too busy rolling in the sheets at the Hay-Adams," I responded.

"You're just jealous."

"Damn right, I am. And for the record, Barker's membership is open to women. I think we have four or five women now."

The cook was busy making pancakes and bacon, and it wasn't long before the aroma had lured everyone to the kitchen. We took coffee and heaping plates into the family room. We ate in congenial silence, the morning peace disturbed only by the moans and groans emanating from Stella's morning class. She had picked up the pace again.

My phone rang again—this time it was Red.

"I leave town for a few days, and you're on the front page of the *Post*. Yes, I'm back in town, and I'll thank you not to ask where I've been."

"Wouldn't think of it. I figure you'll tell me if I need to know," I responded.

Red's voice rang with true appreciation. "Thank you, Jack. I appreciate your discretion." Then it was back to normal. "I thought you'd want to know that Carol never left town."

"I'm not surprised. I invited her client, Rouss, to my briefing this afternoon,"

"You don't sound happy. Anything you want to tell me?"

"No. I've got a lot on my plate. After I present my case this afternoon, maybe we can have a private talk."

"I'd like that. I told Lucy to keep her powder dry until she hears what you have to say. Don't know if she was listening. You know Lucy."

"That I do," I laughed.

"Oh, one last thing—do you have an extra ticket for this afternoon's fireworks? I thought I might send my public relations guy to watch."

"I'll put him on the list," I replied, and after getting the information on his guy we hung up.

Carol's presence in DC could mean only one thing—she would be at the briefing. This was a curve ball I hadn't anticipated. The increasing noise finally interrupted my reverie—I was reminded of a fund drive for public radio. Maggie, Larry, and Micki were all dealing with calls.

"What's going on?" I asked no one in particular.

Maggie put her phone down and said, "I've taken calls from two embassies so far—both are sending attachés. They're calling back to confirm the place and time. Word is getting out, Jack." She turned to her ringing phone.

The *Post* article had done its work. News travels fast in DC, and when one person decides an event is a must-attend, no one wants to be left out. I wondered if the *Post* and the Press Club were getting similar responses. The answer came from Martin.

"Be careful what you ask for, Jack. Security for the bigwigs is all over me. They want to know where they can stand and if they're allowed to bring in firearms. John Robert and I are off to the Press Club now for a security meeting. Don't worry—I have plenty of drivers, and a number of John Robert's friends are watching this place."

I could feel the excitement grow as I watched Beth and Maggie put together a list of attendees. My own phone rang—I was surprised to see Peggy's number. She answered with no preliminaries.

"I'm not happy about it, but the AG has decided we should both come to your shindig. He thinks this whole thing is funny, just laughs every time someone, usually me, objects to your little circus.

"Cotton has been calling all morning, but the AG won't take the call, said to let him stew in his own juice. Lawyers for about a half dozen defense contractors have demanded an immediate meeting, but he waved them off. He asked his FBI detail to make sure we have front-row seats.

"As a result of all the angst generated by the *Post* article and your impending press conference, I have an appointment in the S.C.I.F. for a video conference with State, Defense, the NSC, and God-knows who else to decide what to do if you spill government secrets. Can't you please dial this thing back for at least a few days?"

S.C.I.F., or Sensitive Compartmented Information Facility, is simply the common acronym for a secure room where sensitive information can be reviewed and discussed. I wondered idly how the one at DOJ would match up with one designed by Stella. When I worked at Justice, I always thought individuals impressed with their own importance overused it.

"Please tell me this is all a joke, maybe just a bad dream."

"Peggy, as far as I know I have no government secrets to spill. And there's only one way you can get me to back off. Someone way above Cotton's pay grade has to admit that Rachel was innocent and was murdered."

I heard a deep moan. "Jack, you know the government will never admit that Rachel was innocent, much less murdered. Nor will the government allow you to have this briefing. It's just too risky. Maybe I was wrong. Maybe I should have insisted that the AG take your meeting. But a full-scale press briefing in front of national and international media is out of the question. Call it off, Jack, and I'll try to work something out."

I wanted to trust Peggy and the AG. In fact, I did trust them. But the power of "national security" had closed the door once before and, given an inch, would surely do so again.

"Peggy, I'm sorry this situation is tough for you, but it isn't personal, it's business. Well, except for Rachel and Harold Spencer. You do what you have to do, and I will do what I must."

"Jack, you're giving me no choice. There is no way you're going public this afternoon."

"Peggy, you're wrong. There is no way you can stop me."

75

───◇───

As I put the phone down, I noticed Maggie pointedly tapping her wrist. I realized it was almost ten o'clock, time to leave. Maggie, Beth, and Jeff would go straight to the Press Club. Brian would join them after attending Cotton's press conference. Clovis and Stella would come with Micki and me to Barker's. I'd arranged for a small conference room where we would meet Ken.

We were about to leave, but I pulled Stella aside and said, "Stella, I need you to trust me one more time."

"Well, it's worked so far, and we're all still alive, so what do you need?"

"I've prepared a document that I need you to sign on blind faith. I hope we can tear it up after today." I handed it to her.

She looked it over and asked, "Do you really think we'll need this?"

"I sure hope not."

She took the pen I offered and signed it. "There. I told you it wasn't a big deal."

I gave it to Clovis and said, "Hang back for just a few minutes. Get Beth to gather the attachments referenced in this document and put them wherever we're keeping the original zip drive and Harold's letter."

Clovis looked at the document and grinned at Stella. "Jack always gets paranoid right before a big day."

Micki and I were soon sitting with Ken in a small conference room at Barker's, and enjoying ham sandwiches and the only potato

salad I'll eat in DC. Brian had called earlier to give us the gist of
Cotton's press briefing, but I wanted to hear about it from Ken.

"At first he was all hale and hearty, said he hadn't tried to set aside
the judgment because he was waiting for you to do the right thing.
You know, give back the million dollars voluntarily. What a crock!

"Then he encouraged all of us to ignore your press briefing,
predicting it would be just more whining from a lawyer who lost a
big fee when his client died. He said both government and private
attorneys would be there ready to sue if you defame. I asked him
who the clients were, but he totally ignored me. He went on to say
that his office was considering instigating disbarment proceeding
against you and Micki."

I laughed. Micki looked a little more concerned.

"The rest of his comments were a repetition of what he told me
last night: he didn't know about the account, the inventory was a
low-level assistant's error, probably just poor proofreading, and
the evidence against Rachel was overwhelming. He concluded by
saying the million dollars would be in the government's coffers by
this afternoon. I'm here to tell you it was one weird performance."

Micki responded, "The latter is impossible. If we did return the
money, it would go back into the seized bank account until a Court
determines its true ownership. We couldn't put it in the government's coffers even if we wanted to."

Ken asked if he could quote her, and she readily agreed.

I gave Ken a summary of what I would say and prove this afternoon. After the plates were cleared I asked, "Have I suggested
anything inconsistent with what you've discovered over the last few
months?"

"Rachel alluded to most of it through hypotheticals, but you've
gone way beyond even what she thought was happening. But, no,
your conclusions aren't inconsistent with what I've learned. It helps
to have the letter from Spencer. When can I get a copy?" he asked.

"This afternoon," I answered. I handed him a list of today's
attendees. He hadn't had time to check in with T.J., so he had no
idea who was coming.

Ken gave out a low whistle as he scanned the list. "There's no
way this briefing will come off. They'll lock you up first."

*****

On the way to the Press Club, Micki said, "I don't think I'm dressed for jail. Do you think they'll let me change before they lock us up?" She grinned, but we both knew the joke might be on us.

When we arrived, satellite trucks lined the streets, blocking traffic on both 14th and New York Ave. We rode the elevator up to the 13th floor and, to avoid the mob of reporters and guests, Martin and John Robert whisked us to a private room.

"I'll say this, you sure know how to draw a crowd," Martin drawled.

"Well, it never hurts to have the *Post* backing you."

T.J. rushed in to join us. He was clearly excited.

"So far we have five ambassadors, a bunch of ranking intelligence officials, staffers from three Hill committees, the Attorney General, the Director of the FBI, and more than a few uniforms, all waiting to hear what you've got to say.

"It's almost show time, so let's not keep 'em waiting. Our editor-in-chief will begin with a few words. The rest is up to you."

Micki squeezed my hand and whispered, "You can do this." We got up and walked in through a side door into the First Amendment Lounge.

I noticed Maggie and Beth, who were sitting off to my left. I could see the Attorney General, the Director of the FBI, and Peggy seated in the front row. Carol Madison was sitting a few rows back, next to Eric Hartman, chief lobbyist for Rouss—a slick dude if there ever was one. I also recognized several of the lawyers in the room, including one of my old partners at Banks and Tuohey. He specialized in libel law—I felt sure he would like nothing better than for me to defame his client and suffer the consequences.

The *Post's* editor-in-chief, Ralph Armbrust, stood at the podium. Ken had guided Micki and me to a table next to the podium that was equipped with additional microphones. The editor cleared his throat and began.

"I want to welcome everyone to this unusual event—a press briefing by the lawyers who represent the estate of Rachel Goodman. But before I turn the microphone over, I have a few words to say.

"When the *Post* ran the first story about the arrest of Rachel

Goodman, we reported what we understood to be the truth about
Israel's involvement in her alleged espionage. In fact, we reported
that the Israeli government made regular monthly payments to Ms.
Goodman and suggested that such payments were in exchange for
military secrets. Our newspaper was not alone in doing so."

Many heads were nodding in agreement, and I could hear the
murmur of whispered asides.

"Only yesterday did we learn, and have now confirmed from several independent sources, that Rachel Goodman did indeed receive
payments from the Israeli government." He paused for effect and
the noise level rose a bit.

"But the fact is that those payments had nothing to do with any
alleged spying. The Israeli government employed her husband, and
when he was killed she received a widow's pension from that same
government.

"*The Washington Post* apologizes to the Israeli people and its
government for this mistake. Our failure to check the accuracy of
the information and our willingness to assume the worst led us to
harm the relations between our country and Israel. I believe the
Israeli ambassador is with us today. Mr. Ambassador, on behalf of
my newspaper, I extend our sincerest apologies. A full retraction of
our stories will appear tomorrow in the *Post*. In addition, a full-page
ad paid for by the *Post* and apologizing to the people of Israel will
run in the *New York Times, the Chicago Tribune,* and the *L.A. Times*
tomorrow."

Wow—that was a surprise, and he was just getting started.

"Because of our failure to do our job, and because of the negli-
gence of the U.S. Attorney or someone in his office, my paper has
decided we owe it to both the public and Mrs. Goodman to hear
her version of the facts. As you can see, we also decided not to limit
access to whatever Mr. Patterson and Ms. Lawrence have discovered. It's high time we all listened to someone willing to talk on the
record, rather than taking as truth the words of those who only talk
off-the-record.

"That said, I will turn the microphone over to Mr. Patterson and
Ms. Lawrence."

I paused before rising. The buzz from the press had grown louder. My eyes turned to my team. They looked anxious. Then I looked toward Carol—she was looking daggers at me, as was her companion. I rose, took a deep breath and walked to the podium.

"Good afternoon...."

"Stop!" I heard and then saw Donald Cotton striding toward the podium waving a small stack of papers.

"Stop!" he shouted again. "I have a Court order that says you are to cease and desist from speaking to this group, that you and Ms. Lawrence are under arrest, and that all materials in your possession are to be confiscated."

Bedlam ensued, and while the editor-in-chief tried to restore calm, I took the papers from Cotton and scanned the Court order. There it was in black and white: both the greed and the gall. I handed the Order to Micki, stepped around the table and walked to the front row to confront Peggy, oblivious to the surrounding turmoil.

"I guess I was wrong, you stopped me after all."

"Jack, I don't know anything about this, I promise." Her eyes told me she was telling the truth.

I turned back to see Cotton at the podium. He was shouting into the microphone. "Marshal, restrain Mr. Patterson. Now if everyone will calm down and return to your seats, I'll explain why I had to take such drastic action."

I extended my hands to the two marshals who had appeared with handcuffs. Thank goodness they left Micki alone. Peggy looked aghast and started to rise, but the Attorney General pulled her back. I noticed John Robert and two of his SEALs moving in my direction, but I shook my head, and they backed off.

Grinning in triumph, Cotton was about to speak again when the Attorney General rose and walked directly to the podium. The AG's face was bright red—I don't know that I've ever seen an angrier man. He confronted Cotton head on.

"What is this, Cotton?" He didn't need a microphone.

76

THE MICROPHONE EASILY PICKED UP COTTON'S ANSWER. "Patterson committed fraud by failing to disclose the million-dollar wire transfer into Goodman's account during our negotiations. I went to court to get our money back and to prevent Patterson and Lawrence from exposing national secrets. My sources tell me that's their plan."

"So we throw the First Amendment out the window whenever someone threatens to say something we don't like? Did they teach you the concept of prior restraint at law school? When were you going to let me know about your actions?" the AG boomed.

"I didn't need to. If you remember, the special committee appointed by the Director of Intelligence placed litigation authority in my hands." I was pretty sure that Cotton had just shared confidential information covered by the National Security Act. He had certainly tightened the noose around his own neck.

"Now who's disclosing national secrets, Donald?" Cotton's face turned red, but the AG wasn't finished. "And let me ask you in whose name the asset forfeiture case was brought. If you had read the pleading you filed, you'd know it reads 'In the name of the United States of America by the Attorney General of the United States,' not by some special committee."

Micki cleared her throat and handed the AG the copy of the court's order that Cotton had given me.

"Thank you, Ms. Lawrence. Well, what do we have here? The court order you've been flashing around the room reads, 'based on the Motion for Immediate and Emergency Relief filed today by the

Attorney General of the United States.' Donald, for once in your life, if you have any hope of keeping your job, please find a seat and keep quiet. Marshals, please remove the restraints from Mr. Patterson. He's not going anywhere, and he's not planning to hurt anyone. Are you?" he said, looking at me.

I almost said "No, your honor," but caught myself. "No, sir."

The marshals took the cuffs off, and I walked back to my place by Micki. The AG still had the microphone, and I waited to see what would happen next.

"First, let me say I came today to hear Mr. Patterson out," he said firmly. "I had my doubts about giving him credibility, but given this morning's article in the *Post*, I decided I should attend, as well as my deputy, Ms. Fortson. Now I'm glad I did. Mr. Patterson, are you comfortable proceeding? I will do my best to have the court's order vacated by the time you finish, but you carry some risk by proceeding."

I turned to Micki who winked and nodded her assent.

"Ms. Lawrence and I are prepared to take that risk."

"Well, before we get to your presentation, I have a few questions," he said.

"Fire away," I said, forgetting for a moment the gravity of the circumstance. "I apologize, sir. I'm a little nervous."

He smiled for the first time, then continued, "Do you have anything to say about this order that might help us convince the judge to set it aside?"

"Yes sir, I do. I have not seen the motion filed by Mr. Cotton, so I don't know exactly what he alleges, and I've only had a minute to scan the order, but I do know that the order was time-stamped at nine fifty-five this morning."

The AG asked, "And why is the time significant?"

"Many members of the press who are here are also aware that Mr. Cotton held a press conference at ten o'clock this morning. At that time he told the press he had decided not to seek an order requiring the return of the million-dollar wire transfer because he hoped we would return the money voluntarily."

Most of the members of the press nodded in agreement. Cotton, who had pointedly pulled up an extra chair rather than sit at the table with Micki and me, lowered his head and sat staring at his shoes.

"I would also like you and every person in this room to know we have never contended that the money from oversees belongs to Rachel's estate. Those funds were wired into her account subsequent to her arrest and represent what we believe to be a poor attempt to frame Rachel Goodman for a crime she didn't commit. If Mr. Cotton had used his phone rather than calling a press conference, we could easily have worked out an arrangement for holding the money as evidence of that attempt.

"But Mr. Cotton's deception goes much further than the million-dollar wire. Without notice or a hearing, he convinced a judge that the entire account at Parra Bank should be paid into the General Account of the Asset Forfeiture Division of the U.S. Attorney's office. The Parra Bank account also contained Rachel's widow's pension as well as the proceeds from her late husband's life insurance policy.

"In effect, this ex parte order litigates and decides the whole asset forfeiture case in the government's favor. It even requires the estate to return Rachel's wedding rings and other personal effects to the U.S. Attorney and orders me to turn over the work-product of our investigation. His actions represent over-reaching at its worst." I had gotten a little worked up; it felt good.

The AG brought me back to earth. "All that will be resolved, Mr. Patterson. The order will be set aside, I promise you."

Cotton and his advisors had been caught red-handed. But setting aside the order wouldn't exonerate Rachel, so I calmed down.

"May I say just one more thing about the order?" I asked meekly.

The AG nodded yes.

"The order requires my office to turn over to Mr. Cotton's office all copies of the design of an early warning detection system that is in our possession."

Puzzled, the AG looked at the order and then at Cotton. "Okay, what are you doing with plans for an early warning detection system and why does the U.S. Attorney want it?"

"The system was designed by a computer expert who works for me. The system has protected my team from people who are, shall we say, up to no good. It works so well that someone must want it for his own personal gain."

Cotton couldn't keep quiet, "I was told it was so good that it must have been stolen from our military."

The AG gave Cotton a dirty look and looked back to me.

"Yes, it's good, but it was designed by one of my employees, and I can prove it. I wasn't aware that a U.S. Attorney could demand the surrender of private property on a whim or a tip. But here's the real question, Mr. Cotton. How does your source know about the system's existence, much less how good it is? The only people who are aware of its existence are the people who work for me, two individuals now in military custody who were caught by the system, and those who hired them."

Cotton knew he had screwed up in defending the attempt to steal Stella's system, but I had confused the AG.

"What are you talking about?" he asked.

We were getting ahead of the game, but I decided to forge ahead.

"In the last week, two individuals, on two separate occasions, trespassed on the property where my team is located. One was found carrying a sniper's rifle. The other was found attempting to launch a rocket directly at the house where we are staying. Had he succeeded, the house and those of us in it would have been destroyed, and there would have been no need for this press briefing. On both occasions, the warning system detected their presence."

"Where are these individuals now?"

"They're currently in the custody of military police at a location I'd prefer not to disclose in public."

"You said 'launch a rocket.' One can't carry a rocket around on one's person as far as I know, at least not yet. What kind of rocket?"

"Several Navy SEALs who have been staying on the property recognized it as a prototype of the Pinpoint Missile System sold by a subsidiary of Rouss Military Systems to the Israeli government."

Two men jumped up immediately, oddly crying out "Liar!" at the same time. One was the Israeli ambassador; the other was the lawyer sitting next to Eric Hartman and Carol.

The room began to buzz, but the Attorney General raised his

voice again. "Please, I must ask you all to be quiet. You two, sit down right now." The Israeli ambassador resumed his seat.

When the noise died down, I offered, "Two Navy SEALs are here today who can identify the rocket and the system."

"No, that won't be necessary. Where is that system now? I assume it's not propped up in the back of a closet."

"No, sir," I smiled. "The rocket and its launch system are in the custody of the military police at a location that again I'd rather not disclose in public."

"That is certainly understandable." He smiled in return.

I heard a rustling and watched as a distinguished gentleman who I would soon learn was Deputy Secretary of State Frederick Sumner, stood and said to the AG, "Burt, a word in private, please." "Burt" stepped away from the microphone and joined him near a window behind the podium. The room descended into chaos.

77

PEGGY WAS ON THE PHONE trying to reach the judge's clerk to get the order rescinded. Carol, Eric, and several men who looked like lawyers huddled together, and Cotton was left sitting by himself off to one side, looking lost. I could almost feel sorry for him. I turned to Micki and said, "Still wish you'd brought along a change of clothes?"

"We're not out of the woods yet. No one has offered to take our places," she smiled grimly.

The AG approached and motioned for Peggy to join us. "I have to hand it to you, Mr. Patterson. Almost everyone in this room is pissed at you; some clearly wish you were dead. The mere mention of a Pinpoint Missile System gave the intelligence people heart failure. I also can't have the system or the man who knows how to use it wandering around one of our military facilities, so I need to know more.

"Let me propose that we find a way to empty this room of the press and anyone else who shouldn't be here before I allow you to continue. Peggy is getting the order rescinded, but I think Cotton still has to be in the room. What about the ambassadors?"

"The Israeli ambassador needs to stay for sure, along with the man to his right, Rabbi Strauss. The other Ambassadors represent countries that bought weapons or systems from Rouss in the last few years, so that's up to you and the State Department. Rouss has several representatives here. You will want to witness their reaction. The people from JAG need to stay, as do the people from Pentagon acquisitions," I answered.

"You make this difficult. How do I get the press to leave and make everyone else stay? The staffers from the Hill sure won't leave without a fight. Got any ideas?" he asked.

"How about this? I won't mention specific weapons or systems, nor will I mention which countries bought what. I will give you the exhibits that lay out what we discovered, and you can decide who else should see them, whether it be the State Department, Congress, the Pentagon, or whatever intelligence agency. I will then prove Rachel's innocence and why she was murdered," I suggested.

"We can try it. I may have to stop you, but we can try. Anything else?"

"Yes. A few brave souls are holding three very dangerous men and a missile system at a military base in Virginia. I will give you and the JAG Commander their location, but only if you both agree to detain these men at an appropriate facility and that you won't seek redress against the military police who went out on a limb by agreeing to detain them."

He laughed, "Let's deal with that first thing. I sure don't want anyone wandering around Virginia with a rocket system. I'll call the commander of the JAG—where are they being held?"

I gave him the name of the facility, and he nodded at Peggy, who hurried out of the room.

The AG then stepped up to the podium again. The noise lessened almost immediately.

"Thank you, I appreciate your patience. Mr. Patterson will resume his briefing in about fifteen minutes or so. Anyone is free to go or stay, but I've cautioned him not to get into specifics in a few sensitive areas. I've warned him that if he crosses a certain line I will halt the briefing. Please be back in your seats in fifteen minutes."

*****

Maggie, Stella, and Beth met us in the small briefing room. It felt good to relax, even if for only a few minutes. Stella looked pensive and finally asked, "How did you know that Cotton planned to steal the plans of our security system?"

"I didn't. But I worried that if they were able to seize our exhibits and work product, your plans would be gobbled up. That's why I had you sell Red both the design and plans. I would have made sure he signed the document and paid you for the design, but at least as of the time they seized everything, the system belonged to Red. I had no idea they would be stupid enough to list the system in the court's order. As soon as the order gets set aside, we can tear up the sales agreement."

"Who do you think was coaching Cotton?" Beth asked.

"I don't know, but I'll bet a dollar to a donut that person is in this room or will be soon."

When we returned to our table the room was a little more crowded. The President of Rouss, Dennis Maxwell, had joined Eric and Carol. Lucy was sitting with her staffer and the chair of the Senate Foreign Relations committee. I wasn't surprised to see Red Shaw, sitting with his head of public relations.

Peggy walked up, looking relieved. "The order has been rescinded, thank goodness. I wouldn't want to be in Cotton's shoes the next time he appears before that judge. The judge had asked him if the AG was on board with this, and Cotton assured him he was.

"Also, the JAG commander spoke with your friend at the military base. In collaboration with the FBI, the three prisoners are being moved to a more secure facility, and the missile system will be secured as evidence. When were you going to tell me about the man from St. Louis that Clovis Jones deposited with the Montgomery County police?"

I raised my eyebrows and shrugged innocently. She was not amused.

"He has a lawyer and wants to make a deal. He claims to have information about the deaths of Harold Spencer and Rachel Goodman. Did that slip your mind?"

"I did call and ask to meet with the Attorney General, but I'm getting old and sometimes forget details," I replied. She was still not amused.

Now it was Micki's turn to scold.

"Clovis took an unnamed man from St. Louis to the Montgomery County police? He claims to know about both deaths? Forget her—when were you going to tell your partner? What's going on, Jack?"

The AG stepped to the podium before I had to answer her questions.

"Ladies and Gentlemen, because of national security concerns there will be no questions after this briefing." A groan rose from the press. "I also ask you to refrain from any spontaneous outbursts. Mr. Patterson and Ms. Lawrence have agreed to limit their remarks, also because of national security concerns. If they do not comply, this briefing will end.

"For your information, the order entered this morning at the request of Mr. Cotton has been vacated by Judge Hicks. I can also tell you that three individuals formerly in the custody of the military police are now in the custody of the FBI, as is what appears to be a missile or rocket system of unknown origin or manufacture. A joint JAG and Justice Department investigation is underway surrounding these circumstances." He paused to take a sip of water and clean his glasses.

I glanced at Carol. She was pale and tight-lipped, and she stared straight ahead.

Micki leaned over and whispered, "Who's the woman sitting between the two men on the third row? She's been staring at you the whole time, and she isn't flirting. If looks could kill, you'd be deader than a doornail."

"That woman, my dear Micki, is Carol Madison."

Micki giggled. "The famous Carol Madison? You did move up in class, present company excepted."

"The one and only."

"Got to be awkward," she said, trying unsuccessfully to suppress a laugh.

"You have no idea."

78

The AG gave a little cough and said to us, "Mr. Patterson, Ms. Lawrence, the podium is yours." Micki squeezed my hand under the table, and whispered, "You're on." I returned the squeeze, walked to the podium, and surveyed the crowd.

I was sure my voice quivered. "Thank you for coming. It's been an interesting afternoon. I asked for this briefing because after Rachel Goodman's death, no one, and I mean no one, was interested in determining why a bright, intelligent young American would have committed espionage. Everyone took it as gospel that she was America's Mata Hari, as U.S. Attorney Cotton is prone to call her."

I made it a point to stop and look at Cotton. I so wanted to shove his words down his throat. *Stay calm, Jack.*

"No one, including the U.S. Attorney, lifted a finger when that same young woman was found dead in her cell—the victim of an apparent suicide—when only hours earlier she had been upbeat and in good spirits. I met with her that very afternoon. The last thing she said to me was 'it's not what it seems.' Our meeting, though brief, had convinced me of her innocence. An FBI agent and the Deputy U.S. Attorney witnessed our entire exchange, and I am sure they will back up what I say. So would the video of our meeting, except that after Rachel's death that video inexplicably went missing."

I paused.

"Rachel was held at a military base in Virginia under tight security. Neither the Deputy U.S. Attorney nor I knew where she was being held. On the day of our visit, we were transported to and from her location in a windowless van. So, you might ask, if her own attorney and a Deputy U.S. Attorney didn't know where she was, how could anyone have gotten to her? I learned just yesterday that someone had attached a tracking device to the underside of the van that took us to Rachel's location. My visit to see my client actually led her killers straight to her."

Very few people knew about the tracking device. Cotton perked up a bit. From his look, it was clearly news to him.

"Now that we know how her killers found Rachel, let's turn our attention to why someone wanted to frame and murder her. That story begins two years ago. Rachel Goodman's husband, Ira, was a rabbi working and living in Washington, DC. But he also worked for the Israeli government. The *Post* once described Ira as 'a bright light' trying to bring peace to the Middle East. One day when he met friends for coffee at an open-air café in Sderot, a rocket attack took his life and the lives of twenty others. The Israeli government blamed Hamas, and this bright light for peace was extinguished.

"When Rachel flew to Israel to make arrangements for her husband's burial, she went to see the remains of the café. She saw something there that only an analyst at the Pentagon would notice. Shell fragments from the rocket or missile bore the markings of a weapon made in the U.S. She made notes on everything she saw and brought them back to the States."

The Israeli ambassador interrupted, "Do you have proof of what you say, or are you merely speculating?"

The AG was about to admonish him for interrupting, but I answered first, "I have her notes which I will give to the Attorney General after this briefing.

"At first, she thought an American weapon had been stolen and sold on the black market to Hamas. A logical assumption, but she couldn't find any record of the rocket and its delivery system in our military's inventory. It wasn't a weapon used by any of our soldiers.

"She continued to search until she discovered the weapon, its manufacturer, and why it was so difficult to locate. It was part of a missile system designed, built, and tested by the Pentagon, but ulti- mately rejected. It wouldn't be the first weapon system that didn't live up to its potential, but she knew something was amiss. You see, if a weapon fails testing or is rejected by the Pentagon, the weapon is dismantled so it can't fall into anyone else's hands.

"Rachel had two concerns. The first was that the weapon might have been sold or stolen rather than dismantled. Of equal concern was that the designer of the system had also been awarded the contract to dismantle the system. Longstanding Pentagon policy forbids the company that designs a weapon to either test or dismantle it. Makes sense, doesn't it?

"She contacted a high-ranking employee of the company that had been awarded both contracts and told him of her fear that the system had been sold on the black market rather than dismantled. She also raised the possibility that the Pentagon's policy had been violated. At first, he assured her neither could be the case—he said it wasn't possible, but agreed to look into the matter."

So far I hadn't named names. It was the Attorney General who let the cat out of the bag.

"I appreciate you honoring my request that you not give specifics, but the name of the company that builds a particular weapon system is not a national secret. You can tell us who built the system."

The Deputy Secretary of State didn't look that comfortable, nor did Carol, but I forged ahead.

"The rocket system was designed and manufactured by Rouss Military Systems."

That brought one of Rouss's lawyers to his feet, but he remained silent. We weren't in court.

The Attorney General wasn't finished, and I realized he knew what he was doing. "And who was the high-ranking individual whom she contacted? Is he in the audience?"

"That person's name was Harold Spencer, who was then the head of the testing division at Rouss. I wish he were here today, but he was murdered a little over a month ago." I was careful not to smile.

That was news to almost everyone, and the room erupted with questions. The Attorney General was able to restore calm in short order, but the lawyer remained standing. He'd heard enough.

"My name is Christian Small, attorney for Rouss Military Systems.

I'm not about to sit still and listen to Patterson's lies and slanders. Enough of this fairy tale."

I wanted to tell Attorney Small where to stick it, but this was the AG's show, and he was quick to respond.

"Please sit down, Mr. Small. I may have started this by asking Mr. Patterson for a little clarification, but I'd like to remind you I said no interruptions. No one is forcing you to sit still and listen—you are welcome to leave at any time. I will ask Mr. Patterson to address your concerns. Do you have any evidence that your client ever spoke to Mr. Spencer?"

"I do, and that evidence will be delivered to you this afternoon."

"That's impossible. We—" Small quickly caught himself, but the damage had been done.

The AG raised his eyebrows. "That's an interesting reaction, Mr. Small. I play golf occasionally at Columbia and was aware of Mr. Spencer's death. I believe the investigation into his death is still open. If you or your client has any pertinent information regarding his death, please turn it over to the police immediately."

He turned again to me. "Mr. Patterson, since Mr. Small has questioned your truthfulness, can you tell me what sort of evidence you have that establishes Mr. Spencer's communications with your client?"

"Yes sir, I can. After Rachel's arrest, Mr. Spencer left a sealed envelope with his wife that she was to deliver to me if anything happened to him. He feared for his life, so he wrote a letter setting forth why Rachel had contacted him and what they had discovered over a period of two years."

"A letter. What did it say? And why did he leave if for you?" he asked.

"I feel that a truthful answer to that question might lead us into areas that could compromise future investigations. Perhaps I should show you a copy of the letter and let you decide."

He gave me a quick smile of thanks and called for a fifteen-minute break. Micki handed him a copy of Spencer's letter. He scanned it quickly and motioned for Peggy to join him. She read it, and they sat down to confer.

I went to sit with Micki. "Sorry to steal your thunder; the exhibits are part of your presentation."

Micki smiled. "You're doing fine—we play this one by ear. I'm happy to carry your briefcase this time. Your girlfriend sure doesn't look happy—I wouldn't want to be on her bad side."

"That's where I am, and I'm liable to remain there."

I caught a movement out of the corner of my eye and saw Clovis motioning to me from the side door. Glancing at my watch, I walked over to meet him.

"Pretend you need to go to the bathroom, and meet Stella in the conference room. I want to keep it quiet, so the rest of us will stay here."

I did as he said and hurried to the conference room.

Stella was all grins. "Whoever wiped Rachel's computer should be fired—they did a piss-poor job. She kept a journal, but it's encrypted much like the zip drive, only better. She installed programs I've only heard about that prevent the standard bleaching and wiping systems from eliminating a file. Whoever tried to wipe the computer didn't stand a chance. Rachel sure knew computers."

I couldn't believe our luck.

"What's in the journal? I don't have time to read it," I asked.

"We've just now managed to break the encryption, and I've only scanned the journal, but it appears to confirm everything that's on her zip drive and in Spencer's letter, but in much more detail."

"That's okay. Do we have a copy to give the Attorney General?"

"We do. We also have copies for you and Micki to read when you're through. You may have noticed that Beth and Jeff aren't here. They're in a separate conference room reading it word by word, and will come running if there are any surprises."

"I have to get back, but I could kiss you, Stella. Thanks."

I turned to leave, but she reached out to stop me. "One more thing, Jack. You should know that Rachel believed from day one that someone inside the Israeli military murdered her husband. That's why she never spent a dime of the life insurance or the widow's pension. She was still thinking through what to do with what she referred to as their 'blood money.'"

79

I RETURNED TO MICKI and quickly told her about the journal. We had too much momentum going to take the time to stop and read it. I had to rely on Stella's quick scan, as well as Beth and Jeff's more detailed reading. The AG approached the microphone.

"I have conferred with the JAG Commander, who will now assume the lead in investigating the death of Mrs. Goodman. He will coordinate with the Montgomery County Police Chief who is handling the murder of Mr. Spencer. We are all in agreement that this letter is too important to both investigations to make public. I know the media is disappointed, but I'm sure it will become public at the appropriate time. Mr. Patterson, why don't you continue?"

I approached the podium again and raised the microphone.

"I believe I was talking about Rachel contacting Mr. Spencer. He didn't think her allegations were credible, but since he had worked with her before, he agreed to look into the matter from his end. Rachel focused her research on whether there were other instances where Rouss had been given the contract to both design and dismantle a weapon. She identified five such instances over the last four years.

"She also discovered that in all five cases, a weapons system almost identical to the one rejected by the Pentagon was subsequently sold by Rouss's overseas subsidiary to a foreign entity.

"Meanwhile, Spencer realized that Rouss's revenues for these five contracts made little sense. The earnings for these five projects exceeded normal revenue and profit margins by almost double the company's average.

"Spencer believed these numbers could be explained as accounting errors rather than the double-dipping Rachel suspected, but he did a thorough analysis and was forced to agree with her conclusions. We have this analysis and will give it to the Attorney General this afternoon.

"Now, neither of these individuals went off half-cocked. Instead they worked together to prepare a report for the Inspector General of the Department of Defense. This draft report contained no confidential plans or designs, nor did it draw any conclusions. Ms. Lawrence can give you all a summary of these exhibits."

As I paused, a man rose from his seat on the front row. He didn't look like a reporter. He appeared to be about forty or so, trying to look younger. His hair was closely trimmed, and both his tailor-made suit and expensive shoes were of a certain style.

"Mr. Patterson, until we can review and scrub these exhibits, there will be no further discussion about their content. I have heard enough to believe we are dealing with national security concerns, and our office must intervene."

I said, "I'm sorry, sir, but who are you?"

He stood up a little straighter and walked toward the podium. "Richard Ewing, Deputy Director of National Intelligence. Any further discussion of the contents of those documents, and you'll find yourself in custody."

I looked to the AG and Peggy, who seemed to want to throttle the guy. The AG didn't budge much. "I will review both your credentials and your position before making a decision. We'll take a five-minute break."

The whole room was abuzz, and for the first time the Rouss people and Carol relaxed. I sat down with Micki.

"Maybe we'll need those prison clothes after all."

"What's with the 'we'? I kind of like the guy; he cut my presentation to zero. Do you know him?"

"The Director of National Intelligence is a big deal, reporting directly to the President, but I had no idea there was a deputy. He looks kind of familiar. I might have met him at Carol's."

"If he was at Carol's, you've been keeping bad company," she said, as she elbowed me.

"You don't know the half of it."

Peggy approached us a few minutes later. "Our hands are tied. We can't let you reference a document that national intelligence considers confidential, regardless of whether they've seen it. They've directed us to round up all your documents and turn them over for analysis. We'll fight it, but you need to shut this down before you get in hotter water. Ewing's orders are coming straight from the top."

Her personification of "national intelligence" startled me. It reminded me of *Moonrise Kingdom*, an eccentric but provocative film where a specific state employee was always called 'Social Services,' even to her face. I tried to let it go, but the comparison was troubling.

"Peggy, you know this is the only chance I'll get to exonerate Rachel. Thanks for the advice, and please come see me in jail, won't you?"

Peggy looked at Micki, "Talk some sense into him, please."

Micki's quick, sharp laugh attracted stares from those near enough to hear.

"Peggy, you've known him longer than I have. Please tell me how to do that, will you?"

The Attorney General returned to the podium, hardly able to conceal his disappointment. "Ladies and Gentlemen, the deputy director's decision regarding the exhibits takes precedence today. I don't see how we can proceed. Sorry."

Micki gave me a sharp jab with her elbow, and I rose.

"Pardon me, Mr. Attorney General. You've been very helpful, but I believe this is my press briefing, my show. I won't reference any exhibits, but I would like to finish my statement. May I have the microphone, please?"

He smiled and handed it to me.

Ewing lost his urban chic, whining, "Burt, aren't you going to stop him!"

The Attorney General didn't hesitate, "Nope, not even going to try."

John Robert Spencer had changed into to full dress uniform and now walked down the aisle to stand next to Deputy Director

Ewing. A quick look told me that our SEALs, now all in full uniform had placed themselves in strategic places around the room, No one could miss their presence.

Ewing was livid. "What do you think you're doing, young man?"

"Sir, my name is John Robert Spencer. I am Harold Spencer's son. If you care to hear why my father was killed, I will be glad to escort you to your seat. If not, I'm here to escort you out of the room. Your choice."

Ewing looked around for help, but finding none, returned to his seat, accompanied by Spencer in case he should get lost.

The room had fallen totally silent, so I began. "Neither Harold Spencer or Rachel Goodman ever attempted to sell or give away government secrets. Rather they worked together to find out how weapons that should have been relegated to the scrap heap ended up in the hands of foreign countries. Rachel thought she had uncovered a blatant act of corporate greed, and Harold searched relentlessly for an accounting error. The answer lies in the documents I'm prohibited from discussing, so we can only hope that Mr. Ewing and the intelligence community will make them public one day. I won't hold my breath."

Micki gave me a signal to speed it up. How in the hell was I going to do that?

"Until this afternoon, I was afraid that Harold Spencer's murder would be buried and Rachel would be forever branded as a spy who hung herself in a jail cell. Since the FBI and the JAG have now opened an investigation into Rachel's death, and because the Montgomery County Police now have a cooperating witness, my fears of a cover-up have lessened. If I'm wrong, well I'm not going anywhere, and I hope the press will continue to follow both stories with interest.

"But we still don't know why they were killed. According to Harold Spencer's letter, he feared they were both in danger because they had uncovered a scheme by Rouss to triple dip—get paid to develop a weapon system that failed, get paid again to dismantle and destroy it, and get paid a third time when they sold the system under the table to a foreign country."

CEO Maxwell turned pointedly to his attorney, but this time the man didn't budge.

"But I think the evidence points to a more complicated plot. I believe Rouss was only one player in a much larger enterprise. Let me propose a different scenario that fits the facts, as I know them. When I do, the members of the Senate and House committees will now understand why they were invited today, why the ambassadors from certain countries were asked to come, and why both Rachel and Harold were murdered. They were investigating something more complex than either imagined."

"Let's speak in hypotheticals so I don't violate national security. I'll leave it to you to decide how far off base I am. Let's suppose that an administration or the military, or both, thinks it's in our national interest to put certain weapons in the hands of our allies. This is done all the time. Jet fighters are sold to our allies every year. There's an agency at the State Department called the U. S. Defense Security Cooperation Agency that facilitates the sale of weapons made in the U.S. to our allies. Several members of that agency are here today." I pointed in their direction.

"So what I suggest is not unusual. But let's say the administration or the military doesn't want anyone to know that a certain weapon or weapons system is being sold to an ally. A sale to Israel, for example, might offend certain Arab countries, or a sale to Germany might make Russia nervous. Moreover, all such sales require congressional approval, or at least notice given to certain congressional committees. And we all know that when Congress knows, the whole world knows." I smiled and was rewarded with a few chuckles.

"Occasionally, Congress's refusal to approve a sale can be embarrassing both to an administration and its allies. This occurred just a few years ago when several well-publicized sales weren't approved. The military brass was madder than hell, and the administration was caught with egg on its face.

"So how does an administration get around congressional notification requirements? How does an administration sell weapons to its allies without anyone's knowledge? It would take someone very creative, very senior, and very well connected to pull off such a scheme, right?

"First, you'd need to repeal the Pentagon's policy that prohibits the designer of a weapons system from also dismantling and destroying those weapons. Lobbyists would argue that such a rule was impractical—who better to dismantle a system than the company that designed it? Besides, it would be a money saver.

"We know that in at least five cases the Pentagon's rule was waived or ignored. How exactly the Pentagon's long-standing policy was changed is up to the press, Congress, and others to find out. I only know that it happened.

"I expect there have been other instances where designers of weapon systems dismantled what they built, but Rachel was only interested in projects where Rouss was the designer, so I only know of five. But I don't believe for one minute Rouss is the only contractor that took advantage of the administration's change of heart.

"Next, in order to bypass congressional approval, the administration and the military must develop a weapon that our ally wants and that the administration wants them to have. That part is easy: the military develops weapons all the time. Some work, some don't. Next, the designer must insert a flaw into the design that can only be remedied by the designer himself.

"Finally, the designing company must be awarded the contract to dismantle the weapon. It then simply fixes the flaw rather than scrapping the system. As far as the public or Congress knows, the weapons system no longer exists. The designer then can use an off-shore subsidiary to sell the renamed system to whomever, and no one is the wiser. Except, of course, for the very creative, very senior, very well-connected person who has directed the entire process on behalf of the administration."

I paused a minute, but no one interrupted, so I continued.

"I know that to accomplish what I have suggested, the scheme would need to be far more complicated than I have described. Would it even be doable in these days of transparency? Maybe it's only a hare-brained theory, but before you discard my musings, let me give you a bit of information that comes from public websites on the Internet."

I looked at Deputy Director Ewing to make sure he knew I wasn't about to leak confidential information.

"Rachel identified five projects that Rouss designed and then dismantled. Over the last four years, five identical weapon systems were sold to our allies. The manufacturer of these identical systems was Surplus Military Systems Ltd., an off-shore subsidiary of Rouss. Not one of these sales was submitted to Congress for approval."

I had decided not to mention that Surplus Military Systems was also the source of the million dollars wired into Rachel's account, but I would make sure that both the AG and Peggy knew that fact.

"Let me remind you of another fact. You may think my theory is far-fetched, even fanciful. Those sales could have been legitimate. There could be a logical explanation for them to have been sold without congressional approval. That's for Deputy Director Ewing, congressional oversight, and the press to figure out. But for Rachel Goodman, what happened was neither far-fetched nor fanciful. It was as real as it gets. A rocket designed and built by Rouss Military Systems, that should have been dismantled and destroyed, killed her husband and twenty other innocent souls.

"A rocket, part of a system that cost our government more than six hundred million dollars to develop and build, and more than a hundred million to dismantle and destroy, was sold to the Israeli government without congressional approval and used by someone to murder her husband. It doesn't hit any closer to home than that.

"And when she and Harold Spencer discovered the truth, they didn't receive an explanation, an apology, or compensation. Instead she was arrested, branded a traitor, and they were both murdered.

"Maybe someone who isn't hiding behind the words 'national security' can explain how this happened, because I can't. I only know that Rachel and Ira Goodman, and Harold Spencer are dead, and those responsible for their deaths continue to do business as usual.

"Let me leave you with one more thought. It would be easy to believe only Rouss was responsible—just another contractor caught padding invoices. But that conclusion doesn't make sense. Rouss makes plenty of money. Why take the risk of faking documents about dismantling systems and selling a weapon without congressional approval? I don't believe they would or did.

"The irregularities that Rachel and Harold uncovered would certainly not have been worth the risk. Rouss is an enormous company that legally develops more than a third of our country's weapons systems. My guess is that Rouss was approached by someone within the administration, high enough to speak with authority, and asked by that person to participate, without fear of consequences.

"Couldn't have happened? Maybe not—I've been wrong before. But in this case I don't think so. Someone in this administration ordered Rouss to develop, design, and sell systems without congressional approval, someone involved ordered Rachel and Harold's death, and everyone involved will continue to defy our laws until they are stopped."

I put the microphone down and walked over to the table where Micki sat.

With that, most everyone rushed to leave. A few reporters tried to ask me questions, but I waved them away. I turned to speak with the AG, but stopped when I noticed Ken and T.J. waiting.

"T.J., I can't thank you enough for making this event possible. It took courage both on your part and that of the *Post*." I extended my hand in thanks. "You know, Mr. Chandler here is a fine young reporter, not afraid to take a chance when it's the right thing to do. Take good care of him, you hear?" Ken blushed, T.J. laughed, and they both walked away.

Micki had joined me, and we again turned to Peggy and the Attorney General.

"Mr. Attorney General, I owe you my thanks. Without you I'd probably be cooling my heels in some jail by now."

We all laughed, although Micki still looked a little nervous. "Anyway, it's all yours now. Maggie will get Peggy copies of the exhibits this afternoon."

"You're welcome—you weren't too bad yourself," he said. "The Pentagon and the intelligence community will try to sweep it all under the rug, although they'll catch holy hell from the press. Congress will beat them up for ignoring them, new legislation will be introduced, and I'll do my part to find the killers and bring them to justice. And unless and until I'm forced to resign, I will do my level best to bring whoever is behind all this to justice."

"I appreciate your help, and when people try to convince you that you need to let it go for the good of the country, remind them I'm out there watching. I still have a back-up plan if they try to cover it up."

"A back-up plan? Please keep me out of it." He smiled then turned to Peggy, "Tell me again why you didn't want me to meet with him?"

Must have been a private joke, because she punched him in the arm and they walked away sniggering.

Clovis approached and nodded his head toward Carol, who was now standing alone. "It won't get any easier. Time to say goodbye."

I walked over and spoke, "Hello, Carol, I've missed you."

That caught her off guard.

"Things could have been so different, if you'd only listened."

"True, but I couldn't. It's not in my DNA," I answered.

"Are you going to tell the AG that I was involved?" she asked.

"No. It doesn't matter—it's not my case anymore."

"What do you mean?"

"I mean that Rachel has been exonerated, and the JAG will determine that she didn't commit suicide. That's all I was ever after."

"Too bad you didn't tell me. We could have worked something out. You should have told me," she smiled.

"We had an understanding not to talk about each other's business, remember? But even if I had, it wouldn't have worked out."

"How did you figure me out?"

I ignored her question, and shook my head. "Goodbye, Carol. It was fun."

We didn't kiss, we didn't embrace. There was nothing left. I couldn't help but wonder if the decision to kill Rachel and then me had been made at her place on the Eastern Shore.

At that moment, Eric Hartman walked up beside Carol, draped his arm around her shoulders, and with a shit-eating grin said to me, "I hope you're proud of what you did today. You just made your country weaker, asshole!"

I have no memory of what happened next. The next thing

I remember, Eric was lying on the floor, his faced covered with blood, and Carol was screaming at me, "You broke his nose. You broke his fucking nose!" Clovis was leading me away, and I could hear Red laughing.

80

THERE WAS NO TIME for celebration or admonishments over my loss of temper. We regrouped at the park across from the Press Club. After a few high fives, Clovis, Stella, Micki, and Larry decided to return to Little Rock immediately. Micki needed to deal with members of the local press who were camped out on Ben's front lawn, and Clovis was ready to spend a little more time in his new rocking chair. Beth and Jeff asked if they could stay a day or two, which delighted me no end. John Robert and his SEALs wanted to stay at the compound for a few days to make sure there were no more bad guys hanging around.

After hugs all round, the four of us hopped into the waiting Tahoe, ready to relax at our temporary home by the river. Once we were underway, Beth handed me Rachel's journal. It was heart-breaking to read the part Beth had marked for me to read. Rachel described in detail what she had learned about Ira's death. She and Ira had always known that some factions of the government disagreed with his approach to peace. Her suspicions were aroused when she found shell fragments with U.S. markings at the remains of the café. She knew that the U.S. would never sell a rocket system to Hamas.

Beth and I spent an hour or so wandering the property. We talked about her studies at school, Jeff's plans after his residency, where I should move, and on and on. It was nice to have time alone with her, but before too long it became apparent that we both needed to get back to our own lives.

The "day or two" turned out to be that afternoon. They had

found a flight out that evening and were gone before I knew it. When the SEALs found out that Stella had gone to Little Rock, their enthusiasm waned, and they left the next morning. John Robert offered to stick around, but I told him he needed to get back to his mom and his own life.

Maggie, Brian, and I spent the rest of the week tending to details and enjoying the quiet. Maggie and I took long walks around the grounds. She showed me where the foundation and retreat center would be located, and we talked about how the day-to-day operations of our office should run now that Brian was on board.

We purposely chose to avoid the cable news outlets and Internet news, sticking to the *Post* and the *New York Times,* and the national evening news. Fortunately, the cameras hadn't caught my encounter with Hartman. The administration was in full cover-up and "national security" mode, calling my theory about a purposeful plan to sell arms to allies without congressional approval a "pure fantasy."

Lucy was enjoying another day in the sun, calling for bipartisan investigations and hearings on every news and social media outlet. One thing was for sure—when she got a tiger by the tail, she didn't let go.

Red told me she was irritated because I didn't share everything with her beforehand. He also mentioned that my seat at their wedding reception had improved. I would be seated a few tables closer to their table, and nowhere near Carol and Hartman.

Ken Chandler and the *Post* were relentless in their coverage; they had my road map and a head start. It also helped that Ken had been digging for months with Rachel's help. He had an ample supply of sources within the Pentagon and the intelligence community who helped plug every hole in the story I had painted at the National Press Club. Ken easily discovered that at least five other contractors beside Rouss had engaged in exactly the same activities. Moreover, it was determined that Hartman's lobbying firm was the registered lobbyist for all.

One of Ken's sources had actually been present when Hartman and several other lobbyists pitched the need to do away with the Pentagon's conflict restrictions. The meetings occurred at a posh resort in south Florida attended by high-ranking officials at State, Defense, and the White House. I'm just waiting for pictures to show up on Facebook after those present deny attending.

Peggy reported that the man Clovis brought back from St. Louis was cooperating with the JAG, the FBI, and the Montgomery County police. Within days after his ill-fated appearance at my press conference, U.S. Attorney Donald J. Cotton had resigned—apparently he wanted to spend more time with his family. But time with his family didn't prevent him putting together a committee to explore his chances of becoming Virginia's next Attorney General. In his farewell to his staff, he complimented everyone for helping break open the scandal over the abuses by military contractors and the unsavory attempt to frame Rachel Goodman. What a jerk. I intend to give a healthy contribution to his opponent.

Rabbi Strauss and I had dinner one night at the Bombay Club, one of my favorite DC restaurants. Over tandoori trout and a nice Oregon Pinot Gris, we talked about Ira Goodman. In her journal, Rachel had laid out in exact detail why she thought the extreme right-wing element of the Israeli government had ordered the rocket attack on her husband. I told him I expected the Israeli government to launch a full investigation into Rabbi Goodman's death.

As always, he was non-committal, but promised to do what he could. I reminded him that Ira was an American citizen, and that if there were no investigation, I could sue the Israeli government on behalf of Rachel's estate.

"So that's what you're after, more money for her heirs." He tried to look disgusted.

"No, that's not what I want, and you know it," I said raising my own voice. "Rachel spent two years of her life getting to the bottom of the administration's scheme to get rockets to Israel without congressional approval. She never spent a dime of the money she received from Israel. Her reward was to be labeled a spy and then killed. I want the same thing Rachel wanted—for those responsible for Ira's death to take responsibility. We want justice for Ira. And I want justice for Rachel. One way or the other, I'm going to get it."

Fortunately, Strauss made amends for his erroneous assumption, and we were able to finish the meal in relative tranquility. I doubted that either my threat or my little tirade would have any effect on the Israeli government, but at least I'd given him something to think about.

I had called Ben that afternoon and reached him just as he was cleaning up after the lunch crowd.

"Jack! Good to hear—Yes, ma'am, thank you. Well, we do try— Jack, give me just a second." I could hear the tail end of their conversation, the scrape of chairs on linoleum, then the sound of a door closing abruptly, followed by silence and finally, "Sorry, Jack—I can talk now. What's up?"

I brought up the subject of the money that had been in Parra Bank, and he said, "You keep every dime. You earned it, Jack."

"I can't do that. Even after expenses and paying Micki the fee she deserves, there's more than a million dollars left. I can't just leave it in my trust account."

"Rachel didn't take their money, and neither will I. What would I do with a million dollars? Buy a bigger boat? The one I have is fine. I own my restaurant free and clear, and it supports Linda, the boys, and me. Give it to charity, but I don't want a penny of that money."

It was good to hear the old energy back in the voice. I told him we could talk about it later.

I contacted the lawyer for Rouss, then Peggy, even Carl Clifford, who had taken over for Cotton—no one wanted anything to do with that money, like it was blood money. But money is money, nothing more, and I had an idea to propose to Ben when the time was right.

I enjoyed a long lunch with Red, at Morton's, of course. He made me swear a series of blood oaths before admitting he had spent a couple of days with Judy Spencer.

"Harold had a dark side. He loved to gamble, and he seldom lost. Las Vegas sent a jet for him four times a year for a week of gambling, and he took advantage of the freebies—luxury suites, booze, food, and women. Judy knew all about Vegas because he bragged about his escapades when he came home. He was brutal in his honesty.

"You know, when he wasn't playing cards or bragging, he was a model husband and father. He was well-respected in the defense contracting business, both for his brains and his ability to lead. Many a defense contractor tried to hire him, but he was as loyal to Rouss. He just had a dark side."

"Why did Judy stay with him?" I asked.

"Who knows why one person stays with another. You've met her—she's as smart and classy as any woman I've known. I tried many times to get her to leave him, but she always refused. I knew her way before Lucy was in the picture and chased her as hard as I've chased anything in my life. I usually get what I want, but not this time."

"Is it a problem for you? Now that she's a widow?" I asked.

"That's why I went to see her. I had to know where we stood before I married Lucy. She was as cool as a cucumber. We had a nice dinner, talked non-stop, and she let me fly her to wherever the hell she is now. But she made it clear we had no future together. My ego likes to think she'd had enough of men on account of Harold, but who knows? I know I need to let it go."

"I don't know what to say, Red. I've met her—she's definitely a class act, but some things aren't meant to be. Remember the Rolling Stones? 'You can't always get what you want, but you just might find you get what you need.'" My Mick Jagger imitation was pretty bad— Red almost lost his wine.

"So you think Lucy is what I need?" he laughed. "Thanks for listening. It feels good to tell someone I trust about the one that got away. Speaking of, I hear that Carol and Eric are constant companions now. What happened?" he asked.

"You asking about Carol and me, or the right-cross that decked Hartman?"

"Both, I guess."

"It would be easy to say that punch was about Rachel's murder, or Ira's, or Harold's, because I do believe Hartman was the puppet-master. He's the only one who has the contacts in both the administration and the defense industry to pull it off. But all I remember is seeing his arm around Carol like he owned her, that arrogant grin, and him saying I'd weakened this country. Something inside of me had enough."

Red laughed, "Remind me not to get fresh with your mermaid, if I ever get the chance to meet her."

"As for Carol, we were great together. She is everything a man should want in a woman, but we are both married to our work, and, like Judy Spencer, who knows why something doesn't work out."

"Said like a true gentleman! Why do I think you aren't telling me everything?"

"For the same reason I don't think you're telling me everything about Judy Spencer."

We agreed to leave it at that, and drank toasts to our respective loves and losses . . .

A few days later Maggie and I closed up the house on the shore and returned to DC. Walter had returned from his business meetings, and the three of us enjoyed a nice dinner. He congratulated both of us on the results of our work and gave me hell for involving Maggie in such a dangerous case—all in the same breath. The next day, Brian and I were trying to figure out how to reorganize the office, when Peggy Fortson called, no flirting this time.

"Jack, the Attorney General intends to send his resignation to the President. He's scheduled one last meeting with Richard Ewing, and he wants you to attend."

I asked, "Are you okay?"

"This is tough, but you know me—I'm a survivor. I'll clear you through security. Come to the AG's conference room at three this afternoon. Thanks."

The Attorney General's office was adjacent to a very large conference room—think thirty or forty people—on the fifth floor of Main Justice. A large, ornate table that sat on a very old oriental carpet dominated the room. The carpet still bore the evidence of Brumis, Robert Kennedy's hulking Newfoundland and constant companion. Today, Attorney General Bertram Sharp was sitting at its head. The Deputy Director of National Intelligence, Richard Ewing, sat on his left, and I sat on the right, flanked by Peggy Fortson. My presence was clearly offensive to Ewing.

"What is he doing here? Who asked him?" Ewing demanded.

"I did. My office, my guests." Sharp's tone was steely. "His hard work has brought us to this day, and I want him to hear what I have to say."

He looked at me and said, "Jack, I asked you to come today because I want you to hear my response to Richard's request that I turn over all the exhibits and other information you gave me. He claims they contain classified information and that his office should take possession of them for our national security."

Ewing reminded me of Walter Peck, the pencil-necked character in the original *Ghostbusters*, arrogant, and on the wrong side of right. It occurred to me that he and Hartman might use the same barber.

He turned to me and said, "I might as well tell you, Mr. Patterson, that if you still have copies of any documents relating to this matter, we expect your full cooperation in the return of those documents. Otherwise, we will get a court order that compels you to comply."

I came close to telling him where to put his expectation, but held my tongue. It was the AG's meeting.

"Richard, my office has carefully reviewed your request," Sharp responded. "Not one single document is covered by the Secrets Act, or even considered to be confidential. The press has already splashed about half the exhibits all over the news. Therefore, I refuse to comply with your request."

He raised his arm to fend off Richard's response. "I know what comes next, so I'll save you the trouble. You're about to tell me I work for the President and that, since this issue is a matter of national security rather than criminal justice, I'm duty bound to follow the wishes and the orders of the President. Am I right?"

Ewing shrugged his shoulders.

"Well, if that is the case, and I suspect it is, the President will have my resignation on his desk this afternoon. I won't do it."

Ewing didn't act surprised, but Peggy sighed, even though she'd known it was coming. I felt the bile rising in my gut. It was time to put a stop to Ewing's cover-up of the scandal and the administration's attempt to continue to sell arms to whomever they damn well pleased. I shook my head slowly and cleared my throat. Ewing looked bored.

"Your resignation is unnecessary Mr. Attorney General, because even if you resign and a new AG turns over the materials they want, I control the originals as well as a few other documents I've held in reserve. If you resign, I'll no longer have any confidence that the federal government intends to get to the bottom of Rachel's murder, and I'll have no choice but to put in motion my back-up plan."

Ewing interrupted, "I demand you return the exhibits and documents in your possession relating to this case—originals and copies. You won't get a second chance."

I smiled and calmly replied, "Mr. Ewing, that's at least twice you've demanded that I 'return documents.' Let me make one thing clear before I continue—the documents and exhibits do not belong to you or to the government; never have, never will. They either belong to my client or are my work-product. The United States government has no ownership claim to any document in my possession.

"And before you run off to get a court order that I will disobey, please tell whomever you send on this fool's errand that if they attempt to obtain those documents by court order or by breaking into my office safe, or by any other means, they will fail. I've taken measures to protect them, and should something happen to me, copies will be delivered to the *Washington Post,* the *New York Times,* and *Bloomberg News.* And I don't mean just the documents the AG holds. I mean every piece of evidence assembled by my client or myself over the last two years. You don't want to open that can of worms, trust me.

"Mr. Ewing, should this administration accept Mr. Sharp's resignation before he has time to do his job, I will file a wrongful death and malicious prosecution lawsuit naming Eric Hartman, the defense contractors involved in this conspiracy, the federal government, specific individuals who work at the Pentagon, and certain intelligence agencies, including yours."

I was bluffing just a little—it felt really good.

Ewing said, "You signed a release. You released the government from any claims when we returned her assets."

I smiled. "Interesting that you know the terms of that settlement, Mr. Ewing. You can tell me how you learned of its terms when I take your deposition. But I think maybe you should read that release a little more carefully. You'll find it only releases claims arising out of the asset forfeiture. The release says nothing about malicious prosecution or wrongful death."

Ewing looked totally bumfuzzled.

I turned to Bertram Sharp. "Please don't resign, Mr. Attorney General. I don't have the time or the resources necessary to launch the kind of investigation that will reveal exactly what happened and who was responsible for this shameful scheme. As Peggy will tell you, I'm an antitrust lawyer, and as she so often reminds me, I'm in way over my head."

FRIDAY

Two Weeks Later

81

THE ATTORNEY GENERAL didn't resign. Peggy told me he received a call from the President asking that he stay on and launch a full-scale investigation. Apparently the uproar raised by the press had been enough to cause even this President to temporarily retreat from Twitter. I promised her I'd call for brunch in a few weeks. She said she looked forward to it, but she had a back-up plan just in case.

With Ken Chandler and *The Post* leading the charge, the story wasn't going away. Both the House leadership and the President's senior advisors recommended a total house cleaning at State, including the Secretary. An outraged Congress was demanding heads roll, and both the administration and the Pentagon have been quick to lay the blame on rogue low-level employees at the State Department.

I didn't buy this spin, but it wasn't my battle to fight. I'm still convinced the scheme was Hartman's brainchild and that he used Carol and others to further his ends. I'd spent enough weekends at Carol's place on the shore to know she never bothered with low-level types. Her guests were always generals, cabinet officers, members of Congress, and high-powered lobbyists. The least important person there was always, well, me. I will tell Ken Chandler what I think.

I received several letters from Hartman's lawyers threatening to sue me for assault and battery, demanding that I pay Hartman's medical bills and apologize. I tossed them in the trash—no way would I apologize and his threat of a lawsuit was ludicrous. His lawyers weren't about to give me the opportunity to question him under oath about his involvement in the framing of Rachel and her murder. I don't think he personally ordered Rachel's death or the attempts on our lives, but as the driving force behind the plan to sell arms without congressional approval he was as guilty as sin. According to Ken Chandler, Hartman was spending a lot of time out of the country recovering from the "terrible beating" he received. My bet is he was checking out countries that wouldn't honor a request for extradition.

Two weeks had passed since the press briefing, and I was back in Little Rock to attend a gathering at Micki's ranch hosted by Ben and Linda. Most everyone came. Beth and Jeff drove down from St. Louis for the weekend. Martin and Big Mike couldn't make it, so I promised we'd bring them barbecue. We invited John Robert and his SEALs, but John Robert was out of the country, and the others had returned to duty.

Sam Pagano was there with Jasmine White, who looked mighty fine with her dark flowing hair and enormous hoop earrings. I pulled Micki aside and asked about Kristine. Turns out, she and Maggie had decided Kristine had to go. Once they discovered that Jasmine was both a runner and cyclist, they made sure Sam either attended or participated in every race she entered, an activity totally appropriate for an aspiring politician. Kristine wouldn't be caught dead at such an event, and it didn't take long for Sam to notice Jasmine. When I nudged him a little, he confessed that he hated fundraising events and missed the Faded Rose.

Kristine had moved on to bigger fish. A slick local TV sports commentator, despite having no experience or brains, had decided to run for governor. He and Kristine were made for each other.

After dinner, Jeff took the opportunity to ask my permission to marry Beth. I didn't think my approval made much difference, but the gesture made me feel good, sort of like I was still in control. They're off to Charleston next week to tell his parents. The ring was his grandmother's, and Beth couldn't stop looking at it. They hadn't set a date or place for the wedding yet, but Maggie and Walter suggested that if they could wait a year, the new retreat center would be available. My bet was that Jeff's mother would organize a large church wedding in Charleston followed by a very expensive reception paid for by the father of the bride . . . me.

Beth and Jeff weren't the only couple to get engaged that day. Clovis fell to one knee to ask Stella to marry him.

Her response? "Took you long enough."

They asked me to serve as best man, and Micki as maid-of-honor. Their wedding will be at a trout-fishing lodge on the New River in North Carolina next spring.

I kidded Micki, "Good news comes in threes—you and Larry next?"

She frowned, "We're not there yet. We still have mother-in-law issues to work out."

I feigned disappointment, and she told me they would be in DC more often over the next year. Maggie was so taken with Larry's ideas for the foundation's offices and the Retreat Center, she'd asked if he would supervise the architects and contractors.

"I hope you have a spare desk at your office." She smiled, but looked a bit uncertain.

"My office is yours. We'll put your name on the door if you want." And I meant it.

After we'd heard all the news and everyone had settled in with a drink and old friends, I managed to corner Ben and Linda for a few minutes.

"Ben, it's time for us to deal with all that money that's languishing in my trust account. It can't stay there forever." I'd already sent him an accounting of the money I'd spent, including Micki's fee.

"Keep it. I noticed that you paid Micki, but not yourself," he said.

"I used it to pay every expense I incurred, as well as a bonus to Brian, Martin and his crew, and for a dinner at Morton's Steak House for John Robert and his team. But if you are absolutely sure you don't want the money, I'd like to suggest an alternative. A good portion of that money comes from the manufacturer of the weapon that killed Ira. Rachel and Ira spent most of their adult lives promoting peace and reconciliation. Why don't we donate the money to a non-profit organization that promotes peace in the Middle East along the lines that Ira believed? We can do it in Rachel and Ira's memory."

Ben looked at Linda, and they both smiled before he responded.

"Swords into plowshares—it's a fitting tribute. Linda and I had already been talking along those lines. And we talked about something else as well: the money should be given in the names of Rachel and Ira Goodman. She loved Ira and became his wife. How is her changing her name to Rachel much different from Linda taking my name? She chose to become Rachel, and we should honor her decision."

Ben Jr. had included a few new items from his father's menu for the afternoon. Jalapeno hushpuppies and a black-eyed pea soup with chorizo were both a big hit. But, as usual, Ben's basic barbeque sandwich and dry-rubbed ribs ruled the day.

After dinner, everyone gathered around Micki's fireplace to chat and reminisce. I couldn't help but notice that all my friends were now couples, and the longer I stayed, the more awkward I felt. No one made a fuss when I told them I had an early plane to catch and returned to the Armitage.

The Lobos were playing the Redskins in DC on Sunday, and Red had insisted I join him in the owner's box. The Lobos linebacker, James "the Wall" Stockdell, had guaranteed victory. The Redskins had made the mistake of letting "the Wall" go to the Lobos in the supplemental draft, and he'd been All-Pro since, with a definite chip on his shoulder whenever he faced the Redskins.

My plane landed at National around noon the next day, and I took a cab home, without protection for the first time in what seemed like forever. I took a minute to really look at the house that had been our home for so many years. It was filled with many good memories, but no dogs, no Beth, and no Angie. It looked as lonely as I felt. I was scheduled to meet with Susan on Monday to start the process of putting the house on the market. This time I felt sure about the decision to sell.

The decision to sell my house also made me realize something about my relationship with Carol. I had always used Angie as the excuse as to why I was so conflicted about Carol. Much like I told myself I couldn't sell the house because of Angie, I told myself that it was Angie's memory that kept me from committing fully to Carol, but that wasn't true. Bottom line, Carol wasn't the one for me. I didn't love her. I enjoyed being with her and she was everything a man should want or need, but she wasn't the one. When all was said and done, I couldn't fool my own heart.

I walked into the house, threw my keys on the side table, and flipped through the accumulated mail, most of it, of course, either bills or appliance ads. I heard voices in the background and wondered if I'd left the TV on the whole time I was gone.

Jo Ellen Murphy didn't leave me in suspense. She ran out of the den and directly into my arms.

"It's about time you got home," she said.

I could hardly believe my eyes. Her red hair was its usual tousled mess, and she wore jeans and an L.A. Lobos jersey.

"Boy, have I missed you," she said, giving me a welcoming kiss.

Still in a state of shock, I let her lead me into the den and pull me down onto the sofa. "We have rules to discuss. I've got a reputation to maintain."

It turned out that Clovis had been worried about Jo as well as Beth and Jeff. He'd sent Jordan to Pawleys to explain the danger she could face. Naturally, Jo laughed it off, said she could take care of herself. But Clovis asked Jordan to stay in Pawleys and keep watch until after the press briefing.

"Jordan's an easy guy to like," she said. "My girlfriends thought he was hot and kept him busy while I ran the restaurant. But you have nothing to worry about. He's way too young for me—I prefer a much more mature man."

"Clovis called last night," she explained after she'd laid down her "Rules."

"He said the case was over, and in his opinion you could use company. You were moping around, and everyone was worried you were reverting to your former self. 'Was it possible for me to surprise you?' He even offered to pay for my plane ticket, first class no less. Offended, I said 'hell no.'"

"What changed your mind?" I said with a smile.

"He told me you had skybox tickets to the ball game. I've never been to a pro football game much less sat in a skybox. I figure no one I know is here. I can keep my reputation, and you can show me the sights. I want to see the monuments, the museums, and the Capitol. Don't think it's because I want to see you," she said with a laugh, and we went upstairs to get reacquainted.

The look on Red's face when we walked into his box the next day was worth the price of admission. Her knowledge of the game and her obvious pleasure in being there made Jo an instant hit. The game turned out to be closer than expected, and the Lobos won 33-31 when Billy Hopper made a one-handed touchdown grab in the game's final seconds. Only one of Red's guests was unimpressed with Jo: Lucy. The senator wanted nothing to do with Jo, and Jo reacted in kind.

"That woman needs to see a doctor about removing the stick up her ass," she whispered in my ear.

Red couldn't have been nicer, which was probably why Lucy behaved so badly. He ordered Lynn, one of his two ever-present "advisors," to make sure Jo got a full set of Lobos gear to display in her restaurant. He told her she was welcome to come to a game in L.A., with or without me. He'd even send his jet for her. I laughed; Lucy fumed. When he insisted that we join them at Joe's Stone Crab after the game, Lucy pleaded a headache and bowed out. She blamed the headache on the mess I'd given her and her new Senate committee.

I put off my appointment with Susan for a week, told Brian to hold down the fort and not to call me unless there was a real emergency. Jo and I spent the entire week playing tourists, enjoying great restaurants, and studying the chessboard. DC is a wonderful city if you don't need to get anywhere quickly.

I say "playing the tourists," but it was Jo who mapped out our itinerary. She had planned our days down to the minute, and not just our visits to the Smithsonian and the monuments. We went to the Library of Congress and then walked to the Eastern Market. We visited galleries off the beaten path such as the Kreeger and the Phillips. We spent one morning at Hillside, the museum and former home of Marjorie Merriweather Post, and an afternoon at the spy museum. She made reservations at restaurants I'd barely heard of, and of course, she had to have fresh crabs, so one afternoon we drove to Cantler's, sort of indoor/outdoor crab restaurant near Annapolis that served the best crabs on the East Coast, in my opinion.

She saved the Vietnam Memorial for our last day, and insisted I do an etching of my father's name inscribed in the marble. That night I grilled steaks and she made twice-baked potatoes, a salad, and blueberry cobbler. I opened a special bottle of wine I'd been saving for . . . well, I wasn't sure why I'd saved it. After dinner we stayed up half the night talking and holding each other, neither of us wanted the morning to come, but come it did.

She reminded me of her "rules" on the way to the airport. I still wasn't to come to Pawleys any time soon, but at least her rules were bending. She didn't rule out coming back to DC or meeting me in L.A. or New Orleans for a ball game. I was not to pester her; when she thought she could get away, she'd call—after all, she had a restaurant to run. I sulked as I carried her bag to the security lines. I didn't like her rules one bit.

We stopped for a goodbye kiss, and she whispered in my ear, "You know, Jack, rules are meant to be broken."

*****

ACKNOWLEDGEMENTS

JOHN, LAURA, AND PETE provided me legal advice and emotional support for close to a decade and through my most difficult moments. I will be forever grateful for their legal skills, kindness, and friendship.

Suzy read and edited every draft of this book, and it would not exist without her patience and skill. My children and their spouses offered ideas, suggestions, and encouragement. My Charlotte, DC, and Arkansas friends continue to encourage and support this adventure. This author does not have the words to convey how much I appreciate their unwavering help and friendship.

Terry, Walter, and Caroline read early drafts and acted as sounding boards for sticky health, computer, and legal issues. Jim Frenkel provided sound editorial advice and suggestions.

My deepest thanks and appreciation to Beaufort Books. Publisher Eric Kampmann believed in me and the Jack Patterson series from day one. Managing Editor Megan Trank has been a constant source of support whether it be editing, cover design, publicity, or the hundred other things she does on my behalf. A special thanks to Michael Short for the cover design and Veronica Kelly for her editing expertise.

I continue to be eternally grateful to George and his family.